THE DEATH CLUB

THE DEATH CLUB

CAROLINE PECKHAM

SUSANNE VALENTI

This book is dedicated to Niall's sledgehammer, Mary and her smooth, smooth handle. Her hammer was thick and crushed skulls like a dream— except that one time when she came loose and caused a right fucking mess. We'll miss you Mary, may you rest in murder weapon heaven with that dodgy hatchet Fred who Niall lost last Christmas when he fell in a ditch and you jammed into his thigh. He broke you in two for that, called you a crapchet and shoved your pieces up a man's arse. That guy was a sicko so he deserved it, but maybe you didn't.

RIP Mary and Fred.

BROOKLYN

CHAPTER ONE

There were some things in life which most people believed.

'Santa isn't real.'

'No girl enjoys butt stuff.'

'Killing is bad.'

But not me. I believed the exact opposite of all those things. And you know what? I was happier for it. I'd shoot down Santa in a rain of blood and glory and find one hell of a freaking meaning to that. *Merry fucking Christmas, dickmunch. Thanks for the lack of presents, I'll make up for it with my new set of flying reindeer.* I'd put myself on the naughty list around the time I was eight years old and stabbed my daddy's girlfriend (see: woman who sucks dick for cash) in the tit with my plastic unicorn when I'd found her stealing from his wallet.

My dad was the only good man I'd ever known. He loved red meat, deep fried snacks and cheap beer. So naturally, his heart gave up on my eleventh birthday just after I blew out the candle on the red velvet cupcake he'd bought me. Unlike most little girls, I hadn't wished for a pony. I'd wished for my life to be an endless adventure full of furry animals who could talk, shiny clothes that made you go *wow*, and an invisible friend called Pete who knew the way to Wonderland.

If only I'd wished for my daddy to have a new heart, maybe I wouldn't be here now. Living under a bridge like a Billy Goat. Or was it trolls who lived under bridges? Either way, it was cold and dark down here and looked nothing like the birthday wish I'd made. I mean, I supposed you could count the family of rats as the furry animals, and my ripped blue coat was kinda shiny in certain lights. But I didn't have any friends, and if I asked Stinky Jim the way to Wonderland, he'd only whip his stinky dick out.

So unless my fairy godmother had been bound and gagged by a drunk pixie who liked to mess with my wishes, I was getting the impression mine hadn't come true. Ah, who was I kidding? My fairy godmother was the Devil and he had big plans for me. I just wished he'd get a move on with them, and maybe send a little hellfire into my sleeping bag to warm my chilly ass up at night too.

Guess you could say it was my fault I was a homeless nobody. But I liked to blame my deadbeat uncle who'd taken me in. See, if Uncle Jake had taken better care of me, maybe I would have had nicer clothes to wear to my new school. Maybe I wouldn't have turned up to class unwashed with holes in my blazer that showed through to my white shirt underneath. Maybe I wouldn't have coloured those holes in with a Sharpie to try and blend in a little better. Maybe Penelope Weston wouldn't have noticed I was the definition of dirt poor, and maybe she wouldn't have made me the butt of every joke in the school. Maybe I wouldn't have been bullied for year after year after year by her and her vile, disgusting little gang of followers. Maybe Penelope's boyfriend Andrew Fig and his friends wouldn't have done what they did to me in the woods on the edge of campus.

And maybe I wouldn't have ended up stabbing four of them in a wild rage. Two died. Penelope and Andrew didn't. The ones I'd wanted to die most. That still haunted me to this day, knowing they were out there somewhere living their lives. I'd tried searching for them, but I had no phone, no money, no freaking resources at all. And apparently wandering about hoping to bump into people you like the idea of killing isn't a great method of tracking them down. Who knew?

I'd made a vow on the sky and the moon and all the stars above that someday, somehow, I'd find a way to finish the job I'd started.

Turns out, you're supposed to be remorseful for stuff like killing people. But I didn't regret it. I would never regret it. In fact, it was my best quality. I'd spent a few years in juvie where I went on to taint my record a bit further with some blood splatter - alright, I'd slammed a girl's head into the wall until she stopped squealing, but that had been the third time she tried to shank me. Okay so maybe the dance I did on her dead body had been overkill, but was it really inappropriate to dance on someone's corpse if they'd been a shitbag while they were alive? The warden had seemed to think so. He called me unstable. He said stable people didn't draw cocks painted with blood on the walls and across their victim's cheeks. So long story short, I got committed to Eden Heights Psychiatric Hospital. That was where I officially learned that all human beings are awful. Especially the ones who are supposed to help you.

I was kind of famous for a while. The newspapers called me the Bully Butcher which actually had a nice ring to it. But it was pretty inaccurate really. Butchers cut meat with care and precision, but when I'd driven a knife into flesh it had been savage, jagged, sloppy. I didn't know the right places to strike, I just knew that if you struck everywhere it got the job done. Made one holy hell of a mess though. But I'd never claimed to be a tidy killer.

There weren't many people under the bridge tonight. I refused to learn the names of those who came and went. I hadn't had a friend since my dad had passed and I didn't plan on making any either unless my invisible friend Pete decided to show up. He'd definitely be a unicorn, or a dragon, or maybe a tiny little lion who I could put in my pocket. Being alone was always better than having company though. And if I was gonna take on a friend, it definitely

9

wouldn't be a man. People were awful, but men were pigs. So I lived by the rule that men didn't exist to me ninety nine point nine percent of the time. And when they did, they were already on their last warning. Sadly, I wasn't a lesbian. Even the Devil hadn't helped me out with that. *Like, give a girl a break please, Big Red? Just have a word with my vagina and tell her dicks are devious and pussy is purity.*

I pictured his scalding red abs and knew I was doomed to hunger for dick for all eternity. Though I'd never met a real man who fit my idea of hot. I didn't know if that was because I had a particularly rare craving for athletic physiques infused with pure evil or if all men were just boring. Maybe both. Either way, I guess it worked out for me because no attachment was the way I liked it. Even when the nights got real dark and the void in me could have swallowed up all the bullshit spewing out of every politicians' mouth in the world. Yah, it was *that* big.

Anyways, whatever I needed in life, I stole. I got by. But sometimes in the dead of night, I craved violence more keenly than I craved food or sex or money. Even more than I craved Big Red sticking his Devil dick in me. Yeah, sometimes I dreamed of how it would feel to purge my demons by sending the scum from this world with knives and guns and teeth. If I hadn't needed to keep a low profile, I think I would have killed again by now. It was in my nature. I was a vicious, bloodthirsty savage. I wasn't sure when I'd realised I was different, but I'd never flinched from blood. It had always drawn me a little closer, made me breathe a little quicker.

I had fantasies about becoming a high paid assassin. The cold blooded, beautiful kind who wore slinky dresses and killed men with nothing but her thighs around their necks. It was a silly, pretty dream. But weren't they the best kind? Currently, the closest thing I owned to a nice dress was an XXL men's t-shirt representing the band Scum Drop and I hadn't shaved my legs since…well, let's just say they don't give you razor blades in insane asylums. And I'd been out of that place just over six months now. *You can't catch me,*

I'm the Gingerbread Man motherfuckers.

"Get away from me," a girl hissed somewhere on the opposite side of the underpass, disturbing me as I almost grasped sleep. That bitch was a tricksy mistress to wrangle at the best of times and I didn't need chatty people making it harder. I mean, I was a chatty person when I wanted to be too. But like, most people told me to shut the fuck up once I got going. Especially if they were trying to sleep.

I tilted my head up, glaring out of my sleeping bag as a shadow shifted in front of the girl. *Ergh, great, they're gonna have sex and I'm gonna have to lay here and watch it while I touch myself. I wonder what it feels like to ride a cock. I bet it's way more fun than that popsicle I stuffed up there last summer...*

"Let me see your face," a gravelly voice came from the large shadow, flecked with what I guessed was a Mexican accent.

"No – get away," the girl snapped, her voice ringing off the bridge above. Why was she being so damn loud? Was this some sort of roleplay shit? I'd heard about that. If I ever got the chance to do it, I'd totally dress up as Loki while Thor hammered me from behind.

The two older men who were huddled around a flaming drum cast sideways looks in the girl's direction before pointedly ignoring the situation.

The Shadow leaned down, taking hold of the girl's face and I frowned, sensing something off about this situation. My fingers twitched as I reached for the switch blade in my pocket and I slid it out, snapping open the knife then tugging down the zip on my sleeping bag. I was the furthest thing from a hero that existed. But I also hadn't stuck a man like a pig in a long ass time. Call it my weakness, but if this lurker was a creep, I'd relish the chance to end him.

"Hurry up," another Mexican voice sounded and my head whipped around in the direction it had come from somewhere up on the bridge.

"Woof," the Shadow laughed. "Never mind, cerdita. Your face ain't worth my time."

"She's good enough. Take her. I'm freezing my tetas off out here," his friend called and I pushed myself to my feet, the low lighting keeping me hidden. I was a cat in the dark, surefooted, pissed off and happy to scratch your eyes out for a laugh. *Purr, purr, die.*

"Nah, I want the pretty one. I saw her come down here," the Shadow growled. "I'm telling you, Carlo, this one will make our pockets fat."

"She ain't here," Carlo huffed, stepping under the bridge as he moved toward his friend. "Just take the dog."

The girl on the ground tried to jump up, but the Shadow knocked her down and my heart slammed against my ribs at the sight of the gun wheeling toward her face. In that fleeting heartbeat, I was *that* girl again, lying on my back in the woods as creatures bigger than me held me down. There were strong fingers around my throat, heavy breaths against my face. Hands grasping and groping and people laughing-

I blinked to force the images away and rage twisted through me like a living storm.

These fuckers had given me flashbacks. And I hated freaking flashbacks. *Game on.*

The two old men by the drum scarpered just like that and I reckoned in another life that would have been my cue to do the same. I didn't feel fear like normal people did though. I'd been called odd a lot. Like, *a lot.* But odd served me well out on the streets. Even dodgy people didn't like odd. It made them squirm. *So squirm away little squirmers. The odd one's out on the prowl.* People always hated others for being different, but really they just hated themselves for being average.

The Shadow heaved the girl upright and she screamed in fright. "No! Let me go. She's who you want. *Her*!" She was pointing at me – *me* – and my gut clenched like a fist.

People are awful.

The men whipped around and their eyes locked on me like missiles. My first thought was stupid and irrational. It should have been 'run like the wind, bitch!' or 'shitballs, stab them in the dicks!' but it was actually 'she thinks I'm pretty'. I didn't get called pretty - fuckable, sure. Well, I'd been called that by the gross guy who lived in the bushes at the end of West Street that one time, but pretty? That was what people called cute girls with names like Emily and Amy. I wasn't an Emily and I sure as shit wasn't an Amy. Mom had called me Brooklyn because she thought it was quirky. After she divorced Dad and moved to Vegas with Esteban – fucking Esteban – Dad had wanted to change it. Couldn't blame him really. It didn't suit me. But I'd never found anything that did. *Oh fuck I'm about to die.*

The men ran at me and I lunged forward to meet them with a growl of determination, swinging my knife with all the grace of a three-legged mutt. As I slashed my knife across the Shadow's arm with little skill but absolute brutality, the big guy behind him crashed into me and twisted my wrist so hard that the knife went clattering across the ground. I threw my knee into the Shadow's groin and dove for my weapon with a jolt of desperation. *I don't die on the ground like a pigeon fallen from its perch, I die like a warrior with fire blazing all around me and the whole world roaring my name!*

My fingers grazed the hilt just as strong arms wrapped around my waist. My pulse thudded in my ears and I went full savage, reaching back over my head and clawing at any soft flesh I could find until pained curses left the guy's lips. The Shadow sadly recovered from my attack on his junk and slammed his fist into my gut. Something popped, might have been a lung. *Holy mother of ow.*

"She's a fucking salvaje. Ella es justo lo que le gusta al jefe." The guy holding me laughed and I didn't like that, there was victory in that sound, but I wasn't done yet.

I reared back against him, throwing my feet out and kicking the Shadow in the chest as hard as I could, knocking something from his hand in the same movement. A syringe went tinkling over the ground to buddy up with my knife and the bottom dropped out of my stomach. I'd failed math at school harder than a monkey with a broken calculator. But this was one sum I could do in my sleep. Dodgy syringe + two psychos under a dark bridge = bad news.

They're trying to take me. Run, bitch, run!

I leaned down, sinking my teeth into the large hand locked around my arm and bit deep enough to hear a nice crunch.

"Ah!" the man yelped at the pitch of a boy whose balls hadn't dropped yet and his grip slackened enough for me to throw an elbow into his side.

The Shadow was coming again, but I was suddenly free and I hit the ground running. I'd always been good at that. Running from my problems, running from responsibilities, running from mall security, cops, but call me boastful, my real speciality lay in running from creepy ass dudes under bridges.

I always slept in my boots and this was why. I ran like the fires of hell were burning my ass and shouts sounded out behind me as the men took chase. There was a ringing in the back of my skull like an alarm bell because why the fuck were they still chasing me? They weren't giving up. They wanted something from me that was bad, bad, bad. And I could not let them get it.

One look over my shoulder showed me they were used to running too, and they were fast. Like bats out of Hades fast. The Shadow was out in front, the flames from the drum lighting his face, the wild, lustful glint in his eyes telling me he wanted to ruin my life in every way he possibly could. Too many people had looked at me like that in my twenty-one years of existence. I blamed the wish I'd made on my eleventh birthday. Endless adventure? Fucking dumbass. I'd read enough books to know endless adventure was a curse, not a gift. Just look at Frodo Baggins! He was almost eaten by a giant spider and that wasn't even the worst day of his life. Bilbo had tried to warn him, but did he listen? Oh no, he went off on his little hobbity adventure and look at all the monsters he'd faced. I'd wished for the same, but my monsters weren't spiders – which I actually had a fondness for, just check out the badass tattoo on my forearm of a web and the little spider hanging down by my thumb – my monsters were people. And people were sick. People did psycho stuff for fun. I should know. I was one of them.

I ran into the road – ran into the motherfucking road without obeying the simplest rule of them all. Look left and right. The car didn't hit me hard, but it sure as hell knocked me on my ass and grazed up my legs good. I hissed between my teeth then looked into the blinding headlights, hope sprinkling through my chest like pixie dust. Maybe it was a soccer mom or a priest. Someone who had to pretend to be a decent human being because of societal pressures and all that bullshit.

"Hey!" I called out to them. "Help me!"

The driver's door opened and a smug looking woman with a ponytail stepped out and sneered at me. My heart dipped, my courage waned. Unless this bitch was a nun who'd left her habit at home, I was definitely fucked.

The Shadow made it to the road as the ponytail whore lifted a hand and pointed a gun at me. Thick hands grabbed me from behind, hauling me upright and I winced from my bruised ass.

"I swear if my peachy butt has any permanent damage, I'm gonna be seeking reparations in blood," I told the bitch, pretending I wasn't afraid. I did feel fear, even though it didn't look like it most of the time. And I felt it now like a hungry beast nibbling at my heart.

"Get her in the car," the woman commanded and a needle sank into my neck.

And just like that, oblivion stole me away and my doom surely awaited me beyond it. I hadn't lived a big life. But it had been mine. And I had the heart-wrenching, soul-obliterating feeling that I'd just lost that privilege.

NIALL

CHAPTER TWO

I was happy once. Not that I can recall that feeling now.

When the woman I loved was torn from my grasp, I was thrown into the never-ending fires of hell.

But there's one thing they don't tell you about men without souls when they're cast into damnation. Once we make a home for ourselves in hell, there's nothing left to fear from life. And a man without fear is a man without limits. I hadn't had any limits in ten long years.

Sometimes I felt like an old man, broken by the weight of time and grief pressing down upon my shoulders, though my pa assured me regularly that I was still young. Virile. Had my whole life ahead of me. In fact, he was at it again now, while I tuned him out and watched a pigeon strutting along a rooftop like he owned the motherfucking world. Mrs Pigeon certainly seemed to think he might be right about that if the way she was eyeing him was anything to go by.

"Did you hear me, lad?" Pa's voice bit out, thick with his old Irish accent. There was enough snap to it that I knew he was wishing I was with him in person, so he could clip me round the ear like I was a small lad.

"The line dropped," I replied casually, my own accent more subtle and born from spending years in the homeland as a child before returning here to the states.

My back pressed firm to the window frame as I sat eight floors up, watching the sun rise over the city and waiting for this call to end so I could finish up my job here. Scaling this wall had been no easy feat and I didn't much appreciate the interruption.

"Like hell it did," Liam O'Brien snarled in that tone he used when he wanted to remind me that he owned me. Owned the whole family. The whole fucking world too, no doubt. And I made myself listen because he was right about at least two of those claims and possibly the third.

"I'll be expecting you home for breakfast at nine. Dress sharp, lad, I won't have you embarrassing me," he said in a tone that brokered no arguments and he'd get none from me. It wasn't worth my time, or my life, pitiful as it was.

"Home at nine," I confirmed, taking my phone from my ear and adding a reminder to it. I wasn't likely to remember that shit even if it was only three hours from now. And when he said 'home' he was referring to his mansion of course, my own residence holding no interest to him even if he had known where it was. Which he didn't. The house which I rented and he knew about lay as empty as the day I'd first signed the lease on it, but what he didn't know didn't hurt him. Besides, if he cared so much about the place his youngest son called home, he could have asked to come visit me. Which he hadn't once done in the ten years since I'd supposedly moved in there. "Anything else I can do ya for?"

"Burnley. Is he dealt with?" my pa asked smoothly.

"About to be," I replied, turning my gaze to the closed window beside me where the man in question lay fast asleep in bed. I hoped he was having nice dreams because there was a nightmare coming his way which he wouldn't be waking from.

"What took you so long?" Liam sneered, the suggestion of

incompetence clear in his tone but I couldn't give a fuck about that. I was the most competent man I knew. I just liked to pick my moments.

"I wanted to be certain he wasn't infected," I said with a shrug he couldn't see.

The world was currently held hostage in the grips of the Hades Virus, more than half the population hiding out in quarantine from the sickness that killed sixty percent of the people who got infected with it. But I didn't much care for wearing face masks and in my line of work I didn't come into contact with many people, so I was content to go without and take my chances. I'd gone up against death and won plenty of times before now anyway, I doubted fate was kind enough to let me die sick in my bed.

"What difference does that make? You should be wearing the mask I provided you with regardless."

"Of course I am," I replied – assuming by 'wearing it' he meant leaving it in my car. "But it seemed like letting him suffer through the virus might have saved me a job. Anyway, he got the all clear, so I'm doing it now."

Liam tutted and I could imagine him stubbing out a cigarette while he thought up ways to punish me. "Home. Nine." He hung up and I considered tossing my phone all the way away. There was a man walking along the street and if my aim was true I'd likely kill him with the damn thing from this height. He had the look of an asshole about him so in all likelihood he deserved it.

Perhaps it wasn't the brightest idea to consider using a phone that could be linked back to me as a murder weapon though. *Pity that.*

I shifted on my perch, my gaze sweeping out to take in the rising sun again as the pigeons stopped dancing around the subject and got down to fucking. I gave them a moment to have at it. No need to ruin their day after all.

With the coos of pigeon pleasure calling out to me, I looked at the sun and thought of the time me and Ava had trekked up that fucking mountain in Ireland and watched it set. She said it was the most beautiful thing she'd ever seen and I'd promised to take her up that mountain every year so she could see it again. Not that we ever went back. And she didn't get much of a forever. That was the curse of loving me.

Of course, thinking of my wife made me think about the state her corpse had been in when I finally got her back. Too late. Too fucking late. Time hadn't meant a whole lot to me since that day.

The pigeons finished up their fun and I offered them a round of applause. That noise right there was Burnley's chance to wake up, spot me, scream, run, beg - but he must have been a deep sleeper because he just slept on.

I sighed, shrugged one shoulder and slid the little wire I'd been holding beneath the bottom of the sash window. Honest to donkey dicks, I didn't know why people were dumb enough to have these old piece of shit windows still in place on their properties. It was like they assumed being eight floors up and overlooking a busy street was enough of a deterrent to psychopaths who might wanna crawl in their window and take a shit all over their lives.

Not so, my friend. Not so.

With a twist of my fingers, the curled end of the wire hooked around the catch at the bottom of the window and I gave it a sharp tug to unlock it. The thing gave way easier than I'd expected and I came damn close to falling all the fucking way down to the street below.

No such luck of course. The Devil didn't want any competition so he'd refused my admittance to hell more times than I could count by now. He'd done me the courtesy of making sure I lived within my own personal hell at all times though, so I guessed he was winning.

The window slid up with a bit of muscle and a grinding noise that really should have woken Burnley. But no. Maybe I was about to find him dead and my work completed for me. Unlikely, but I supposed it was possible.

I dropped down into his fancy pants room with its bachelor pad grey on grey on grey on - oh shit is that a bit of red? Kinky fucker. Right above his bed too.

I tilted my head to one side as I tried to make sense of the splashy splotchy piece of art, but I'd be damned if it looked like anything other than a cat's arsehole to me.

I took the hammer from my belt and gave it a few casual test swings as I approached the man of the hour, whistling a bit of that song from the advert with the cat and the duck playing the violin. I wanted to say it was for a tin of something. Peaches maybe? Nah, no one advertised tinned peaches. Tuna? Lima beans? Sweetcorn? Well, fuck me, I couldn't recall. That was gonna eat at me all damn day.

My gaze moved to the red blob art thing and I decided I wanted to know what it was. I reached out gently with my hammer and used it to peel the comforter away from Burnley's sleeping form.

He was a middle-aged man, stout of stature and sporting some rather stylised chest hair. I couldn't say I'd ever considered growing my chest hair into a pattern before, but I guessed it was a conversation starter. 'Oh hey, Wendy, did you hear I manscaped my chest hair into the shape of a heart? Does that make ya wanna fuck me?' I had to say, I couldn't picture it flying so well, but maybe the women Burnley liked went in for that. Or men. Not judging. I was an equal opportunity serial killer. All races, genders and sexual orientations catered for.

"Is it meant to be a vagina?" I asked loudly and Burnley jerked awake with a shriek an eighty-year-old granny would have been proud of.

He lurched up, seeming inclined to run and I pressed the flat head of my hammer to that fancy heart shaped hair on his chest to force him back down onto the mattress.

"What do you want?" he gasped.

Always with those same questions. 'What do you want?' 'How did you get in here?' 'Is that my wife's hat you're wearing?' 'Did you just piss on my rug?' 'Why do you have a knife?' blah, blah, blah. I wasn't in the mood for the old usuals today, so I just jerked my chin at the painting, getting him on track with my thought process.

"So, a vagina then? Or a never-ending portal to nothing and nowhere? A dog on a bench? What is it?" I asked and he craned his neck to look up at the painting for a moment.

"I-I don't know. It was expensive and I liked the look of it, so-"

"So you just plastered a huge vagina on your wall without even knowing it was a vagina? I mean, do you think you subliminally had vaginas on the mind that day or are you generally in a vagina mood?" I asked.

"W-why do you keep saying vagina?" Burnley stammered. I heard a lot of stammering in my line of work, begging, pleading, bribing, lying. Saw a lot of people piss themselves too. And shit themselves. Killing wasn't pretty work, that was for sure. Aside from all the red of course. My favourite colour.

"Well, if you've got no answer to my question, I guess I might as well get on with it." I heaved my hammer back, lining up the best strike as he screamed again.

"Why?" he wailed, cringing away from me.

"I'm Liam O'Brien's boy," I said with a shrug and his eyes widened in realisation. Yeah, there it was, he'd just figured out that fucking over the biggest crime family in the city was a bad idea. Why was it no one ever had to tell people not to stick their dick in the garbage disposal and yet they needed reminding not to play games with mobsters which they couldn't win?

"I've never seen you before," he breathed, shaking his head.

"I'm Niall," I explained, stowing the hammer in my belt and offering him my hand to shake. He did because he was one of those well-bred bastards and I gave him a good old squeeze because I appreciated manners even if mine were few and far between. "The youngest."

Burnley's eyes widened as I shook his hand vigorously and his whole arm kinda flopped up and down before I released him.

"The...unhinged one?"

"You've heard of me?" I asked, smiling widely because who the fuck didn't like being famous?

"I thought you were a rumour, a myth. You're never at corporate events or meetings, everyone says you don't even exist and you're just a lie they tell to make people fear them."

"Well, turns out I'm no legend - just a hot blooded man with a bloodstained soul. I'll be killin' ya now then," I warned him, hefting the hammer in my grasp once more and giving him a moment to process that fact. "It won't be fun and it won't be pretty. But if you wanna write out a quick note to your mammy or whoever to say goodbye, then I'll give you a moment to do it. But don't go gettin' any daft ideas about mentioning me in your note. Because then I'd have to cave her head in after I deliver it. And I hate killing mammies because of stupid fuckers like you."

"I want to live," he gasped. Why didn't they ever take me up on the offer of writing that note? I'd wanna remind the people I cared about that I loved them if I knew I was gonna die. Or at least, I imagined I would if I gave half a shit about a single soul on this planet. Unfortunately, I wasn't convinced I did, so maybe I wouldn't take up the offer of the note either.

"Are you sure about that? Because I can make it swift if you wanna accept it. But if you're so certain you wanna live then we can make a time of it. I have a few hours to kill before I'm to meet my pa for breakfast and no doubt you'll be begging for death before I have to leave."

Burnley tried to run and I struck him with the hammer, straight to the temple. Hard enough to stun him a bit, but not enough to finish the job. He'd said he wanted to live after all, so it made sense to put that to the test.

He fell back against his pillows, pressing a hand to his head where I'd hit him like he couldn't quite believe I'd actually done it. I cocked my head as I watched him, waiting for that lightbulb moment - the one where he'd look up at me and see the devil I was. And as his gaze met mine again, I got my wish. Bingo. Total terror – wait a moment, was that ad for corned beef?

Burnley lurched out of the bed and I let him go this time, following him from the room as he staggered away, making a predictable run for the door. I'd have gone for the kitchen knives personally. Better to give yourself a fighting chance and all that, but maybe Burnley just didn't have any fight in him.

He reached the door and started struggling with the lock just before a blow from my hammer sent him crashing to the floor with a cry of pain. I grinned down at him as he stared up at me like I was a monster, trying to do a kind of backwards elbow crawl wriggle away thing, like that would make a jot of difference.

The next time I struck him, I was fairly sure I fucked him up good enough that he wasn't with me anymore, but I let my inner animal loose and made a blood bath out of it all the same. I hit him over and over, not stopping until my arm was aching and the job was complete.

I stowed my hammer back in my belt and took a knife out next, removing a finger for Pa.

I had a fancy little gift box all ready in my pocket to put it in and everything. He'd never actually asked me to start bringing him proof of death when I killed for him, but I liked to present it as a gift and tell him I had a no returns policy. He just accepted it these days. Besides, the true meaning behind my presents for him was a joke I'd only ever told myself and I still found it really fucking funny. Because I didn't just pick any finger. Oh no. It was the middle finger, just so that I got the pleasure of knowing the mark was flipping my pa off when he opened the box to see it. Little pleasures and all that.

Once that was all wrapped up with a bow, I strolled away from the bloody lump of flesh that had once been Burnley and headed into his bathroom to take a shower and wash the blood off. Apparently it didn't do to stroll around town covered in blood, though I did feel that I shouldn't have to hide my lifestyle to conform to social ideals. Were there any occupations that had to deal with so much hatred as psychopaths? Where were the equal opportunity protesters who flew my flag? Although I had heard that there were some people who liked reading stories like mine about fucked up men like me and fantasised about taking them to bed, so maybe that was where I'd find my people. The readers who understood that sometimes a bit of choking was perfectly acceptable or maybe even desirable and wouldn't judge me for it.

Once my dirty blonde hair was no longer tainted with red streaks and the only stains marking my skin were the countless patterns of ink which I'd put there permanently to coat my muscular frame, I dried off and pulled my jeans back on. I stole a blue button down from Burnley - because let's face it, he didn't have use of it anymore anyway - and I strolled my ass right on out of his apartment with my bloody shirt balled up in my hand and the freshly rinsed hammer tucked into the back of my pants.

I strode down the street to my cherry red muscle car and hopped on in, wondering if I could find somewhere to get a burger at this time of day. The Hades Virus sweeping the world really had fucked with my eating habits. Though I guessed lockdown made it a hell of a lot easier to sneak about and kill people seeing as there weren't any witnesses out and about to take notice. Silver linings.

The ventilator mask I'd promised to wear sat in the footwell, glaring at me with its glassy black eyes and whispering, 'you could be sick, you stupid bastard'. I stamped on it to shut it the fuck up, pulled a pack of cigarettes from the glovebox, lit one up and turned on the radio as I started the engine. Luck would have it that that fucking tune was playing, the duck quacking along so we didn't forget about him in the audio version of the ad and the whole thing ending with an enthusiastic man suggesting I buy his tomato soup.

Fuck no. Who wanted food that came without chewing? He could keep his soup and his fucking tune too. I was just glad my question had been answered and it had been purged from my brain.

Daisy by Ashnikko came on as the ads finished and I inhaled deeply, nicotine searing my lungs and giving me a moment's reprieve from the monotonous misery of my life. It wasn't that my life was oh so fucking terrible really, more that it was oh so fucking empty and pointless since I'd failed the only woman ever foolish enough to love me.

Thirty fucking two and I swear I'd lived more of life and learned more of its lessons than men three times my age. I was so tired all the damn time and yet I never actually felt awake. Never felt a whole lot of anything if I was being honest.

I leaned my head back against the headrest, carving my fingers through my hair and filling the car with smoke, sighing as I equally hunted down the memories and wished they'd leave me be.

"I'll love you forever and a day," Ava breathed, looking up at me from beneath those blonde bangs which always got in her eyes and I smiled before stealing a kiss.

"I'll love you until death and beyond, my girl," I promised her in return. And oh how fucking right I'd been about that.

I took my phone from my pocket and opened it up, scrolling to the video I watched too often, the one they'd sent me. The one that had damned me for all of time.

My thumb hovered over the button to play it and through some sense of repentance or insanity or just pure fucking misery, I pressed down.

I watched as Ava was hauled into the room the camera was aimed at. She was naked, her body battered and bruised, cut and beaten. They told her to beg for me to save her. She begged for me not to instead.

"I'm already gone, my love," she wheezed out. "Don't let them take you too."

Tom Nelson backhanded her before the clip ended and that was the last time I'd ever seen my wife alive.

My phone started buzzing and flashing and I growled at it as a notification popped up over the image of my wife's tearstained face, telling me to get my ass to my pa's house or else.

That handy reminder made me realise the time and the fact that I was going to be late. Really fucking late. *Goddammit.*

I tossed my phone on the chair beside me then took off at high speed, cranking the music to drown out my grief and singing at the top of my motherfucking lungs to That Bitch by Bea Miller to make sure I was thoroughly purged. I liked learning the lyrics to as many songs as I could – it kept my brain busy and the darkness out. Sometimes. It wouldn't do me any good to face off against the old man with my heart raw and battered over ancient scars though, so I needed all the help I could get.

Thanks to the lockdown, the streets were empty and I sped through downtown Hemlock city, breaking every speed limit I passed through before racing out to the sprawling estate where my father and the rest of my unwholesome family resided. Well, all of them aside from my nephew Kyan who was currently enrolled at Everlake Prep - some fancy ass school for posh boys where he was meant to rub shoulders with the future leaders of our country and no doubt further Pa's plans for world domination too.

Kyan was about the only member of my family I trusted. He wasn't blinded by Liam's power or desperate for his approval like all the others. He was his own man and the only one I cared for these days – I could write him a deathbed letter come to think of it. I was one of nine siblings and every single one of them was a conniving prick who I'd happily see dead.

I sped past the private security Pa had in place at the gate to his grotesque mansion and parked up right outside the front door, opening it myself instead of waiting for one of his staff to do it for me. I swear the old man had so many of them that he must have employed a few purely to wipe his ass.

I spotted his housekeeper Martha as I strode down the obnoxiously grand central hallway past countless priceless paintings. She subtly pointed me towards the dining room so that I'd know where to find the old ass.

I strode right on in, glancing around at the long table which only had four places set for the breakfast he'd been so keen on me attending. Seeing as the thing was long enough to seat all eight of my siblings and their spouses, plus some, the gigantic room looked particularly ridiculous set for four. There was a fire roaring in the fireplace though and the scent of food beckoned me forward, so I ignored the posturing in favour of filling my belly.

I didn't hesitate to approach the table despite the supposed risk these strangers might pose to me due to the Hades Virus, because I knew there wasn't a chance in hell they'd be here unless my pa was totally certain they weren't infected. I might not have been worried one way or another about catching it, but my father certainly was. He wouldn't wanna go and die just to do me a favour or anything.

There was a woman sitting beside him but I ignored her, my eyes on the man who had sired me as I took the gift box from my pocket and placed it before him on the table.

Liam O'Brien was well into his eighties with dark grey hair but was just as intimidating as he'd ever been. Tall, refined and perfectly put together in a sharp suit with a cigarette hanging from the corner of his lips like always. I once again sent a silent prayer to the lord of nicotine to finish him the fuck off.

Apparently his guests weren't privy to the kind of work I did for my father's organisation though as he merely pocketed it and offered me a tight smile that said he planned on making me pay for the three minutes I'd made him wait. Funny that, most of the time he didn't give a shit about the time I chose to arrive but on the odd occasion he'd lose his shit over it. These people were clearly important to him in some way.

"Niall, my boy, I want you to meet Anastasia," he said, his voice warm in an utterly bullshit way that told me he was up to no fucking good as he pointed me towards the chair beside the woman. "You may remember her father, Vlad, from some of the other business dealings our families have had with one another."

I dropped into my seat, glanced at scary ass Vlad with his slick, black hair, prominent jaw and no doubt supposedly terrifying face tattoo. It was of a skull that appeared to be crying tears of blood and I would have suggested he look into getting a better artist thanks to that wonky as fuck detailing, but the woman spoke before I could point it out.

"It's a pleasure, Niall," she said in a soft Russian accent, her hand brushing over mine and making my skin prickle with unease.

I pulled back and gave her a sweeping look too. Blonde, fake tits, fake lips, fake lashes, fake smile. Nice dress, but I doubted it would fit me.

"Pleasure," I echoed, just tossing the word back at her and meaning it a whole lot less.

I reached out to start loading my plate with a bunch of the breakfast options that had been laid out, taking a handful of fancy French pastries and filling my cup with coffee before dunking one of them into it then pushing the whole thing into my mouth.

Liam cleared his throat and gave me a warning look which I frowned at. He hardly ever gave me shit over my crappy attitude, knowing full well that it was better to keep a rabid dog on side rather than waste time trying to tame it.

I brushed a flake of pastry from the corner of my mouth and sat up a little straighter, willing to play his game in order to figure out what was going on here.

"We were just discussing a union of our blood," Vlad said, eyeing me with far too much interest considering we'd just met and he was a dude. I didn't swing that way unfortunately for him, though my dick didn't exactly swing any way these days aside from into the company of my own hand.

My gaze flicked to my pa again, wondering what the fuck he was cooking up now and he smiled tightly.

"Vlad suggested that one of the best ways for our families to come together in partnership would be to create a bonding union between us. Making sure that we are all in fact tied together should anything try to divide us."

"And I'm here because..." I bit down on another pastry and Anastasia giggled like she thought me tearing into my food was amusing. Or maybe that my ignorance was. Either way her laughter was as fake as the rest of her and I wasn't buying it.

"I don't have any other unwed children," Pa supplied. "So if we want this union to go ahead-"

"You've got plenty of single grandsons," I pointed out, a coldness creeping beneath my skin that almost always ended in death.

It wasn't panic; my fight or flight instincts had been cut off at the neck when I'd realised that death would actually be a relief for me, but it was a dangerous state for me to be in and if my father knew me at all then he should realise he was treading a fine line with me right now.

Anastasia pursed her lips, clearly displeased by my utter lack of interest in her, but I guessed she didn't realise that I wasn't interested in any women. Not in a long fucking time. It wasn't a comment on her perfectly presented package, just on the damnation I had brought on the woman I loved.

"You assured me this would be a good match," Vlad growled, his gaze on my pa as I drained my coffee, wishing someone had had the forethought to lace it with liquor.

"It will be," Pa said, his tone not giving away so much as a hint of his rage, but the darkness in his eyes promising I'd pay if I didn't fall in to line right about now.

Respect for the son of bitch who had fathered me had been drummed into me every damn day of my life since the moment I was born. It was a part of who I was. Ingrained in me so deeply that it was damn near impossible to carve it out. Family. Honour. Respect. It was a fucking cliche and yet here I was, biting my tongue and giving the faintest nod of my head, which I doubted Vlad or the daughter he was here to whore out would even notice. But it was enough to make my father drop his death glare.

"Martha!" I called out, knowing she'd be close by. "I need some more coffee. Can you get me a pot?" I didn't need to spell out to her that I wanted it to be more whiskey than coffee - she'd know that well enough.

I leaned back in my chair, the food no longer holding much interest for me as Liam O'Brien engaged the Russian gangster in some discussion about import taxes which was no doubt a cover for discussing the latest shipments of drugs they were waiting on being delivered.

He'd been working on his relationship with the Russians for a while, the two families uniting in peace over their hatred for the Italians. I probably should have seen this coming if I'd taken more of an interest in his bullshit.

My mind drifted to the hammer still hooked through the side of my belt and I wondered how quickly I could kill the three of them and be gone. Sixteen seconds was a good bet. Maybe eighteen because Vlad's skull looked kinda chunky and he might take an extra hit or two. But then I'd have to clean house because the staff all knew I'd been here and that would be a royal pain in the arse.

Martha delivered the spiked coffee and I gave her a winning smile. It was a mask, but I'd been wearing it so long that I'd forgotten where the bullshit ended and I began, so neither of us made comment on it. She was a sweetheart though and it would be a damn shame to have to kill her in the clean up. I sighed as I let that idea drift away like a feather in the wind.

While our fathers sat talking business like we were irrelevant additions to the room, Anastasia decided to press her luck, leaning close to me and whispering in my ear.

"We're all just pawns on their chessboard, aren't we?" she breathed, her Russian accent faint but still present. I guessed my pa wasn't the only mobster who liked to ship his kids off to the homeland while they were young. He hadn't bothered so much with the grandkids, but for me and my siblings, we'd lived a life between homes, hopping back and forth across the Atlantic more times than I could count. Don't get me wrong, Ireland was a beautiful place and if I'd had a say in it, I may well have chosen to stay there. But Liam's part of the O'Brien empire was firmly run stateside, so I'd long since made my bed with living here.

"If you're only just figuring that out then I pity you," I replied to her, not bothering to look her way as I drained my coffee, the whiskey burning my throat on its journey down and going some small way to taking the edge off of my souring mood.

"Perhaps it wouldn't be so bad to be united," she said, reaching out to place her hand over mine, letting me know she wasn't opposed to fucking me at the very least.

I stilled, caught for a moment in the surprise of her touching me so boldly as she trailed her hand up over my forearm. The feeling of her touch on my skin was so alien and unwelcome that I almost snarled like a beast as she skimmed her fingers right over the tattoo I had of my wife's name. Anastasia didn't know that of course, my shirt sleeve hiding it, but as her fingers grazed over the point where the swirling script which spelled out *Ava* marked my skin, I came so close to killing the lot of them that I swear I actually blacked out.

When I came to, I was on my feet, my coffee cup smashing in the fireplace where I must have hurled it. I was surprised to see the three of them alive and staring at me, Pa's eyes lighting with anger at my behaviour.

"It looks like you've got the arrangements well in hand," I said, smiling widely and curtsying for them just to throw them off. No one ever knew how the fuck to respond to that kind of behaviour and it suited me well. "So I'll be taking my leave now."

I strode from the room before any of them could say a word to stop me and kept going until I was back in my car and tearing the fuck away from them. I didn't know what the fuck I was going to do. But I did know I wouldn't be marrying that woman. Been there, done that, got the ring and fucked it up. Never. Again.

BROOKLYN

CHAPTER THREE

I was in a room. A dark room. A dark, stinky room. It smelled like smoke… misfortune and…eggplant. *Ew. No one likes an eggplant.*

I pushed myself up on the black silken sheets and my skull rattled with the mother of all headaches. My mouth was parched and the low, red light from the weird ass black skull chandelier above me barely lit the little slice of hell I'd just woken up in.

"Hello?" I called, my voice hoarse from lack of moisture as I got to my feet. "Satan? I looked after those demons you planted in my head well all these years, baby. Let's not be a dick, kay?"

No reply. Either I wasn't dead or Satan was a tight lipped bastard who didn't have much to say to me. I mean, I hadn't expected a tea party, but he could have at least stuck a hot poker up my butt and made a comment or two on my sins. *If I die a virgin, you'd better at least pop all my cherries down in hell. Nipple sucking, BJs, sixty-nines, all the eating – back door and front door. All of that before the main event. Don't hustle me, Big Red. I want the works.*

The door opened and a man stepped into the room who was built like a brick shithouse, with huge shoulders and an equally large gut. He had black, luscious hair, an equally luscious moustache and his eyes were deeply overshadowed by his brow. He was squeezed into a fine suit and behind him was the woman with foxy features and a light brown ponytail who'd hit me with her car, plus the big, hairy guy I recognised as the Shadow.

"New stock," the Shithouse spoke to his friends, his voice warbling and thickened by a Mexican accent. The word 'jowly' sprang to mind. This guy was definitely jowly.

His dark brown eyes were void of emotion as they roamed down me and as I followed his gaze, I realised for the first time I wasn't wearing my beat up jeans and woollen sweater anymore.

Someone, some fucking handsy creepazoid had put me in a hot pink dress which hugged my slim figure and meagre cleavage. I wasn't exactly living on three meals a day. Two if I was lucky. But worse than that, far fucking worse was how smooth my legs felt. And not just my legs, the silky sheen continued up between my thighs and though I definitely wasn't going to be putting my hand up my dress to check with this freakshow watching me, I had a feeling I was now as hairless as a naked mole rat. Everywhere. Pussycat and all. Except my head obviously. My ebony hair actually felt as soft as feathers against my cheek so that was nice, but nothing else about this was.

They stared at me like I was a hunk of meat, but I'd been looked at worse. Like I was still a live and kicking critter with its back legs broken.

"Who are you?" I demanded, chin high, spirits low.

This wasn't hell, but I had the feeling it might just be worse. I'd take the hot poker up my ass over the way the meathead was sizing me up. Ah who was I kidding, I'd take the hot poker just for fun. *That's a promise, Satan. Just in case you're listening.*

"She's thin," Shithouse commented, ignoring my question as he spoke to Ponytail.

"She's a project, señor." Ponytail shrugged. "Besides, some of the men like them skinny."

"She's petite…muy pequeña," Shithouse said assessingly. I knew I wasn't the first girl he'd looked at like this. From the critical, no nonsense way he eyed me up, I'd guess I was somewhere in the two thousand and eleventh region.

"Five foot exactly, señor," the Shadow supplied. "We measured."

Somehow that felt as violating as the shaving. Alright, not quite. But who the fuck measures people in their sleep? Aliens? *Oh my god, I've been abducted by aliens. Wait, do aliens speak Spanish? I mean, they could have learned it. But why would they pretend to be Mexican? Unless they just want to distract me with their sultry accents, catch me off guard and shove a probe up my butt. And I didn't want that. Not from these creeps.*

"Alright, let's get a better look then." Shithouse waved a fat hand and the Shadow turned the lights up so the red glow grew to fill the room.

The three of them approached me and my throat thickened as I instinctively did a sweep of the place for a weapon. Nothing. Fists it was then. Good ol' fisty cuffs. They'd never let me down. Well, okay they had. I could land a decent punch, but it was hard to build muscle when you spent your days living between meals and running from the cops.

"I asked you a question," I growled.

"Off," Shithouse commanded, gesturing to my body with one finger. "*Ahora.*"

"'Scuse you?" I hissed, refusing to take a step back even though I didn't like how his sweet, liquorice scented cologne was seeping under my nostrils as he moved into my proximity.

I'd always hated liquorice. Who thought making candy taste like gasoline was a fun idea? Not me, that's for sure. But those tempting colours still lured me in, convincing me I might just like them if I gave them another try. *Deceptive little bastards.*

"Fernanda." Shithouse nodded to Ponytail and she stepped forward with intent, reaching for my dress.

I slapped her manicured hands away with a sneer. "Back up, E.T. I know what you want and you're not getting anywhere near my ass."

Fernanda threw a tired look at the Shadow. "A hand, Rafael."

The Shadow –Rafael – lunged forward to grab me and I threw my first punch at his face. It cracked against his jaw and he snarled, snatching my arms and twisting me around. I kicked and thrashed, leaving scratches, bites, bruises, going full animal in my desperation not to be touched. My heart was hammering, my mind was flashbacking. I saw the woods, the moon, shadows shifting in the dark. I didn't like it. "Stop. Get off me, stop – stop!"

He tore my dress, ripping it down the back and fear ratcheted through the centre of my soul. *No. Not again. Never again.*

His greasy hands pawed at my bare flesh as he threw the horrid material to the floor, leaving me bare. I wheeled around and went for his dick. I'd wound it beyond repair, crush the slithery thing he wanted to violate me with in my fist. *But what if aliens don't have dicks??*

He shoved me away before I got close, the force he used sending me crashing to the floor, my dark hair flying around me.

"Look at the little ratón, she thinks she can take on the cartel single-handedly," Fernanda laughed callously. *Oh shit, they're not aliens. They're people. And that's worse. Much, much worse.*

"Enough," Shithouse said calmly and the icily cold kiss of a knife slid under my chin. He applied pressure, making me tip my head back as he gazed down his nose at me. "Up," he growled.

I didn't obey, my breaths coming heavily as I remained in a heap on the floor, naked and bruised. Hell, my ass hurt. It had collided with the concrete hard when that car had hit me. I bet it looked like a BDSM-loving peach right now.

"Get up or I will have Rafael here break you in for the clients. He will not be gentle. He will leave more bruises. And not all of them will be on the outside."

My lungs crushed as I gazed up at this monster who had me in his snare. His emotionless eyes were the worst of it all. Like he'd seen every horror under the sun and none of them made him so much as wince. I could see what he was now as clear as day. He was a businessman who traded in pain and I was his latest asset.

Rafael unbuckled his belt and I got up with a steadying breath. I was ready to fight with all I had, but there were three of them here and I didn't have a weapon. Men did not touch me on their terms though. Not for a long fucking time. And that wasn't going to change today. They'd have to kill me first.

"I am Señor Castillo, and you will do precisely as I say. Do you understand?" Shithouse asked, his voice detached, rehearsed.

His eyes were still studying my body critically and Rafael wet his lips in the corner of my eye. My pussy ziplocked itself and I raised my fists like I'd seen boxers do on the TV. *In for a penny, in for a potato. Or whatever the saying is.*

Fernanda laughed and I lunged at her like a wild cat, grabbing her ponytail and yanking with all my strength. "Stupid, ponytail bitch, is there a horse's ass under here?" I snarled.

She shrieked, her nails raking up my back and I was suddenly knocked away by big hands. Hands that touched my shoulders then my boobs. Rafael was smiling darkly as he squeezed and his fingers dug in painfully. I screamed and threw my head forward in an effort to headbutt him, but he knocked me back again with brute force. My ass hit the bed and Señor Castillo gazed on with vague boredom, like I was the least interesting thing he'd seen today. *Well, let's change that shall we?*

I let the demons in my head come out to play, lunging at Rafael and sinking my teeth into his ear, ripping and snarling as I tore the flesh away. His fist cracked against my chest and I hit the bed in a sea of stars, spitting the chunk of ear from my mouth. Rafael screamed as his blood seeped over my tongue and I lifted my hand to wipe it clean. *What a beautiful sound, I wish I could add it to my Spotify playlist. Shame I don't have the app. Or a phone.*

"This is all getting very messy," I hissed as Rafael cupped the side of his head in agony. "Just so we're clear, I don't do being touched without consent."

Mr Castillo regarded me with mild intrigue like this new development simply changed my value to him somehow. I got the feeling my situation hadn't improved, in fact, I was pretty sure it had just worsened. He gestured to Fernanda and she strode forward, taking a gun from her waistband and levelling it at my forehead before pushing a pill into my mouth. "Swallow."

I toyed with the idea of letting her blow my brains out just to defy her, but I still had unfulfilled dreams on this earth. Ones which might earn me more favours with the Devil when I met him. No slut-shaming, but he was the only man I planned on spreading my legs for on command. I'd just spread 'em like a well-paid whore and sing Don't Stop the Devil by Dead Posey while he went to town on me. It'd be so damn hot. Like, literally. I'd probably catch fire. But it'd be so worth it.

I swallowed the pill, figuring a glass of water wouldn't have gone amiss, but hey, there were worse things in life I guessed. *Bleugh, scratch that, no there weren't. Dry-swallowing uncoated pills was officially up there with eating rusty nails.*

It wasn't long before the drug took effect and colours seemed to melt together in front of my eyes.

"Ponytail…bitch," I panted as the drug rushed into my blood, causing a strange numbness to fill me.

My head swam, but I didn't pass out, my mind just sort of disengaged from my body so I was no longer in any real control of it.

Seconds turned to a blur of time I couldn't comprehend. There were flashing lights, a woman painting my face, sexy black underwear pulled onto my body. The kind of stuff I'd only ever fantasised about wearing. But this was not how my fantasies had gone. In my last dream there had been at least one man choked to death by my thigh lock and another pretty one with a big dick who'd done all the crazy things to me which I liked. Before I killed him too, because *pa-chow* that was just the kind of badass bitch I was.

"Does anyone know the time?" I asked in a mumble as I blinked and found myself in a row of girls dressed just like me, checking an invisible watch on my wrist. "What use is a watch if it's invisible? I bet Pete the unicorn could read it…"

The girls all had collars around their throats with a large silver ring dangling from the centre of each one. Every now and then an ugly fucker of a man appeared, locking a chain to one of their rings and tugging them away through a dark curtain. I didn't want to go beyond that curtain. There was cheering and hollering and someone banging a gavel beyond it. My brain was too foggy because of the drug to figure out what that meant. *The drug, Brooklyn, the drug!*

"Who said that?" I slurred.

Oh right, *I* said that. My 'in the brain' me. And I had a point.

I stepped away from the line-up of girls and stuffed two fingers down my throat in a shadowy corner. I twizzled that little dangly thing that lived back there in my mouth, but that didn't work because I had no damn gag reflex, so I just thought about the Shadow's rancid cock and up came the contents of my stomach. Which happened to be the remnants of that gross tasting pill and half a bag of fries I'd stolen off of an old woman at a bus stop. She'd said I was the problem with the youth these days and I'd thanked her for the compliment before I munched down on her late night snack. Screw getting old. If I wasn't able to do backflips when I was ninety, life wasn't worth living. Not that I could do backflips now, but I almost could. So by the time I was ninety I should definitely have it down.

My head throbbed as I straightened and I casually wiped my fingers off on the nearest girl's panties. She was as high as a bee in a bird's nest, so I doubted she noticed, and it was probably the least of her problems anyway considering the chain man who kept coming and going to take us beyond that curtain.

I still felt all kinds of fuzzy, but clarity was coming back to me piece by piece. And one thing I knew for sure was that I needed to get out of here. I was tiny, I could totally slip out unnoticed. Maybe if I just crawled through a side door no one would see. I could wrap myself in a blanket and curl up in a ball any time someone looked my way. But where could I find a blanket...

A clipping noise reached my ears and I looked down to find a chain had just been bolted to the collar around my neck. The chain man had come to collect another soul and my brain had been too distracted to notice. *Stupid fucking brain, now look what you've done.*

"Mmm, you should fetch a nice price," he purred then yanked the chain to make me follow him, my head jerked forward with the force he used.

I started struggling as some of my strength returned, but my arms felt like they were weighed down with silverback gorillas and my feet just sort of plodded along beneath me of their own accord. *Bad feet, stop it. Turn back this second. Or at least do something to stall for time. Do a tap dance.*

My big toe twitched on my right foot. *Poor effort.*

I was pulled up onto a stage and a spotlight blinded me, glaring down from above. I could hear a crowd but couldn't see them beyond the light as I winced against the brightness, holding up one hand to shield my eyes.

The robed man knocked it away from my face, angling my chin up toward the light. *Balls*, it was as blinding as the fucking sun.

"The bidding starts at ten thousand dollars," a deep voice filled my head that I recognised as Señor Castillo. Man, that voice would be sexy if it wasn't trying to sell me. He could make a killing on audiobooks for sure. But I guessed human trafficking paid better.

A clamour broke out and the bids kept rising and rising while I focused on summoning a demon or two to come save my ass. Shame I didn't have any chalk to paint a pentagram.

I squinted through the light and took in the row of men at the front of the seats, watching me with disturbing looks of intrigue. I memorised as many of them as I could, etching them into my brain and marking their lives. *You don't know who you're messing with, you pack of perverts. I'm the Bully Butcher. And I'm friends with the Devil. Like really good friends. Soon to be more than friends actually. He's got my back.*

"Sold for sixty five thousand!" A gavel hit a block and my head rung from the noise.

Holy mother of fuck.

As my mind started to slot back together, fear crept up my spine like tiny mice in spiky shoes. Me and this pretty underwear had just been bought by someone out there beyond the blinding light. It wasn't one of the front row perverts, but a couple of them had bid on me. What kind of mystery monster had won?

The chain man yanked on my collar, towing me off stage as I tried to pull back, making me cough from the force he used to drag me along. I was marched down tight, winding corridors full of doors with sultry red lighting above. I was deposited in one of the rooms and my heart thrashed as I took in a strange contraption in front of a large bed. It was some sort of bondage bench with straps to hold down my legs and wrists. *Nope. No thank you. One ticket to literally anywhere else please.*

I swung around just as the chain man slipped out of the door and locked it, leaving me alone with the chain still dangling from my throat.

My breaths came unevenly as I gazed around the room for a weapon, but there was nothing but four black stone walls and the sound of my own heart crying. *Hush, Heart. Brain will hear you. And you know how Brain gets when you lose your shit.*

My body at least seemed to be cooperating now, but I wasn't going to be able to tap dance my way out of this situation, no matter how much talent I could conjure for the plan.

The door opened and a man walked in who was twice my age with a red beard and eyes which were too close together for my liking. It gave him a shifty look, not that I needed the hint towards this guy's moral compass. He'd just bought me in an auction and had me delivered to a sex dungeon. *People are awful.*

He locked the door, slipping the key smoothly into his pocket, an action I took thorough note of. His shifty eyes trailed over me as he peeled off a pair of leather gloves like a creeper and I wrinkled my nose.

"Kneel on the bench like a good girl," he ordered and I laughed coldly. "What's so funny?" he snarled.

"I don't take orders from men," I said icily. "And I'm not a good girl."

"Hmm," he hummed, his eyes lighting up. "They said you were spicy."

"Sweetness is overrated. And I'm a Carolina Reaper Pepper, spicy man. You can't handle me. No one can."

He took a step toward me and I backed up to buy myself time, considering my chances against this asshole. He was tall, but he didn't look particularly muscular. I wasn't exactly a bag of muscle myself, but I had a healthy dose of crazy on my side which he wouldn't be ready for.

He lunged at me, grabbing the chain hanging from my throat and dragging me over to the bench. I snarled, tearing gouges into his arms as he forced me in front of him, shoving my knees onto the padded cushions of the bench and pressing down on my back to force me to bend over it. My breaths came heavily as I fought to get up, but he was even stronger than he'd first looked. And I hadn't even had a meal to fuel my body since I'd thrown up those fries.

He released the chain so it came tinkling down beside me. *Oh hello baby, how would you like to team up and get murdery with me?*

I jerked my elbows back, slamming one into the guy's head as he managed to strap my right thigh in place. *Yee-ha!*

I hurried to unclip the chain from my throat and took hold of it with both hands, reaching behind me and looping it around his neck as he fought to get my other thigh strapped to the bench, panting and laughing as he enjoyed my struggle. But I kept winding the chain around his scrawny neck again and again in furious movements then yanked it tight as he tried to shove me off. I kept hold of both ends and wrapped them around my wrists, using my body weight as I bent over the table to yank it tight. His hard dick ground against my ass and I grimaced, wishing I could rip it off and throw it far, far away over a mountain.

"*Whore*," he choked out, punching my sides with furious blows and I grinned as I felt his hard on fading while I choked the life out of him. *Bye bye, shifty dick.*

"I'm death's whore, baby," I growled. "And he wants to play with us."

Everything hurt as he battered me, but I absorbed the pain, letting it fill me up and awaken every dark spirit that was housed in my flesh. The fight slowly went out of him and my arms ached from the strain of holding the chain taut. His heavy body weight settled over me, crushing me to the bench and a sigh of relief left me just as his final breath fluttered against my ear.

I held on for a good few minutes after just in case he decided to come back from the dead for one final, bad guy showdown. But as I turned my head, I saw his tongue was hanging out of his mouth, blue and swollen, his eyes lifeless and fixed in shock. Damn, that felt good. The rush filled me like an orgasm. No, it was better than that. No one had ever made my body feel as good as a killing high did.

"How's that for spicy?" I hissed, dropping the chain, my wrists aching and bruised from how tight it had been wrapped around them. *Good work, chainy-pie.*

I threw my weight back with a grunt of effort and the asshole collapsed to the floor, his creepy leather gloves falling out of his pockets. Were they driving gloves? I mean, ew. Who wore shit like that? I'd wear the fuck out of some lace, fingerless Madonna gloves obviously, but for driving? Hell no.

I unstrapped myself from the bench and squatted down to rummage in his pockets, taking out the key and breathing in deep as I checked myself over. My ribs were reddened and the bruises were starting to show already from the asshole's assault, but I didn't give an owl of a hoot. I was alive. And I wondered if the Devil was peeking out of hell right now to check on me.

"Don't you worry about me, Big Red. Just keep those horns sharp for when I come down there to rock your world."

I realised my hands were shaking and I rubbed them together as the adrenaline subsided. I wasn't scared. I mean okay, maybe I was a little. I guess when I thought about it, I wasn't really afraid to die though. I didn't want to obviously, but what really scared me was losing control while I was still breathing. Being owned by some leather driving glove wearing freak. Yeah, this one was dead. But there were more of them out there. Maybe an endless amount. The world really was a lonely, cruel place to exist in when you were me.

I headed to the door but before I could unlock it, it opened. My heart did a somersault as Señor Castillo strode into the room followed by a man in a shiny black mask that made my skin crawl.

"Are you satisfied?" Castillo asked his companion as I backed up and they took in the dead body. The masked man nodded once, saying nothing which was scary as shit. He had Chainsaw Massacre eyes and everything about him screamed *run*.

"He fell," I deadpanned. They ignored me. "Who's this guy?" I demanded of Castillo.

"He's the man who bought you," he announced, his eyes twinkling with dollar signs as if I'd somehow just earned him and his moustache more money. "This was a test."

"Guess I failed," I said boldly, still hunting around for some kind of weapon. My hands were all bruisy and I didn't fancy my chances fighting these guys without at least a blade or two.

The chain was latched around my last victim's throat and unless I wanted to challenge one of these pricks to a duel, the leather gloves were no use either.

"You passed actually," a cold voice spoke behind the mask, sending a tremor of dread through me. This guy wasn't Mexican. He was American, posh and deadly in some way I didn't understand yet.

Two more masked men walked in behind him and I knew I was fucked before I even saw the syringe in one of their hands.

"She'll feature in our next event if you're interested in attending," the masked man told Castillo before nodding to his lackies. "Take her to the club, boys."

NIALL

CHAPTER FOUR

It had been a long damn time since I'd drunk myself out of consciousness, but when I finally came to after my descent into oblivion, it was clear I'd managed just that.

I swiped a palm over my face, cursing the mother of our Lord as I sat up from my position on the couch. Not that I truly felt a mother should be blamed for the sins of the son or anything like that – my own ma had been a damn saint and look at me. Plus I wasn't religious. All in all, that meant my curses fell on deaf ears to serve no purpose, so I took them back.

My neck was stiff and my head pounding, and I wondered why I couldn't have just drunk a bit more and finished off the job of poisoning myself. I guessed that was a boring way to go though, even if I was feeling low enough to have embraced it right about now.

My tongue was thick with the taste of day old whiskey lingering on it and I heaved a deep breath as I placed my feet on the floor, knocking the empty liquor bottles rolling away from me as I glanced around the room.

It was a beautiful big farmhouse that had been converted with a healthy influx of money into something much more modern. The living room where I'd passed out had tall ceilings which reached up above me to reveal wooden rafters and one wall made entirely of windows that looked over the swimming pool outside and the hills beyond. Green hills which rolled on and on into the horizon without another house or soul in sight which was why it suited me well. I was better alone, less dangerous when my bad moods couldn't so easily be directed towards someone close by.

I hadn't bought much since I'd moved in. The previous owner hadn't had any use for any of his things after we'd met and had left them in my care. Besides, I couldn't summon the energy to give a fuck about soft furnishings even in my best of moods. A couch was a couch, a bed was a bed, and all toilets were just there to flush away the crap no one wanted to look at. Or step in.

I'd made it my own in the ways that counted. I had my rooms in the basement which served me for work purposes and the rest of the shit here suited me well enough to keep me comfortable. Or at least they did when I made it up to bed instead of falling asleep on the burgundy leather Chesterfield couch which had turned out to be an unforgiving mistress indeed.

I glanced over at the couch on the other side of the room, the big grey one that was soft and covered in cushions and looked out over that view. Why the fuck did I pick this one for my bed when that sweet sanctuary was in sight?

I knew the answer to that though. I was punishing myself. Forever punishing, repenting, prostrating myself and yet never coming any closer to redemption. Because there was no coming back from sins that burned as deep as mine and there was no making up for what I'd cost that innocent soul.

I massaged my neck one handed, glancing down at the colourful jester inked on my left side and wondering what the fuck he was so damn happy about.

It was cold in here and I looked across the room, noticing there was no fire burning in the grate either and I wondered vaguely how long I'd spent chasing the dark at the bottom of a bottle.

My phone started ringing and I shoved the empty pizza boxes on the coffee table aside until I dug it out from among them. The thing was running low on charge and I'd have been tempted just to cut the call if the person ringing had been anyone other than my favourite nephew.

"What the fuck have you done now?" I asked as I answered it, wincing a little at the sound of my own voice thick with gravel.

"You sound like shit, Niall. What's wrong? Did you stay up past OAP hour watching The Bachelor again?" Kyan asked, laughing at his own joke. Fucker was lucky he wasn't within stabbing distance, coming at me with the headache I had going.

"Get to the point before I lose interest," I replied, pushing to my feet and striding across the room to get a look out at the view. I was only wearing a pair of grey sweats and the chill in the air had goosebumps rising across my brightly inked skin.

"I was hoping you might be up for helping us with a little project," Kyan replied and I could tell this wasn't just some bullshit, so I gave him my attention. I had to smirk at the use of 'us' in that sentence, the little gang he'd built up with his friends around his girl had apparently become a single entity now. They liked to call themselves the Night Keepers and I had half a mind to get them all matching capes for when they went out avenging or whatever the fuck messed up rich boys did for shits and giggles.

"What project?" I asked, wondering if I was in the mood for projects. Pancakes, yes. Projects? Undetermined.

"I won't beat around the bush with you. We wanna take down Royaume D'élite and seeing as only members can get in there, I'm a little short on help. I figured if anyone I knew had an axe to grind against those fucked up people, it'd be you. Besides, I know you don't generally need much persuasion to help spill a little blood."

I barked a laugh, pushing my fingers into my dirty blonde hair and glancing at the Ava tattoo on my forearm. Yeah, I had good reason to hate the kind of men who liked to use their power to rape and kill innocent women. In fact, if my pa hadn't been so damn keen on keeping the rich bastards who ran that club in line then I probably would have made myself a job of taking out their sex trafficking, lecherous members a long time ago. But if I had one good quality left in me then it was loyalty, and I was still clinging onto it for some reason.

"Pa won't like it," I pointed out as I thought it through.

But why was I clinging to the idea of loyalty to that old prick so hard anyway? I was just a chained attack dog to him, not a son. He didn't love me. He used me. I knew it and I had my own reasons for staying loyal all the same, one being that I knew he'd never just let me walk away and the other being that if I killed him, I would be expected to take his place running the family. And I had no desire to run his empire. Nor did I have any desire to see any of my rotten siblings don the crown. Especially Dougal. Or Connor. Or Ronan for that matter. And there was no fucking way I'd ever let Dermot rule over O'Brien empire. In fact, I'd sooner kill each and every one of my eight siblings than see any of them hold that power.

So I'd stayed my hand, played my part, had been satisfied to stick to the role Pa set for me. But maybe I wasn't satisfied anymore. Especially with that shit he'd pulled on me the other morning. He knew how I felt about Ava. He knew that the last thing I'd ever want to do was marry another. And yet he was looking to force matrimony upon me anyway. To some fucking woman I'd never even met before too. Some Russian with her own agenda and own mafia wannabe family and a father with a shitty tattoo artist. I'd never trust a man who wore bad ink like that. Never. So what had my loyalty to him afforded me? Fucking nothing. Perhaps it was time I switched allegiance. I could be loyal to someone else and still call it a virtue. Right?

"Liam doesn't have to know," Kyan said and I could practically hear him smirking at the idea of undermining the head of our family.

"I suppose he doesn't," I agreed with a smile of my own. I was in the mood to shake a few coconuts from a tree anyway. "And in all honesty, I'm thirsty for blood so this could be the perfect project for me right now," I added, leaning my shoulder against the glass and looking out at the pool. The clouds were grey and threatening rain and I wished they'd just get the fuck on with it or not. Procrastination made my brain hurt.

"Do you want payment?" Kyan offered and I scoffed at the insult.

"We're blood," I growled. "Don't try and pay me for help. If I choose to offer it, it's not based on any profit I may make."

"A favour then?"

"You know I'll always take one of those." I rapped my knuckles against the glass beside me and made my decision "Fuck it, I'm in. If Pa has an issue with me hunting down rapists and gutting them then he can come to me directly about it. There won't be any witnesses to tell him it was me anyway."

Kyan laughed but I could hear the relief in his voice which gave away how much he'd been counting on me and I smiled widely. I liked helping him. I liked having someone who actually thought I was good for that too, that I was reliable and trustworthy. Even more so now that I knew his motivations weren't selfish like they used to be. The boy was in love, that doe eyed, burn the world down, desperate kind of high school obsession that I could almost remember feeling if I just closed my eyes and forgot my life. Which of course I couldn't.

"I'll see you at the next event then?" he confirmed.

"'I'll be the one in the mask," I agreed and he snorted a laugh before cutting the call.

I looked down at my phone and cursed as I realised I'd been in the dark place for three whole days. There was a chunk of my life I was never getting back. Ah well. I dropped the phone onto a desk lined with unopened mail which wasn't addressed to me and decided a shower might be the best thing to start my day.

I headed for the bathroom but paused as I heard the furious screams coming from beyond the basement door at the foot of the stairs. Holy fuck I'd almost forgotten the guy I had down there. Where was my goddamn head at? The poor fucker was probably wondering where the hell I'd gotten to.

I opened up the door that led down the basement and took an axe from the wall before hefting it over my shoulder and whistling as I strode down the stairs. Best to make a mess before having a shower instead of the other way around. Lord knew bloodstains were a bitch to get out of the sheets and my next port of call was going to be my bed. I'd sleep off this hangover and be bright and dandy for my trip to the psycho fun house they liked to call Royaume D'élite.

The journey to Royaume D'élite was a torturous exercise in rich bastard posturing that had me bored to tears as I was forced to head to a random location and then prove my membership to the arsehole who turned up to collect me. Once inside the blacked-out car, I got the joy of dressing in an ebony hooded robe with a black and gold skull mask to cover my face while he drove me around in circles so that I wouldn't know where the club actually was by the time we arrived.

Rich people were fucking strange. Not that I wasn't one of them really, but I'd spent enough time in the gutter through work and choice to decide that I much preferred it in the dirt. The so-called dregs of society knew a whole lot more about life than the upper crust in my humble opinion, and this kind of showboating bullshit left a vile taste on my tongue which had me hungering for something real. Or blood. But I was always partial to a little murder and mayhem, so I was inclined to think it was the former.

The car eventually rolled up outside the sprawling mansion which housed the elite club for the fucked up and I stepped out without waiting for my driver to open my door. He handed me a little device with a button on it which I could use to call him whenever I was inclined to leave, and I had half a mind to press it right now. Or to shove him back into the car and use the thing to bash his brains out...

Before I could get carried away with that little fantasy, I turned away from him, remembering that I'd made a promise and that I was a man of my word - at least when I remembered to be anyway.

My robe had a shiny number two-thirty gleaming on the chest of it, which was the only defining thing about my outfit, allowing me and all the other members of this secret society to remain anonymous in our participation of the fucked up sports which took place here.

I was only a member myself because my pa wanted the family to have a footing here. He liked us having a place at the big boys' table, rubbing shoulders with senators and judges, billionaires and businessmen. Who better to help those corrupt fuckers with their illegal dealings than the Irish mob? I found little appeal in it myself, but I was just the trained attack dog after all so my own preferences were negligible.

A diligent little worker bee hurried forward to greet me like I was some great lord, his skull mask plain black, void of the gold detailing on mine, marking him as a member of staff rather than a member of the club. Though I guessed he was partial to the same oaths of secrecy which I'd sworn to when obtaining my membership. Not that I gave a shit about keeping the secrets of the men who ran this place, but I also hadn't been inclined to spill them before now either.

"I'm meeting a friend here," I said before the man could make a fuss out of welcoming me. "Number...ah shit, I don't remember. His name's Kyan Rosc-"

"You mustn't speak the names of the members!" the guy cried, grasping my arm in an attempt to silence me.

Unfortunately for him, I wasn't a fan of people touching me and I quickly twisted his arm around behind his back before driving him up against the door with enough force to break his nose. He screamed as I exerted pressure and there was a loud crack as something broke. The screams that followed that were damn near musical and as another man came racing outside to find out what was happening, I dropped the first guy, my heart pumping fast as a wide grin split across my face beneath the mask.

"Seventy-seven!" I said loudly, snapping my fingers as it came to me. "I remembered, the man I'm meeting is number seventy-seven. Be a lamb and tell me where he is." The man at my feet just screamed again which was damn rude so I gave him a sharp kick. "Did ya hear me?"

"Seventy-seven is yet to arrive!" the new fella interrupted, moving closer but clever enough not to lay his hands on me like the screamer. "If you'd like to head into the club, I'll be sure to come and find you once he does."

I shrugged like it was no skin off my nose and jogged up the steps and into the mansion, leaving the screamer behind without a backwards glance. It was darkly lit inside, the sound of some thumping dance music grinding through the walls and making me pause as I tried to figure out what song it was.

It was something dark. Something I'd killed someone to, I was fairly certain – maybe that guy with the funny eyebrows who I'd choked out in the men's room at Pam's Pizza that time. Or the one in the elevator at that country club, although come to think of it that place wouldn't have been playing this kind of music so maybe it was the skateboard kid who I'd bludgeoned with his own shoe. Hmm, it was gonna drive me fucking nuts if I didn't – got it, ice cream man! I totally won a bet with myself that day – turns out you can kill someone with an ice cream after all. Anything is possible if you just believe. Still didn't know what the song was but I didn't even like it, so who gave a shit?

I headed through the closest door, finding a room full of men in robes just like mine. They all stood in a circular formation, looking towards the centre of the space and I shoved a few of them aside to get a look at what held them so enraptured.

In the middle of the room, a stone altar had been set up and there was a naked girl lying on it, her eyes wide and pupils full blown as she seemed hardly aware of where she was or what was going on.

A man to one side of the room drew my attention from her as he reached up and spun a wheel like some kind of demon gameshow host and I cocked my head to one side as it slowly came to rest on number thirty-one. One of the robed figures stepped forward eagerly, moving to stand between the girl's thighs as he unzipped his fly and his stumpy little cock emerged from the folds of his robes. Was there anything worse than an ugly dick? Maybe a cake that had been used as a sex toy, but aside from that I couldn't think of a damn thing.

My lip curled back as he tugged the girl closer and I looked into her deadened eyes as she pawed at her breasts and moaned unintelligibly. She made no complaint as he started fucking her, instead moaning more like she was enjoying it and more than a few of the men around me pushed their hands into their pants as they got off on the show. She was likely a whore, well paid for her participation in this, but I found my skin prickling as I met her unfocused gaze. The girl was clearly high as a fucking kite and I wasn't convinced consent could really be given in that situation. Besides, I was bored. And when the bastard blew his load into her without even making her come, I made my mind up about him. *Dead man walking.*

I slipped between the bodies in the crowd quietly as he moved away and the wheel was spun again.

I could be a wraith when I wanted to be. A shadow in the dark which no one ever saw coming. Not that I could strike while I was here. There were rules about killing other club members and I'd accidentally stabbed one the last time I was here, so I probably shouldn't rock the boat. But I could add him to the list.

You could wonder how someone comes to accidentally stab a person, but it was quite simple really. He smacked into me then demanded I apologise for him sloshing his beer all over me. Then he fell on my knife. Repeatedly. Damn tragedy that.

I stalked my prey out of the room and up a set of stairs into a dark corridor. Unfortunately for him, there was no one else here. He didn't even get a squeak out before my hand tightened around his throat to the point of stopping all air from passing through it and I whirled him around to slam him against the closest wall.

"Boo." I grinned as he flinched, then remembered I was wearing the damn mask and sighed at the fact that he couldn't look at the face of his own death.

People didn't tend to recognise me at first. I didn't participate in a whole lot of family business and I had no interest in the meetings and dealings my pa and siblings did behind closed doors. No, my infamy was restricted to a tight circle of dead folk. And I enjoyed giving new targets a good look at me before I came back for the kill. Maybe I was sadistic, but I just loved the idea that I might be featuring in their nightmares before the main event. No doubt they'd all be waiting for me in hell when my time finally came but until then I'd just keep searing the memory of my face into bad men's eyes during their final moments and enjoy the anticipation of seeing them again in the seventh circle when I got there.

My grip tightened as I pinned him to the wall, adrenaline surging through me as he tried to fight my hold, fingernails biting into my hand as he struggled. He was almost as tall as me and as broad too, but despite his size he was weak in all the ways that counted. Plus everyone knew you should go for the dick kick if a fella was choking you out, didn't they? Apparently thirty-one didn't though. More fool him.

I waited until he was a moment from passing out then flipped his mask up so that I could get a look at his face. I had a damn good memory for faces even if I was inclined to forget all else and now I had this specimen marked. If he ever crossed my path again, I'd finish this little game we were playing.

"I'll be seeing you, thirty-one," I breathed in a menacing voice and the panic that flared in his eyes was really akin to poetic. It almost made me feel something. Almost.

I dropped him, letting him fall to the floor as he wheezed and gasped for breath and I was gone before he even began to recover.

"Ah, your friend is just arriving!" that handy little staff member called out to me just as I descended the stairs, and I arched a brow as I wondered how he'd known how to find me. "If you wish to wait in the entrance hall, he will be here momentarily."

I nodded, following him back towards the front door and situating myself against the wall as I waited for my nephew to appear.

I glanced around at the old artwork hanging from the walls, all of it no doubt priceless even if I found old paintings of orgies a little boring. I mean sure, everyone in them was nude, but they always looked bored as fuck too. I was fairly certain people shouldn't look that way while fucking. Though I wasn't entirely certain I remembered it right, so maybe I was wrong.

The doors opened and Kyan strode in, his huge physique unmistakable even if it was entirely covered by the robe which stopped me from seeing any of his heavily inked form. In fact, I wasn't sure if he had more ink than me now. I needed to count. And then he'd need to count. And then I'd have to rectify it if he'd managed to out-tat me. For no other reason than it would make me feel like a lazy asshole if an eighteen-year-old had managed to beat me in the art of scarring his flesh when I'd had fourteen more years than him to coat my own.

I grasped his hand, his grip strong enough that neither of us managed to crush bone despite our efforts to do so, and I grinned even though he couldn't see it beneath my mask.

"Uncle," he greeted in a clipped tone which gave away how much he hated this fucking place.

He needed to work on that. Lad always had been too hot headed, wearing his emotions on his sleeve. Not that I contained mine all that well, but the only things I gave away were superficial. I was a smiling widow. The kind who laughed to bury his pain because if anyone looked at the truth of me, they'd fall apart weeping uncontrollably - much like I would myself. Better to be the clown with the butcher's knife than the mourning man with a target on his back.

My gaze slid from my nephew to the girl at his side. The one who had caught his heart and set it aflame. I liked her, even though I hardly knew her and I reached out to give her arm a squeeze, trying to convey to her that the fear in her eyes was unnecessary. She had two devils guarding her tonight and even in this pit of hell, we wouldn't allow any harm to befall her.

"Hello, lass," I purred affectionately and the look in her eyes beneath the mask covering her face let me know that she was both pleased by my affection and fully aware that I was a deranged psychopath. Clever girl.

"Please remember not to use each other's names or titles," the escort clipped as he dared shoot a glare my way. Perhaps he was looking for a blade to the eye? "We all go by a single name here."

"And what's that?" Tatum asked, her attention shifting to him and stilling my hands even as my finger twitched for the feel of his throat clasped in them. It was a brave man indeed who spoke to me like that.

"Master," he breathed, like a deranged zealot. "For we are all the masters of our own destiny at Royaume D'élite. Here we are free to become our truest selves. We shed our skins at the door and step into a realm where anything is possible."

I rolled my eyes at his bullshit and clapped him on the shoulder, squeezing hard enough to bruise. "Great, lad. Now where can my truest self get a stiff drink?"

"Down the hall and to your left," he answered, bowing his head to us. "Have an exhilarating evening." He strode away and I let him go, reminding myself that killing every annoying fucker in the world wasn't feasible before releasing a calming breath.

I'd been adding some yoga to my training regime recently and they encouraged a lot of that. It was meant to free the shackles of the soul or some shit. Or maybe I was muddling up my yoga and that weird palmistry show I'd been watching while I was drunk the other night. Or was that the other week? Fuck knew. Didn't matter anyway. I was practically the king of meditation now. The other day I'd taken a whole thirty seconds to compose myself before stabbing a fella who'd pissed me off.

Kyan glanced at me, less familiar with the layout of this place than I was and I decided we all really did need that drink, leading him and his girl into the depths of the club in search of it.

I had a feeling that I was going to do something life changing tonight. It had begun with coming here without telling my pa, knowing it would rile him up something rotten. And I was certain it was going to end with something even bigger. But until I figured out what that was, I was happy enough to offer backup to my nephew's plans and ride the wave of the evening. No doubt an opportunity would present itself soon enough, and when it did, I'd be ready to grasp it by the balls and tug on them until I made it my bitch.

BROOKLYN

CHAPTER FIVE

I'd woken in the trunk of a car blindfolded, gagged and hogtied while being transported who knew where. After I was carried inside some building, I'd been untied and put in a cage in a dark room where the sobs of other prisoners had been my only company. They themselves had been pretty useless even when I'd tried to rally them as an army. My speech hadn't gone down well. Maybe I'd rambled on about the liquorice scented man Castillo for too long, or maybe I'd lost them when I'd side-barred onto my childhood and my need for a mother who hadn't up and left me and Dad for a man called Esteban. It might have been when I'd spent a healthy forty-five minutes discussing my lengthy issues over craving a family and yet was held back by the fact that children kind of creeped me out. They were just small people, stumbling around like they were drunk. And if you upped and left them, they'd just sit in a room and die. What the hell was that about?

I couldn't be responsible for something that helpless. Even a monkey could probably let itself out of a window if I went AWOL for a few days. I guessed deep down, I knew my need for a family wasn't really about kids though. It was company I wanted. But men were inherently untrustworthy, skeevy little bastards who I had no time for beyond the odd orgasm (potentially) and women just didn't do it for me – believe me, I'd tried to make it work with a sweet gal called Wanita once. She hadn't been totally aware of my advances and when I'd gone in for a kiss, she'd called me devil woman in Spanish and told me to stop blocking the queue to her burger van. At least I guessed that was what she called me. I didn't actually speak Spanish, but I was pretty intuitive and *devuélveme mi bolso* definitely meant that.

I wished just once in my life I could meet a man who didn't want to rob me of something. My innocence, my body, my life. It was exhausting fighting to own stuff that was supposed to belong to me inherently.

Anyway, a woman in the cage below mine had screeched at me to shut up and eventually I had, falling into a brooding silence as I awaited my doom in the dark. At some point, a masked man showed up and given us all a couple of slices of bread each. I devoured mine like a starved crow, but a few crumbs had fallen down to the cage beneath me and apparently the girl in there didn't like that either. I'd even worked to eat them out of her hair and that had only made her angrier. There was no pleasing some people.

There wasn't a clock in here as far as I could tell, yet there seemed to be an endless tick-tocking in my head as my life appeared to draw closer to some inevitable conclusion. It was either death or fate calling, and I couldn't decide which I preferred. Fate rarely called my name unless she was looking to have a laugh at my expense. So if that bitch was showing up now, it would mean nothing good.

"Get them upstairs for the bets," a guy called as the door opened and light spilled into the room.

I flinched away from it, the sudden brightness hurting my brain as I squinted through it to get a proper look at my surroundings.

My cage was on the top of a two-high stack and in a room that looked like a big stone basement. People started crying, screaming, cowering and whimpering around me. But I just cocked my head and eyed up the men pouring into the room. They all wore robes and the same creepy black masks of the one who'd bought me from Señor Castillo.

I curled my fingers around the bars of my cage and watched them approach while the largest guy at the back called out numbers.

"Fifteen, sixty-four, thirty-two, forty-" he kept going and I realised his lackies were reading numbers on the cages. A lump rose in my throat as prisoners around me were hauled out and shackled together, bags shoved over their heads as they were filed out of the door.

I reached through the bars, turning around the little wooden number hanging there just as the boss guy called it out, "One-fourteen."

My cage door was yanked open and I leapt forward with a snarl, falling down on top of the closest guy, but before I could land a single hit on him, a taser slammed into my side and a thousand bolts of fuck-me-with-a-donkey-dick electricity blasted through my body. I was half aware of hitting the cold floor and jerking around like a fish out of water as pain shot into every corner of my being.

It stopped just as suddenly and I heaved in a couple of breaths before laughing like a mad woman.

"Holy fuck, Batman," I gasped, my chest heaving. Now that the agonising pain was gone, I was all tingly and fuzzy. "Do it again."

"This one's broken in the head," a guy said as he grabbed me up from the floor, my limbs still like jelly. My muscles were all floppy and relaxed, it was like I'd had a full body massage from the inside out and I'd definitely peed myself just a teensy bit.

I was dragged out of the room, my wrists put in chains and locked to the back of the line of the prisoners just before a black bag was tugged over my head.

Okay, how do I get out of this? And how do I pocket one of those tasers for personal reasons?

My foot hit a step and my face bumped into the back of the woman in front of me as we were led upstairs. We kept going and going and going while I occasionally yanked on my restraints or swore at my captors.

We finally stopped and someone pulled the bag off of my head, the sound of a crowd filling my ears as lights swept over me. I was on a stage looking out across a sea of black masked faces and suddenly a round of bidding began, voices hollering out and making my ears ring as they fought to win the man at the front of our line.

By the time they got to me, I was as pissed as a bobcat in a net. I was getting bid on again? Seriously? I was third-hand goods at this point. Didn't someone wanna keep lil ol' me? I mean, I knew I wasn't much of a prize with my skinny arms and hobo lifestyle. And I didn't actually wanna be owned obviously. But this was getting insulting now. I needed a target who stuck around long enough for me to kill them and escape. Why was that so much to ask?

The bidding started again and a man gripped my face, turning it toward the crowd. When his other hand slid down to my ass, I sank my teeth into his fingers with a growl, tearing into his skin until I tasted blood. He back handed me so hard I knocked into the girl beside me and sent her flying. As I fell down on top of her and started kicking and spitting at anyone who tried to pull me up, the bidding grew more frantic. One man kept shouting out louder than all the others and eventually bellowed, "Fifty thousand dollars for her as my proxy!"

Um, what?

No one bid higher and as I was finally tugged upright by two sets of hands, I saw my winning bidder standing in the audience with his eyes set on me behind his mask.

"One-twenty-three, you're in the club if she wins," a booming voice called to the winning bidder and I memorised that number, marking his life. *You just bought your death muchacha.*

We were led off stage and a clanging noise sounded just before we were shoved through a barred door. The space wasn't cosy exactly. More like a cage of untold misery. But at least we were all untied before we were left standing together in front of a set of black drapes hanging from the bars ahead of us.

Above us was a fancy balcony ringing around what I guessed was the massive room we were in. The ceiling was an artwork of creepy paintings of ugly gargoyles and the masked assholes were all walking up to the balcony railings to watch us, seeming riled up by something. Whatever they were happy about couldn't be good. There was definitely gonna be a hungry tiger beyond those drapes. Or maybe a pack of angry badgers. *How many badgers can I take on at once? Twelve? That's a lot of badgers. But if I landed every punch, I could do it. But what if there's thirteen? Or a hundred? Shit, I can't take on a hundred angry badgers.*

"The rules are this!" a booming voice called to us and my head snapped around to locate a tall man in a gold mask staring down at us from the balcony. "Only one of you will leave the game. If you are not the last one standing, you will *all* die."

Some of the people around me shifted nervously, sharing glances, but others seemed unphased by what they'd been told, like they'd been expecting it. I did a quick headcount and tried not to panic. Fifteen. This was fine. Totally fine. I was just in a death game with a bunch of desperate prisoners who all wanted to live as much as I did. Plenty of whom were big ass men who seemed ready for a fight as they limbered up and I noticed numerous scars across their bare chests and backs.

O...kay. I'm not gonna be facing badgers. So let's do a quick assessment of how fucked I really am –

A klaxon sounded and a cage door slid open ahead of us, the black drapes whipping back simultaneously. There was a table full of weapons ahead and the big motherfuckers ran for them like they'd known they'd be there.

The woman in front of me fell to her knees and started crying. I leapt over her like a heartless bitch, shoving people aside and racing to that table with every ounce of strength in my body. *Don't stop. Dodge, weave, push, snatch.*

A massive guy with a skull tattoo on his neck swung around with a machete and I ducked it fast, but the spray of blood over my back said some unlucky fucker behind me had met their end.

I scrambled between the meaty man's legs and reached up to grab a weapon from the table, my fingers closing around the hilt of a freaking ninja sword. *It's killin' time, baby.*

I crawled under the table and started slashing the legs of as many of the massive assholes as I could. *Slash, slash, slasheroo. Buh-bye advantage.*

My heart pounded to this beautiful tune as violence descended around me, screams ringing out, death and carnage everywhere. This wasn't cool though. I was definitely aware of that. But I also wasn't going to die here like a rat in a maze. Survival instinct wasn't gonna let me. And my morals were shady on the best of days. I'd heard the rules like the rest of them had. It was me or them. So it was gonna be me.

Someone grabbed my ankle and hauled me out from under the table on my back, kicking the hand which held my sword and sending it flying away from me. *Nooo, come back Mr Slashington!*

The huge man swung an axe down at me and I jerked sideways, the blade slamming into the stone floor with a clang that reverberated through my skull and a cheer went up from the crowd.

I threw my head toward his junk and my forehead crushed his dick, making him stumble back with a roar and drop the axe. Some men could be the biggest, baddest motherfuckers in the world, but they still had an off switch sitting between their legs like all the others.

I snatched up his axe, wielding it over my head and bringing it down on his skull with a juicy thwack that finished him. My new axe got stuck and before I could race off into the labyrinth of shipping containers and cages that made up this twisted little arena, strong hands wrapped around my throat from behind and squeezed.

I clawed and scratched at their fingers before they shoved me up against the mesh face first and started choking me while bashing my head into the bars.

Holy.

Mother.

Of.

A.

Twat.

I fought like mad to try and get free, but this asshole was not letting go and stars were bursting in front of my eyes.

Satan, your girl is in trouble! Give her a hand, kay?

The guy released me and screamed in pain. I wheeled around, finding a woman burying a knife into his back again and again and I gave her a free pass, leaping away from her. But she finished her kill and took chase like a two-faced snake. *There's what being nice gets me. P.S. Thanks for the help, Big Red. Keep sending me those positive vibes.*

I raced off into the maze, sprinting through a shipping container, the top replaced with bars so the audience could keep watching and they cheered in excitement as they peered down at the contestants from walkways that crisscrossed overhead.

A weirdly dark patch on the floor made me slow and I pressed my toe to it, feeling some sort of material dipping under my weight. It was camouflaged with the floor and screamed dodgy to me, so I turned back only to find the knife-wielding girl racing inside and trapping me.

She ran full force at me and there was really only one thing I could do. I screamed at her like a banshee and grabbed her outstretched hand where she held the knife, swinging her around behind me. The knife came loose from her fingertips and clattered at my feet as she fell backwards onto the material. It dropped beneath her and she tumbled into a pit trap, her cry cut short as she was impaled on sharp spears sticking up from the ground. *Ick, that's no way to die. Glad it wasn't me.*

Hoots and whistles came from the crowd along with a few catcalls and I spared a moment to offer them my middle finger before grabbing the knife and heading back the way I'd come.

I moved through the cages, expecting a fight at any moment as my muscles tensed and flexed. My breaths were heavy and I could taste blood on my lips that wasn't mine. It was totally gross. But I also kinda liked it.

I rounded into the next cage, but a huge weight collided with me as a tattooed guy knocked me to the ground. He punched me in the head and pain burst through my actual brain. He laughed like he was enjoying himself, but then I slammed my knife into his side and his laughter turned to squeals as I kept stabbing. *In out, in out, shake it all about, do the hokey cokey and – oh he's dead.*

I wriggled out from beneath him and took a moment to gather my wits as I headed on into the maze. I was shaken for sure, but not stirred. I'd been hungering for a chance to kill again for a while, and so long as these assholes kept coming at me, I was going to keep enjoying myself. I might as well get something out of these shitty circumstances, because honestly if I thought about it too much I was going to start panicking and getting all woe-is-me.

I padded around the next corner on silent feet and two bitches descended on me at once. One of them grabbed my arm as I slashed at them with the knife, fighting to get it from my grip as the other one swung a baseball bat at my head. I ducked it before it could connect and snarled as the other girl bit my hand to make me let go of the knife.

She snatched the hilt before it fell from my fingers and I kicked her in the stomach to get her away from me before turning and running for my life. I wasn't stupid enough to stand there and take my chances without a weapon.

The bite on my hand stung and I cursed as my body hummed with all kinds of bruises and cuts. If I made it through this with all my limbs intact, I was gonna need a hug. I couldn't remember when I'd had my last one of those, but I'd craved plenty on cold winter nights. It was just a shame so many humans were unhuggable. Was it so much to ask for one snuggly one who didn't wanna see me in pain?

I lost the girls by running through the maze at my top speed, having outrun far too many cops in my time to let them catch me. *I'm a pony with a rocket up my butt. I can outrun anything.*

I turned into another cage and spotted a corridor out beyond it with people casually walking along dressed in robes. I ran toward it, colliding with the bars and wrapping my fingers around them.

"Hey!" I hissed. This place might have been full of assholes, but they all seemed to enjoy death. So they might help me if they thought it could mean I'd spill more blood for their entertainment. "Are you carrying weapons? Give me something to help!"

Two bright blue eyes peered at me from beneath the nearest mask, the girl dressed in some tight ass catsuit thing that accentuated her curves. Girls were sometimes less assholey than men. Like ten percent of the time. She gazed at me with a desperation that almost matched my own and hope bloomed in my chest.

"I'm sorry, I don't-"

Her male companion yanked her away from me as a guy in a black mask strode forward and took a baton from his hip. For a second I thought he was going to give it to me, then he whacked it down where my hands were gripping the bars and I cursed, stumbling back and sucking my middle finger which had caught the worst of the blow.

I heard heavy footfalls coming up behind me and wheeled around in alarm, spotting a huge, bearded man running toward me like the beast from the east. I raced off into the maze before he could get his hands on me, letting out a little squeak of fright. *I need a weapon dammit.*

I made a few circles through the cages to make sure I lost the yeti on my heels and suddenly heard female voices up ahead.

"It's just that big hairy guy, the man with the crow tattoo and the girl I took the knife from left, Greta," one of them said and I peered around the corner of a large crate I was hiding behind. *Thanks for the info bitchtits.*

My gaze fell on Greta as she crept up behind her companion with her bat held above her head. She swung a furious blow and didn't stop there even when her apparent friend hit the ground in a pool of blood. *People are awful.*

I watched the sickening show as my gaze hooked on the knife that had clattered away from the dead girl's hand. *My* knife. *Hello, pretty, I'm coming for you. Just wait right there.*

I slinked out of the shadows, moving silently up behind Greta as she made a show for the audience then waved her bloody bat triumphantly at them. A bunch of the masked observers were laughing and I was pretty sure I was the reason why.

I swiped up the knife from the floor behind Greta's feet and jammed it into the back of her neck before she even knew what had happened. She hit the ground as she died and I was about to steal her bat too when the yeti came charging toward me from around the corner and my heart lurched into my throat.

He had a crowbar in his hand ready to beat my head in like a piñata, but there was no candy inside me. If he ripped me open, only sharp stuff would fall out.

I whipped up the bat, throwing it hard at his face, making him flinch aside. I ran at him, stealing that teeny tiny moment of advantage, but his fist smashed into my gut and I hit the ground like a sack of shit. *Plan failed. What's my Plan B? Um, badgers? No that's not a plan. Foxes, cockerels, squids, great crested grebes – why am I just naming animals?!*

The crowbar smashed into my leg and I screamed wildly from the pain, but he'd caught the fleshy under bit and I was pretty sure my bone had survived. He grinned, about to hit my leg again, apparently thinking he was going to finish this slowly, put on a parade of death for our audience. *Seriously bad move, yeti man.*

I slashed at him with the knife and he gasped as I cut his stomach, seeming surprised I'd managed to land the strike. He swung the crowbar toward my head and I stabbed the knife at his arm, cutting him again and making him drop the bar before he could land the blow. He reared away with a yell of pain and I leapt up, continuing to stab and stab and stab and stab, not giving him a chance to use his superior strength against me. "Yeti-ki-yay motherfucker!"

Shock filled his eyes. The fact that he'd thought I'd be easy prey for him to play with was funny really. And if I hadn't been sweaty, bleeding, and gasping for breath, I might have laughed. *Oh wait, I am laughing.*

He fell at my feet and I looked around the audience for a timer, but there was no sign that told me how long I had left. So I kept running through the maze as I hunted for the final guy, blood pissing down my leg where the crowbar had struck me, but at least I was still walking so it definitely wasn't broken. Hurt like a bitch in a blender though.

Footsteps sounded behind me and I darted into a shadowy corner to hide, holding my breath as a man appeared a beat later. He was tall but he definitely wasn't the guy with the crow tattoo. *Goddammit, Greta, how dare you count wrong? How many assholes are left in this game with me? Can't you do anything right?*

I crept silently toward the guy and leapt up, slashing my knife across his throat, needing to conserve my energy because I was getting seriously knackered now. Gah, why hadn't I put in more time at the gym when I'd had the chance to up my stamina? Oh right, because the gym was just that dirty alleyway full of used condoms where Bert the Shitter lived. And yeah, he had that name because there was always shit on his pants. And no, it wasn't actually a gym. So I really wished I hadn't paid the join-up fee of two pickles and an egg.

The not-crow-tattoo dude fell at my feet and if I'd been a remorseful kinda girl, I might have wondered whether he had any sort of life waiting for him outside of this place, if there was someone missing him or whatever. But I wasn't so, meh.

A loud clang caught my attention and I crept out into the next cage, frowning at the sight of the masked guy who'd just fallen from the balcony to land on top of the bars. I gazed up at the dude who'd clearly pushed him, now stepping back from the edge and adjusting his mask. The man beside the pusher was laughing so loudly I could hear it all the way from here and I really liked that sound for some reason. It was all rough and wild and free and it made me want to capture it in a jar to listen to later.

A savage smile pulled at my lips as I took in my new prey writhing on top of the bars of my prison. He was one of the fuckers who'd put me in here, so it seemed right that he'd come to play.

When life gives you assholes, make assholeaid.

NIALL

CHAPTER SIX

Kyan and his gang of ferocious friends were much subtler beasts than me. I'd kept watch for him and his girl while they broke into an office and hunted for the information they'd need to take this place down. I had to wonder why they were bothering. Give me an assault rifle, some kerosene and a match and I'd have this place gone before the night was up.

In response to my suggestion of doing just that, Kyan had said something about this building not being the end of it and them needing to expose the members before they could take it apart. I would have just insisted that my plan was better, but he then pointed out that the people they kept in cages here probably wouldn't do so well in a gun fight. Or a fire. And though I may have been a man without morals, there were a few lines I wouldn't cross. Killing innocents was one of them. And women who had been kidnapped and coerced for use as sex toys would never fall prey to violence at my hands.

So instead of setting this place alight, I'd trailed them while they conducted their plans, hunted in offices and then we'd caused some minor mayhem. But now my skin was beginning to itch with the need to do something more. Something important. It was like the beat of music I could hardly hear but hungered to dance to and I needed to know where following it would lead me.

We'd made our way through several of the rooms in this place while they conducted their plans, then I'd brought the two of them to my favourite. Where they held death games. Kyan and his girl had followed me up a flight of stairs onto the mezzanine level where metal walkways ran across the caged area below so that spectators could watch the people within the maze as they fought for their lives and we'd stopped to watch.

I'd fought in there once myself. It was how I'd earned my membership to this elitist club - by being the last man standing. And I had to say no one in my game had posed me much of a challenge. But occasionally I'd seen men and women of merit fighting down there. Most of them weren't potential members of course, just poor folk looking for a pay out by playing as proxy for a rich sponsor. I couldn't say I knew a whole lot about the ins and outs of it. It had never caught my attention, though now that Kyan had decided to take an interest in destroying this place, I found my interest piqued.

My pulse was thrumming violently as I watched the spectator Kyan had just launched over the railing start crawling away across the top of it, my laughter ringing out loudly. Damn I wanted to know what the fella had done to make my nephew toss him over the side but whatever way, this was shaping up to be one hilarious fucking show.

The guy struggled to move on top of the cage and to my delight, down below him a wolf was hunting, one of the players in the game sensing fresh meat as she crept out of the shadows beneath him.

As I looked at the girl, a shiver raced down my spine and my smile widened as I saw something in her that caught hold of me and just wouldn't let go.

With a cry like a warrior charging into battle, she leapt up with her bloody knife in hand and slammed the thing straight into the member's gut.

He howled and screamed as she clung onto the bars beneath him and stabbed and stabbed and stabbed, blood pouring down on her like rain while the officials all yelled and screamed instructions to try and save him.

But it was too damn late for that and I howled another laugh as I watch the fucker get stuck full of holes by the pocket-sized girl in the cage, fascinated by the show she was putting on.

She was wild, brutal, clearly untrained but also full of that fire which I recognised so easily because it burned in me too. She was a kindred soul. Someone so full of pain and hate that the only cure for it was violence. I knew that feeling well. And I wanted to get a taste of hers.

It was hard to get a good look at her besides the mane of ebony hair and the blood which now coated her skin from the murder she'd committed, but I wasn't certain if I'd ever seen such beauty in the making. There was something captivating about her which drew me in like nothing had in so long that I couldn't even draw a comparison. She was this itty bitty girl, probably no more than five foot nothing and yet she'd damn near won this game with savage brutality and pure talent. Some people claimed that killing wasn't a talent, but they were damn wrong. It was an art form that was wildly underappreciated, but I could tell she knew that as well as I did. She got it.

My hands curled around the metal railing before me as I watched her, leaning right over it so that I was in danger of falling myself as I strained to get a better look, wanting to see the glint in her eyes as she bathed in the glory of the kill.

"Ho-ly fuck, I think I'm in love," I announced loudly as I couldn't help but laugh again while the guards on the outside of the cage shot my little firecracker with stun guns which sent her crashing to the ground in a heap.

I snarled like a beast at the sight of that. The motherfuckers were in no danger from her on their side of the fence and I had a general dislike for long range weapons at the best of times.

She twitched and convulsed beneath the effects of the electricity they'd shot her with, but I was pretty sure I could hear her cussing them out, naming them cock sucking toad fuckers and wart faced ball sacks despite the clear agony she was in. Yeah, she was a kindred spirit alright. Girl after me own heart.

Movement caught my eye as the final contestant in the death match spotted her lying there and raced forward to try and take his shot at her while she was down. I whistled sharply at her, half tempted to call out a warning before deciding I'd rather just see if she really had the fight in her I thought she did and watching with rapt attention instead.

Her opponent charged at her with death in his eyes as she made it to her knees, trying to grasp the knife she'd dropped when she was hit with the stun guns. But it was out of reach and she clearly hadn't fully recovered. It was all but over and I snarled angrily at the idea of that. I wanted to see her get her shot, not watch her get taken down because of those damn guards.

The fella swung a rusty metal pipe at her head and that should have been lights out - except she managed to roll beneath it somehow, her reflexes clearly those of someone who had been born to fight even if her form was all over the fucking place. She snatched her knife as she came up, her strikingly blue eyes flaring with something so much more intoxicating than the need to survive - that was the ache to kill I saw flaring within her soul.

She didn't allow her position on her knees to be the end of her either, stabbing the guy right in the dick and snatching the rusty pole from him as he screamed like a babe. There wasn't a beat of hesitation as she swung the pole with all her might and caved his head in like a pro and I found myself laughing loudly again as she was announced the winner.

I felt wide awake for the first time in fuck knew how long as I looked down at the bloodstained girl and I knew that this was exactly what I'd been searching for tonight.

I stood tall, turning away from her and spotting a group of robed men striding towards us along the walkway looking like a squadron of pissed off enforcers and I clapped a hand down on Kyan's shoulder to draw his attention to them too. No doubt they were here to give him a spanking for tossing that fella down to his death, but I was feeling generous today, so I decided to take the heat for that little accident. Besides, an idea had just occurred to me which wouldn't let up in my mind and I was fairly certain I was about to do something which was ill advised.

"Well lad, that's my cue," I announced, eyeing the robed figures as I decided on how best to play this.

"Shit," Kyan muttered, and I was guessing he hadn't really wanted to bring too much attention down on himself tonight. Or more likely down on his girl, and I fully understood his desire to protect her.

"What do we do now?" Tatum asked nervously and I smiled before remembering the mask meant she couldn't see it and cursing it in my mind.

"Just leave this to me," I said firmly, leaving no room for discussion on the subject. "I haven't spent nearly enough of Pa's money recently and I think that beautiful little specimen down there is worth the gold."

"What's that supposed to mean?" Tatum demanded and I was almost offended at the clear concern in her voice before remembering that she'd once seen me drop two decapitated heads onto a dinner table, so her low opinion of me was well enough earned.

Either way, there wasn't time for me to reassure her of my pure intentions. And I wasn't certain I could really claim purity anyway. All I knew for sure was that I wanted that girl down there. I wasn't certain what for yet, but I wanted her and I wasn't leaving her in this fucking place. She was mine, I just needed to negotiate the hows of that or figure out who I needed to kill to make it so.

"Just get out of here, lad, and take your sweet girl with you. Let's hope neither of you ever have to come back," I said firmly, focusing on my nephew and I strode away from them towards the robed men without letting them argue. Now wasn't the time for it and I was really rather keen on my new idea.

I opened my arms wide like I might be inclined to hug the men who were pissed as hell over the dead chap down there and I called out to them placatingly as I approached. "Sorry lads! But that asshole had it coming, he was refusing to pay up on a debt he owed me. And I couldn't have known the lass would stick him full of holes now, could I? What say we get together over a whiskey and discuss what reparations you need me to pay to make this right again. And while we're in discussions, I'll be wanting a price for ownership of that girl down there."

"You are aware of the rules against killing other club members?" the man who I guessed was in charge ground out and I nodded, placing my hands together like I was praying for them to forgive me. Not that I cared either way if they did. "Like I said, I'm good to cover the costs and I'll happily take that little killer off of your hands too."

They exchanged some looks and I was guessing they hadn't expected me to come so quietly, but as they surrounded me and turned back the way they'd come, I fell in with them easily enough. Five against one wasn't great odds, but I was fairly certain I could take them all down without too much trouble if needs be. I just had more interest in my new purchase than I did in breaking their necks right now.

I glanced back over my shoulder, glad to find Kyan and his girl gone before I let the men lead me downstairs. They could get themselves out of here and continue their plotting in safety while I let this night play out and I got the feeling that it was going to go damn well.

"The Grand Master will charge your account for the cost of the clean up on the deceased member," one of them said to me and I nodded easily enough. It was my pa's money anyway and he would pay it without complaint to keep his connections with the powerful men who ran this club in place.

Personally, I was of the opinion that they could all get fucked. Let them come at the O'Briens if they really thought they could take us on. We might have been a bunch of savages who hated each other's guts, but we'd band together and fight to the death for this family we all detested if we had to. I'd like to see a bunch of judges and senators come out of that fight on top. But Pa enjoyed his scheming, putting powerful men in his pockets and making friends in high places, which was fine for him and didn't matter enough to me for any kind of fuss to be made over it.

"And what about the girl?" I asked, not really giving a shit about the so-called trouble I was in over the death of some prick. There wasn't any punishment left for me in this world that compared to what I'd already suffered through anyway, so they could bring it on.

"A night with one of our winners is priced at-"

"You're misunderstanding me, lad," I interrupted. "I'm not looking to spend the night fucking her to then just give her back to you when I'm done. I want ownership."

"Ah, I see. So you'd like use of one of the studios?" another masked man suggested and I pursed my lips at not being able to even see their faces. I'd be marking them for making this difficult if I had.

"What's a studio?" I asked, a little curious though I was fairly certain they still weren't offering what I was asking for.

"Just a private space where you may take one of our products to use as you require... until their death. The price is particularly high of course because of the loss of stock, but if that is what you require then it can be arranged."

"Oh, so I can just fuck her and do whatever else until I kill her in there?" I asked, starting to see why Kyan hated this place, my hands curling into fists. I was feeling all kinds of murderous right now and I had to wonder if I could just take this place down like I'd planned or if I should let Kyan execute his plan with his friends. It was hanging on a coin toss right about now for sure.

"Yes. Of course, if necrophilia is more to your tastes you can always-"

"That is not to my tastes," I interrupted him with a warning growl.

And frankly I'd seen plenty of dead bodies in my life, not one of which had tempted me to stick my dick into them. Dead people shit themselves a lot of the time aside from anything else and I'd never gotten hard over the stench of shit. "I want to purchase her and take her home with me."

Silence.

Not a fucking word.

"That's...rather unusual. The security risk involved with allowing a live-"

"In case the accent hadn't clued you in - it may be worth mentioning that I'm an O'Brien. Not one witness has ever lived to testify shit against my family and I'm hardly likely to make the mistake of allowing that girl to become the first. Now fuck off and ask someone more important than you how much it's going to cost me to take ownership of her or you'll find yourselves taking part in a death game which isn't held inside of a cage."

The men muttered between themselves before scattering, only one of them staying with me as he cleared his throat uncomfortably, obviously concerned I might really flip on him. *Clever boy.*

"They will get an answer for you from the Grand Master," he explained a little nervously. "Would you like a drink while you wait, or-"

"I'd like to meet my new property," I said firmly. "So perhaps you could be a duck and take me to her."

He nodded before leading me further into the dark corridors, moving us away from the sound of music towards the parts of the club which I guessed were more designed for the staff. It wasn't as fancy down here and people were hurrying back and forth around us as we walked.

The light brightened as we headed through another door and I strode downstairs into a room with cages all around us, holding men and women in various states of undress. Most of them cowered away from the bars of their cages, trying to hide and not draw any attention as I prowled into the room. I guessed that being selected by someone in a set of robes like mine wasn't necessarily very desirable to them, but they had no need to fear me, unlike most other people I came across.

There was one prisoner who didn't seem to have the faintest desire to remain ignored and forgotten, and my lips lifted into a smile as the killer I'd come here for rattled the bars of her cage and screamed curses my way.

"I won your fucking game!" she yelled. "Now let me out of here before I rip one of these bars off of this cage and ram it so far up your ass you end up choking on it."

She was still covered in blood, dressed in revealing black underwear because that was what they liked to make the girls fight in during the games and her dark hair was sticking to her face. She was bruised, cut and battered too which made my blood burn with a feral kind of rage. But as the people directly responsible for those injuries already lay dead, I forced aside my need for bloodshed at the sight of them. None of that was what captured my attention most though. The look in her electric blue eyes was what held me captive. She was wild and furious and filled with a need I knew too well. She wanted to make the world bleed. And she may just have met the man able to help her do it.

I didn't say anything as I stood watching her, listening to the insults she tossed my way and smirking at them while she riled herself up beyond the point of return. She started to throw herself against the bars with more and more force, no doubt injuring herself in the process, not that she cared.

A man appeared from another door and hurried towards us. "The Grand Master has accepted your request. He requires five hundred for her and a guarantee that she will never be allowed to speak a word of this place to anyone."

"Done," I agreed, knowing he meant five hundred thousand and not batting an eye. "Just add it to the bill you send my pa. But don't itemise it. Let him think the entire fee is for the death of that prick I pushed."

The man hesitated, seemed to realise I'd gut him if he didn't agree to that then nodded. "As you desire."

While my focus was on him, the other guy shot my latest purchase with a stun gun I hadn't noticed before reaching through the bars and injecting her with something.

"What the fuck are you doing?" I roared, my fist colliding with his jaw as I knocked his mask half way from his face and sent him crashing to the floor.

The girl's eyes met mine for a moment before she passed out and there was a question in them which I couldn't fathom.

"It's procedure for us to sedate and clean any stock who are bought," the man said in a rush, raising his hands defensively.

"Fuck procedure. And I doubt the girl wants your fucking hands on her. I'll take her bloody and I'll take her now. Open the cage," I snarled.

The men exchanged a glare then hurriedly unlocked it for me, seeming to accurately guess that I wouldn't hesitate to kill them if they continued to piss me off and doing as I'd said.

I didn't wait for their approval before stooping down and picking the girl up. She was skinny and her flesh was cold beneath the wet blood that smeared across it where I touched her.

I held her close, offering her a little body heat and her head lolled over my arm as I turned and started towards the exit, having gotten what I'd come for.

"Call my car around!" I yelled over my shoulder, not looking back as I strode away from them. They were just fucking lucky I wasn't currently in the process of gutting them.

By the time I made it outside, the car was waiting for me and the driver pulled the door open to let me get into it. I dropped into the backseat, propping the girl up beside me and taking off the cloak I was wearing before wrapping her up in it. It wasn't any form of kindness on my part, I just had no desire to leave her dressed up like a whore.

I closed the door behind me and was plunged into darkness behind the tinted glass as the driver pulled away from the club and started on the journey back to my car. I wasn't entirely sure what I was going to do with my new pet when I got her home. All I knew was that I hadn't wanted to leave a girl who fought like she did in that place to be destroyed by the monsters who frequented it.

I guessed I'd just have to figure the rest out.

Ah well, the best ideas were always formed of chaos and spontaneity. And I got the feeling this might just be one of my greatest decisions yet.

BROOKLYN

CHAPTER SEVEN

I ran toward the unfortunate fucker who was about to get some payment for watching me down in the death fight. He was screaming like a wounded animal, his arm clearly broken as he tried to drag himself along to get off the cage roof.

I mentally tipped a salute to the man who'd handed me one of the dickwads who'd been enjoying watching this fight, then I jumped up, catching hold of the bars underneath him and drove my knife up into his big gut. I stabbed and stabbed, letting his blood flow as he screamed and tried to roll away. But one final slash ended him for good and my fingers peeled off the bars before I dropped down to land in the pool of his blood that had collected below.

My foot slipped, but I caught myself as the crowd shouted out in anger and excitement above me, chaos reigning.

Guards appeared at the side of the cage to my right and I tried to move before they shot at me with stun guns, but I fell to the ground under the assault of their weapons. Electricity raced through my limbs and pain scorched the inside of my skull. I twitched and jerked, light bursting in front of my eyes and making me sick. This wasn't sexy like the taser. These things *hurt more than anything I'd ever felt before. They were burning me from the inside out.*

The pain suddenly stopped and a shadow leered over me. I scrambled to my knees, hardly able to see as I sensed death breathing down my neck. I hunted blindly for my knife, my head spinning and my gut rolling.

A whoosh of air told me something big was being swung my way. I dropped backwards and rolled on instinct alone, trying not to retch as my hand landed on my knife.

Oh hello beautiful, where have you been hiding? *I reared up, stabbing madly and a scream told me I'd met my target just as my vision was restored. And what a target it was. My knife was buried in the guy's groin and he fell back with a scream of agony, dropping the rusty pole in his hand.*

I grabbed it from the ground, leaving my knife deep in his junk and jumping up to finish him off with a vicious blow to the head. He died at my feet and I swallowed the bile in my throat as a din of shouts filled my entire skull, making my brain rattle and bounce all over the place.

Someone was announcing me as the winner as I tossed the rusty pole aside and gazed up at the sea of monsters above. I may have won, but the fight wasn't over. Because I knew I hadn't just earned my freedom. I'd just traded one type of hell for another.

My gaze caught on the masked face of the laughing man as he whooped and hollered for me and somehow, I didn't mind his excitement the way I did the others. It felt like he was cheering for *me not* at *me, and the intensity of the look he was giving me from within that mask set my skin alight with fire. If I didn't know better, I would have said the Devil had come to watch me prove myself.*

My fingers twitched as consciousness slid back to me and I realised I was no longer in the death game. I'd won. I was somehow alive, clinging to this world like a cockroach with a tiara.

Music pounded in my head and I vaguely recognised it as Bad Memory by K.Flay as a rough male voice with an Irish accent sang along word for word somewhere nearby. My head throbbed and my injuries from the death game were stinging, burning and itching. The one on my leg in particular was screaming for attention, but I wasn't sure if I was going to live long enough to fix it up. I unfurled my hands where they were tightened into fists and the blood of my opponents cracked where it had dried on my knuckles. *Man, I was having a rough twenty-four hours. And I couldn't even celebrate my victory in the death game because now it looked like I had someone else to kill. Jeez, you wait for people to murder then ten come along at once.*

I kept my eyes closed as the effects of the drugs wore off, taking in my surroundings with my other senses as my body was jostled around in the seat of some vehicle, a belt across my body telling me I was strapped in. There was a robe wrapped around me and I had the icky feeling it was one from that freak club.

The singing was coming from my left and as the grogginess slipped from my mind, I peeked through my eyelashes to assess my latest captor.

His robes and mask were gone, revealing the beast of a man who had hidden beneath. He had messy blonde hair and an athletic physique, his black t-shirt was drawn taut around his muscular arms which were heavily inked with colourful tattoos, and my gaze caught on the horns of a devil devouring souls on his forearm. I swear Big Red winked at me and I was almost tempted to wink back. *Hey there, baby, still watching the show? I hope you like the bastards I sent your way. Are you cooking them up on a barbeque? You're such a bad boy.*

My gaze flicked up to the guy's face, the blonde stubble on his jaw, and his eyes which were crocodile green and sort of captivating. My eyes widened further as I studied the depths of them, finding something temptingly familiar there which called to the darkest piece of my soul. But then those eyes flashed onto me and I realised he'd stopped singing and had noticed I was no longer unconscious. *Crapcakes.*

"Good evening, Spider," he said, that Irish accent thicker in speech than it had been in song and I kinda liked that, but my upper lip peeled back at this creep who'd bought me for his own pleasure. And despite his size, he looked hungry. Like a stray mutt which had been starved for years, living on scraps. "Now let's just get a couple o' things straight-"

I shrieked like a wildcat, lunging at him and tearing at his face with my nails. The SUV he was driving was going way too fast down a narrow lane between trees, but fuck him if he thought that was gonna stop me. I'd drive him off the road and crawl out of the burning wreckage like a zombie. The Devil would protect me, but this motherfucker was going down.

He started laughing, shoving my hands off of him and pumping the gas with a roar of the engine. I snarled like a savage, fighting against the restraint of the seatbelt as I tore at him, punching and scratching as he batted my hands away like we were play fighting.

I landed a solid punch to his jaw and he threw out a hand with a growl, locking it around my throat and shoving me hard back into my seat. *Ooh la la, I shouldn't like that but I hella do. Gah, focus. He's a creep. Creepy McCreeperson the fifth.*

His eyes remained on me as he continued to accelerate like crazy and he bared his teeth at me. "No. Bad, Spider," he barked like he was telling off a dog.

"My name's not Spider, you freak. And get your filthy pervert hands off of me." I clawed at his arm as his tattooed fingers tightened around my neck then I leaned down to try and sink my teeth into his flesh, but the angle was too damn awkward.

"I could say the same to you, lass," he laughed then glanced back at the road, taking a turn at high speed so gravity pushed me back against the window.

My heart leapt and started bashing its little veiny fists on the walls of my chest to try and get out before this car went tits up. *Sorry, bud, you're locked in for the ride.*

As we rounded the lane, we drove out of the trees toward an old stone bridge that crossed a lake and beyond it I could make out the lights of a house.

The moon was glittering on the water and giving me just enough brightness to tell me this property was large and had no neighbours in sight. It was a murder house if ever I saw one.

I fought harder, panic rearing up in me. If this man got me in his home, he'd do what he wanted to me. He was big, far bigger than me or any man I'd killed before. And he was as strong as an ox with metal bones.

He released my throat and I swung my feet up, trying to ignore the blinding pain from the cut I'd gotten from that fucking crowbar, needing to get free no matter what. Death would be preferable to what he wanted from me. I couldn't go back. I couldn't be that girl again. The moon was reminding me of that night, it looked just the same, just as useless and mocking as it watched with its big fat eye, waiting for my world to go up in flames.

"Fuck you, you piece of shit!" I screamed at the moon, the guy too.

I kicked him in the chest then aimed for his groin, my bare feet making my blows less effective, but I still didn't stop kicking. My heel landed on his junk and he snarled like an animal.

"You wanna play like that, then here's my move," he growled and as we drove across the bridge, he turned the wheel violently to the left and I screamed in fright as the SUV went sailing over the edge of it. *I'm dead, I'm dead, I'm dead-*

We hit the water hard and an airbag exploded in my face, powder coating my tongue as icy water rushed into the vehicle in the footwell.

I swung my legs away from the psycho who was laughing in his seat as he observed us going down like the captain of the Titanic, saluting us outa this world. I clicked my seatbelt button, tugging to pull it free, but it was stuck. *No, life, this is not cool. You do not get to do this to me today after all the shit I've survived. The audacity of you right now. The audaaaacity.*

The water rushed in faster, already up to my calves, stinging that bastard cut and terror caressed my heart, the Devil making no move to help me out here. *Hey, er, Satan? Your fave girl is in a tight spot. And she'll show you her tight spot in return if you come give her a hand...Big Red? No? Fuck.*

"So, I'm Niall. What's your name?" my captor asked casually and I glanced at him as I wrestled with my bastard of a seatbelt.

The water washed over my stomach, rising fast and my breaths came heavier as I was faced with the fate of drowning. Because even if I got this fucking seatbelt off, I couldn't swim. I had never had a lesson in my life. That was a rich people thing. And on the scale of poor to rich, I was somewhere in the once-considered-eating-an-eraser-shaped-like-a-hotdog-because-I hadn't-eaten-for-two-days region.

"I need a name or yer'll be Spider, last chance for an opinion on the subject," Niall said, frowning as the water reached the dashboard and the music cut out.

"Is this what you bought me for?" I snapped. "To die in this fucking pond with you?"

"It's a lake actually, and yeah, maybe I did. Or maybe I didn't. I haven't decided yet. Death doesn't want me, lass, but maybe I'll force his hand today."

I shivered against the cold, letting his words fall over me and I stopped fighting with the belt. My breaths fogged before me as I fell still, staring my fate in the eye. Much to my disgust, this creep's words had kinda resonated with me. Death wasn't my enemy. It liked to run circles around me, test my limits, see what I'd do to avoid it. But if today was the day I didn't escape it, then was that really the worst thing in the world? My horned boyfriend-to-be was waiting down there in the afterlife. I wouldn't be alone when I was with him. I mean sure, he probably had a few side pieces. But I'd rock his world and he'd forget they existed for the most part. And I didn't have to go monogamous with him anyway. He was gonna be busy torturing souls and shit. So I'd have plenty of spare time to make some friends. Sexy friends.

I sighed, leaning back against the headrest. This was definitely better than getting raped, but I really wished I'd been able to have my favourite sandwich here to see out my last moments on Earth. Hardboiled egg, avocado, red grapes – the crunchy ones not the squishies – on a honey oat baguette slathered in mayonnaise. I'd only had it once in my life after I'd stolen it from a soccer mom who'd told me she'd call the police if I came near her kids. As if I wanted to go near her brats anyway, I'd smelled her heavenly home-packed sandwich of dreams and snatched it from her handbag. Food always tasted better when it was stolen from a bitch wearing crocs. Croc wearers didn't deserve tasty sandwiches. Fact.

"Mmm," I hummed as I craved it. Then just as I was getting cosy with the idea of taking a trip to hell and warming my frozen ass on the flames, the asshole started talking again.

"Why've you gone all quiet like?" he asked, seeming surprised. And I got the impression this guy wasn't surprised often.

"I was trying to spend my final moments in peace, but some yappy kidnapper just ruined it," I snapped, shooting him a glare in the shadowy depths of the car. Ergh, I couldn't believe I'd been bought by this guy just to join him in some weird ass suicide ritual. "Did you really buy me just to kill me? There's literally ten thousand things you could have done with me and you chose this." I shook my head as the water level rose and my heart fluttered uncomfortably. *No point in panicking, heart, we can't get out. Drowning won't be nice, or quick, or – well I'm gonna save you from hearing about all the things it won't be. But it will be over soon. Ish.*

"Enlighten me," he asked. "What sorta things could I do? Maybe you'll change me mind." He put his feet up on the dashboard as water climbed up over his chest, the weirdo seeming totally at home here. It was kinda hot actually. If he'd been literally anyone else in the world that is. Because ew.

I was not into thirty-something-year-old men who kidnapped me and made me drown with them. But if I was, I guess he wouldn't have been a terrible option.

"I don't really wanna spend my final minutes giving you ideas about how to torture me before you kill me. I wanna have a word with my boyfriend."

"Boyfriend?" he mused. "Who's that then?"

"Well, he's not my boyfriend exactly. Not yet anyway. But he will be when we meet."

"Ya haven't met the lad?" he questioned curiously.

"No, he's kinda…incarcerated right now," I said, trying to block him out, but Niall kept watching me and his bright green eyes made me feel all weird inside.

"Righto, so what's his name?" he asked, taking a cigarette box from his top pocket and lighting up. The smoke was thick and enticing, making my belly all knotty. I'd always liked the scent of them, but every time I'd tried one they'd made me nearly cough a lung up. I had no idea how people smoked several a day, but I guessed this guy had figured it out.

"Satan," I answered simply then shut my eyes as he released a booming laugh. His hand clapped down on my thigh underwater and I jolted, smacking it away with a yelp.

"Don't touch me," I hissed, shrinking back from him. "You wanna die, then hurry up about it."

He grinned, his face shadowed in the dark and his eyes igniting in an orange gleam as he toked on the cigarette in the corner of his mouth. My lips parted as I was captivated by this incarnation before me, looking like the first real demon I'd ever seen in my life.

"Your boyfriend's not the Devil, lass, and he ain't deep in hell neither," he growled, his voice roughened like sandpaper. "Because he's right here and he's got big plans for you."

He reached out and I noticed his hand was curled around a knife. He slid it under my chin and I almost moaned as the blade kissed my skin. His words wrapped around me, luring me in like a lamp before a rabbit. I was blindly leaning into his madness, sure I really could see the Devil in his eyes in that second. Fuck, I was turned on and terrified and all the bad things. Maybe he actually was Big Red, maybe he'd come personally to drag me down to hell and he wanted to make me commit the seven sins before we left.

"Is it gonna hurt?" I asked, more curious than afraid.

He toked down the last of his cigarette as the water lapped against my throat, splashing over the blade. I was numb from that point down, but where the sharp edge touched my skin, I could feel everything. More than I'd felt in months, no…years. I was so awake it was like the strength of a thousand souls were fuelling my body. And I ached to be worth that many too. The Devil was the only one who'd value mine now. There wasn't a person alive who'd pay a dime for it. But Big Red? He had to be different. He'd see some value in me. He had to.

Niall spat his cigarette into the water and it hissed as it went out. "I can make it hurt so bad you'll think your skin's turning inside out," he purred in a way that had me panting. "But this ain't the day you die, Spider." He lowered the knife under the water and slid it beneath the belt, slicing through the material to free me.

I gasped as he grabbed my waist, throwing me over his lap and shoving me out of the open window beside him. My head went under the water instantly and I started kicking on instinct as I fell into the depths of the lake.

My head somehow broke the surface and I screamed, flapping my arms as I went under again and the deep water tried to claim me. He wasn't just gonna let me sit there and die in a comfy chair, he was gonna watch me panic. Watch me flap and flail and fight to live. He was sick, sick, sick in the head. A head I wanted to cave in and gouge the eyes out of. I'd keep those alluring green eyes in my pocket though. They were too luscious to throw away.

I went under again, the water glittering with moonlight as I thrashed and tried to keep my head above the surface.

"Can't yer-"

I went under again before I heard the end of that sentence. Not that I cared to hear what he had to say. He wasn't the Devil. He'd have killed me if he was, taken me down into the roaring flames and made me his. He was a dirty con-artist, and I wasn't gonna fall for those pretty monsters in his eyes again.

"Swim?" he finished as I came up again and dragged down a lungful of air.

No, not like this. I'm cooler than this death. I don't wanna drown like a rat in a barrel of rainwater. Let me go out in a blaze of glory. Let me rip off a dick or two. Let me be cool in my final moments!

I answered him with a snarl, vaguely lunging toward his voice as I tried to land a blow on the asshole. His hand caught my wrist and I was tugged flush to a hard body. I wrapped myself around him, holding on like a damn spider monkey because if I was gonna drown then this motherfucker was coming to the depths of the lake with me.

"You've still got blood in your hair," he commented, my face all too close to his for my liking as my nails dug into his back. He grabbed hold of me, dunking me under the water like a rag doll and scrubbing his knuckles over my head.

My lungs burned as he held me down, a stream of bubbles leaving my lips as his calloused thumbs rubbed over my cheeks, my forehead. I scratched at every piece of his flesh I could reach as my vision started to darken. He yanked me back up above the surface just as I was about to pass out, then assessed me with a satisfied smile.

"That'll do. Off you go then, lass." He threw me away from him and I cried out as I hit the water once more, immediately going under the surface. My limbs were still exhausted from the death game and as I sank deeper, my legs couldn't kick hard enough to get me back up.

I screamed and water poured into my mouth, only making my panic rise. The moonlight on the surface was getting further and further away and darkness cloaked me like a second skin as death whispered in my ear. *Time to go.*

The next thing I knew I was lying on the grass with the beast man looking down at me with his head cocked to one side. "I thought you were getting it there for a sec, little psycho, but then ya just sank like a stone."

He grabbed my hand, standing up and started dragging me up the grassy hill on my back.

"Hey!" I snapped, my voice sounding hoarse from all the screaming and the near dying I'd been doing in the past half hour. The robe he'd put on me had been lost to the lake, so I was back down to the lingerie from the auction and I had to think this week was going from bad to worse. It all had started with a dodgy burger. *Fucking Wanita. She'd kept my change too. And I'd stolen that change off of a particularly feisty busker who'd hit me with his violin wand, so it was extra annoying.*

I yanked my hand free of Niall's grip, my wet palm giving me a chance to get it loose and I leapt to my feet. I turned and ran like a frog outa hell, but he was upon me in seconds, lifting me up and throwing me around his neck, holding my feet with one hand and my wrists with the other. I wriggled wildly, but it was no good and my head pulsed with all kinds of horrible memories from my past as he walked inside the large farmhouse and kicked the door shut behind him.

He strode through the place and I barely took it in as he made it to a basement door, adjusting me over his shoulder as he unlocked it and started carrying me down into the dark.

I wasn't a beggar, but if I had been I'd have been pleading right now. Saying all kinds of things like 'please don't', 'help me' and 'have mercy.' But I hadn't spoken those words in six long years, not since I'd been held down and screamed them into a sweaty palm while my body was tarnished, gilded in eternal ruin.

"I'm thin and bony," I told him. "I don't make a good lay. My pussy feels like a haystack full of needles. Ask anyone."

He reached the bottom of the stairs and dumped me down so I fell on my ass. I raised my fists like I had in front of Señor Castillo and his freaky friends as I pushed to my feet. I wouldn't go down easy, but from the size of him, I was sure I'd go down.

"I'm not gonna fucking rape ya, Spider," he said seriously and my throat thickened.

I stood my ground, unsure if I believed that. He'd bought me from creepsville and shoved me in his basement. He'd tricked me into thinking he was the Devil then watched as I'd almost drowned in the lake. I didn't know what to make of him, but he wasn't bringing me down here for a bowl of Coco Pops and a movie. He was gonna try to force himself on me like every other person who'd kidnapped me recently.

I willed my pussy to grow razorblades, calling on the power of Big Red to help me out with that, but I didn't feel any kind of stirring down there. Unless you counted the good kind, because dammit this asshole was hot. And I was apparently fucked up enough to keep noticing. But that didn't mean he could touch me. No way hose-ay.

He grabbed my shoulders and I clocked him in the jaw with a sloppy punch that made him howl a laugh.

"Stop it," I spat. "Don't laugh at me."

I went for a knee to the balls and he shoved me back, twisting me around and clamping me to his chest with a muscular, inked arm.

His mouth dropped to my ear and I shivered from his heated breath on my neck. "I will not lay a hand on you, Spider. Not like that."

"Why do you keep calling me that?" I hissed, relief filling me even though I wasn't totally convinced he was telling the truth. But rapists didn't tend to waste time pretending they weren't rapists just before they raped you, did they?

"Because of this." His hand slid down my arm, turning it over to reveal the spider tattoo there. I'd gotten it a few months ago when this dude found me sleeping in the doorway of his tattoo shop. He'd said I could get some free ink if I let his trainee practice on me and had added in a burger as a sweetener. I'd been in it for the burger, but it turned out his trainee guy had been a pretty good artist and I kinda loved my inky wincy spider. "Gotta call ya somethin' and as you've given me no name, I'm sticking with that. Last chance to gimme your real one."

"You said that last time," I growled and he grabbed hold of my chin, turning my head to the left as he flicked on a light and I took in the basement properly for the first time.

There was a large double bed there with white sheets and comfy looking pillows. Beyond it was an open door that gave me a glimpse of a small bathroom. "That side is for if you're good." He yanked my head around to show me the right side of the basement and my stomach clenched at the sight of a big cage in a dark corner. There was a huge figure inside, sitting hunched over in the shadows and though I couldn't see his face, I felt his eyes on me like they were tearing into my flesh and devouring everything they found beneath it. "That side is for if you're bad."

Fuck me, who's that beast in there? And where the hell's his soul, because I sure as shit don't sense it in this room.

Niall walked me across the basement to a red door with a reinforced glass window in it, shoving my face against the glass. My heart stammered as I took in the huge stone room inside; a table was laid out in the centre of it with all kinds of torture implements hanging on the walls. There were a couple of wooden chairs too and bloodstains on the floor. My pulse elevated as I pictured being held down in there, ripped apart piece by piece. I was all for heavy spanking and the odd vaguely sharp object inserted into my butt, but I didn't fancy being cut up and melted down in a vat of acid, no matter how much I wanted to visit the Devil. Okay, so I hadn't exactly had the butt experience to claim I liked such things. But I had the feeling it'd be my jam.

Niall's breath on my ear was making me squirm and it was for a mixture of reasons which my depraved soul wouldn't admit to.

"Lemme guess, this room's for if I'm really, really bad?" I questioned, keeping the concern out of my voice.

"Nope," he chuckled, tugging me away from the door. "That one's for if you're boring, little psycho."

He pushed me toward the bed and I dug my heels into the floor, my spine straightening as I pictured him throwing me down on it and taking, taking, taking from me until I broke and screamed and begged for him to stop. *No, no begging, Spider. Oh my god, I called myself Spider in my own brain. Do I like it? Dammit I do.*

I swung back toward Niall with a savage growl, slashing at him with my nails, but he caught my wrist in a vice-like grip before I could get close.

"I'm not gonna rape yer," he said through his teeth. "I'm not in the least bit interested in my cock going anywhere near ya, so get that in yer head and make it stick."

"What do you want then?" I demanded, tugging on my wrist, but he didn't let go. I was slightly offended about his cock not wanting me too. Why not? I was cock-worthy, right? Not that I wanted his cock. My gaze fell down to his crotch where the wet denim was making his jeans ride low on his hips, revealing a deep V that plunged beneath his belt. The words *all paths lead to hell* were inked over his right hip bone and I found myself in need of that road map.

"Right now, I want ya to get changed and say hello to your roommate. There's clothes in that cupboard over there. And Mateo will tell you what happens to boring people in case your imagination isn't up to the job." He smirked, leaning closer and lowering his voice to a whisper. "I'll give ya a clue, it ain't pretty."

He turned, whistling loudly as he headed up the stairs and out the door, a sharp click sounding as he locked it.

I wheeled around to look at Mateo, sensing him still watching me, but he was as silent as the grave. And just as full of death by the feel of the aura around him.

"Hello," I said, stepping toward his cage. Nothing. "Um…hey?" He still made no sign he'd heard me at all and all I could see of him was that dark silhouette, the single light in the room was dim and aimed towards the 'good' area with the bed and shit, leaving him in shadows.

"Are you deaf? Or a mute?" I tippy-toed closer still. "Do. You. Speak. The. English?"

Silence.

"O…kay, well I'm gonna just change out of this underwear, you have no idea what a day I've had. Seriously, I had to kill so many people. Then that asshole bought me like I was a cow at a market, then he tried to drown me, but *then* he didn't drown me and now I'm here. So weird, right? How's your evening be- oh, well I guess you've just been in that cage so I'm gonna imagine it was a solid two on a scale of one to ten. Things can always get worse though, am I right?"

This was why I had no friends. When I did make an effort with people, they saw how weird I was. I'd never really understood social conventions so that made me an awkward plus one at the best of times. One of the few birthday parties I'd ever attended, I'd eaten half the birthday cake before it was brought out of the kitchen to do the sing-song thing and apparently that wasn't okay, and my dad had to come pick me up. No one really liked me after that. I didn't personally see it as a crime to eat a tasty cake when you found it lurking out in a kitchen all alone, in a box, in the fridge, behind a wall of orange juice. Seemed more like destiny to me that someone left it lying around like that unattended.

There was a single cupboard beside the bed and I opened it, finding clothes folded inside in all sizes. They were all the same type, grey joggers, shirts and hoodies. I plucked out a couple in the smallest sizes and slipped into the bathroom, switching the light on. Call me crazy – and lots of people did – but this was kind of a turn up for the books today. I'd been sleeping on the streets for weeks and bathrooms were hard to come by. This one was small, but clean and had actual, honest to shit shampoo and conditioner in the shower.

I shut the door behind me and gazed around at my little bubble of privacy with a smile before stripping out of the underwear which had left red marks on my skin from the underwire and straps, then I moved into the shower and turned it on. The noise that left me was so sexual, it could have been a soundbite in a porno. I lathered up my hair in the papaya products, groaning lustfully as I washed out the blood and the dirt. I washed the cut on my leg and pouted at the ouchy as I inspected it. It wasn't too deep and the cut was pretty clean, so I hoped I wouldn't have to chop it off. I mean, I'd make a good pirate for sure, but I'd have to cut out an eye too and get an eyepatch, and the whole thing just seemed like quite the identity shift, so I was cool with keeping the leg if possible.

I planned to spend a seriously long time in this shower. And when I was done, I'd be a new woman. A kidnapped, captive woman with a psycho for an owner and a scary, soulless mute for a roommate. But it wasn't all bad. At least I'd smell good enough to eat. But Niall better not be planning on eating me or I was gonna give him the worst indigestion of his life. Period.

MATEO

CHAPTER EIGHT

I listened to the sound of the shower running while the girl loudly discussed the benefits of washing her tits with conditioner for extra softness and I was gifted the image of her standing beneath that running water and massaging them with the slippery substance.

My throat was thick as my mind conjured images of that, her tanned skin dripping wet and her hands slowly sliding across her flesh.

She moaned a lot and it wasn't hard to imagine her with her fingers between her thighs in there, the thought alone making my pulse beat harder.

It had been a long fucking time since I'd even thought about a girl, let alone seen one in the flesh.

Niall hadn't brought a pretty girl like her here before. In fact, he hadn't brought anyone here and left them alive up until this moment. Any time he had shown up with some doomed pendejo, he'd just dragged them straight past me into his killing room. No introductions or bullshit like he'd just offered her. The closest I'd come to interacting with any of them had been me listening to their screams while they died.

But now he'd left her here and hadn't so much as lifted a fist against her.

Was she meant for me? A trap? A trick? A new form of torture for the poor bastardo locked in this fucking cage? Was she here to tempt me and make me ache in new ways, to give me ideas of all the things I could do to turn her moans to screams?

It felt like something was changing here and in the monotony that had been my life for months on end, the prospect of that was its own special kind of exhilarating.

I hadn't moved since he'd arrived with her. Had barely even drawn breath. This one, single change in my circumstances had shifted everything. Or nothing. I wasn't certain yet.

But my fingers were twitching with the desire to wrap tight around that slender neck of hers and see how long it took her pleasure at my hold to switch from exhilaration to panic. Demons crept out from the darkest crevices of my soul as they hungered for that too.

I sat on the small wooden bench which was the only piece of furniture within my cage, forearms resting on my thighs as I leaned forward and my hands hanging before me. My head had been dipped while I sat alone in the dark, my mind still, calm, empty. But now that she was here, there was light.

My eyes stung from the dim glow emitted by the bulb on the other side of the room and I tried to remember how long he'd left me in the dark this time. Long enough for my eyes to be more comfortable without it anyway.

It was fucking cold in this basement, but I was long since used to the chill, especially as I was rarely given anything to wear beyond the grey sweatpants I currently had on. My chest was bare, offering up a view of the scars that bastardo had given me down here in hell and my bare feet were forever frozen against the cold, stone floor.

I spent my days dreaming up all the ways I'd destroy him once I broke free of the shackles he'd placed on me. I'd repay him for each and every cut and burn and scar on my flesh tenfold and bathe myself clean in the sounds of his screams. Everyone had heard stories of estúpido people who kept wild animals caged in their homes, and when they finally got out the beasts devoured them whole. The difference between me and those animals was one thing only. I'd relish the kill for nothing other than my own pleasure, not for food or instinct. Just for the sweet, sweet taste of revenge. I'd show him why an army of men were hunting me and what happened to anyone unlucky enough to find me.

The idea of hot water pouring down so nearby opened up an ache in my chest, but I refused to be tempted by memories of a life outside of these iron bars. That was the quickest way to despair. I didn't think about the things I missed, and I didn't worry about the things that bastardo would do to me the next time he decided to question me over the money I'd stolen.

I just shut down, kept my mind clear and worked out until I couldn't anymore. Exercise gifted me oblivion when all else failed and it wasn't like there was anything else I could do with my fucking time.

Though that was never going to be enough to stop the darkness from creeping in. From the memories of my past to the desires I held for my future. I was a bad man with a wicked soul and there was never going to be any escaping that. And even when I tried to convince myself I wanted to escape it, I knew I was only lying to myself. I enjoyed the dark in me. I revelled in it. And it had been a long, long time since I'd had a woman to fantasize about sharing in it with me.

I didn't trust this one, but I never trusted any woman. No man who thought their kind were weak knew what he was talking about. Physically women might be weaker than men, but they were far crueller and capable of so much worse. I should know. I'd survived the very worst of them and more. I'd survived - but I'd come out the other side scarred in ways you couldn't see.

The shower shut off and I instantly tensed, fingers curling into fists. I'd been alone down here for so long, I didn't know how to contemplate company. I hungered for it and didn't want it in equal measures. Down here only the demon who possessed me knew where to find me. And aside from his whisperings, I'd grown too used to silence.

A few muttered curses came from within the bathroom and the door suddenly burst open, the little livewire falling backwards out of it and landing on her ass. She'd pulled the grey sweatshirt on over her head already, but the pants were tangled around her ankles and there was a whole lot of tanned legs on show.

A growl caught in the back of my throat as I watched her, my imagination going wild as I drank in the sight of her down on the floor and wondered if she'd like it better if I was pinning her there.

My gaze caught on a swollen, bloody wound on her calf and anger tangled in my gut as I pictured Niall doing that to her. I fucking hated that man. Sometimes, that was the only fact about myself that I was certain of these days. I. Hated. Him.

Lo vería muerto sin importar lo que me costara.

"Motherfucking octopants," she cursed, throwing herself down onto her back and kicking her legs up into the air as she dragged the sweatpants up and managed to poke her toes out of the holes at the bottom. "Got more testicles than a squid."

My brows pulled together minutely before I realised she must have said tentacles. But I guessed that it wasn't such a surprise that my brain would play those kinds of tricks on me. I was a hot blooded man who had been denied a look at a woman in far too long and now here she was, this creature of the night who moaned lustily in the shower and made pulling sweatpants over her ass look like origami.

She got up with a huff of irritation and pushed her long, wet hair away from her face before snapping around to stare in my direction. She either had the most beautiful features I'd ever seen, or I'd been alone longer than I realised. Her lips were full, her eyes brightest blue and her nose a slender, delicate thing. There were bruises on her jaw and neck, disappearing down beneath her clothes and I had the feeling the trend continued where I couldn't see.

I wondered if she'd show them to me. I wondered if she liked the way they hurt and might enjoy me bruising her more when she gave her body up to me and I taught her the meaning of sin.

Te arruinaría hermosamente. I would ruin you beautifully.

Her eyes narrowed on me for a moment before she turned away again, dismissing me in my cage in the dark in favour of exploring the little area around the bed.

A growl rumbled low in my chest as she turned away from me like that. The man I'd been before I entered this cage could have killed her for such an insult. No one ever would have dared to risk my wrath like that. Where I came from everyone knew who and what I was, they knew my role in the Castillo Cartel and they knew better than to ever risk turning their back on me. If I wasn't in this cage, I could have snapped her neck already. But as I watched her, I knew I wouldn't have. Not right away anyway. There was something about her that drew me in and made me want to know her inside and out. I wanted to peel her open and dissect all of her secrets before branding my name on her flesh and making certain she never underestimated me again.

There wasn't much surrounding the bed. Just the soft mattress, the fluffy rug on the floor beside it and the little white nightstand. I'd never been allowed to sleep on that side of the room. It was a slice of torture of its own while I slept on the hard concrete and gazed over at that comfortable space. I'd been certain it was only there to mock me until now.

She opened the nightstand drawer and pulled out a pencil and a notepad, raising the pencil to her lips and taking a moment to think before writing something on the first page of the book.

She tore it out when she was done and balanced it against the wall, the word *good* looking back at me and making my brows draw together.

She dropped the notebook onto the nightstand and pocketed the pencil before whirling around to look at me so suddenly that my teeth clenched.

"Here, kitty, kitty," she purred, making little kissing noises and holding her fingers out in front of her like she might have a treat in them.

I didn't move, the locked leather collar around my neck feeling heavier than it had in a long time as I watched her drawing closer.

If I was free, I could have been on her already. I could have her at my mercy and find out what move she'd make when she found herself there. Would her confidence shatter or bloom then?

"Are you a good kitty? Or the kind that rolls over to draw me in for a tummy rub then savages my arm like a fucking psycho? I knew a cat like that once. She was called Susan. That name should have warned me. Fucking Susan." The words coming out of her full lips were touched in sin, her voice husky yet dipped in honey. That was the kind of voice I could devour for hours on end. I didn't even care what she was saying, but she was still talking and as I hadn't had any form of conversation with anyone beyond Niall in months, I found that I wanted to listen. "Of course, I really should have known she was a little cunt because she had that look in her eyes, you know? Wait, what am I asking? Obviously you know, you've met the man upstairs and he definitely has it too. That I-could-kill-you-at-any-moment-and-the-only-real-question-is-when thing he's got going on."

She tipped her head back to look up at the ceiling and pointed, clearly meaning Niall.

If she'd seen the dark in him so easily, no doubt she'd recognise it in me even faster. But not yet. She was too curious at the moment, even the cage and the chain not enough to warn her about my nature. But I could assure her, it required this and more to keep me caged.

I wondered what he wanted her for and how long it would be until her screams coloured these walls. With a voice like that, I'd bet she screamed beautifully.

"Can I see your eyes?" she asked, looking back over at me and stepping out of the ring of light that surrounded the nice side of the room as she moved into the shadows that surrounded me and my cage.

Did she know she was slipping into the water with a shark? Or was she a shark too?

My gaze dropped to her bare feet as she stepped off of the fluffy rug which ran along the floor beside the bed, walking across the cold concrete and my frown deepened. I knew well how cold this floor was. I slept on it every night – assuming I slept at all. And every morning it took me over an hour of working out to banish that fucking chill from my bones. But she didn't flinch, and I got the feeling she was no stranger to the cold or hardships like that.

So what was she?

"I want to know if you've got it too, Dead Man."

I almost reacted to that name. It was surprisingly fitting. I did feel dead here, like an empty, forgotten ghost of the man I'd once been, but perhaps she was going to revive me. I certainly hadn't had the attention of a woman this beautiful in a long time. In fact, I couldn't remember laying eyes on one who captured me so wholly as this creature.

Soy hombre muerto - I am a dead man. But maybe not for much longer.

She didn't stop coming, walking right up to the bars of my cage and curling her fingers around the freezing iron as she looked in at me in the dark.

I didn't move, my gaze roaming over her hungrily as I drank in her tanned skin and the alluring sound of her voice. I wondered if she might be a spy sent here by Santiago Castillo, the man who had once owned me, but then I dismissed it. He already had Niall working to rip my secrets from me, he wouldn't send a girl like this. Honey and sugar wasn't his preference, something so sweet wouldn't be to his tastes.

She tilted her head to the side, leaning so far over that she probably would have fallen if she hadn't been holding onto the bars. I watched her hungrily, drinking in her movements and wondering what I'd done to earn this treat. This was how wolves at the zoo must have felt, staring out at a curious little human meal they couldn't get their teeth into. One who wouldn't be standing anywhere near as close to them as this if the bars of their cage vanished.

"Sometimes seeing people upside down gives you a clearer perspective," she said as her dark hair brushed against the floor. "You know, like you can see if they're two faced before they flip on you."

I didn't know. But I wanted to. Something about her was rousing the beast in me and I got the feeling it wanted more than just her flesh. This girl was different. I just hadn't figured out how yet.

I licked my lips slowly, my mouth as dry as a desert and this girl a raging pool of water. I wanted to drink her up. Every last drop.

"Did Niall cut out your tongue?" she asked and I guessed she still couldn't really see me. "He seems like the type. I bet he has a tongue necklace hanging in his boudoir for special occasions. Though it would be a shame if he did. Because then you'd be no good for licking and licking is one of those pleasures in life that I'm really not certain I'd want to go without. Like, how do you eat an ice cream? Do you just go bananas and deep throat that sucker? I don't really have a gag reflex, so I feel like that could be hazardous for me because I could accidentally inhale it. And then there's like…huh, I can't think of other things I like to lick. Isn't that odd? Maybe it's just ice cream then. Do you like ice cream? Because if you don't then I guess the lack of tongue isn't an issue after all."

The sweatpants she was wearing were too big on her and while she spoke, they slipped down her hips until they were barely staying on her frame at all. Though it looked like her ass had taken on the job of holding them up.

I'd lost the thread of what she was saying as she continued to discuss the finer points of owning a tongue and I forced my gaze up from the bare skin above her sweats to look at her again just as she ran her tongue up the length of one of the bars.

Santa Madre de Dios.

My cock had been rock solid from the first moment she'd opened her mouth, but I'd been able to tune it out for the most part until that moment when it jerked in my pants and almost made me groan.

At this point, I was fairly certain the thing thought I'd forgotten all about it because it hadn't gotten any fucking action in all the time I'd been locked down here. Niall let me shower once a week in cold water and he watched me the entire time while aiming a shotgun at my dick. So that made those times seriously unappealing for jerking off and I wasn't gonna get cum all over the floor of my fucking cage. So here I was, cock aching and out of practice, watching a girl lick an iron bar and wondering if I was dreaming.

"Mmm, tastes so metally. But I guess you wouldn't know, without a tongue and all," she said, sighing like that disappointed her. Or maybe like she pitied me.

Perhaps she should have been more worried about herself though because she'd fully captured my attention now and there was a damn good reason why people didn't want to be noticed by me.

I shifted the tiniest amount, my broad shoulders tightening as tension moved though my limbs and she stilled, eyes widening then narrowing like she was trying to interpret the meaning of that infinitesimal movement.

"Where do you pee?" she whispered before her eyes fell on the bucket on the far side of my cage and she found her own answer. "Shit?" She looked at the bucket again then nodded. "Could be worse though, right? I once tried to take a shit in the woods and a stalky squirrel turned up for the show. Can you believe that? He had no freaking boundaries. Said he just wanted to check if I had any nuts and I had to yell at him that I had a pussy before he'd fuck the hell off."

My gaze fell back to those low riding sweatpants as she mentioned her pussy and I experienced a pang of jealousy over a squirrel. *Oh, how the mighty have fallen, Mateo.*

If my papi could see me now, he'd roll in his grave. But the Castillo Cartel took him out long before I got a chance to show him what a disappointing man I could grow into. Not that I was supposed to know that, but I imagined I knew a lot of things Santiago had never wanted me to know. He was a monkey sitting on a throne he didn't deserve, and I'd been undermining him for years before I cut my losses. Even the money I'd stolen from them didn't taste so sweet anymore. Not since Niall had shown up anyway.

"This one time, I was put in a cage like yours, but it was way smaller," the livewire said, rubbing her hands up the length of the thick bars until she was gripping them above her head and leaning forward to look in at me. "I couldn't stand up and I was dressed in nothing but underwear. It fucking sucked. I was like fuck, I don't wanna be in this cage, you know? And that was only like... a few hours earlier on today - so if you've been in there longer than that then you must be all like fuuuuck, I *really* don't wanna be in this cage. Right?"

I looked into her eyes though I was sure she still couldn't see mine in the darkness that lived on this side of the basement. There was an innocence to her which was tempered by violence and I found myself wanting to know more about that.

The two things didn't marry up and yet there she stood in the perfect little package, bursting with energy and life while somehow seeming broken and falling apart all at once.

This girl could be my ticket out of here. But it had been so long since I'd made any sound beyond roaring in anger or pain that I wasn't entirely sure I knew how to form words anymore. I'd lost them when I gave in to the dark in me and I wasn't certain they'd find their way back. No matter. For now, I'd just wait and see. Figure out how pliable she might be and find a way to bend her to my will. If she could be of use to me then I'd gladly use her. More than gladly. Every last piece.

"Are you afraid?" she whispered and I couldn't help but notice that she didn't seem to be. Fear wasn't something I'd ever given much stock to. It seemed to be a fairly pointless concept to me considering self-preservation had never been too high on my list of priorities. I just wanted to live well and fuck over the Castillo Cartel for what they'd done to my father. And for a while there, I'd done it. Until Niall showed up and put me in this dungeon.

There was a sound from the top of the stairs behind her and she whipped around, leaning back against the bars and giving me the perfect opportunity to strike.

I stood, almost silently aside from the chain attached to my collar clinking metallically. But I was fast and my hand curled around her throat before she could jerk away, yanking her back against the bars as my broad frame pressed up against them from the other side.

Her skin was hot against mine and the rampant flicker of her pulse in my grasp had me drawing in a deep breath which enveloped me in the scent of the papaya conditioner she'd used to wash herself.

I leaned forward and ran my tongue up her jaw to the sweet spot behind her ear, tasting her skin and marking her as mine.

Si, chica loca. I have a tongue.

She gasped as my tight grip flexed around her neck, but she didn't flinch or beg or cry. She just whipped the pencil from her pocket and slammed it into my thigh with an angry snarl.

I grunted as it embedded itself in my skin, letting her go and moving back a step as she whirled around to glare at me. My cock really was straining for attention now, more interested in her than ever, this tiny little thing so full of fire and lacking in fear. I wondered how far I would have to push her to get that feeling from her. Would she break for me or just bend? Could I get her panting and begging for more or would she be soft beneath this outer layer which blazed so ferociously?

Silence hung between us for the first time and she panted as she reached up to touch her neck where I'd been holding onto her.

I yanked the pencil out of my thigh and tossed it back to her, the pain of the wound insignificant after months in Niall's care. Though I was more used to hurts that didn't bleed. Not to say he'd never cut me, because I had plenty of scars to prove he did. But he preferred methods like electrocution or near-drowning for me. Mostly because he wasn't ready for me to die and he didn't want the hassle of patching me up too often.

The pencil rolled away across the floor and we just stared at each other until it stopped. The wolf and the lamb. Though for the first time that I could recall, I found myself wondering which of us was which. There was a power play at work here and I couldn't help but wonder how she was wielding so much of it.

The livewire's fingers moved to touch her jaw where I'd licked her and I could have sworn her eyes flared with something so tangible that it sent a rush right through me.

Did you like that, little one? Are you wondering what more I could do to you?

"You *do* have a tongue," she accused like she thought I'd lied to her and was endlessly offended. But I'd never been the one to say I didn't. She stooped to pick up the bloody pencil before looking at the blood on my thigh where it stained my sweatpants, no flicker of anything in her gaze, certainly not remorse.

"Hmmm." She turned away from me and moved to the nightstand beside the bed, picking up the notebook again and levelling a glare on me as she wrote something in it.

She ripped out the page she'd been writing on then tossed the notebook aside along with the bloody pencil.

The girl lifted the page and turned it towards me, and I looked at the word written in my blood.

Tongue.

Amusement tugged at me for the briefest of moments and I was so taken aback by it that all I could do was remain still and stare at her.

I hadn't felt anything so real as that in a long, long fucking time. Far longer than I'd spent in this cage. Far longer than I cared to remember. Yet here she was, poking and prodding at me in ways I couldn't predict and pulling more of a reaction from my emotions than they'd shown in longer than I could remember.

Could she taste the danger hanging in the air between us now? Could she feel it humming all around her, caressing her body and making it buzz and ache for me the way I was for her? Had she realised yet what was so painfully apparent to me? That she was a fly in my web, I'd caught her and was on my way to inject the poison into her veins that would forever stain her as mine.

I could.

I could scent it, taste it, feel it, foresee it.

She was mine one way or another. Mi presa. I would feel her bowing for me, drink in the moment she broke and then ruin her so thoroughly that she would never be even close to the same again afterwards.

I was a man of few words these days, but actions spoke louder anyway. And when it came time for me to act, this little chica wasn't going to know what hit her.

BROOKLYN

CHAPTER NINE

I woke in the softest sheets I'd ever slept in, moaning as I stretched my whole body out into the huge bed. I had never, in all my life, been in a bed this big or this comfy. Sure, I was a prisoner in a basement and I was probably gonna die yada, yada, yada. But right now, I was in heaven and I'd learned a long time ago to live in the moment. Because all the good ones didn't usually last very long, so I liked to suck the goo out of them and make them really worthwhile. I wasn't going to think about being dragged into that murder room later today and peeled open like a banana on a chopping board. That was later's problem.

I sat up, tugging the covers down and checking on the ouchy on my leg. The skin had stuck itself together and there was no more blood or oozings, but the bruising around it was now as colourful as a rainbow. I bent forward to kiss it better then pushed out of bed, stepping onto the cold floor with a shiver and heading to the little closet to grab some clothes, tossing a quick glance at Mateo who was curled up sleeping on the floor. It looked real uncomfy down there. *I oughta give him a pillow or something.*

Sleeping on the ground was never fun. The closest I'd come to comfortable sleeping on the streets was that time I'd found a balloon tied up all alone, shaped like the number five. Just sitting there like it had no friends in the world, all shiny and pink. I'd cut it off of the arm of the kid it had been tied to and ran away with it to set it free, but then I'd been attacked by an army of tiny children all dressed as princesses and shit. I'd had to make a quick exit through a bouncy house and slashed it with my pen knife, escaping out the back of it and capturing all the little beasties within it. That balloon had served as the best cushion ever for almost three weeks before the air went out of it. I organised a funeral and told all the bridge hobos to come. But none of them did. Then a dog pooped on its grave while I was doing my speech. I missed that balloon.

I took one of my pillows and pushed it through the bars for Mateo then marched into the bathroom for my morning poo and to brush my teeth. It sure beat pooping in a bush while Stinky Jim tried to sneak a peek at my butthole. I'd sharpened the end of my toothbrush for that reason alone, but my new toothbrush was smooth and rounded, not made for scaring off pervert hobos. And yes, I brushed my teeth while I pooped. Things like that were best done simultaneously to save time in case of attacks.

I showered again just to enjoy the hot water and the scent of all those yummy products on my skin then dried off and dressed in some fresh sweats. Then I took out the pencil I'd stashed in the pocket of my yesterday pants, running my finger over the tip which was now stained with Mateo's blood. "Well hello little stabber, and how are you today?"

I headed out of the bathroom and Mateo's eyes drilled into me. He was sitting on the wooden bench with his elbows on his knees and his face cast in shadow. Again. He liked watching me and he still hadn't spoken yet. He'd pushed the pillow back through the bars in a clear refusal.

"Good morning, don't you like your pillow?" I called, but he said nothing. That was okay though. I had plenty to say for the both of us. "It looks ouchy in there on the floor. Kinda cold too. Does Niall let you sleep in the bed sometimes? Do you think we'll have to share occasionally? Are you good at sharing? I'm not really. I don't have any brothers or sisters. Do you?" I raised my eyebrows but he didn't answer any of my questions. Not one. And it wasn't a no-tongue issue because he'd gone all licka-tongue on me yesterday, so what was it? "Well maybe you can teach me how to share sometime if you do. This space is both of ours now I suppose. But I do like sleeping in the bed alone. But I also think you look all sad in there on the floor so if you want to share when Niall lets you out, I think I'd be okay with that. Are you a cuddler? I've never been cuddled by someone who wasn't my dad. He died, you know? It's okay, it was a long time ago. It was on my birthday though, so that was traumatic...do you have a dad?" He blinked so I was gonna take that as a maybe. "Anyway, I'm kind of curious about cuddling. I think I'd like it. It looks nice when I've seen couples doing it on the streets. But the problem is, I don't like being touched." I laughed at myself. "Silly, isn't it? I should get over it really." I grabbed the pillow from the floor and positioned it in front of his cage as he just stared at me.

It was still crazy dark over here in the corner but as I sat down, more of the light made it over my head from the nice side of the room and I could see more of his face. He was...tasty to look at. Did that make sense? His skin was the most delicious shade of brown, all warm and making me think of sunshine and sangrias. I'd seen those in a magazine once with an advert for vacations to Mexico. He looked like the guy who'd been sunbathing in that photo with inky black hair that was smooth and sleek, but also long enough to tuck behind his ears. His jaw was thick with a dark beard which looked nice and scratchy and his enormous body was like this naked statue I'd slept under once outside a museum. The sign had said the statue was of Adonis, although Mateo had scars on his muscular body where the statue had been all smooth. It was hard to make out many of the details in the dark, but it looked like he had a big crucifix right over the centre of his chest – not like a tattoo, more like it had been burned there long ago. His dick also wasn't out, and I wondered if it was as small and shrively as that statue's had been. *Holy fucking Gatorade, if you say Adonis backwards, doesn't it spell Mateo? No way is that a coincidence.*

My gaze dropped between his thighs to the bunched material of his sweatpants as I hunted for evidence of his teeny weeny. I had a lot of dick curiosity generally, but apparently asking guys to show you theirs equalled them trying to make you touch it and waggling it around in your face. I could thank Lanky Bob for that mental trauma and because of him, I didn't ask to see Mateo's. Lesson learned.

"Can I tell you a secret?" I bit my lip and he frowned, seeming curious but he still didn't reply. I guessed he didn't mind. "I have all these fantasies about things I think I'd like to do. Some of them are really trivial. Like hand holding. How cute is hand holding?" I threaded my fingers together to show him. "Like this way. Not the parent way. This way is how I want to hold hands with someone. I think that would be quite nice, don't you? I have a problem though. And it's a really big problem which means I can't try this with anyone." I lowered my voice further and I swear he leaned just a little closer to catch my next words. "People are awful. I've never met a good one since my dad. He was nice to me, but maybe he was a dick to other people. I'm not really sure. I hope not. My mom was one hundred percent, no shadow of a doubt a dick though. She ran off with *Esteban*." I lifted my hand and wiped his name from my tongue, scraping it against my palm. *Yuck*. "Anyways, since Dad died, I've only met bad ones. They do nasty things or they try to. Don't worry, I killed some of them. Not all though…" I shuddered, thinking of the Eden Heights Psychiatric Hospital I'd been locked up in. "I went to a home for crazies after I killed some people. Isn't it funny how you get locked up for stabbing people who ruined your life? Doesn't seem fair to me. Shouldn't we be allowed to stab people that hurt us? The law is stupid. That's why I don't pay attention to it. Anyway, Mr Judge didn't agree when I told him that it was my right to kill monsters and had me sent for a special assessment where the world decided I was crazy."

Heat built up in my cheeks as I met Mateo's eyes again, hunting for what he thought of that. People didn't like the word crazy. I didn't like it either. It made me an 'other.' An outsider who didn't slot into society's norms. The funny thing was, 'normal' was a concept that everyone was trying to squeeze into so hard so that they didn't stick out, while all I'd ever wanted to do was shine brighter than all the norms and be uniquely me. The world didn't like that though. Being weird scared people. I scared people. But that seemed like a them problem, not a me problem.

"When people are scared of you, they want you gone," I told Mateo in a dark tone. "They want you buried deep, deep, deep underground somewhere they can't see you. Somewhere they don't have to worry about you slipping into their lives and making them uncomfortable. So they put me in a room with padded walls and fed me drugs that made my mind all fuzzy." I reached out to wrap my hands around the bars, staring in at him intently. "Do you know what giving someone power over other people does to them? It makes them bad, Dead Man. Because no one's looking," I whispered, glancing over my shoulder as if I could feel the horrible, drilling gaze of the head nurse on me now. Then I looked back at Mateo and found him frowning. "They made me feel small, like they made everyone in that place feel small. Tiny, little specks of dust who mean nothing to no one." Anger rose in me as I thought of those bastards and especially of Madam Lucille who'd been in charge of my ward. She liked to make me squirm, and cry, and suffer. She liked to make all the patients do that when she got the chance. "I stopped taking my pills, managed to hide them under my tongue and spit them out. I cut a little hole in my mattress and put them in there so I got my mind back. I might be crazy by the world's standards, Dead Man, but my mind is still mine. I like being me. Those pills took me away. They smothered me as good as dead. So I reclaimed myself, woke my mind up and then I saw the reality of the hell I was in."

His jaw began to tick and I sensed danger coiling out from him like leeches from the water. His eyes were dark, deep, deep, deep, dark pits that drank in all the light and made me want to dive in too. He really was a dead man, those shadows lived right there in his eyes and they wanted to drink me up. He was a wild animal caged in a zoo and he hungered for his keeper's death. But I didn't think he hungered for mine. Not right now anyway.

"Lucille and her awful team used to push us around, laugh at us, treated us like we were their playthings whenever the other nurses weren't there," I went on, revealing one of my darkest secrets as the ghosts of my pasts crept up my spine. "They called us the monsters, the freaks, but it's them who are the monsters, Dead Man. It's the ones who keep order. They're the real enemy. And you know what was sad?" I inched a little closer as he watched me, listening to everything I said without comment. I wasn't sure if I'd ever had such an attentive audience, most people told me to shut up once I got started on a conversation. But not my dead man, he was all ears and I liked that. It felt good to be listened to after so many years of being ignored. "I think some of those inmates might have been able to be friends of mine. I liked Angry Jack. He was so big and so, so angry. But he'd had his mind stolen like they'd all had their minds stolen by those drugs. They weren't really there and I couldn't save them. I'm not a hero type, but I don't like people being in pain when they don't deserve it. I still think about them sometimes. Because I got a chance to run. And I left them all behind. People are awful, Dead Man. And I'm people too."

His lips parted and I thought for a sweet, hopeful moment that he was going to say something, but then the door to the basement banged against the wall as it swung open and the pounding of loud footsteps came down the stairs. I slid my hand into my pocket, taking out my pencil and sliding it up my sleeve as my heart thrashed harder. My captor was coming. My latest monster. He was in charge of us, and maybe that meant he'd be just like Madam Lucille. Power went to people's heads when they thought no one was looking. And no one was looking here. Mateo and I were like ferrets in a barrel. And I didn't wanna get shot.

Maybe Niall planned to drag me into his murder room, but I really didn't want to die yet. Satan was being awfully quiet on the matter, so I couldn't be sure what he had planned for me. He wasn't the best at answering my call. I guessed you couldn't expect much from a guy who worked twenty-four seven and had millions of souls to torture for all eternity. But a little check in from time to time wouldn't have gone amiss. *Hey, Big Red, did I ever tell you I'm a virgin who needs corrupting? Yup, you heard me correctly, baby. Just gimme a little helping hand to escape and I'll save myself for you, kay?*

Niall appeared in jeans and a dark green shirt which brought out the colour of his eyes and hugged his muscular frame in all the right ways.

I pushed to my feet as he gazed from me to Mateo in his cage, seeming curious about me being so close to him. "Come over here, lass," he ordered.

"And what if I say no?" I questioned, brushing my thumb over the sharp tip of the pencil. If he tried to get me in that bloodstained room, I was gonna fight like all the demons of hell resided in my body. He was gonna have to shove a crucifix up my butt to get them out of me. I'd like it too. Which would only make it more awkward for him.

"Then I'll respect yer wishes, but I have somethin' I wanna ask ya, and I'd rather do it over here." He gave Mateo a dark look and I shrugged, heading over to him, my pencil poised for a good stabbing. One decent shot to the neck could be all I needed to kill the big guy. But he wouldn't die quick, so I'd need to stab and run.

I got within a foot of him, eyeing the blonde stubble which coated his jaw and ran down his neck and deciding on where to aim. My heart suddenly scrunched up as a familiar scent carried from him and I sniffed the air to be sure. *No, how can that be possible??*

But it was. He definitely smelled faintly of Coco Pops and a pang of utter longing filled me from my childhood. Fuck me sideways with a rollerblade, did he have Coco Pops in this house? *The* Coco Pops? Not some knock off Krispies American thing. I was talking fully British, fully fucking perfect Pops. I'd been on one big vacation in my life and it was to London, England with my dad just after Mom had left him with hairy-ears-Esteban. We'd had Coco Pops for breakfast every freaking day. They. Were. The. Shit. Like I-will-die-for-the-Pops good.

Dad had bought up a bunch of mini boxes to bring home with us and I'd been careful to make them last for weeks. I'd taken my final box everywhere with me. It was the holy grail and I'd been saving it for Christmas day. But then – *then!* - the day before mom had left for Vegas with her new boyfriend, I'd had to stay over at their place to say goodbye and swallow up her fake promises that I'd see her every second weekend of the month. *Bleugh.* Liar. I'd gone for Dad's sake because he'd wanted me to have closure or some bullshit. But *then* disaster had struck.

The next morning, I came downstairs to find Esteban polishing off the last of my – MY!! – Coco Pops like they were nothing. *Nothing.* The box was already in the trash. My backpack was sitting open on the kitchen counter which he'd apparently gone through for no other reason than to destroy my entire life. That was the first time I'd gone full savage on someone, but not the last. He'd just wanted to 'try' them Mom had said. But he'd sniggered at me while she pulled me away from him. I'd heard it. He *knew* what they'd meant to me, he must have. So he'd taken them. Swallowed them down his greasy pipe and eaten a piece of my soul along with them. *I shall never forgive you, Esteban. I curse you a thousand times.*

So the question was, did Niall have Coco Pops in this freaking house? My stomach growled at the thought of it, fucking ached. If they were here, they were mine. Nothing would stop me from getting my hands on them. This had to be fate, the Devil's little nod to me that he was building a happier life for me. It was all coming together, I just had to keep my head and play this right. Because nothing could jeopardise me getting those Pops.

New plan: stab him in the neck, get upstairs, lock the door, steal coco pops, run for my life.

"I was thinking you could join me for dinner this eve-" he started and I lunged at him with a shriek, my hand flying toward his jugular, pencil poised, teeth bared and a furious energy pumping through my veins.

Niall caught my wrist a second before I could land the strike, ripping the pencil from my fingers and eyeing it with a smirk. "As I was sayin'…" He dropped the pencil into his pocket and I pouted as he knocked my arm away from him. "I'd like you to come to dinner with me this evening, Spider."

I frowned, my failed murder attempt making me moody. But I was always up for eating. Especially if it would give me a chance to scope out the location of the Pops. "What kind of dinner?"

"Takeaway," he said.

"What kind?" I folded my arms like I had standards. But honestly, I was up for any and all kinds of takeaway. I'd have kebab on a pizza, pizza on a noodle, noodles on a burrito.

"Chinese," he announced and my mouth watered. I groaned, actually groaned, dropping my head back. Because I was weak. I wanted Chinese food *so* bad. "That a yes?" he chuckled.

"Yes, it's a yes," I growled, looking back at him. Chinese food with a side of death. I was gonna go upstairs into a house full of objects. Some of which were pointy. And I only needed one to stab in his eye then I'd grab the takeaway and the Coco Pops and run like the wind. Maybe I could even stab him with a chopstick…

"Good." He reached into his pocket, taking out a chocolate bar and handing it to me. "Breakfast."

"What about Mateo?" I asked as I snatched it and shoved it up my sleeve so he couldn't take it back again.

"He's in the naughty cage, he doesn't get breakfast," Niall said simply. "You can have it if you gimme that location though, eh el burro? Or maybe

I'll just feed you one o' those god awful protein bars I found upstairs, that'll be torture enough to get it outa ya," he called loudly and Mateo didn't reply, but scowled intensely. Niall stepped closer to me, lowering his voice. "Has he been given ya any trouble?"

"No, he's a sweetie pie," I said, shooting Mateo a grin. "Aren't you, Dead Man?"

Mateo said nothing but I just smiled wider. Maybe I was projecting a personality onto him that didn't exist, but at least while he was in that cage I could imagine he wasn't awful like everyone else in the world. It was a pretty little fantasy I was happy to buy into. But I must never, ever truly believe it. That was when awful people struck. They could get under your skin and make a nest there like a racoon, then they'd have babies and their babies would eat my flesh from the inside. No, I couldn't let Mateo give birth to racoon babies in my chest. But I could pretend like he wouldn't do that while he remained behind those bars. Ignorance is Swiss after all. And the Swiss are notoriously happy.

"Dead Man?" Niall laughed, slapping me on the shoulder and making me stumble a step.

Woah he was strong. Like hold-me-down-and-bury-your-dick-in-me strong. Not that I wanted that. I was absolutely anti-that happening. Like, unless I was onboard with it. I had always wondered what that might feel like. Actually, was it a totally insane idea to try and seduce the psyxy (psycho sexy) Irish man *then* run away? It wasn't a terrible plan. I'd definitely had worse plans. Like that time I thought it would be a good idea to bungee jump off the bridge using a selection of men's dress ties that had fallen off the back of a van. I'd knotted them all together and asked Pervy Tim if he wanted to give it a go first. I was pretty sure he still hadn't forgiven me for losing his leg.

Anyways, this plan wasn't like that. Maybe I'd be able to get closer to Niall. Straddle his hips post-Chinese food and get all hair-flippy porn star on him. I'd lick my lips all hot like and draw him in to my honey badger cave. I might even take a little taste, see how far that wild wind carried me before I skewered him on one of his own kitchen knives. The thought of all that got my cheeks flushed and Niall just looked at me like he didn't know what was going on as I fanned myself with my hand and turned away. *Oh yes, I can be psyxy too.*

I walked away from him, swinging my hips and looking back over my shoulder at him, biting my lip. "Well I guess I'll see you for dinner then, Hellfire," I purred in my huskiest come-fuck-me voice.

Niall looked turned on, or maybe just confused. I wasn't the best at reading people's expressions. But he was still looking at me so maybe it was working.

"I'm just gonna spend the day doing some Pilates," I told him, bending forward and touching my toes, swaying my hips from side to side as I gazed back at him through my legs. "If I don't practise daily, I'll lose my flexibility. And we wouldn't want that, would we Hellfire?"

"If that's something that's important to ya, then I guess you'll wanna keep up yer routine," Niall agreed.

He looked good upside down. Like he was hanging from his ankles about to be whipped. He scratched at the Devil tattoo on his forearm and a tingle ran through me. I wanted to rake my tongue over that mark and whisper to my evil ruler that I was doing his bad work. Or maybe I wanted to tell Niall that right now. He looked terribly like the big bad hellion I'd pictured for years as my boyfriend. Minus the horns and the red skin.

I started lowering down into the splits, still looking back at Niall between my legs as blood rushed to my head. I got two thirds of the way down then winced as my body refused to go any further. It hurt like a bitch and a squeak of alarm left me as I pressed my hands to the floor.

"Oh holy mother of a bitch," I gasped, trying to get up as I attempted to stay sexy while my hip flexors screamed no. I flailed like a mad thing as I tried to stand up, but it was no good. I was stuck and my feet were slipping across the floor. I was going to do the splits whether my body liked it or not now. It was happening. Ow, ow, ow-

Big hands grabbed my waist from behind, tugging me up and I found myself staring at a wide-eyed Mateo as I was held against Niall's strong body.

Niall flipped me around to face him and my pants fell down over my hips, my ass not quite holding them up as they slid shamelessly down to my thighs. I decided to roll with it, twirling a lock of hair around my finger and batting my lashes. "Do you like that, Hellfire?"

"Do I like your sweatpants falling down over your ass because they don't fit ya?" he asked, reaching down and grabbing the hem, yanking them up so hard that he wedgied me. "That'd be a weirdly specific thing to enjoy."

"But did you, Hellfire?" I purred, releasing a girlish giggle. I was great at this. Being a sexy assassin was in my blood.

His face twisted as his gaze dipped to my mouth then back to my eyes. "Why d'ya keep callin' me that?"

I reached out, my heart rioting in my chest as adrenaline kicked in, unsure if I was about to die for this. I ran my hand down his arm to the Devil tattoo and caressed it in circles. "You remind me of him."

He stared at where my hand was moving against his flesh, seeming perplexed before he casually knocked me away from him and I stumbled back a step. "Here." He grabbed the drawstring of my sweatpants and yanked it tight, knotting it over and over with deft fingers so they were firm to my waist. "Problem solved. See you at dinner, Spider. Dress up nice."

"Oh, I will. And I can't wait to eat with those chopsticks!" I called after him. "Can't wait to run my fingers up their long, hard shafts."

He glanced back at me as he moved onto the stairs. "Just don't try and stab me with them, eh?"

I laughed loudly, pretending he was soooo hilarious. "You're so funny."

He headed upstairs with a snort and I was sure he'd be thinking about me for a while after that excellent performance. A bang made me turn around in surprise and I found Mateo standing at the front of his cage, his hand against the bars like he'd just hit them. He looked mad and confused, but mostly mad.

"Did you see that?" I whispered excitedly, jogging toward him, though not too close after he'd grabbed me last time. "I'm gonna get us outa here, Dead Man. I'll seduce Niall then stab him up good. Do you think I should wait 'til after he's fucked me?" I asked, considering that. Was I gonna live out my fantasies with my big scary captor? Was he gonna be the first guy I let do dirty things to me? My instinct should have been no, that was a stupid idea. But it wasn't. Everyone was a piece of shit in this world, so it wasn't like my first time would be with some angel. And in my darkest imaginations, I didn't want it to be. But it still made me feel all jittery and silly.

Nah, I wasn't gonna do that. Was I?

Mateo smashed his hand against the bars again, his upper lip peeling back.

"Duuude, calm down. This plan is fool proof. Did you see how sexy I was back then? I don't think he noticed the little blip with the splits. I totally played it off as part of my act, didn't I?"

Mateo growled like an actual beast and my heart juddered at that carnal noise.

"Ooh, shit, did I turn you on too?" My eyes dipped to his sweatpants where sure enough there was a huge bulge pressing against them. My throat thickened like it was full of cotton wool and I just stared at the perfect outline of his boner as heat crawled along every piece of my flesh. *It's so big, how would it fit in my pussy? In my butt?* "Oh my god, I don't know my own power."

NIALL

CHAPTER TEN

I pulled on a fancy white dress shirt that I found in the closet, rolling the sleeves back to reveal my inked forearms and staring at myself in the floor length mirror, studying the way it looked with my stonewashed jeans.

To be totally fair, I was pretty sure 'hot mess' summed up my look but I was down with that.

Dress up or down, lad. In between makes my fuckin' eyes hurt.

My pa's voice echoed through my skull and I smiled to myself as I mentally told him to get fucked, staying in my mismatched combo and loosely hanging a tie around my throat too before tying it. I didn't button the shirt though, leaving it hanging open and enjoying the mental images I got of good old Pa losing his shit over the state of his youngest.

I probably gave a little too much of my focus to trying to spite the old bastard in ways he'd never even hear about, but my petty ass couldn't summon the energy to give a fuck, so I just carried on with my day.

Last night had been a long one and after washing off the lake water and drinking half my bodyweight in whiskey, I'd passed out for way longer than I should have.

I almost could have forgotten that I had a new house guest, but that little spider was hard to forget. So seeing as I'd crashed out on the couch again after delivering her breakfast then slept through most of the afternoon and forgotten to feed either of my pets lunch and then gotten drawn into a documentary on gold mining, I decided to be gracious and order extra for dinner. She was probably fucking starved down there, not to mention Mateo needed feeding too. Couldn't forget to feed my prisoner. I needed that bastard alive and kicking so that he could tell me what I needed to know. On that note, I really needed to change his shit bucket too.

I wondered how buckets were made as I thought about that. Did a man stir molten metal on the end of a pole while doing a hula hoop kind of manoeuvre? Did you just grab a big old blob of metal and stomp on the middle of it until a bucket dip was formed? There had to be welding involved. I could google that shit, but the stomping thing had credibility and I was willing to trust my brain over some computer man.

Takeout was pretty much my go to, especially now that half the city was locked down and I couldn't cook for shit. The doorbell rang to tell me it was here as I pushed my blonde hair back out of my eyes and contemplated the best ways to hunt down my next mark. The job had been waiting on my email this morning and I still hadn't totally decided to take it on, but the fact that my mind was working out how best to kill the fucker already was usually a fairly positive sign that I'd end up pulling through. I'd give it a little more thought before I took it on though. I had my hands kinda full with my new house guest after all.

I strode across the walkway that connected my enormous bedroom to the staircase, looking over the glass railing at the lounge area below where the fire in the stone fireplace burned low.

I jogged down the stairs, grabbed a butcher's knife from the coffee table and crossed to the door. You never could be too careful, and I had a lot of fuckers who ached for my death. It kinda came with the job description. Yet another way that I was persecuted for my profession. Personally, I thought it was dumb as shit when men came hunting me for retribution after I'd killed their *insert relative or friend here*. They may as well blame the bullet or the knife or the blunt pole I'd shoved up the arse of their loved one. I was a weapon just the same. I rarely killed anyone I personally wanted to see dead. Well, okay maybe not *rarely*, but the motherfuckers I liked to hunt down for the sheer pleasure of it didn't tend to be loved by anyone who might seek vengeance. As for the rest of them, they were jobs. If they wanted revenge, they should go take it out on the fucker who ordered the hit.

Of course, the likelihood of anyone showing up here to try and kill me was damn low. No one knew about this place or its location aside from me and Mateo. He was the only asshole I had to worry about trying to kill me around here and I really wasn't worried about that at all. He had his collar and his chain and his cage, and if he hadn't escaped in all this time then I couldn't see it happening any time soon. Might be fun if he did though. I did love a good fight to the death.

I glanced at the screen showing the view from the security cameras that ringed the house as I made it to the door, pressing a button that shot a firework into the air at the foot of the long drive and watching it burst into green sparks on the monitor. I wouldn't ever be fooled by a looped feed. Hell, I wouldn't ever be fooled by anything. I was crafty like that.

I palmed the butcher's knife, hiding it behind my arm and glancing at the takeout kid on the screen, sizing him up as he half leapt out of his skin thanks to the bang of the firework. I deemed him harmless and pulled the door open.

"Where the fuck have you been?" I demanded loudly even though he wasn't late, but I just loved to watch the little bastards leap outa their skin when I yelled.

"S-sorry, Mr Buttsniffer," he muttered as he dropped the bags of takeout onto the step and backed up six feet, his eyes wild above the medical mask he wore. *Oh right, pandemic.*

"What did you call me?" I growled, loving the way the fear grew in his eyes.

Had I given them that name to put on the order? Possibly. Had I insisted the guy address me by it? Definitely. Was I going to be scaring the living shit outa him because he'd done as instructed?

Might just be.

"M-mister, I'm just trying do my job," he said, backing up like he could see the psycho in my eyes.

I sighed, realising this one was just like all the others and would only crap himself if I pushed him much further. I was always hoping for a chancer who'd try to kick my head in, but I guessed delivery kids just weren't wired that way.

I broke a grin, one with too much teeth and no joy to it then screwed up a hundred dollar bill and tossed it at him.

"You already paid," he murmured, stooping to snatch it up.

"That's a tip," I said with a shrug like I was always generous like that. But it was just some cash from a jar I'd found hidden in the back of a closet in the house and I was guessing the original homeowner wouldn't mind. Or maybe he would. Ah well.

"You want another?" I offered.

His head bobbed up and down and he gave me the puppy eyes, instantly forgetting I was a god-awful cunt.

"Here's your tip then," I said, twisting my hand and brandishing the butcher's knife at him. "Run."

He shrieked louder than a new born babe and ran for his damn life while I roared a laugh. I watched him race towards his piece of shit car, falling over his own feet before scrambling back upright and diving in behind the wheel. His eyes lifted to meet mine with fear flaring in them as I continued to grin from the doorstep and I slammed the knife into the centre of the front door, earning myself another of his screams before he gunned it the fuck outa here.

I was damn tempted to give chase just for shits and giggles, but the smell of the food reached me and I scooped up the bags and headed back inside instead.

An empty stomach waits for no man. I'd once paused to eat a sandwich halfway through killing a fella. He hadn't wanted a bite which was all the better for me because I hadn't been in the mood for sharing and feeding a soon-to-be-dead man seemed kinda wasteful.

I strode into the fancy ass dining room I never really used and dumped the bags down in the centre of the long oak table. It was big enough for ten people but I never had guests and had no friends even if I wanted guests, plus I hated most members of my fucking family and... There was a point to that thought when I started out, but I'd circled back to my stomach rumbling so I forgot it and snatched a spring roll from a paper bag instead.

I grabbed two sparkling clean plates plus knives and forks, wine glasses and some blood red serviettes I'd found in a drawer a while back. The place looked nice as shit. Fit for a queen.

Laying out a date night, now are we?

I frowned at that errant thought. No I was fucking not.

Ava must be turning in her grave. You cause her death then just forget about her and start going on dates like she was nothing and no one?

Of course that was followed by the all too vivid memories of me finding my wife's butchered body and realising that I'd been far too fucking late to save her. Everything following that was dark in my mind. I'd snapped, lost it, killed more people than I could count and painted myself in more blood than would ever really wash off. Hadn't brought her back though.

I bit my tongue, huffing out a breath as I glanced over at the corner of the room where I always imagined Ava to be standing. Not that she was. I couldn't see a damn thing there apart from shadow and failure.

"Never, love," I promised her, wondering where the thoughts had gotten that idea anyway.

That wasn't what this was about. Spider was a means to an end. Nothing else.

I pulled my phone from my back pocket and put some music on to stop the muttering in my mind, Anaconda by Nicki Minaj pouring from Alexa and giving my tongue something to do as it bent around all of the words and I drowned out the whispers in the back of my skull.

I couldn't give in to those thoughts, they were likely to get someone killed and I didn't wanna squash my little spider. Mateo still had too much juicy information about the Castillo Cartel and all of their missing riches locked up in that pretty head of his, so I needed to hold back with him too. Damn, I shoulda gone on a job today, I was feeling all kinds of riled up and that was never good for anyone who got close to me.

Oh shit, I forgot to put shoes on. I stared down at my bare feet for a long minute, jaw ticking and I grabbed hold of one of the wooden chairs sitting around the table, hurling it at the door and smashing it good.

My smile was back as Nicki kept running me around lyrical circles and this time it was a little less fake. If I even knew how to do less fake anymore. Who knew?

I tossed all of the takeout boxes down on the table and grabbed four of them at random before piling them in my arms and heading towards the basement. I paused as I reached the basement door and unbolted the four deadbolts before taking the key from my pocket and turning it in the lock. It was a noisy as fuck process that would give them plenty of time to shit themselves over my approach, but I could do it silently when I wanted to. Then I could sneak down there while they were sleeping and wake them up however the fuck I pleased.

I stepped inside and locked the door behind me before jogging down the wooden stairs.

Spider sat on her cushion beside Mateo's cell again and I arched a brow at the two of them.

She had her back to me, the blanket from the bed wrapped around her but she turned her head and sniffed at the food.

"Is it time?" she asked, looking genuinely excited and I guessed that was on behalf of her stomach, not in anticipation of my company.

"This is for Mateo," I said, stacking the boxes beside the bars of his cage. The moody fucker just scowled out at me, but he'd snatch 'em up and eat the lot the moment I was gone. I hadn't given him any chopsticks though, so he'd have to use his hands like a dog. "Maybe you should have your shower first though?" I asked him with a smirk.

His eyes moved to Spider for a brief moment, still wrapped in her blankets and I leaned closer, gripping one of the bars in my fist and looking in at him.

"What's the matter? You don't want the lady seeing your little cock?" I teased and he bared his teeth at me. "Are you still salty about me sticking that cattle prod up your arse?" I asked with a heavy sigh. "You know you could just start singing if you don't enjoy our play dates."

Nothing. Nada. Zip.

Wait...dogs don't have hands. Well, he'd just be eating like a man without chopsticks in that case. Still, point to me. I probably shouldn't have given him such nice food all the time, but I just couldn't be fucked making him something different to what I liked so he got takeout. Did he thank me for it though? Never.

Ungrateful. That's what he was. In fact, he could wait an extra day for his shower. I didn't want my food getting cold on his account.

"Come then, Spider, let's go eat away from the overriding stench of silence." I held a hand out for her and the big motherfucker lurched forward suddenly, slamming his hands against the bars and glaring at me like he hungered for my death more than anything in the world. More than he had even when I spent that afternoon hitting him with a kipper and electrocuting him through those funny little metal nipple clamps.

He growled like a feral beast and fuck me, the bastard had a voice. It had been so damn long since I'd heard it that I'd forgotten it. And his growl had a little accent, though I hadn't quite caught any words in it, unless I imagined it, but I didn't think I had because I'd heard it and he was only fucking Mexican!

Oh wait, I knew that. Mateo. Cartel. Stolen treasures. Reason I was here.

Fuck me, the things I forgot sometimes were damn worrying. Never Ava though. I could never forget her and what I'd caused her. Maybe that was the problem.

I barked a laugh as Spider pouted at him. "I don't need your advice, Dead Man. I'm going for Chinese food now."

I wasn't certain how a growl was advice but maybe she could speak raging madman. It would be handy if she could because then she'd speak my language too.

I turned my back on her and strode away as the sound of the blankets falling to the ground came from behind me and I jogged up the stairs.

I unlocked the door again and held it open like a proper gent, waiting for the lady to arrive. Only when she did, I found myself lost for fucking words.

"You told me to dress up," she said, arching a brow at me as I stared at her in my brown leather killing apron. And if her bare arms and legs were any indication then she didn't have a scrap of clothing on beneath it. "I didn't have many options though, so I worked with what I could find."

She did a twirl for me, revealing her bare arse and back as she looked back over her shoulder at me and gave me an exaggerated wink.

Shit. Why did she look good in that thing? It should have been weird. I wasn't supposed to like it. But then I liked a lot of things I wasn't supposed to, like killing and maiming and My Little Pony.

How old was she anyway? She wasn't my nephew's age. Bit older. Maybe in her twenties. Late twenties? Hopeful. Wait, why would I hope for that? I didn't give a shit if she was a two-year-old with impeccable language skills and astounding hand-eye coordination. Made no difference to me.

I ran my nails over my jaw, scratching at the stubble there as I found myself utterly stumped by her. But as my eyes fell to her arse again an uncomfortable lurch in my gut made me bark a laugh.

"Well, fuck me, Spider. You're certainly something else," I teased, slipping my open dress shirt from my arms and catching her hand before forcing it into the sleeve.

I didn't need to be looking at her perky little arse while my wife's ghost was hovering nearby.

"Don't you like my outfit?" she demanded, whirling away from me with the shirt hanging from one arm and I shook my head, laughing again as my gaze caught on the swell of her tits which were being pushed up by how tightly she'd tied the apron.

Jesus.

I swallowed thickly and gave her a reply.

"It looks a little windy in the whistles," I said with a shrug, pointing her away from the basement as I locked it up again quickly.

She didn't seem inclined to take my advice on the outfit, so I grabbed the back of the shirt and hoisted it up and around her as I made her walk with me. She muttered curses at me, slapping my hands away and I ignored her as I forced her into the white material just as we made it into the dining room. She didn't button it up but at least her arse was covered and the apron was hiding the important bits in the front. Mostly.

"Sit," I commanded, pointing to one of the chairs with a plate in front of it and she plopped down onto it.

"Do you have Coco Pops?" she asked as I dropped into the seat at the head of the table beside her and I stilled.

"Why?"

There was no way she could know about my Pops imports. I ordered them in bulk from the UK because those fuckin' Krispies things you could get here were not the fucking same, but I'd never revealed my stash to anyone. Not a soul. They weren't for sharing but somehow, she'd figured out that I had them hidden here somewhere.

She narrowed those strikingly blue eyes at me and I narrowed mine back. So it's a Pops war you want, is it missus?

"No reason," she said, eyes darting towards the door and back to me again. But she wouldn't find them. Unless she looked in the kitchen of course.

"Hmm." I dragged a box of takeout towards me and jerked my chin towards the others to let her know she was welcome to do the same.

She grabbed one at random as I leaned back in my chair, using the little disposable chopsticks to tuck into the noodles and watching her as she tried to use her own.

She raised a noodle out of the box, dangling from a stick and lunged forward to claim it, but it slithered back off of the chopsticks before she could and she cursed, digging them in for another turn. I watched her as I continued to eat, lines forming on her brow as she tried to figure the chopsticks out and her food kept falling off of them.

"You gotta think of 'em like two stubborn little bastards who won't get along," I told her. "Force them together and don't let them back off until they've had a baby."

Spider's chin lifted as she took on that stellar piece of advice and she lifted a heap of noodles from the box with a triumphant grin, leaning forward to eat them. But at the last moment, they all fell free of the chopsticks and slapped down into her lap. Seeing as she wasn't wearing any pants, the piping hot food hit bare thigh and she cursed like a sailor, hurling the entire takeout box across the room where it crashed against a mirror and sent noodles spraying everywhere.

She leapt up with a huff, knocking her chair flying and I threw a glass of water into her lap to help her out.

Her full lips popped open as her eyes widened on me in shock and what I was pretty certain was utter rage. She shrieked as she launched herself at me, disposable wooden chopsticks raised like a spear and murder in her eyes.

She dove on me and I laughed as my chair tipped back, tossing my own noodles onto the table half a heartbeat before we fell crashing to the floor.

I ended up flat on my back with her straddling me, one of her hands closing around my throat as she swung her other arm back and aimed the chopsticks at my heart.

I caught her wrist before she could land the blow and she actually growled at me as I grinned up at her.

"Well hello, killer," I said, my other hand landing on her hip as I gripped her tightly and kept her in place.

"I don't like chopsticks," she snarled, her grip on the ones she'd tried to turn into a murder weapon tightening and a sharp crack sounded as she accidentally broke them.

"Cheap throw-away ones like these don't make for much of a weapon," I agreed as she squeezed my throat with the hand I wasn't immobilising. I let her do it because in all fairness, she needed to get a bit of that rage out of her and she also wasn't near strong enough to choke me single handed. "In fact, I can't say I've ever killed anyone with a chopstick. Did use a teapot once though. I smashed it into the fucker's face and it shattered all over the place. Then I pinned him down kinda like you're doing to me right now and just kept smashing and smashing and smashing it into his ugly face until he stopped kicking. The handle never did break. I named it Bert," I sighed at the memory. That teapot handle had stayed with me for a while, but I'd ended up shoving it up some prick's arse when he cut me off at an intersection. Poor

145

Bert probably got surgically removed from his crack and tossed away like yesterday's trash. Fucking tragic that.

"You pinned him down like this?" Spider asked breathily, her grip on my throat tightening even more and my gaze slid from her parted lips to the way her tits were trying to burst out of that killing apron and for a moment I just wanted to-

Your wife died because of you.

"Yeah. But I'm a big fucker, so when I'm on top of someone, they tend to have more trouble getting me back off again than I'd have with you."

She seemed to realise her attempts at choking me were going nowhere fast and glanced down at my chest for a moment before shifting her grip to my tie which hung over my shirtless torso. That psycho look flashed in her eyes again as she grabbed my tie, yanking it tight so that it cinched up around my neck.

My grip on her hip tightened and she gasped, shifting her weight right over my crotch and making me grunt through the tight hold the tie had on my throat. *Not gonna think about her wearing no panties.*

"You still think you can beat me, Hellfire?" she purred, looking so damn cute and proud of herself that I almost felt bad about bursting her little power trip bubble. I wasn't entirely certain what she expected though, she was five foot nothing and I doubted she weighed more than a hundred pounds. Meanwhile, I was six foot five and at least double her weight – mostly in muscle. Not exactly a fair fight, but I'd never had an issue with fighting dirty.

I bucked my hips, unbalancing her and knocking her onto her back before rolling over on top of her and pinning her down easily. I snatched her hands into my grasp, transferring both of her wrists into one of my hands and grinding them down into the carpet above her head before grabbing the flick knife from my back pocket.

I snapped the blade open and her eyes widened in fear as she gasped, wriggling and thrashing beneath me, screaming like a damn banshee.

I kept my hold on her, my weight far too much for a little thing like her to overpower in this position.

I slipped the blade between my throat and the tie, cutting through the fabric and nicking my skin, making me bleed in the same move.

The moment the tie fell away, I pressed the bloodied knife to her throat and grinned down at her.

She really was panting now, her eyes sparkling with an endless kind of heat that drew me in, hungering to know more about her. I wanted to peel her open and find all of the secrets hiding in her dark places. I wanted to know if they were as dark as mine. Or darker. Was there a darker? Maybe.

"You're dead," I said to her, my blood pumping faster at the mere thought of it. I'd have killed her then if I didn't enjoy her so much. I shifted the blade to press the tip against her heart. "Dead again." She sucked in a breath, watching me like a feral cat, poised to attack and I smirked as I touched the blade to her stomach over the leather apron, showing her all the places I could stab her if the mood took me. "Dead. Dead. Dead. Dead. Stuck like a pig and bleeding out - you could survive this one though assuming you got help fast enough." My blade was low down on her stomach now and she was still watching me with that heat in her eyes.

"You'd kill me good wouldn't you, Hellfire?" she asked breathlessly and there was at least as much curiosity there as fear. Maybe something else too.

"Real good," I assured her and she smirked at me like she could think of worse ways to go.

She tugged on her hands again and I released one of them, wondering how she was going to try and best me this time and kinda loving this game. No one ever wanted to play killer with me. Even when I was a kid, my older brothers wouldn't join in. Apparently I got too stabby. But what was a bit of blood between siblings?

I watched Spider as she reached for me, her fingers brushing against

147

my throat and making me still at the minor pain I felt when she dragged them over the cut I'd given myself.

Her fingers came away bloody and she touched them to her lips, licking the taste off of them and making my heart race furiously as she closed her eyes with a soft moan.

She was a beautiful girl. It had nothing to do with why I'd taken her, but it was hard to deny it when I was looking down at her like this, breathing in the scent of her and watching her with more interest than I'd had in anything in a long damn time. Ebony hair spilled over the carpet all around her and those full lips glistened with the red of my blood. I kinda wanted to take a bite out of her and find out if she tasted as good as she looked.

"Your death tastes sweeter than Chinese takeout," she whispered and my smile widened.

"I damn well hope so. I've been waiting on it for a hell of a long time," I replied, closing the flick knife and pushing it back into my pocket. "I want it to be a good death. The kind people remember. So if you kill me one day, little spider, promise you'll make a fine mess of me."

I hopped up again and offered her my hand, hoisting her to her feet no bother on account of how damn small she was. Honestly, how had such a little thing won that fight in Royaume D'élite? I was looking at pure talent right here, all wrapped up in a five foot package.

"I'm so wet," she said, her voice husky, bright blue eyes drinking me in and for a long moment I just stared at her, the kind of thoughts I hadn't had in a long damn time trying to push their way into my brain until she spoke again. "Can I get a towel or something?"

Jesus.

She pointed at her legs and I looked down automatically, clearing my throat as I realised she was referring to the glass of water I'd dumped in her lap. That kind of wet. Obviously.

I grabbed a napkin and tossed it at her then righted her chair for her and sat back down in mine. The crotch of my jeans was considerably tighter than it had been, but I paid no attention to that as I reached for a few more takeout boxes and dumped food out onto the plates.

When spider was done drying herself off, she sat down and I handed her a knife and fork with a grin.

"I wanted to master stick eating," she sighed in disappointment, casting a glance down at her broken chopsticks on the floor before digging into her meal.

We ate like we were racing to be the first to finish, and I fought her for the last spring roll, giving in and letting her have it when she tried to bite me. *Little hellcat.* She pushed it into her mouth and grinned broadly as she chewed, leaning back in her chair and sighing.

"I like noodles," she said decisively.

"Me too," I agreed. "And I think they make a nice addition to the wall too." I looked over at the splattered mess which had mostly fallen onto the carpet now and she nodded seriously.

"I should probably clean that up," she said, biting down on her bottom lip and widening her eyes at me.

"Nah," I replied dismissively, but she was already on her feet, moving around the table towards it, swinging her hips wildly from side to side so that my shirt flapped around her arse and gave me a glimpse of more skin than I should have been looking at.

"Did you hurt yer hip in that fight at Royaume D'élite?" I asked her, wondering if she needed some kind of medical attention. I had a doctor I could take her to off the books if needs be, but I tended to let Mother Nature do her worst with my own injuries. I hadn't died yet so I figured she was in on the joke with the Grim Reaper, the two of them punishing me with this lingering life for fuck knew how long.

"No," she replied, frowning back at me. "Why?"

"Yer walking weird," I replied.

"No. This is my normal psyxy walk." She winked over her shoulder at me and I cocked my head, wondering what the fuck that was. "Have you got a feather duster?" she asked.

"To clean up noodles?" I frowned and she nodded.

Huh, maybe she knew more about cleaning than I did. Couldn't say I'd ever tried using a feather duster to clean up blood though. It just didn't seem like the right tool for the job.

"There's some cleaning shit in the kitchen. Come on." I jerked my head, grabbing the dirty plates and crockery and she followed me out of the room.

As soon as we made it into the huge open living space in the centre of the old farmhouse, she turned and tried to bolt for the door, but I caught her wrist and swung her back around towards the kitchen. Neither of us commented on it and we kept going until I was pulling the cleaning closet open for her.

The kitchen cupboards were all shiny and grey and the big window that ran above the sink looked down the drive and into the valley beyond. We were on top of a hill here and the views all around were stunning, but better than that, it was damn near impossible for anyone to sneak up here without being seen. Aside from me of course. I'd happily taken the place from the previous owner after sneaking in while he was sleeping. But I was a ghost. It was damn hard to predict what I'd do at the best of times, not least because I generally had no fuckin' idea meself.

"I have a proposition for ya," I said, dumping the dirty crockery into the sink and leaning back against the marble worktop as she rummaged in the closet.

"Oh?"

"Yeah. I want you to work for me."

"Doing what?" she asked suspiciously, turning to face me with a feather duster in hand like she'd wanted.

"I want you to help me kill people."

Her eyes lit up like it was Christmas Day and Santa had just hand delivered a selection of vibrators right to her bed. It was a damn cute look on her.

"Like stabbing and maiming and chopping them up?" she breathed, her voice somehow getting even huskier as she considered it.

"Yeah. I was thinking it'd be good to have someone help me out from time to time and I fucking hate having to work with my family. Being a part of the Irish mob can be a royal pain in the arse."

"Mob?" she asked, sharp as a whip.

"Don't worry yer pretty head about that," I said dismissively. "The point is, I wanna keep you out of my family. As much as I can anyway. Start my own thing. Like a team."

"Or a club?" she asked. "I've always wanted to be a part of a club. Stacey Briner had a girls' club when I was in middle school but she wouldn't let me join because she said I had cooties. But I got my cootie shot. I. Got. My. Shot. Fucking whore."

"Wanna kill her?" I offered, not liking the hurt that flashed in Spider's eyes at that memory.

"Nah," she sighed. "I heard she got knocked up by Conner McGrath. The guy always stank of farts and ate way too many Cheetos all the damn time. She's already in hell."

"Sounds like it," I agreed and she smiled brightly at me before turning and starting to dust the worktop opposite me, bending forward and walking weird again.

"Tell me if there's anything in particular you want polished," she offered, pouting at me over the feather duster and doing more of that funny walk.

"You sure you don't need to see a doctor for that leg?" I asked. "I killed a doctor once. Nasty fucker who had been going all power of god on

151

his patients. The woman who hired me wanted me to make him suffer and I can tell ya, he screamed and screamed and screamed before-"

"I hate doctors," Spider snarled viciously, brandishing the feather duster at me like it was a gun. "You can't make me see one. I won't. They can't have me back."

I realised she was about to bolt again a second before she tried it and I grabbed her, whirling her around and pressing her back against the sink as she thrashed and kicked.

"You can't make me go back!" she screamed, smacking me with the feather duster and making me cough as dust fell over both of us from the damn thing.

I ripped it out of her hand and flung it away, lifting her up and slamming her arse down on the worktop beside the sink as I tried to contain her.

"You don't have to-" I began but she managed to snatch a fist from my grasp and lunged towards the sink.

I threw my weight onto her, forcing my way between her thighs and mostly pinning her down before she grabbed something out of the sink and stabbed me in the arse with it so hard that I yelled a curse.

I snatched her wrist into my grip, transferring both of them into one hand again and slamming them against the cupboard above her head as I leaned in close and snarled at her.

I could feel whatever the fuck she'd stabbed me with still very much lodged in my left arse cheek, but I didn't remove it, grasping her chin with my free hand and forcing her to look at me as panic flared in her eyes.

"No doctors," I swore, making sure she was listening to me and feeling some of the tension leaving her body as she did.

"Promise?" she breathed and there was something so innocent about the way she said that word that I just stilled for a long moment.

"Cross my heart and hope to die," I growled firmly.

We stared at each other for the longest time, chests heaving, breaths mingling and some kind of understanding growing between us. If there was such a thing as a kindred spirit in this world then I was almost certain I'd found it in this wild girl.

"I should change your name to Chaos," I said roughly and a smile touched her lips.

"You don't know the half of it. You've brought a hurricane into your home."

"Work for me," I demanded.

"What makes you think I'd be good at it? No one ever thinks I'll be good at anything."

"For a start I watched you win that death tournament," I replied. "And I can see you've got the instincts for it. But you need to work on a lot of shit if you wanna be able to do this work and survive it."

"You want to teach me?" she asked, her eyebrows rising and I could have sworn she sounded excited about that.

"If you wanna learn," I agreed. "Besides, you owe me half a mil anyway so you might as well start working off your debt. I won't be able to let you go until you do."

Technically that was my pa's money and I had no intention of paying him back a cent of it, but I didn't give a shit about that and I wasn't going to mention it.

"How do you figure that out?" she scoffed, shifting and reminding me that I was still very much between her bare thighs. I hadn't been between a woman's thighs since...

I released her suddenly and stepped back, grabbing her knees as I did so and firmly pressing them closed without letting myself think about the fact that she had no panties on.

"I bought you, remember," I replied.

"I never asked to be sold."

"And yet you were. That makes you mine."

"You paid half a million for me?" she asked, her brows pulling together in confusion.

"Sure did." *Well, Pa did.*

"Half a million *dollars*?" Her eyes narrowed with suspicion.

"No, potatoes," I deadpanned.

"Oh," she laughed. "That makes more sense. I'm worth half a million potatoes for sure."

"No, of course dollars," I snapped.

She frowned again, all confused like as she took a moment to scratch her little nose. Then she roared a laugh, pointing at me. "You got ripped off, Hellfire. I'm not worth a dime." She clutched her sides, laughing harder. "People would actually pay me to go far, far, far away. You must feel so stupid right now."

"Not really, Spider. Pretty sure I got myself a bargain actually." I huffed out a breath as she seemed confused by those words, reaching behind me and yanking the fucking fork out of my arse. Yes, a fucking *fork*. It hurt like a bitch, but the fact that she'd managed to wound me like that said a lot for her potential. She needed to work on her damn aim though, there had been a kidney right there for the stabbing and she'd gone for a chunk of flesh that was never gonna be fatal.

"You stabbed me in the fuckin arse with a fork," I growled, tossing the offending piece of cutlery into the sink beside her again.

"Well I'm not gonna kiss it better," she snarked back, folding her arms and pushing her tits up even more. I didn't notice them though because I wasn't looking. "Besides, it's an ass, not an arse."

"It's on my body so I think I know what it is," I replied darkly.

"No. I have one too and it is definitely an *ass*," she replied stubbornly.

"An ass is a donkey," I replied. "My arse is my arse."

"Ass," she hissed, making my temper flare because she was very fucking much wrong.

"Arse," I growled.

"Ass."

"Arse."

"Ass."

"Arse."

"Ass."

"Arse."

"*Ass*."

"That's it!" I barked, lunging at her. "I warned you what would happen if you were bad."

She shrieked and tried to escape, throwing a plate from the sink at me and I barely blocked it as it crashed into my arm and fell to the floor with a loud smash.

Dammit, why wasn't I wearing shoes? Rule one of feet. Wear fucking shoes.

Spider leapt off of the counter and ran for it, but I was faster, jumping over the shattered plate and winding an arm around her waist then throwing her over my shoulder before she could escape me.

She kicked and screamed, grabbing hold of one of the cupboard doors and yanking it open.

I laughed as I tugged on her legs while she clung on and she reached into the cupboard where I kept a load of candy, snatching something out before I tore her away from it.

I carried her back to the basement door and unlocked it while she thumped my back and tried to aim for my bleeding arse cheek.

"Shoulda been the kidney, love, then I mighta had an issue."

She cursed wildly and I chuckled as I ignored the way she was fighting me. "You'll have an issue when you sit down on that ouchy ass cheek, Hellfire. When you're doing a poo, you'll think of me. And maybe that's just what I wanted!"

I got the basement door open and carried her down the stairs inside, flicking the light on and walking straight up to the naughty cage where Mateo lunged to his feet, glaring at me and the girl dangling over my shoulder.

"Down, boy," I warned him as I unlocked the barred door and he scowled deeply but said nothing. Silent bastard. I'd crack him one of these days though. Every nut cracked in the end.

I dropped Spider onto her feet and she quickly shoved the packet of jellybeans she'd stolen into the pocket of my killing apron. I pretended not to notice because she was skinny enough and I liked her, despite her not knowing how to say arse.

"It was just a little fork," she protested as I kept hold of her arm and pushed her into the cage before locking it up tight again. Mateo couldn't reach her if she stayed right there. The chain attached to his collar wouldn't allow it, so I was pretty sure she'd be fine. Probably. And she needed to learn her lesson.

"It's not about the fork," I growled, meeting her defiant gaze. "It's about the arse."

She pouted and I grinned.

"You hurt her and I'll kill you," I said to Mateo, making sure my words were laced in malice and he had no doubts at all about the truth of them. "It won't be quick either."

"Wait," Spider called and I looked back at her. "I want you to know that you're saying it wrong. It's *ass*."

"Fuck you," I replied, barking a laugh as I jogged back up the stairs and left her there, but she shouted after me all the same.

"ASS!"

I locked the basement door and couldn't quite wipe the grin from my face. That girl was going to be all kinds of trouble. And that was exactly why I liked her.

BROOKLYN

CHAPTER ELEVEN

My lower lip stuck out in outrage. It was just a little fork in the ass, what about that made me deserve the naughty cage? I'd done worse to people hungover with a chest infection. That wasn't naughty, that was freaking foreplay. I think so anyway. I wasn't exactly sure what the word foreplay meant. But that was my best estimate.

I growled under my breath then stilled as a large body shifted behind me, a lump rising in my throat. *Oh tits. Mateo.*

I slowly rounded toward him and his dark eyes burned into me unblinkingly. As I moved, his gaze followed and I got the exact same feeling I did when I was watched by a hungry dog. I'd fed the strays out on the streets whenever they looked at me like that. A starved beast was better your friend than your enemy. And if you didn't respect that, you might just end up as their next meal. Luckily for him, I'd stashed a bag of jellybeans in my pocket from Niall's candy collection and it looked like I was gonna have to share. He was no shitty little Susan the cat after all. He was definitely more canine. So I was going to try a different approach because fuckballs, he was scaring me with that expression.

I'd killed a bunch of people in my life, but this guy looked big enough to eat me alive. And I didn't even have my pencil in defence anymore. No, all I had was my wits. So I was going to need to convince him I was just a harmless little dandelion who desired no trouble in her dainty spring flower patch, because if he caught the whiff of a killer on me, he might just attack first.

"Hey there, boy," I said softly, approaching him at a steady pace, keeping low to show I meant no harm. I was gonna guess he'd be a rottweiler with all that rippling muscle and savagery. I made kissy noises with my lips and he frowned at me as I got closer. "I got ya something."

I took the jellybeans I'd stolen from my pocket, kneeling down in front of him and shuffling closer. He smelled like sweat and blood and the combination was kinda scrummy. It looked like he'd been working out the whole time I'd been gone. He did that a lot. Dude had hobbies. Silence and working out. Fancy.

I wasn't into dogs, but if I had been, this one might have turned me to bestiality. Alright, alright, I knew he wasn't a pooch. But it made approaching him seem a lot easier if I tried to believe that. It took a lot to unsettle me and this guy was about two hundred pounds of bottled scary. And as we were now cellmates, I didn't wanna wake up dead tomorrow.

I tore the packet open and poured a few into my hand. "Do you have a favourite?" I asked and he growled deeply in response as adrenaline surged into my blood.

"Shhh, puppy." I held the selection up to him on my palm, folding my legs as I inched a little closer, my knees brushing his. The apron wasn't best designed for this position but unless he leaned all the way over, he wouldn't get a look up it to my vag. "The green ones are the best," I whispered conspiratorially.

His upper lip peeled back and I took the opportunity to slide a green one between his lips, meeting a wall of teeth. The feeling of his mouth against my fingertips had my skin going all duck-bumpy and I shivered in a way that was half scared-little-lamb and half give-me-more-big-bunny.

"Open up," I sang and he growled again. That was a scary sound so it shouldn't have been making me feel all hot and prickly, but what could I say? Me and danger had always been a good combination.

I popped another green one between his lips, keeping my eyes averted from his as he stared in that intense way of his. He'd have to chew eventually. All that sugar was gonna start melting and he wouldn't be able to resist it. I was finding it hard to resist it myself.

I placed another green one with the others then sat back and waited for him to eat them. He didn't.

I pouted. "Maybe you like a different colour?" I guessed, but he gave me no indication that was the case. *O...kay.*

I leaned forward, hooking the green ones back out of his mouth and stuffing them into mine instead with a grin. It was like a firework of sugar on my tongue coated with beastly man mouth.

"Mmm, so good," I sighed and his eyes lit up at the noises I was making, full of some wicked emotion I couldn't place. I hadn't had anything sugary since I'd stolen a pack of churros off an eight-year-old a few weeks back. Kid had had one mid-way to his mouth, his eyes gleaming with excitement. Excitement I'd wanted to steal. So I had. I guessed shoving him onto the floor was overkill, but I'd had to wrestle that final churro from his meaty fingers.

"Do you like red?" I offered, holding one up to his lips.

I lifted my eyes to meet his gaze, trying to read him a little better even though I knew that was a bad idea with wild animals. He lunged toward me suddenly and I dropped backwards in alarm, bending all the way over so my spine hit the ground as he reared above me. My heart thrashed as I fell still like a rabbit in the headlights. That worked for them right? Cars totally swerved around them when they did that. Right? Right??

He crawled up my body, his leather collar tethered to the wall so the chain went taut as he stared down at me. He was all monster with a healthy dose of barbarian thrown in. My kind of fantasy man. Though it was slightly more unsettling meeting him in the flesh rather than in the safety of my own mind.

I dropped the jellybeans in my hand and they skittered out around me. I quickly brought the pack to my mouth, tipping a few between my lips. If I was gonna die, I wanted a mouth full of the rainbow when I went. It was always best to hold onto something sweet when life got bad. And it looked like things were about to get really, really bad. If he hurt me, I'd fight. I was a spring coiled and loaded. But I was still holding onto the hope that my tactic of playing vaguely dead was going to work.

His shadow consumed me as I lay awkwardly beneath him, his body dropping down until his chest brushed mine, pinning me there as he just freaking stared at me. He was so close to my face, I could feel his breath on my lips, could taste the completely masculine, murderous scent of him everywhere. His beard tickled my jaw and it was such a nice beard, I wanted to climb right into it and live there like a baby bird. I'd burrow deep and dig out his smile. I bet he had a nice one, the kind I wanted to eat.

I placed the jellybeans down and reached up slowly, not wanting to make any sudden movements as I tried to tame this rabid beast. My heart jack-hammered as I pushed my fingers into his dark hair and gently stroked him.

"Good boy," I purred. "Are you lonely in here, poor baby? I'm lonely too." *Sometimes I'm more lonely than the moon who's all the way up there in the sky without a friend to love her.*

A deep V formed between his eyes. Eyes which were like melted dark chocolate with shavings of copper in their depths. *Satan, if you're listening. I know this one was made by you. And bravo. He's a work of art. Did you sculpt him out of the same clay you made Niall with because ho-ly fuck I'm not sure which of them gets me hotter. P.S. you're still planning on getting me out of this right? Because these demons might be pretty, but I have the feeling one of them is going to be my death. And if you're planning on bringing me to hell that way, I'd appreciate the heads up. Otherwise I'm gonna go full savage on them, kay?*

"I'll be your friend," I whispered as he inhaled, seeming to breathe in a piece of my actual soul. I didn't really plan on making a friend out of him. That would require trusting him, which I did not. And frankly, seeing him as a dog was about the only way I could keep myself from freaking out. Because if I thought about it, I was in a cage with a giant man who could kill, rape, mutilate me, or all three if the notion took him.

"Friends," he grunted, a note of amusement in his tone and fuck me with a tin opener, he had a voice. And not just any voice. It was deep, sinful and sprinkled with a Mexican accent that did all kinds of wicked fuckery to my body. He sounded like a monster from the deep and I wasn't immune to its effects at all as it rumbled down into the centre of my body. "That's a big word."

"It's only seven letters. There's bigger words. Like onomatopoeia," I said and he wet his lips, eyeing mine. Did he want me? Some part of me definitely wanted him. In another reality, my V Card might have been in my palm ready to be signed with his name.

I wished I'd had a girl friend or a mother who wasn't a running-away-with-Esteban-whore to talk about sex with. I'd seen a few pornos on Stinky Jim's phone (I was pretty sure it wasn't his actual phone and that he'd stolen it from someone because he totally wasn't charging it using that old piece of hose like he'd claimed) and plenty of pictures in dirty magazines, but I wasn't exactly prepared.

I knew I'd figure it out quick though. I'd like *all* the stuff. My imagination always took me to dark places and it was no different when it came to sex, I just wasn't entirely sure if my fantasies fit reality because no one had ever had a conversation with me about it. Like, obviously I knew where the D went. And I'd found my clit when I was fifteen. But I wasn't sure on the little details. I'd figure it out, I guessed. Porn suggested that dicks were great fun and that cum tasted as good as these jellybeans, so I was sure I'd take to it like a duck to water.

I wasn't going to let Mateo screw me though. If I ever found a trustworthy enough guy to do that with, I'd like to have a weapon somewhere close and maybe they'd be beneath me instead of the other way around. It wasn't that I didn't fantasise about being held down and claimed by guys like this, it was that whenever I pictured it, I was fucking terrified of them doing that against my will. Of me not having an exit plan, a knife stashed up my sleeve. Seduction was power. But it always seemed like sex meant someone had to relinquish that power. And I never wanted to lose control. Not again.

"He calls you Spider, what's your real name?" he growled in that thick, gravelly voice again. Hell, between him and Niall they could have started up their own baritone subsection of an acapella band.

"That's a secret," I breathed and he reached up to clasp my throat in his grip, feeling me swallow thickly beneath his roughened palm.

"Tell me it," he insisted, his eyes flaring with the need to know, but I hadn't spoken it in a long time to anyone. And for a damn good reason.

"You'll tell Niall," I hissed. "And I don't want him knowing." Not least because I was a convicted criminal with a bounty on my head and Niall just might hand me in for the cash if it suited him.

"Why would I tell that piece of shit anything? He's been torturing me for months and hasn't gotten a word out of me."

"You're not loyal to me," I said as his fingers flexed against my neck, just tight enough to keep me there. My hand was still in his hair and I started stroking again, trying to soften the hardness I saw in his eyes. *Come on, puppy, be my new bestie. Then when I get a chance to escape, I'll unleash you on Niall like an attack dog and use the distraction to run. All's fair in love and gore.*

"I might come to be," he said, pressing his weight down on me and the hard ridge of his monster cock ground into my bare thigh through his sweatpants. *Holy fucking biscuits.*

His weight crushed me and suddenly I was breathing too heavily. I liked it. I liked it too much. No I didn't. I didn't like it at all. Terror was bundling up in my heart at being trapped like this, held in place. Fuck, it was confusing. I wanted to be bent to his will almost as much as I wanted to drive a knife into his chest and run for my life.

My head started buzzing with memories, hands on my flesh which I didn't want, but they blurred with the feeling of how good Mateo's weight felt. I jerked against his hold on me, trying to blink back the flashes of yucky, monstrous memories in my mind. *No, no, no. It's happening. I'm going back there again. I don't want to go back.*

Laughter rang in my ears and the sticky night air clung to my skin. I was small, small, small. An ant beneath crows which were pecking at my flesh, tearing at my clothes. They were laughing and prodding and touching me places I didn't want them to touch.

I thrashed beneath Mateo, starting to shove and kick and his hand slid away from my throat.

"Get off- get off!" I screamed. "Get away from me, Andrew!" I bellowed, unsure what reality I was living in for a moment as I saw the moon through the trees or was it a light between the bars of a cage?

A large hand prised my eyes open and banished the nightmare I was trapped in. Mateo's dark gaze blazed into mine and my breathing slowed, my hands falling to rest on his shoulders where bloody scratches were torn into his skin. He'd lifted his weight off of me so I was no longer trapped, but his body still surrounded me as he knelt either side of my bare legs.

"Who's Andrew?" he growled dangerously. "What did he do to you?"

Andrew was one of the bad ones. He'd survived, but others hadn't. I drew on the memory of driving a blade driving into Luke Damsey's gut, stab, stab, stabbing as he screamed, seeing his death in my eyes. It was a beautiful memory, one I owned every piece of. His death was a balm on my heart, and my breaths slowed as I remembered he was no longer in this world and Satan was probably ripping his spine outa his butthole right about now. I just wished Andrew could have joined him there.

"He's my enemy," I replied and he nodded slowly, considering that.

"He hurt you?" he grunted.

"Yes," I said, letting him know. It was obvious anyway. I'd just freaked on him like a raccoon in a rage, so it wasn't hard to put together. I brushed my fingers over the marks on his skin, the scratches kind of beautiful on his olive flesh. "Sorry."

"Don't be," he said, his voice too delicious, my skin peppering with goosebumps again as it washed over me.

I didn't know if I wanted to arch into his touch or build a wall around myself so he could never lay his hands on me again.

I started scrambling backwards out of the cage of his arms, but he caught my ankle before I could get too far out of reach, dragging me back towards him. His hands on me were sinful, making my heart race and heat flood to the depths of my being. But I didn't like people touching me. When they touched me, they did bad things. Things that hurt, things that made me scream.

"Stay still," he commanded, and I listened because I had no weapon and I didn't have a death wish. He sat back then took my hands, dragging me toward him into his lap. My knees settled on the concrete either side of him and his rock hard length rested between my thighs as he held my wrists in one of his. I didn't have any panties on and the way his gaze intensified said he knew. He watched me as my breaths came in furious little pants, fear driving into my core as the instinct to run gripped me.

His fingers slid between mine on my right hand and locked together. *Oh.*

The newness of the feeling made me pause. I shouldn't have liked it. I really, really shouldn't have. But as terrifying as it felt to be touched by this powerful man, it was suddenly so good too.

He said nothing, going mute on me again as he rested our intertwined hands on my knee. I didn't wanna move in case I disturbed his huge dick, but heat was soaking between my thighs and my head was starting to spin. Maybe the nurses at the Eden Heights Psychiatric Hospital had had a point. Maybe I really was crazy. Because right now this forbidding creature beneath me wasn't just touching me in a way I liked, he was turning me on too. And I wanted to lean into the madness swirling inside me and see how recklessly insane I could really be with him.

I was getting nervous and when that happened, I started talking. The word vomit was coming, and I couldn't stop it because I had questions. Lots and lots of questions. "Does it feel good when your cock gets hard like that?" He arched a brow with the ghost of a smirk, remaining quiet so I hurried on. "Or is it sore like you just have to touch it – or have someone else touch it. Or lick it. Is licking it weird?" I shifted on his lap and he groaned lustfully. "That wasn't an invitation," I backtracked in alarm. "I just wondered if that was what it needs. Or is it just a tight hole it wants? Is it any tight hole? Or does it have to be a vag or a butt? And is it hard because it wants *my* vag or butt? And by *it* I mean you and – shit don't answer that. I don't wanna know. No wait, I do wanna know. Do you like me, or is it just because you've been stuck in here alone for a century? If I was an old, old, old, old grandma would you still want me then? Do cocks rot if they don't get used for too long? And is blue balls a real thing? Are they actually blue? Can I see? No wait, I don't wanna see. None of this is an invitation."

"You mentioned that," he growled, his eyes full of darkness as he watched me and I sighed. What was I doing? This was true insanity. The type that grew like ivy inside you, wrapping around everything you were until it all looked so pretty that you might as well just leave it hanging up.

"Why are you holding my hand?" I demanded suddenly, narrowing my eyes on him. "Is hand holding like consent? Did I just consent to something? Because I rescind my consent."

"Jesus fucking Christ, chica loca," he growled and I wondered why he was calling me a chicken head. I spoke fluent Spanish, Tiny Juan had taught me. He always said 'por favor deja de hablarme' whenever we started chatting, and that definitely meant 'hello, how are you.' "You brought me Jellybeans so I'm paying you back. You wanted to know what hand holding was like so I'm showing you, that's it. *This* is what it's like."

"Oh," I breathed. As simple as that? Nothing was as simple as that.

I looked down at our clasped hands and an ache of longing filled my soul. No one had touched me like this before. No. One. And it awoke some deep need in me that had always been there, yet I'd somehow tuned out. It hurt to feel it. But I wanted the pain right then, because it reminded me I was just a girl with wants and wishes and I didn't have to pretend they didn't exist.

I gazed at Mateo as his muscles flexed like he was trying to restrain himself from doing something. Though I wasn't sure what. Probably killing me. But hey, that meant I'd trained the dog. He hadn't bitten me. He did something nice for me. Sure, he could turn on me at any second with sharp teeth and claws, but right now he wasn't. Was this how trust was formed? People doing nice things over and over again for each other until one day they could predict nice things from them in future? But how did you know they'd keep doing those nice things forever? What if they did fifty nice things then one really, really bad thing? What then?

"Time's up." He tugged his hand free and pushed me off of his lap.

My ass hit the floor and he retreated into the darkest corner of the cage, sitting with his back to the wall. My hand tingled from his touch and I gazed after him for a long moment as I wondered if anyone would ever touch me like that again. His hands balled into fists and his breaths came heavier as he looked pointedly away from me.

"You have a nice voice," I told him.

He said nothing and I had the feeling he might be done talking again for a while. People usually got fed up with me eventually. He'd stuck out my ramblings longer than most. But then again, he was trapped in a basement with me. So he couldn't escape even if he wanted to. He was just a lion trapped in a cage with a wildcat and he didn't fancy eating me yet.

I scooped up the jellybeans from the floor and pushed them over to him, nudging them against his hand when he didn't take them. "You didn't even try them yet."

He picked them up and I scooted back to lean against the bars opposite him, holding my breath as I waited for him to eat them. He glared at me as I didn't blink, gesturing with my hand for him to taste one. He poured the entire contents into his mouth and started chewing, a deep, beastly groan leaving him as he ate.

My heart expanded to two times its normal size as I watched him enjoying them, eventually swallowing them down and shutting his eyes as he seemed to savour the lasting taste of them.

Silence stretched out and after a while, I cleared my throat. "So... my seduction didn't go totally as planned upstairs," I told him with a sigh, pushing the apron down between my thighs as I folded my legs. "But I'm gonna keep trying. I don't think I'm Niall's type, but he's gotta have needs, right? Maybe I'll do a dance for him next time. A striptease."

"No," Mateo snarled forcefully. "Don't do that."

"It's not like I can't dance, Dead Man. I've got moves." I rolled my eyes at him. I'd outdanced a fox in an alley once.

"That wasn't my p-"

"I'll grind my ass on him then he'll peel my sweatpants down and he'll be all like 'great leprechauns, that's the finest arse I've ever seen'," I did a perfect impression of him but Mateo didn't crack a smile. "Then I'll let him have his wicked way with me and stab him in the eye!"

"You. Will. Not. Fuck. Him," Mateo spat venomously, and my heart leapt in surprise.

"It's not like I want him to fuck me," I scoffed. *Wait, that didn't sound convincing. Say it again.* "It's not like I *want* him to fuck me." I dunno why it kept coming out like that because I really, really, really wanted to fuck Niall – didn't want to fuck Niall. *Goddammit.*

"Why did you say that twice?" he growled.

"Some things are better said twice." I shrugged, looking away. I wasn't sure why I was getting so cagey about it. Maybe it was because I was in a cage. Because of *course* I didn't want my kidnapper to fuck me. Of *course* I didn't want to feel his cock driving into me while he recited the alphabet in that beautiful accent of his. Obviously. I wasn't *that* fucked up.

"Just trust me, Dead Man," I implored and he fell quiet again, staring. Always with the staring.

I kinda liked the attention though. Most people acted like I was invisible. Not him. He acted like I was the only thing in the room and I was shiny and interesting.

I wouldn't be falling asleep easily tonight though. This guy looked like he could make a balloon animal out of my body. And just because he hadn't hurt me yet, didn't mean he wasn't going to. He was in this cage for a reason. And his eyes alone told me he was no stranger to violence.

MATEO

CHAPTER TWELVE

I didn't sleep and I was fairly certain she didn't either for most of the night. Niall had left the light on so I could watch her where she sat on the far side of the cage, leaning back against the bars, her head nodding as she dozed off at last. She looked so fragile, her neck so delicate. I couldn't help but picture myself sliding my fingers around it and seeing how it felt to hold her life in my grasp.

I felt myself hardening at that thought and squeezed my eyes shut to force that image out of my head. But it always crept back in. Even more recently because it had been so, so long since I'd exorcised my demons and her appearance here of all places had awoken that need in me more fiercely than ever before.

Whenever she was close I couldn't help but stare at her, hungering for the opportunity to get even closer. But I knew if I did, I wouldn't be able to hold myself back. Of course, I could just snap, give in, overpower her and do whatever the beast in me wanted. But if I did that, her death would be all but inevitable, and I wanted more than that, I wanted to own her. I'd known it that first day when she'd set those bright blue eyes on me and taken me captive in them.

But as it stood, I wasn't certain how to achieve that. She didn't act like any woman I'd ever known and I didn't think she'd be won over so easily either. So I sat and I watched her and I tried to figure her out. Tried to figure out how to make her body bend to mine so that I could bury myself in her and make her flesh burn and writhe for me. I'd feel her tight pussy come around my cock then I'd take hold of her throat and watch her panic rise as she wondered whether or not I was going to let go.

I growled beneath my breath at that thought. It wasn't me. Not really. It was the demon who resided in my soul. The one my mamá had tried to rip out of me. But she'd failed. All the things she'd done had only made sure it only clung on deeper, burrowing into the centre of my being where it could never be cut free.

Hours of silence had passed between us and I'd been surprised to find she was capable of it. But I'd gladly listen to that husky voice of hers all day and night, on and on forever even if she hadn't stopped talking. I'd had more than enough of silence.

Her head bobbed forward one last time, hanging low at an awkward angle and her deep breathing filled the silence.

I watched her for several more minutes, then I pushed myself up onto my hands and knees and slowly began to move towards her.

My heart pounded as I closed the distance between me and this tempting little creature, and I moved so slowly that even the chain attached to my neck didn't give me away. I was a predator on the hunt and my prey was already caught. Locked in this cage with me. She couldn't get out. And I could kill her in countless ways before Niall made it down here. He would only appear at all in the scenarios where I let her scream. There were far more where I kept her silent until her final breath fluttered against my palm.

But I didn't want that. I didn't want her fighting and begging and breaking beneath me. I wanted her drawing me closer, not pushing me back, pulling me in and moaning my name as she let me destroy her. And I would destroy her. That was the one certainty in all of this.

I came to a halt right beside her, the scent of freedom clinging to her skin alongside the papaya scent of the soap she'd used, and I leaned in close until my nose was brushing against her throat. I breathed her down into my lungs, slowly running my nose up the arch of her neck and over her impossibly soft flesh until I reached that tender patch of skin right beneath her ear. I inhaled deeply, drawing the essence of her into me to tangle with my soul and draw me back from the edge of the end. Her pulse thrummed like the wings of a tiny bird. *Podría destruirte tan bellamente - I could destroy you so beautifully.*

A soft moan escaped her and tension lined her limbs for a moment, causing me to draw back, just enough so that I wasn't touching her. She settled again and I forced myself to maintain this small distance, just watching her, drowning in her.

In the months I'd spent locked up and alone down here, I'd sometimes fallen back onto the teachings of my childhood. My mamá had been a devout Catholic woman, bringing me to Sunday service and taking communion weekly. She'd drummed her faith into me and tried to raise me to be a good, pious man, even when she saw the evil in me. But she knew full well who and what her husband was, and she was desperate for me to be unlike him. She knew that if I was going to keep my faith, I'd be making a habit out of the confessional booth. A habit which she also adhered to weekly.

Our priest liked to encourage the women of his church to confess the sins of their flesh to him and the day I'd caught him with his hands down his pants while listening to such stories had been the day my faith had faltered. I'd told my papi about it and Father Ferdinand had disappeared that very day. The new priest didn't do that. He seemed nice enough. And that had been the day I'd begun to wonder about a god who allowed his own devoted servants to abuse their position like that.

But my mamá hadn't liked that. She hated me for sending Father

Ferdinand away and refused to believe what I'd seen. My father had beaten her for her part in it of course and no doubt her rage at me was linked to that too. But that was the day she first looked at me like there was no hope for me at all. Like all she could see in my soul was dark with rot and corruption. That was the day she'd started her work on trying to force the Devil out of me. And the day I'd first realised that women weren't the weaker sex at all. They were smarter, crueller, more vicious and cunning and more able to hurt you in all the ways that couldn't be healed.

But down here in the dark, I'd sought out God once or twice. Not to ask for a ticket to salvation or even for any help in escaping my circumstances. I just asked him for a little light in my dark world. And I was beginning to think he'd answered my prayers.

My mamá's work in exorcising my demons had fractured something in me though, so I knew I had to tread carefully if I didn't want to snuff out this little light of mine. Most of the time, I could control that darkness in me, or at least aim it in the right directions. It was what had made me so good at my job while I worked within the cartel, what had put me in the position of power I'd held. But it was also the reason why I'd always known that I would flee one day. Every rotten thing in me had been born in that place, on those streets, in the monastery I had to pass all too often and my parents' home and everywhere in between.

Every time I saw those women in their black and white habits with their crucifixes and rosaries, I was right back there at their mercy. And it hadn't taken me long to find a way to let that darkness out, to give in to it just enough to stop it from consuming me and setting me on the path of damnation. Because if I'd really done what I wanted to do, then I would have barred every door on that building and burned those women alive within it long before the day I'd left.

Instead, I punished myself and I punished others and I revelled in every moment of it. Which was precisely why I couldn't rush this. I couldn't risk it. I wanted to keep her, destroy her in my own way but only in a way that I could repeat time and again.

I'd come close to killing women in the past when I'd taken them to my bed. Flashes of my childhood horrors liked to haunt me when I was in my most intimate moments, and sometimes I couldn't contain that monster within me when it happened. And since the first time that had happened, I'd made sure someone stood in the room with me whenever I claimed a woman, needing them to drag me off if I ever went too far. There were women who liked that. Women I paid. The transaction made it easier. They liked the fantasy of the beast in me, but none liked the reality. When I had to be torn away from them as I lost control and came too close to killing them, I saw the fear in their eyes as clear as day. The realisation that this was no game. That this was a deep and broken thing in me which I couldn't always fight. And if I got lost to that darkness, then they'd be dead at my feet before I even realised what I'd done.

Mi sol, I thought because that was what she felt like, my own little bit of sunshine, brightening up this dark place.

Inky black hair tumbled around her and I reached out to brush my fingers over the tangled strands.

Why are you here? Where did you come from? Are you here to test me? Because if I'm not supposed to own you then I think I might just fail.

I reached down, my fingers itching with the need to curl them around her throat. I'd squeeze just a little. Just for a moment. Enough for a taste of what it would feel like to have her at my mercy and no more.

The locks on the door at the top of the stairs banged open and she flinched awake, gasping as she found me so close and swinging for me with a feral snarl.

Her fist crashed against my jaw and I caught her wrist before she could try to strike me again, baring my teeth as I reared over her.

"I won't get lost to you, Dead Man," she growled in warning, but she stopped trying to fight me and my grip on her relaxed as I nodded.

I backed away, retreating to sit on the hard, wooden bench in anticipation of Niall's arrival, my gaze glued to the girl as she massaged her wrist where I'd held her. Not like it had hurt, more like she was trying to memorise the way it had felt. My heart beat with a ferocity I couldn't contain as I eyed the place I'd touched her. I ached to feel her skin on mine again. I wanted her body almost as much as I wanted her submitting to me. She'd be branded by me in all the ways that counted. In life, in death. *Mia - mine.*

Footsteps thumped down the stairs and Niall leapt from the last one, smiling broadly as he approached the cage.

"Morning, Spider," he said cheerfully. "You'll be glad to hear I can't sit down this morning thanks to the holes you carved in my arse with that fork."

"You mean the ones in your *ass?*" she snarked and his smile widened.

"Maybe I do," he admitted and she hopped up, smiling back at him in a way that made anger build in my gut.

I didn't like her plans to seduce him. He was a vile creature, and she was too damn good for him. If he fucked her, I was going to kill him. I didn't know how or when, but I knew in my soul that I'd want to kill him for that more than any of the tortures he'd bestowed upon me.

Pedazo de mierda.

I watched him as he carried a tray of food across the basement, setting it down on the bed, the scent of coffee from a single mug reaching me and twisting around my lungs like a vice of pure temptation.

He'd never brought me coffee before. Though I couldn't say the food had ever been particularly bad. He gave me takeout most of the time and the worst that ever happened was when he overslept or went away and forgot to leave me enough food. Sometimes I would have to roar and rattle my cage, just to gain his attention and remind him to fucking feed me. The man was loco. I swear he genuinely just forgot I was here sometimes. Who the fuck could forget they had a person locked up in the basement? In fact, on occasion I could be looking right at him and it was like he wasn't even here either.

"Have you given my offer more thought?" Niall asked and my little chica loca shrugged.

"I have some demands," she said, folding her arms over the dress shirt and leather apron she wore and I watched her, my gaze drinking her in as I wondered what he really wanted her for.

If he only wanted to fuck her, he could have just taken it already. And if he needed information from her like he wanted from me then he would have been trying to force it out of her by now. But there was no torture, no signs of hatred or anger in his eyes when he looked at her.

There was hunger though. I just couldn't decide what he had a taste for yet.

"Speak then," Niall offered, moving the tray to the nightstand and tossing a piece of toast in my direction before throwing himself back onto the bed. He cursed, muttering something about his arse and quickly rolled onto his front instead, watching her, waiting.

I eyed the toast on the floor just outside my cage for a moment and luck was on my side because miraculously it had landed butter side up. He'd also slathered it with strawberry jelly which he gave me because he didn't like it, so he saw it as a punishment. I liked it just fine though and I had to wonder why he'd never asked. Not that I would have answered him.

"I want Coco Pops," she growled and Niall narrowed his eyes.

"And?" he asked, not seeming like he was totally sold on the Coco Pops thing.

"And...errr, yeah there's an and... And I want to go back into the good girl side of the basement."

"I came to let you out anyway." Niall shrugged and she pouted.

Why wasn't she asking for freedom? What kind of bargain were they

179

striking here?

"I need some clothes," she said suddenly. "Fancy shit. All the things, like thongs and head kicker boots and a really, really, really nice hat."

"Anything else?" Niall asked, running a hand over his jaw while he considered it.

"I'm thinking on it," she said, glancing at me like I might add to this conversation, but I wouldn't utter a word while he was in the room and I didn't know what she wanted from me anyway.

"Fine. Think and shower," Niall said, rolling off of the bed and approaching us, taking the key from his pocket.

He unlocked the cell door and she slipped out, leaving me alone again, carving a hole in my chest and leaving it barren. But that was probably a good thing. Better she be out of reach in case I had one of my nightmares while she was locked in with me, because the Lord knew I wouldn't have been able to stop myself if that happened. I'd held my demon at bay and somehow spent a night with a girl without killing her. She had no fucking idea how close I'd come to breaking though. If I had, Niall would be punishing me now for disobeying him and I'd relish every blow against my corrupt soul, knowing I fully deserved it and that my darkest desires would never be tamed.

I watched her walk away and she swung her head around suddenly, almost whipping Niall in the eye with her long hair before stopping with her hands on her hips and grinning up at him.

A growl escaped my lips as he watched her with keen interest, and she frowned over at me like I was spoiling something for her, but I just glared right back.

"Shower. I'll go get the Pops," Niall said, reaching into his back pocket and pulling out a hairbrush. "And I got ya this."

She gasped in excitement, taking it and hugging it to her chest before trying to run it through her hair where it promptly got stuck in all the tangles and she hissed in pain.

"Why would you get me a broken hairbrush?" she demanded, slapping Niall's chest and making my lips twitch with amusement before I could stop them.

"It's not the brush that's the issue. It's the crazy ass bird's nest you call hair - which is why I got you the brush," Niall tossed back, reaching out to tug the brush from her hair again while she hissed and cursed and slapped him some more.

Her hand clapped across his cheek just as he ripped the thing free with a tangled lump of black hair still in it and he shoved her back against the bathroom door with a wild laugh while she cursed him.

"I think it's gonna be easier to just cut it all off," he announced, locking a hand around her throat to keep her back and examining her hair by lifting a lock in his other hand. "I'll go find some scissors while you shower."

"You wouldn't!" she gasped and he shrugged.

"Creatures are gonna start living in there soon if you don't sort it out one way or another. Nasty little bastard creatures who whisper mean things in your ears."

"Like geckos?" she asked in horror, wide eyed as she patted her crazy hair like she was hunting for them.

"Yeah. And a little arsehole of a wasp called Claud," Niall agreed. "Now hurry up and get washed while I find those scissors and make a quick phone call."

He strode away without so much as a glance at me and she sniffed as she glared at the hairbrush on the floor, snatching it up before grabbing a fresh tracksuit and darting into the bathroom.

That was about the best opportunity I was going to get to relieve myself in peace and I moved over to the fucking bucket I had to use for a toilet and quickly lifted the lid before taking a piss. I sighed as the stream of urine escaped me after spending the entire night holding back. It wasn't like there was much humanity left in me, but I was going to make whatever effort

I could to avoid using the fucking bucket while she was in here.

I glanced over my shoulder towards the bathroom door where the sound of running water was spilling into the room and blew out a breath of frustration as I dropped my pants and turned around to squat over the damn bucket.

"Dead Man!" my chica loca's voice made my heart leap as she burst back out of the bathroom with a wail and I jolted upright, tripping on the leg of my sweatpants and managing to kick the bucket of piss flying.

I scrambled away from it, yanking my half splashed pants up and cursing in Spanish as I looked up at her.

She was standing there, dripping wet with the white dress shirt pulled over her otherwise naked body. She'd half buttoned it up again, though she'd misaligned them so that it hung unevenly. The wetness made the thing partially transparent and I couldn't help but stare at the outline of her nipples through the fabric, tracing my gaze over her bare thighs beneath it and swallowing thickly at the idea of seeing more.

"Oh no," she breathed, her blazing blue eyes widening as she looked between me and the upturned bucket. "Were you trying to take a shit?"

I growled, hating Niall so fucking much in that moment that I was damn near grinding my teeth to dust in my mouth.

"I'm like that squirrel, aren't I?" she whispered, biting on her lip. "Peeping on you pooping." It almost seemed like there were tears in her eyes as she stared at me and I frowned as she made a move to head back to the bathroom.

"Why did you call for me?" I asked her, my voice still foreign to me after the months I'd spent in silence, not mentioning the puddle of piss creeping across the floor. The slice of toast was floating in it now so that was it as far my breakfast went. *Perfecto.*

She paused and looked back at me and the movement drew my attention to the hairbrush that was now hanging from her black hair, completely tangled up within it.

"I don't want him to cut my hair," she said with the barest hint of a pout, reaching up to tug on the brush and giving up when it refused to come loose. "I thought if I brushed it in the water then it might come out, but now it's living in there with the wasp."

My frown deepened as I tried to figure out why that had meant she called for me and she walked over to pick up the mug of coffee Niall had brought her.

She lifted it to her lips and took a sip before her face scrunched up and she spat the mouthful back into the mug again.

"He's trying to poison me!" she gasped. "He wants me to be bald and poisoned!"

"I doubt that," I murmured.

I didn't know what Niall wanted her for, but I very much doubted it was to give her an easy death like that and to make a wig out of her wild hair.

She looked back to me then jogged over to face me on the other side of the bars, still holding the mug of coffee in her hands.

"Sniff it," she said, holding it up for me. "It smells so strong and weird and gross."

She held it beneath my nose and I inhaled deeply, downing my senses in the heady scent. Damn, I missed coffee.

"It's meant to smell like that," I told her.

"Oh - is that to cover up the poo stink from you using the bucket then?" she asked and I growled in disgust at myself and my fucking situation. If Santiago Castillo could see what had become of the man who had robbed him blind and disappeared like a ghost in the night, I was certain he would be well satisfied with the work Niall was doing to destroy me.

"Do you want it?" she added, looking at the coffee like it was way more disgusting than a shit in a bucket before offering it up to me.

I wondered if she had any idea what this kindness she kept showing me was doing. Did she intend to keep drawing me closer? Was she hoping to captivate me the way she was? It was such a dangerous game to play. She had no idea. Because the more she drew me in, the closer she came to that darkest part of me which wouldn't tell her to stay away. I wanted her close and vulnerable and belonging to me. I'd do all I could to draw her in and when she was mine and I couldn't hold back a moment longer, I'd let her have all of me. Every piece, all that I was in all my glorious, disgusting cruelty. But if I lost control with her, she'd fast regret the day she'd ever dared to trust me. And I'd have to face the truth of what I was more plainly than I ever had before.

I stared at the coffee in her hands for a long moment and she shrugged as she made a move to step back, but I reached through the bars suddenly and caught her wrist.

I stole a moment with her skin pressed to mine, my fingers tightening as I gazed at her tempting lips, lust and violence rising in me sharply and fighting each other for dominance. There was such heat and strength in those blue eyes of hers, but I could see how close she was to shattering too. I wanted that. I wanted her to break for me so that I could gather up the pieces and lay claim to each and every one of them. But not today. So I took the cup from her hands.

"Sorry I spat in it," she said and I snorted. If she seriously thought I had a problem with drinking something that had been in her mouth then she was deluded. I thought about her mouth way too often and I had no issue being close to it at all.

I lifted the mug to my lips and drank every last drop of the rich tasting drink, sighing as the caffeine permeated my veins and helped my senses to sharpen after my sleepless night.

When I looked back at my little livewire, she was trying to tug the brush from her tangled hair again, that sad look returning to her face as she failed.

My gaze roamed over her body as I drank in the sight of the wet shirt plastered to her flesh and tried not to groan. She seemed completely fucking oblivious to the way she looked, and my cock was throbbing with the urgent need to claim her as it tented my sweatpants while I fought against the urge to reach for her.

Was this why she was really here? Temptation? To drive me to insanity looking while I battled with the raging monster inside me who wanted her pleasure first then her pain next?

She didn't even seem to notice as I held the mug out for her to reclaim, tugging at the hairbrush again and sniffing.

"Is there conditioner in there?" I asked, pointing at the bathroom and her eyes snapped back up to meet mine.

"Yeah. I like to wash with it all over because it makes me slippery everywhere."

My gaze dropped down her body and my jaw ticked. That mental image was here to stay now then. "Go get it."

She considered that for a moment then hurried away to grab it, leaving my coffee mug down on the nightstand as she went before returning quickly and handing me the bottle of conditioner.

"Come closer," I said, wondering if she would keep following my commands no matter where they led her, my heart thumping harder at the idea of that.

She slid her foot forward slowly before suddenly stepping forward with the other one so that she was just on the other side of the bars to me. Luckily the puddle of piss was keeping to itself to our right as all we could really do was ignore it right now.

I eyed her for a long moment. Too long really. But she either didn't mind or didn't fully appreciate what kind of creature I was. She should have known better than to get this close to me, though perhaps after surviving a night in a cage with me she was inclined to trust me a little. More fool her.

I reached through the bars and she stilled as I caught her waist in my grasp, slowly turning her around until her back was to me. She glanced over her shoulder at me, watching, waiting and I reached up to squirt half the bottle of conditioner all over her head.

"Stay still," I commanded, handing her the bottle before using my fingers to smear the papaya scented conditioner over her hair and around the brush.

Once I was done, I used the lubrication to tug the brush free, meaning to just hand it to her once I'd finished, but as my fingers skimmed against her neck, a breathy moan escaped her and I stilled, my cock twitching, my demon purring.

"Do you like me, Mateo?" she asked in a small voice. "Because people don't like me very much."

I didn't have anything to say to that. Did I like her? She was like a breath of fresh air in this prison. A ray of light that had reminded me life still went on out there. No. I didn't like her. My feelings towards her were much less healthy than that. I was sorely tempted to consume her. And I would. In time. Fighting the darkness in me was always useless. It had already taken over, blotting out any hope of me resisting the call of her. But I'd take my time with her. She was special. And I wanted to mark her thoroughly, own her entirely and have her aching for me to claim her just as much I was aching to do it before I would.

I raised the brush and moved it over her hair. The knots caught and broke, snagging over and over again, but she never flinched. This was a creature who understood real pain. She wouldn't flinch at this. Would she flinch when she saw the full might of the darkness in me? When I was reared over her, my hand tight around her throat and my cock deep inside her, what then? Would she try to back away or would she find she liked it there? At my mercy and under my control.

Several minutes passed in silence as I tugged the brush through her long, black hair over and over again until the conditioner was splattered over everything close to us and the knots were all gone.

My fingers skimmed down her hair a final time and I brushed them along the side of her neck too, just needing to feel the warmth of her flesh for a moment. I'd been down here so long that it was tempting to believe that she was nothing but a fragment of my sanity that had splintered off and taken on this enticing form just to taunt me. But even my imagination wasn't this fucking good.

She looked over her shoulder at me, long lashes silhouetted by the dim light on the far side of the room and with a surge of determination, I withdrew a step, tossing the brush back through the bars.

She raised two fingers to her lips and pressed a kiss to them before touching those same fingers to the bar of my cage and leaving it there for me. I watched her as she grabbed the brush and scurried back into the bathroom, leaving drips of moisture in her wake from her wet shirt and as the door banged closed behind her, I released a low breath.

My gaze moved to the bar where she'd left my kiss and I stepped forward again, leaning my cheek against the cold metal and inhaling the scent of papaya and heartache she'd left behind. The rough beard that had grown to coat my jaw during my incarceration scratched against the slightly rusting metal and I closed my eyes as it dragged across my skin with my movements.

The door at the top of the steps banged again and Niall returned, looking more pissed than usual as he spun a pair of scissors on his finger and carried a laptop beneath his arm. I recognised that look in his eyes, seeing the depths of his darkness on full display as something ate at him. I'd noticed that look before when he'd taken calls or been away from the house and it usually spelled pain for me. I didn't retreat from my position by the bars though and as his bright green eyes fell on me, the smile that lifted his lips was full of dark intentions.

"You ready to tell me where you hid your treasure, El Burro?" he asked, stalking towards me and spinning the scissors on his finger again.

I gave him nothing. I never did. On some level I got the impression he actually liked that about me. Probably just because he knew it meant he could keep me and use me to get his kicks for longer.

He snipped the scissors at me, his green eyes roaming over my bare chest like he was considering exactly what he might do with them, but the bathroom door banged open before he got his chance.

The girl appeared in a fresh grey tracksuit, grinning widely before bending down to touch her toes then flicking her hair back over her head as she stood suddenly again.

"No more tangles," she announced proudly, her gaze moving to me for a moment with that smile widening.

I didn't react at all, but of course Niall noticed, swinging around to look at me then her again with the air of a shark that had just scented blood in the water.

"Where's my Coco Pops?" the little livewire demanded, noting the distinct lack of cereal in Niall's possession.

"I couldn't find any Pops," he replied, stepping away from me and turning his back on me like I was nothing. The man I'd been before I met him would have killed him for lesser insults. The man I was would have disposed of him more thoroughly than he could even imagine. One day. One day soon. I tugged on the thick leather collar around my neck and cursed him to hell for what he'd done to me.

"No Pops, no deal," she hissed like a cat, her eyes dropping to the scissors in his hand before she plopped down onto the bed and folded her legs beneath her.

Niall snipped the scissors open and closed over and over again, the sharp snick, snick, snick filling the air with the promise of violence before he stopped suddenly.

"Fine," he snapped, sounding pretty pissed about it. "Did you decide what else you want?"

"I told you I need a hat to-"

"Yeah, yeah, you can have full access to my platinum card and go online shopping to yer heart's content for fancy sandals and tiaras," he agreed dismissively dropping the laptop down in front of her and I frowned as I tried to figure out what was going on between the two of them. What did he want from her? What deal were they coming to? "What else?'

"I want..." She chewed on her full bottom lip then raised her eyes to me and an idea seemed to spark in them. "I want the poo bucket gone. I don't like living in a cell with a bucket of poo. It's stinky. I don't like it."

"You said you don't like it twice," Niall pointed out.

"Because I double don't like it," she replied firmly.

"But then Mateo will just be shitting on the floor. Believe me, I've given this a bunch of thought meself," Niall huffed. "I don't enjoy emptying the damn thing, but what am I supposed to do?"

"Let him use the bathroom," she suggested with a shrug and I stilled, utterly, entirely, stilled. Was she seriously bargaining on my behalf?

"If I let him off of his chain he gets ideas," Niall said, talking about me like I wasn't even here. "Starts thinking he's the big man who can take me on. Then I have to stab him or taser him, or hit him over the head with a chair - it's damn tiring, lass. I don't have the energy for it. I'm just an old man."

She scoffed, folding her arms. "Oh please, you don't look a day over forty."

"I'm thirty-two," he growled and I was surprised to find that he was actually a year younger than me. I guessed I'd never given it much thought, but there was a darkness in his gaze that had made me assume he was older than that.

"Then I'm right. Not a day over forty," she replied, lifting her chin.

"How old are you?" he asked, stepping closer to her. "Not that I care."

"Then why ask?"

"Because my dog wants to know," he replied.

"You don't have a dog," she accused.

"I do. He's called…Claud."

"Like that wasp you said was going to come live in my hair?" she hissed suspiciously.

"No. Obviously not," he replied. "He's actually called…Brutus. Big fucker he is, likes long walks on sandy beaches, enjoys going out – and staying in. Has a preference for tuna."

"Like a cat?"

"No. Like a dog who enjoys tuna." Niall raised his chin, daring her to call him out on his bullshit.

"What colour is he?" she demanded, narrowing her eyes.

"Dog colour."

"That makes sense," she conceded, nodding finally and I frowned.

"So? Are you going to tell Cl-Brutus how old you are?" he pushed.

"I'm not sure," she replied with a shrug. "I lost count. It's either twenty-one or fifty-one though."

Niall grabbed her chin and tilted her face back and forth as he looked at her, humming low in the back of his throat even though it was damn obvious which she was. "Twenty-one, I think. Probably. What were we talking about?"

"The poo bucket situation."

"Right, yeah. I can't let him off of his chain." Niall jerked a thumb in my general direction and a growl of hatred rumbled in my chest.

"You could just put a thingy for his chain in the bathroom," she suggested. "Problem solved."

Niall lifted a hand to his chin, rubbing it thoughtfully as he glanced back over at me and spotted the upturned bucket and puddle of piss which was coating the concrete floor to my right.

"Oh, for the love of Christ," he snarled, pointing at it. "Who the fuck is going to clean that shit up?"

"That's what I want," she said firmly, drawing his attention back to her. "Coco Pops. All the clothes. No more bucket."

"If you're good you won't even have to use the bucket because you won't be in the bad girl cage," Niall pointed out.

"I know," she said. "But when I came out of the shower the first time, Mateo was trying to do a poo in the bucket and he looked me in the eyes and I saw something in his gaze that no one should ever have to see. It happened to me once with that pervert squirrel and I can't become that bushy-tailed beast. It can't go on. That's my final demand."

I huffed out an angry breath as Niall howled a laugh at my expense and I folded my arms across my broad chest, glaring at him.

He held a hand out to the girl and she grinned as she slapped her palm into his to seal their arrangement. Niall used his grip on her hand to yank her up onto her feet and even standing on the bed she was only just eye to eye with him.

"We have a deal, Spider. Just don't go disappointing me with your end of it," he growled, his face mere inches from hers as she looked him right in the eyes.

"I guess we'll find out about that once I've got my Pops," she breathed.

Niall's smile was slow and predatory as he kept a tight hold of her fingers and raised the scissors in his other hand up to her hair.

"Don't," she warned him fiercely and he tilted his head to the side as he hesitated there, scissors poised beside her ass length locks.

"People don't tell me what to do and live to tell the tale very often, Spider," he warned.

"Well I'm not people," she replied firmly. "I'm your spider. And I like my hair long."

A tense silence filled the room then Niall shrugged, withdrawing the scissors and releasing her hand, giving her a little shove so that she fell down onto her ass on the bed and bounced.

"Use the laptop to order whatever clothes you want. Just fill up the basket and I'll check it out when you're done," he said and her eyes lit up with excitement.

"Whatever I want?" she breathed.

"Whatever you want," he agreed easily before turning away from her and jogging back up the stairs.

But as the door fell closed behind him, the sound of the locks engaging never came and my heart stilled.

"Run," I barked at her as she lay back on the bed and started moving her arms and legs like she was making snow angels. "He didn't lock the door. Get up there and kill that motherfucker."

"Err, Mateo, I think you've forgotten something," she replied, pushing herself up onto her elbow so that she could look at me. "He's getting me Pops. I don't think this is the time to be riling him up."

"Are you loca?" I growled at her and she narrowed her eyes at me.

"No I'm not a...actually what does that one mean again?" she asked with a frown.

"It means you're crazy," I snapped.

"I don't like it when people call me crazy, even if they do it in a sexy accent," she warned. "It makes me stabby. Real fucking stabby."

The door opened again at the top of the stairs and this time it did lock before Niall jogged back down them, a bowl of the chocolatey cereal in one hand and a mop and bucket in the other. I had to bite my tongue to hold back the curses aching to burst free of me at that missed opportunity and I was sure she could see how pissed I was, but she just shrugged innocently.

"I'm wondering if I've been out bargained here," Niall said as he dropped the mop and bucket and stalked towards the girl who bounced upright and reached for the cereal with a feral kind of hunger in her eyes. I had to admit the smell of them was making my stomach rumble too, but I would never fucking mention it.

"You have, sucker," she announced, snatching the bowl and almost spilling the milk in her desperation to dive on them.

She started eating like a creature possessed, the spoon flying back and forth between the bowl and her mouth so fast that I couldn't help but stare. But then suddenly she stopped, the spoon hanging in the air half way between her mouth and the bowl, loaded up with cereal as she narrowed her eyes on them.

"These. Are. Not. Pops," she snarled, dropping the spoon back into the bowl and thrusting the whole thing back at him.

"Cocoa Krispies are the exact same thing," Niall said with a shrug but he wasn't looking her in the eye. "It's just a different name for the American version and the-"

"Don't try and palm me off with this shit!" she yelled, pointing a finger at him and getting to her feet again as rage burned in her eyes.

Niall pouted, entering into a stare off with her before suddenly snatching the half eaten bowl of cereal away and cursing.

"Fine," he said. "They're those gross Krispie things like you say. But I'm not sharing my Coco Pops hoard with a girl who hasn't even proven herself yet."

"Ah ha! So there is a hoard!" she announced triumphantly.

"Dammit," Niall cursed, dropping the bowl down onto the nightstand before looking back at her. "Fine. I may have a box or two of genuine Pops *but* I'm only gonna give them to ya if you manage to impress me. Until then it's Krispies or nothing."

She looked inclined to argue for a moment but then her eyes brightened and she nodded her agreement. "I just so happen to be really damn impressive, so you're on, Hellfire."

Niall gave her a lingering look then pulled another set of keys from his pocket and crossed the basement to his killing room.

The sight of those keys in his hand made an involuntary shiver track down my spine but outwardly I didn't react at all.

I swallowed thickly and watched as he unlocked his torture chamber and disappeared inside.

The girl jumped to her feet and moved across the room after him, tilting her head curiously as she followed and tension spilled through my limbs.

"Don't," I growled in a voice I hoped was low enough that he wouldn't hear me.

She paused, giving me that curious look that always earned all of my attention as she lingered close to the door. "Why not?"

"No one goes in there and comes back out alive." No one apart from me anyway and I wasn't certain I counted. I gazed at this girl as rage writhed in me over the thought of Niall stealing her from me in that room. There was a searing flame rising in me, a fire that begged me to stop her from going through that fucking door for possessive reasons that consumed me.

Her eyebrows rose like that made her want to see the room even more and she darted across the remaining space to the door just as Niall stepped out and closed it behind him. He had a drill and some other tools in his hands and she skidded to a halt before him, eyeing all of it with interest.

"You wanna know how many ways you can kill a fella with a drill like this?" Niall offered, smiling darkly as he lifted his gaze to me.

I knew my death called to him. I knew he hungered for it just as certainly and forcefully as I hungered for his. Our fates were intertwined in that. This bond had formed between us which was greater than any force on Earth. One of us would kill the other. That was set in stone. And though the odds were squarely stacked against me, I was hoping on a wild card to shift them in my favour. And as I looked back to the girl standing before him again, I couldn't help but wonder if she might be it.

"Nah," she replied. "I like stabbing best. I think I should focus on stabbing."

Niall smirked at her, reaching out to tussle her damp hair as he strolled past her to the bathroom. "You've got a lot to learn, little psycho."

She hounded after him and followed him into the bathroom, grabbing the laptop as she went and the door closed between me and them.

I stood there, staring at the door and waiting for her to emerge again, my heart racing as I listened to the sound of the drill as it was driven into the wall.

Minutes ticked by slowly as all I could hear was the sound of that drill and I wondered if he was seriously going to give me access to the bathroom. Why had she bargained with him on my behalf? Was I a fucking idiota for believing she had nothing to do with the Castillo Cartel? Maybe she really was a spider, and I was being drawn into her trap. *Well I'll draw you into mine first, mi sol.*

The drilling finally stopped and the door opened again. Niall returned his tools to his killing room and reappeared with a stun gun in hand.

My grip on the iron bar in front of me tightened imperceptibly as he approached and I tried to prepare myself for the bolt of pure fire that would come from that thing. He always used it when he wanted to move me. Usually when I recovered from the immobilising shock of it, I woke up strapped to something in that fucking room. And as much as I refused to give him an inch of my fear, there was nothing to enjoy about being tortured. Death was a delicate, refined art but Niall was just a child with buckets of paint, splashing them on the walls to see what happened.

Niall grinned at me as he jammed the bastard thing into my gut and a torrent of cursing spilled through my mind in a mixture of English and Spanish as I hit the floor.

I was vaguely aware of him coming into the cage and unlocking the chain which was bolted to the wall then hauling me out again, dragging me through the fucking piss.

He dumped me in the bathroom, locking my chain to the new bolt in the wall beside the door and leaving me there as my body slowly began to recover.

I could hear the two of them murmuring something, his laughter ringing out alongside the sloshing of water as he mopped and a loud comment about how much he'd hated the fucking bucket anyway. The girl told him she'd finished her online shopping spree then his footsteps poured away up the stairs again.

I growled a curse as I fisted my hands, panting through the pain of that strike and opening my eyes to find her standing over me, hands on her hips as she leaned forward and her long hair hanging down towards me.

"How good did that hurt?" she whispered.

I rolled over suddenly, pushing to my knees as she backed up and I looked around at the little white bathroom. There was nothing particularly special about it, but it was a massive improvement on the cage.

"Niall says you have to sleep in the cage still," she said. "Which I actually think is kinda cool. Like, you know those rich people who have bunnies and they stay safe and snug in their cage at night, but then in the day they can go run on the grass? The bathroom is your grass, little bunny."

"Nadie me había llamado conejito antes," I muttered as I managed to get to my feet.

"Did you just curse me like a witch?" she whispered, sounding kinda like she hoped I had.

"I said that no one has ever called me a bunny before," I supplied, tearing my gaze from her for the first time since she'd arrived here and looking around at the white tiles, basic shower, sink and toilet. Who knew a taste of heaven could be so fucking simple?

"Oh, sorry, you need to poo. I won't squirrel you," she said suddenly, backing out of the room and leaving me there alone as the door was pulled over, drifting open a crack again as she moved away.

I swiped a hand down my face as I tried to take in this change. For more months than I could remember, I'd existed in that fucking cage, my only reprieve being my weekly showers in here and the trips to the room next door where I was tortured for information I'd never give up. This change was unsettling. But also liberating and I needed to make use of it to its fullest.

I moved to the sink, frowning at the reflection of a man I hadn't seen for too long in the mirror. My hair was a long mess of black strands and the rough beard coating my jaw filled me with irritation. I looked older. Bigger too. Which I guessed was to be expected after so long with nothing to do but work out. If there was one small saving grace for my captor, it was that he didn't starve me aside from the meals he forgot. I guessed he wanted to keep me strong so that I didn't die on him before he got his answer out of me, but I wasn't going to refuse the calories out of spite.

I stripped off, dropping my dirty sweats to the floor and turning the shower on. I'd used it countless times, but Niall had always been watching, making me twist the dial to cold and barely giving me enough time to scrub the grime from my flesh.

I turned the dial to hot before stepping in and I rested a hand against the tiles, groaning as the rush of the hot water spilled over me. It reminded me of the noises of pleasure the girl had made while showering and at that brief and all enrapturing thought of her, my cock was hard and aching.

I scrubbed soap over my body, trying to ignore that need in my flesh for several achingly long minutes before realising I didn't have to. I was alone here. There was no crazy Irish man watching me and aiming a gun at my dick. If I ignored the collar around my neck, then I could almost pretend I was free.

I slicked my hand around my cock and it jolted in my hand, relief finding me at finally being able to do this.

I almost groaned again as I stroked my hard length, my mind on her the moment I began. I thought about those full lips and the way her tits had looked through that white shirt while they were all wet and turning it transparent. I thought of her husky voice and those big blue eyes and I groaned as I pumped my shaft, hungry for this release. Then my mind went to that darker place where all my monsters lived, crawling into my head as the gates were pushed open. I couldn't stop them even if I'd tried. I imagined her beneath me, pussy tight around my shaft and spine arching as I locked my hand around her throat and squeezed so tightly that she couldn't even scream when she came all over my dick, those blazing blue eyes locked with mine the whole time as I ruined her.

I growled as I came after hardly any time at all, hot cum spilling from my cock and my gaze moving to the door as I felt the prickle of eyes on my flesh. I never had knocked it closed behind her when she left and as I found those electric blue eyes wide and fucking sparking, staring right at me as I came for her, and I couldn't find it in me to care.

I liked looking at her and if she wanted to look at me too then she was welcome to. All that I was would become hers anyway once I lured her in, let her consume me until it was me who consumed her.

She sucked in a sharp breath as my gaze collided with hers and she darted away, leaving the view through the door empty as she retreated and I was left to finish my shower.

I turned my back on the door, scrubbing at my skin until it was the cleanest it had ever been and washing my hair thoroughly too.

When I got out, I wrapped a towel around my waist and moved toward the sink again, pushing my black hair back and finding the brush she'd used. My hair had grown long enough to need it so I used it to get the knots out, the water slicking it back over my head and leaving me feeling more like the powerful man I'd once been than I had in a long time.

When I was done, I used the toilet in peace and headed back out into the room where the girl sat on the bed, looking up at me as I appeared. I could only take five steps out of the bathroom before the chain attached to my collar pulled tight and I leaned back against the wall with an internal sigh. It was the smallest taste of freedom, but it wasn't nearly enough.

"Wow, Dead Man, you had a forehead hiding under all that hair," she breathed, moving to sit with her legs crossed as she looked at me. "It's a nice one too. I once knew a girl with so much forehead she was practically a bowling ball, but you've got just the right brow to hairline ratio going."

I just stared at her, drinking in the sound of her voice and letting her fill the silence. I liked it when she spoke. She said the kinds of things people didn't usually say and there was something about that which captivated me. Or perhaps it was the way that she sounded. And looked. Or some combination of all of those things.

"Do you want some pants?" she asked. "I'd offer a hoodie too, but you have that whole collar thing going on."

I didn't say anything but she hopped up anyway, opening the closet and taking out some grey sweats just like hers. She chewed on her bottom lip as she selected three pairs then approached me cautiously. Not like she was afraid exactly, more like she wanted to be ready to fight if she had to. *You could fight, mi sol. But you wouldn't win.*

She slung two of the pairs of sweats over her shoulder then held the smallest pair out to me, lining them up with my hips, her fingers brushing against my waist above my towel. They were clearly too small, so she tossed them aside and tried the next pair, her hands brushing my skin again and her eyes flicking up to meet mine for a moment before she tossed them away too.

As she lined the last pair up against me, she knocked my towel loose and it fell at my feet in a heap.

"Oh," she breathed, looking down at my cock which was very much solid again with her so fucking close to me. "Sorry." She quickly hung the sweatpants from my rigid dick like it was a clothes' peg before whirling away and I had to snatch them to stop them from falling.

In the same move, I caught her wrist before she could escape, tugging her back around and making her look at me.

"Why?" I asked in a rough tone, my fingers biting into her skin as those startlingly blue eyes peered into mine.

Her gaze stayed where it was for several long beats before slowly dropping to my cock again.

"It seemed like a handy place to hang them," she replied, biting that lip again and if she didn't stop, I might just bite it as well. *I might just keep biting too until I'd fucking devoured this girl.*

"I meant why did you bargain to get me out of that cage?" I pressed.

"You saved my hair, Dead Man," she replied, raising her eyes to meet mine again. "I just wanted to save you from the bucket."

I stared into her eyes as I tried to find a lie there, but she was a mystery to me and I couldn't find anything hiding within them. I tugged her closer, breathing her in as danger curled through my flesh. *I should tell her to stay away. I should listen to the only piece of my soul which has a conscience.* But the darkness was louder than the light in me. And no warning would pass my lips.

"Do you want a cuddle, Mateo?" she asked, seeming hopeful and a deep growl rumbled through my chest.

I want everything from you. And I'm going to take it.

I took a breath and the cloying darkness receded just enough for me to regain control.

"No." I released her and she stepped back with a crestfallen expression as I pulled my pants on.

"Where did he find you?" I asked suddenly and she shrugged.

"He bought me. I think they ripped him off."

She backed up further and dropped down on the bed, silence falling between us as I thought on that. I knew plenty of men who bought and sold women and none of them had good intentions.

I had to assume the men who'd sold her were sex traffickers. But where had she come from? What had she lived through? I found I wanted the answers to all of those questions and more. I wanted to know why she asked for Coco Pops instead of freedom. I wanted to know why her hair meant so much to her. I wanted to know why shadows danced in the back of those blazing blue eyes. And most of all, I wanted to know why she'd ended up here with me.

I couldn't think about anything else. From the moment I'd first laid eyes on her she'd been owning my mind and tempting my body and I needed more. I needed all of it. And when I had her, I'd feed her to my demons and let her sate their wicked cravings.

NIALL

CHAPTER THIRTEEN

I slid my picks into the lock at the back door of the huge house and hummed beneath my breath as I twisted them in the hole juuuuust right. The click sounded like a death toll in my ears and I smiled as I tasted blood on the air.

This one would be sweet. Not quite as sweet as killing the men who'd taken my Ava from me. Those men had died hard and suffered harder, and still hadn't gotten half of what they'd deserved after ridding the world of the only truly good thing I'd ever known. The only woman I'd ever loved or ever would. But they'd also been the key to unlocking the darkness in me to its full potential.

I'd been re-born in the blood of her killers, painted red with it for all the world to see. Now, no one could look at me and see anything other than a monster. And I was the kind who hungered for more blood at every opportunity. Always spilling it for her. Always trying to make right what I'd caused with my weakness. Because I knew now that that was what it had been. I'd orchestrated the death of that beautiful creature first by loving her, and secondly by allowing a man who harboured me ill will to run from me. I thought he'd send a message home to his friends, teach them to stay the fuck away from me. But of course, all I'd done was bring her death to our door. And nothing I did now would ever come close to paying reparations for that. But I tried my damn hardest all the same.

What else was I if not a demon born in vengeance for her? Sometimes I could have sworn I even heard her whispering to me while I killed, begging me to do my worst, make them bleed, make them suffer. Just how she'd suffered. And I always answered her call.

I slipped into the kitchen of the sprawling mansion and eyed the knives in the rack, wondering if short and sweet was the best plan here. Or if I should make him suffer the way I liked to.

Then again, this kill needed to go down without a hitch. I couldn't risk him surviving. I needed it done. And fast was always the best way to ensure that happened. Not least because I had no doubt that I'd be dead before I even made it off the property if I fucked this up. These kinds of people knew how twisted they were which meant they invested in guns and often security teams too, though it didn't look like he'd gone in for the last one. I had a few questions to ask him before he died, but if things got dicey, I'd end it fast. After all, there was a girl locked in my basement who would starve to death if I didn't make it home tonight. And El Burro I guess.

Perhaps I should have told someone she was there before I set out on this task. But it was too late for that now. Ah well, like the last greatest Irish man I ever knew once said to me: all is fair in death and chaos - and if my time has come to pass, let me go with a blade in my hand, and without any class. My great uncle had technically been insane, but I felt he made plenty of good points.

My nephew Kyan had asked me to do this job and I'd been quick to take him up on it even if I wasn't getting paid for this one. But we were family, so I didn't mind a trade of favours. And if I was being wholly honest, that boy was the only member of my flesh and blood who I'd mourn to see pass outa this world. So I guessed in part I was doing it for that.

It was an equally simple and difficult task. Kyan had a vendetta against that club where I'd found my spider and he was determined to bring them down. Couldn't say I blamed him. That place had never been to my taste, old men buying and selling people like livestock and trading in sex like they had a right to buy it. I'd had words with my pa about it before, made threats, considered just going in there myself and cutting some cocks off. I had no tolerance at all for rapists and perverts after Ava, but he had cut me down before I'd even begun. And I'd bowed to the might of the O'Brien empire just like I always did.

Not because I had any real sense of family or belonging within the gangsters who shared my blood. More because there were just some men you couldn't kill. Not easily. Not without it coming down on yer head. And I didn't want to live under the shadow of my father's death forevermore. He was one of the biggest players in the state. Hell, he was one of the biggest players in the country. His death would create a power vacuum and there were only so many ways it could be filled. Most likely by one of my brothers. And the day I saw one of those arseholes step up and take over the family would be the day I died, because Liam O'Brien might be bad, but his offspring were all monsters.

I was the only decent one, and I killed people for a living.

No, I wouldn't see one of them put in his place and I wouldn't step into the role myself happily either. It wasn't that I feared the power, more that I had no desire to wield it. I was the master of my own destiny. At least as much as I could be while being caught beneath my pa's thumb. He didn't hold my leash too tightly though. He knew mad dogs needed to roam free. So long as I showed up when he called and killed whoever he set me on, he let me live away from the rest of the family who had all made a stronghold out of a private community near the city. He let me come and go as I pleased and take on my own work. It wasn't freedom, but it sure smelled like it when the wind turned the right way.

So I had to listen to my pa's orders not to attack that club. But I'd never made any oaths that promised I wouldn't figure out some of the members' identities, sneak into their homes in the dead of night and make them squeal like little piggies for me.

See, it was all about looking at things from another angle. Rules were made to be bent after all.

And now here I was, hiding in the dark in some unsuspecting fucker's house about to see if I could make him sing so that I could hand Kyan some more information on Royaume D'élite and how it was run. Maybe I'd be able to give him and his friends what he needed to bring the place down, or maybe I'd need to hunt down more motherfuckers and gut them for that information. Either way, I was good with it.

The sound of a fridge door thumping shut made me still and I took a step to my left, looking to the far end of the long kitchen where a man stood staring right back at me. It was dark so I couldn't make out a whole hell of a lot about him aside from his saggy check boxers, beer gut and silver hair which shone in the light spilling in from the moon outside.

Shit on a mushroom.

We entered into a stare off for all of five seconds then he screamed something unintelligible, dropped his bottle of OJ and ran for it. I threw the kitchen knife with all my strength and it whipped through the air before embedding itself in the drywall where he'd been just a moment before.

I cursed as I took chase. He was going for a gun. They always went for a fucking gun.

I slipped in the gobshite orange juice as I ran through it, skidding along like I was on an ice rink before catching the wall and launching myself around the corner after him.

My boots pounded down the wooden corridor behind him and he wrenched a bookshelf from the wall, sending it crashing into my path with books scattering everywhere.

"Stay away from me!" he yelled, darting into a room on the right of the hall and slamming the door behind him.

The sound of a lock clicking into place followed and I cursed him as I vaulted the bookshelf and grabbed a heavy encyclopaedia from the mess. It was the letter N and I grinned at that. Damn good letter that was. All kinds of great words started with N, like nirvana and nifty and nub and Niall of course, the best of all.

I roared like a beast as I charged towards the door, slamming into it and making the hinges rattle. I bounced back off of the heavy wood, charging it again just as gunshots tore through the air.

The door crashed open and I tumbled to the floor, luckily without any bullets finding a home in me.

I grabbed an apple out of my back pocket and launched it towards the arsehole who was shooting at me with a yell of, "Grenade!"

He shrieked in alarm, diving over his desk and landing right in front of me as I got to my feet.

My boot stamped down on his hand where he still held the pistol and I swung a heavy kick into his side with the other foot.

He cried out, trying to lurch upright, but I slammed the encyclopaedia down into his throat with all my strength and his head crashed back down against the wooden floor as a gargled sound of agony escaped him.

I continued to grind my heel down on the hand holding the gun and I smacked him either side of the head with the heavy book, listing animals that began with the letter N so that we could both get a bit of education in with this.

"Newt. Narwhal. Nightingale. Nuthatch..." I paused, standing upright and looking down at his bloodied face as I tried to think of another one but I had to say, there weren't a whole hell of a lot of animals with an N name. *Fuck me, that's sad.* "Can you think of any more?" I asked him. "I'll let you live if you do." Not for long, but he didn't have to know that.

"N...n...n..." His busted lip trembled as he struggled to think of one and I lifted the heavy tome to finish the job. Although on second thought, I had some questions for him so I guessed I couldn't kill him yet. "North American Bear!" he gasped, making me pause.

"I'm unimpressed," I told him. You could just toss 'North American' on the front of any animal name and call it a win. If that was the case, I'd have said North American possum or North American flea or North American weasel and I never woulda run outa animals. But I flipped the encyclopaedia open to check because I'd made the man a promise after all.

After flicking through a few bloodied pages, I found it. Just a single line that said *see American Black Bear,* but it was there. "Hmm, not a great answer but not an entirely incorrect one either."

"Is this about my wife?" he asked, his voice all kinds of fucked up because of that encyclopaedia to the throat, but I'd heard my fair share of death gargles in my time, so I was used to interpreting them.

"You tell me." Three simple words that always made idiots sing. Why was that? They just assumed I already knew everything so they went and blurted it out, but I hardly ever knew shit. I was a gun for hire. People didn't need to give me details, though I always asked for enough of a reason to make sure I wasn't killing someone who didn't deserve it. Fun fact though: a lot of fuckers deserved it. There were so many kill-worthy arseholes in this world it was unreal.

"Did Eric send you?" he asked and I gave him silence because that always made a talker outa fuckers too. "Her brother?"

"Maybe." But also no.

"Look, I...I know I shouldn't have done what I did to her. B-but she was going to divorce me, leave me for that *gardener*. And I just didn't want that whore taking all of my stuff, you know? But I've got plenty of money. More money than Eric is paying you. I'll double what he offered, triple even. No one knows where I buried her. No one knows."

Ah, a wife killer. I had a special kind of hatred for these fuckers.

"Tell me about Royaume D'élite," I growled, managing to contain myself long enough to ask that question. The blood dripping from the encyclopaedia helped, but I was about to lose my damn shit any moment then the walls would be painted red.

"What?" he asked and crown me with a daisy chain, he sounded genuinely confused.

I squinted down at him in the darkness, trying to see beyond the blood and broken nose and frowning as I failed to spot any familiar features.

"Are you Lionel Barnes?" I asked, suspicion creeping up my spine.

I'd used my contacts within my criminally organised family to find this arsehole and I'd spent several hours tracking down his office and stalking him a bit while I figured out what way I wanted to kill him. Then I'd paid off one of my nephews, Shane, to take over from me and follow him home. The kid was only thirteen but he had the O'Brien blood and could boost a car as well as anyone I knew, so I'd given him this shot at proving himself to me. But I was starting to think the little gobshite had gone and followed the wrong fucker home. If I wasn't very much mistaken, this was the wrong fuckin' man.

"B-barnes? No - he's my business partner. I'm Henry Smythe." Hope shone in his eyes then, the poor fool.

"But you did murder your wife and bury her somewhere because she didn't wanna fuck ya anymore, right?" I confirmed.

Smythe whimpered and I nodded my head. I raised the encyclopaedia to batter his brains in, then got a better idea. I needed to assess my little spider and this fucker needed to die. He was big enough, strong enough and wily enough to cause some problems for her and make it a worthwhile fight. This night didn't have to be a total write off after all.

I ground my heel down into his hand until he released his grip on the pistol and I plucked it from his fingers before jamming it in the back of my jeans.

I gave the side of his kneecap a solid kick to slow him down then strode across the room to find my apple.

It was probably gonna be bruised after its grenade impersonation but I was hungry, so I was gonna have to deal with that. I found it, polished off a bit of blood splatter then sank my teeth into it just as Henry made it out the door.

I stalked after him, whistling loudly just to make him shit himself and I followed his limping, beaten arse to the front door.

I waited patiently while he fumbled the locks murmuring, "Oh God, oh God, oh Jesus, please help me."

Did God have a special place in his heart for wife murderers? I knew for a fact he loved a kitten. Had to have a fondness for lambs too what with them being all fluffy and stuff. And I was guessing he had a certain soft spot for mould because why the fuck else would it grow so happily in shitty places. But wife murderers? Guess we were about to find out.

I glanced to my right and noticed a little something orange sitting on a table just inside the room beside me and I moved in to snatch it, grinning as I found a pack of Reese's Peanut Butter Cups. *Yoink.* I'd been eating some of these in a park once when I saw this running man in all his fancy Lycra slip over and roll down a hill. Over and over and over he'd gone, screaming like a new born babe while I howled with laughter. He'd been crying and yelling and begging for someone to call him an ambulance. But no one had been about to hear him. Fucking funny that. I wondered if he was still there now.

The sound of the door unlocking at last reminded me of why I was here and I pocketed my Cups before stepping back into the hall. Henry finally staggered through the door and stumbled out into the dark, so I followed on after him, keeping my pace casual as he ran for it, racing off down the long drive and saving me the trouble of dragging his arse all that way.

I swallowed a bite of my apple and pulled it away from my mouth to call after him.

"Five!" I yelled loudly. "Four. Three-"

He screamed for help at the top of his lungs, but that was the problem with buying fancy arse houses in the countryside. Only the owls could hear you scream. And they didn't even give a crap. Owls were selfish fuckers. They'd sooner shit on you than cut you a break.

I took off the moment my countdown ran low, whooping and laughing as I bounded after him. The moonlight shone off of his pale back and his checked boxers flapped in the wind over his saggy arse. *What a day to be alive.*

Henry screamed again, sobbing and running while I gained on him. A smarter man would have grabbed his car keys before he made it outside, but a smarter man he was not.

I pounced on him as I made it to the end of the drive, tackling him into the mud and grinning as I pinned him on his back beneath me.

"Shh, don't worry," I said, placing a finger to his lips as he tried to buck me off of him. "We've got somewhere to be."

I pulled my car key from my back pocket and pressed the button, the headlights flashing once as it unlocked and revealing its presence hidden within the trees. Luckily, I'd brought the BMW 3 Series tonight and it had a good, hostage worthy trunk. I had a stop off to make before I headed home, so he'd be in there a while.

On the note of cars, I'd totally forgotten to get the car I'd brought Spider home in outa the lake. Hmm. I hadn't seen it on my way out though, so it musta sunk good. I guessed that was the problem solved then. Handy.

I stood up, giving Henry a kick to roll him over and fisting a handful of grey hair into my grasp before jamming his own gun against the back of his head.

"Come along, wife killer," I encouraged, making him walk with me to my car as I popped the trunk.

The BMW was black of course, very hitman standard of me, I know, but

I liked to lean into the odd cliche from time to time. I once wore a red tartan plaid shirt while chopping with my axe like an honest to shit woodcutter. I mean, I hadn't been chopping wood, I'd been chopping legs off, but it still counted.

I kept a ball gag in there for occasions such as this and I had Henry strap it on while I kept the gun to his head then made him climb inside. It didn't look great on him, I had to say, but luckily I wasn't planning on fucking him so it didn't matter.

I grabbed the bag of tools out, not really wanting to leave him with access to saws, hammers and whatever other shit I had in there just in case he used some of it to get himself out. It would be damn annoying if he leapt on me like a zombie rising from the dead while I was driving. Kinda funny, but annoying.

He said something around the gag as he stared up at me in fear and I couldn't make it out, but I knew the drill. It would be something like, *please don't do this*, or *I can give you money*, or *oh my what a handsome serial killer you are*. I hadn't actually heard anyone say that last one yet, but I was holding out hope for it one day soon.

"Don't piss yourself," I warned him, pointing a finger in his face. "It's a bitch to get that stink outa the upholstery and I'll have to kill you worse for it if you do."

Wide, fearful eyes stared back at me like I was a monster and I laughed as I slammed the trunk on him.

I dropped into the front of the car and sighed as I found a cigarette in the glove box, finishing off my apple before I sparked up.

The engine growled to life and I chose to play Tantrum by Ashnikko on the stereo, not needing anything too complex right now and just enjoying it as I sang along. The ghosts were always sated by a bit of bloodshed, so I didn't need too much to distract me from them while I was speckled in red droplets.

I leaned back in my chair and glanced at the time. Pa had been expecting me for dinner an hour ago, but the drive to his place wasn't all that long from here and he was never too fussed about my lateness when he knew I was working. Someone had to keep the body count up for the O'Brien empire after all. He'd said something about a party after dinner, but I had no plans to hang about for that.

By the time I pulled up outside his sprawling mansion, I was on my third cigarette and the volume was cranked high enough to drown out the screams from the trunk. Screaming was such a funny thing – some people did it beautifully while others just shrieked in the most irritating fuckin' way. Henry was practically begging me for a hard death with that din he was making around his ball gag.

I left the car parked at the foot of the steps, not bothering to lock it because I knew from experience that when people were thrashing about in the trunk of a car, they set the damn alarm off.

I took the steps two at a time, wrenching the door open before one of the staff could get there and cupping my hands around my mouth as I shouted into the depths of the house.

"Is there a little underling hanging around here somewhere who needs a job?"

It took a few minutes, but then two of Dougal's boys, Douglas and Donald, appeared, both of them preteens with mean streaks and foul tempers. I always forgot which was which and I knew that annoyed the fuck outa them, but I didn't give a shit because Dougal was maybe my least favourite brother and his offspring were little cunts.

"I got a fella in the trunk," I told them. "Watch the car. Don't touch."

I didn't wait for any kind of reply. They'd do it. Every O'Brien knew their place in the family hierarchy and most of them were beneath me. Aside from my siblings and my pa - though most of my siblings fell in at my commands too. They just didn't like it.

Pa's house servant, Martha, came scurrying out to greet me, waving a damn testing kit at me and giving me a hard look. Yeah, yeah, pandemic. Why wouldn't anyone let me forget about that?

I sighed as I let her toss it my way, wondering if it might be a blessing to just catch the damn thing and let it take me. The Hades Virus didn't sound like a fun way to go though, so I decided against that and took the damn test. Pa wouldn't let anyone come see him without getting a negative result and it wasn't worth the headache to argue. Of course, he also insisted I wear that damn mask while I was out on jobs and I didn't. If death wanted to come for me, I was always ready to welcome it with open arms.

I made small talk with Martha while we waited for the test results and she didn't even mention the blood speckling my bare arms and grey wifebeater. It was probably all over my face too actually. Never mind though. It served a purpose. I never wanted any members of my family to forget who or what I was. I wasn't the kind of man for them to try and bring to heel or ally themselves with. I was the crazy motherfucker with a taste for death and that was all they needed to know.

The moment the test revealed that I was as healthy as a buck, I bid Martha goodnight and headed down the long hall towards the dining room.

Dougal was sat at the table to my pa's left and Connor was on his right. Both of my brothers levelled glares on me that spoke of the rivalry between me and all of my siblings, but I couldn't summon a fuck to give. We all looked fairly similar, dirty blonde hair and strong jaws but I was clearly the good looking one. And definitely the only one who paid enough attention to taking care of my body. They were lazy because they never thought they'd have to run for their lives or fight for them in any way that didn't involve a gun. But maybe one day the cartel would come calling, or the Italians or the Russians. Who fucking knew? All I could say for sure was that they wouldn't catch me, and they wouldn't beat me either. My brothers though? Here's to hoping they were strung up by their ankles and had a stick of dynamite rammed up their arses before going boom and ending their insufferable lives.

"Move along, Connor, your brother is hungry," Pa said and I withheld my smirk as I stalked into the room and Connor was forced to move down a spot for me.

My pa was a conniving old bastard, and he knew full well what moves like that did to his children. He wanted us at each other's throats. He wanted us fighting for dominance and he refused to name a successor for that very reason. The old bastard wouldn't reveal which one of us he'd selected to rule in his place until he was six feet under and we were listening to his will being read.

I hoped it wasn't any of them. And I hoped with all my heart it wasn't me. Not sure who that left it for exactly, but I'd figure that out when it mattered.

"You look like shite, Niall," Dougal said, sneering at the state of my bloodied wifebeater while adjusting his tie. He was clean shaven and his cheeks were kinda shiny like he'd polished them. I wouldn't even be surprised if he did, fucking weirdo that he was.

The three of them were all perfectly presented in smart suits of course but I just shrugged, not caring what I looked like. I always got a free pass when I'd been on a job and I knew my brothers fuckin' hated that.

"He's been working," Pa growled. "Which is more than can be said for either of you today."

Connor scowled at me like he used to when we were kids and I grinned right back. His blonde hair was long and tied in a ponytail at the base of his skull. Whenever I saw it, I wanted to pull it. Maybe today I would.

Martha appeared with a heaped plate of food she'd kept hot for me and I tossed her a wink as I dug into it. She was a nice woman so far as I knew and Kyan was definitely fond of her, but when I was in this house I preferred to just keep to myself, so I'd never gotten to know her much.

"I've got a live one in my trunk," I said around a mouthful of potatoes.

"So I can't stay the night." *Or for the party, what a shame.* I smirked into my food and kept eating.

"Nonsense," Pa said, almost sounding casual but using that tone which said there wouldn't be arguments on this. "We have more guests coming after dinner as you know well and you have to stay to entertain them. Besides, I can hardly arrange your entire wedding for you without your input."

I froze and Dougal gave me a gloating smile from across the table as I lifted my gaze to meet my pa's. He hadn't said a word about the damn wedding when he'd invited me to this shindig. Likely because he knew I wouldn't have shown if he had.

"I thought you mighta forgotten about that," I growled, everything about me screaming killer as I set him in my sights. "You know I have no desire to-"

"Are you an O'Brien or not?" Pa asked, his tone arctic cold and cutting. There were no half answers to that question though and as Dougal casually placed a Desert Eagle on the table, I knew he was hoping I'd say no and give him the excuse to kill me. But there was no way in fuck I was letting one of my brothers be the end of me. Anyone but them. I'd take death by field mouse over allowing them that accolade. I bet I could find a little one angry enough to do it if I looked hard enough.

"I am," I snapped. "But how does-"

"I'm not asking you to love the girl. I'm just telling you to marry her. Fuck her with your eyes shut and think of your poor dead bride if you must, but you will marry her," Pa said coldly.

I glared at my father, hatred burning like acid in my veins as I fingered my butter knife and considered just taking control of this family here and now. I could kill the three of them and be done with this bullshit. But as Dougal raised his gun and casually pointed it at me, I knew that wasn't how it would go. They'd been waiting for this. Hungering for it. Hell, I wouldn't have been surprised if it wasn't one of these bastards who had whispered the idea of marrying me off to the Russians into our father's ear in the first place. All they'd have to do was sprinkle in the odd comment about it being a test of my loyalty and he would have leapt at it. They knew I'd freak out over this. It was my one, guaranteed trigger and they were hoping it would give them an excuse to take me off the board.

"Fine," I gritted out, but it wasn't fine. And it wasn't fuckin' happening.

I went back to shovelling food into my face and Connor sniggered a laugh beside me.

"What would sweet Ava think of that?" he murmured and I snapped.

I was out of my chair in a flash, the thing skidding away across the floor behind me and my hand around the back of his neck as I forced his face down into my dinner plate and waited to find out if someone could drown in mashed potato or not.

He kicked and flailed and I jammed my knee down between his shoulder blades to keep him there before slamming my free fist into his ribs over and over and over until they cracked.

Dougal still had the gun pointed at me, but it looked like he was hoping I might kill Connor before he had to shoot me so that he could get rid of the two of us at once.

"Enough," Liam growled eventually, and I raised my head to bare my teeth at my father.

"Ava was an O'Brien," I snarled. "If he insults her, I can kill him for it."

Dougal looked like he was hoping Pa would give him the okay to pull that trigger and finish me, but of course he wasn't that lucky. None of us ever were when it came to our father. He knew exactly how to keep the lot of us balanced on this edge of hatred without ever letting us tip one way or the other into murder or friendship.

"Apologise, Connor," he commanded, waving a hand at me to make me release him.

217

By some miracle, I managed to calm the beast in me enough to do it, shoving away from my brother and backing up as he pushed himself out of the potato, gasping and wheezing and clutching his side. He was fucking covered in gravy and mash and there was a carrot stuck to his cheek.

"Sorry, Niall," Connor ground out, not sounding sorry at all.

I gave him my devil's grin as I took a photo on my phone, reminding him why he shouldn't try and play killer with me and he spat mashed potato from his mouth before grabbing a napkin and trying to wipe the rest from his battered looking face.

"Go and get changed before the Russians arrive," Pa commanded me. "You have half an hour to make yourself presentable and paint on a fucking smile. If you don't, then you'll be coming back to live here permanently until you remember your place in this family."

I cut him a mocking bow then turned and strode from the room with rage burning a hole in my chest.

Me and my siblings all still had rooms in the ridiculous fucking palace our Pa had built himself and I made my way to mine, just glad of the excuse to escape their company.

When I arrived in the room, I picked up the phone hanging on the wall and called down to the kitchen staff, telling them to bring me more food and a bottle of whiskey. If I was going to have to tolerate the company of my so-called fiancé, then I'd be doing it shit faced.

I ripped my clothes off, having an angry shower as I blasted music from the Bluetooth speaker beside my bed and pushing myself to sing along to Eminem at his finest and most pissed off while trying to wash away this sick feeling in my gut.

I dried off and dressed automatically in a navy suit that hung in the closet just for these kinds of bullshit occasions.

Just as I was about to pick up the phone and ring down to the kitchens again to tear someone a new arsehole for making me wait on that booze, I noticed the bottle I'd requested and a plate of sandwiches sitting there on the desk for me. I guessed some helpful little Benson had dropped them off while I'd been showering and I decided to drown the voices screaming for blood in the back of my mind with liquor.

I unscrewed the cap and tipped the bottle up into my mouth, ignoring the fancy glass that had been left for me with little ice cubes in it. Of course, sometimes instead of drowning, the voices only got louder when I drank. Those were the kinds of nights where I woke up bloody and broken and couldn't even remember who I'd killed. No doubt it was some deserving fucker, but I always worried about how sloppy I might have been on those kinds of nights. And I doubted I could get away with murdering the Russians.

Unless… No. Not likely. Not here anyway.

I forced myself to stop drinking just shy of utterly fucked up and demolished my food before I tossed my tie aside and headed for the exit.

One night. I could endure a single night in the company of my future in-laws, then I'd head home to my spider and offer her up that tasty little fly I was keeping cosy in the trunk of my car.

Sorry about that, Henry, it's a shitty way to spend your final hours. You are a royal prick though, so there is that. I bet your wife is all kinds of okay with it.

I blew out a breath and headed down to meet with my pa and the Russians. No point hiding from it now after all. But I'd be doing whatever I could to get out of this so-called wedded bliss. I was not a creature destined for any form of bliss and I was content to linger in torture for all I'd done. I wouldn't be marrying someone to add insult to Ava's memory as well.

I strode into the huge conservatory at the rear of the house, noticing Connor first, my brother now dressed in a new suit and glaring at me with barely concealed hatred.

I decided to rub salt in his wounds as I strode straight towards him, ignoring the other guests at this little party that was in the midst of kicking off. I'd taken a cursory glance around, enough to notice more of my brothers in attendance with their wives as well as more Russians than I had any interest in ever knowing.

I was never usually required to attend bullshit like this and with the lockdown that was in effect across the country, none of these people should have been here. But no doubt Pa had gotten them all tested, and I could readily admit that this tiny law was the least of all the laws the people in this room had broken.

Actually, on that note, were there any laws I had yet to break in relation to killing? I had to think not. But maybe. Like there could be some super specific weird law about not murdering your brother by forcing a dirty toilet brush down his throat and tickling his tonsils with it until he choked.

I smirked to myself at that visual and Connor glowered as I strode up to him. We were all fairly big lads, but I was the biggest and that rankled my older brothers to no end. They fuckin' hated it. The youngest one, who should have been the smallest and weakest, pushed to the bottom of the pecking order by nothing more than just the fact that I had the disadvantage of age was by far the most notorious O'Brien aside from our pa as well as the biggest and strongest.

And I was willing to bet people knew that I was more terrifying than Liam O'Brien too. Not because I was more ruthless, but because I was fearless, totally, utterly without fear or care or compassion or anything soft at all. Those things had been torn from me long ago and the fact that I was missing them was a horror of its own.

"Did you enjoy yer dinner?" I asked him, smirking as I reached out and took his drink right from his hand.

He was left with the choice of making a scene or allowing it and he gritted his teeth as he gave it up. I drank the lot then spat in the empty glass and handed it back to him.

"Wanna play a game with me, big brother?" I asked and no matter how drunk I was right now, I still didn't slur. No one ever could tell when I was shit faced aside from me. But I was definitely more volatile with half a bottle of whiskey pouring through my veins.

"I can only imagine any game you want to play would end in bloodshed, little Niall," he said, trying to bait me the way he had when we were children, and he used the seven years he had on me to his advantage when we fought. Of course, that hadn't helped him so much the time I'd slipped a noose around his ankle and hung him from the rafters in the old work shed out back while hitting him with a stick until he cried.

"You wanna whip your cock out and find out which one of us is the little one?" I offered, not bothering to lower my voice.

The people at this party were all of the fucked up variety, no matter how much they might enjoy playing pretend. A cock or two between the cocktails weren't gonna make them blush.

"I could be the judge," a woman purred in a soft Russian accent and I stilled as my gaze was drawn to my future bride.

"Here she is," I said, smiling widely and looking her over. She was wearing a figure-hugging dress in blood red, which just so happened to be my favourite colour and her tits were pushed up until she was practically resting her chin on them. "Anastasia."

"Niall," she replied like I didn't know me own name.

"Ah, the poor woman who is to be saddled with my youngest and most irritating brother for a groom," Conner interjected, offering her his hand.

My brother was known for fucking anything with a pulse, so no doubt he was having wild fantasies about fucking my bride too. I was sure he would love plunging his cock into her even more because with every thrust he would think he was fucking me too - not literally fucking me because I was his brother and that was a bit too twisted for even O'Briens - but fucking me over. He'd love that alright.

Funny thing was, if she started riding his little cock right here and now in front of me, I wouldn't be able to summon a shit to give about it. I'd just offer them a round of applause, steal that fancy diamond bracelet she was wearing and leave here a happy man. Well, not happy obviously but a whole lot happier than I was in their company.

"Ah, but you are clearly the ugliest, so at least Niall doesn't have that burden to bear," Anastasia replied smoothly and I barked a surprised laugh which she took as an invitation to sidle closer and wrap her arm around mine, giving my bicep a squeeze.

The killer in me got ideas about that but I locked them down on account of...well, probably not being able to kill all fifty of the people in this room without dying. I mean, if anyone could then I'd put money on it being me, but likely not. I'd spotted enough barely concealed weapons to know it would probably just end with me eating a bullet and I had responsibilities now. I had a girl in a basement.

"Well," Connor spluttered, thrown off by her lack of interest in his dimples and cutting me a glare which said that was somehow my fault. "It looks like the two of you are as poisonous as each other. So at least it's a good match."

He strode away before I got a chance to pull his ponytail and I dislodged my arm from Anastasia's grip, inhaling the scent of roses that clung to her and coughing. I fucking hated flowers. All they ever made me think of was the mountain of them that had been piled on top of Ava's grave, then I just thought about the way her body would have rotted away by now and how she was nothing and no one anymore thanks to me.

"I need a drink," I said, crossing the room quickly, though not quick enough to dislodge my little Russian stalker clearly as she followed behind me.

"Ah, there you are, Niall!" my pa called as I found one of the wait staff and made him stand still for me so that I could work my way through the entire tray of champagne flutes he was carrying. He looked around at the feel of my hand on his shoulder like he was planning on telling me he needed to keep moving, but backed off sharpish when he saw who had stopped him.

I turned to look at my father and Vlad who were cutting through the crowd to us while downing my first glass.

"We're ready to make the announcement. Here's the ring." Liam clicked his fingers at the serving boy to dismiss him and I snatched another glass before he could escape, sinking that quickly too.

The moment I finished it, my pa stole my empty glass and replaced it with a ring box.

I stared at it mutely while Anastasia clapped her hands and put on a good show of being excited. Maybe she'd always dreamed of having a husband who couldn't stand her, killed people for a living and wasn't in the least bit attracted to her. Who fuckin' knew? Strokes for all folks and that.

Vlad seemed a little less impressed with me and he clicked his fingers before my face, making my vision swim as I looked at that ugly as fuck tattoo on his cheek. I'd kill him for that alone. Chop him up into tiny little pieces and feed him to a monkey. I'd have to go to the zoo, but it'd be worth the trip.

On that note, I fucking loved a tapir. Crazy assholes they were with those big old noses and fat arses. Fucking loved 'em. Where was a tapir when you needed it though?

"Are you man enough for my little girl?" Vlad demanded. "I won't agree to a match for her to some fool with a drinking problem."

Okay, so maybe it *was* possible to tell when I was shit faced. I'd thought the room was the one swaying, but in all fairness, there was a good chance it was me.

"I can assure you, my son is the most worthy of all my children," Liam growled. "If I were to make a final decision on which one of them was going to succeed me after my death at this very moment then Niall would be the one. Hands down. Your daughter may just end up queen of the O'Brien empire one day. Niall is his own brand of interesting, but I assure you once you get a taste for him, you won't be able to get enough."

"That's true," I agreed. "People tend not to like me because they know how easily I can kill them. Once they get past the fear, they think I'm a fucking riot – until I kill them that is. Then they remember why they didn't take to me initially."

Anastasia giggled, flipped her blonde curls and grabbed my arm again. Woman was gonna need to stop manhandling me or I'd be breaking something pretty damn soon.

Vlad surveyed the way his daughter was panting all over me like a bitch in heat and nodded once in satisfaction. "Let's do it then. We'll seal our families together in blood then we can look towards the Castillo Cartel and their destruction together."

Always with the war mongering for these powerful arseholes. That was why I hated them. They never got their own damn hands dirty.

Vlad turned away from us and yelled something in Russian at the gathered party goers and my pa grasped my shoulder, steering me forward as all eyes turned to us. Anastasia was still hanging from my arm like a used condom stuck on the side of a dumpster and I forced myself not to throw her off as I looked at the assorted gangsters who were staring at us.

"It is with great proudness that we can officially announce the joining of our two great families!" Pa called out. "O'Brien and Novikov are to be united in marriage and through that bond we will forge an unbreakable alliance. To Niall and Anastasia!"

The rest of the room raised their glasses and Anastasia snatched the ring box from my hand, gasping as she pulled out a ring. I didn't even look at the thing as she jammed it onto her perfectly manicured finger, and I bit my tongue against the venom I wanted to spew from my lips.

I pasted on a smile and accepted bullshit congratulations while in my head all I could hear were the roaring of as many songs as I could cram in there and the little voice in the back of my skull which was screaming out for me to kill my pa, stop this, set myself free. If Mateo would just tell me where he'd hidden all of that lovely treasure of his, I could be on my way any day now. Probably needed to up my torture regime on him to be honest. Sometimes I just needed a TV day though, you know? Like, I'd wake up feeling all 'I'm gonna waterboard the fuck outa that asshole in me basement today', but then I'd accidentally get hooked into a dramatic episode of Ice Road Truckers and before I knew it the day was gone. *Notes to self: focus on escape plan more often - give more serious thought to murdering the family.*

I didn't though. It just went against all the things I'd been raised to be. But I was having more and more of those thoughts recently and I had to wonder if one day they might stick.

Fuck knew how long I managed to stay there, fighting against the desire to murder every fucker in that room before I sketched a mocking bow and just walked the fuck out.

I stumbled a little as I strode away down the corridor, the booze numbing me as I put all of this bullshit into a box at the back of my skull to deal with later.

I kept going until I was outside in the perfectly manicured garden, leaning against a cold brick wall with a cigarette hanging from my lips and smoke spiralling up into the sky.

It's a fucking mess, Ava.

She didn't reply and when I tried to picture her face, I found it missing. She wasn't there in my memories anymore. Not really. I tried to keep hold of her, but it was like keeping water cupped in my hands. It had been so long. All I really knew for certain was that I never should have married her and dragged her into this fucked up world of ours. I never should have painted a target on her back. I never should have let the Nelsons get the chance to snatch her away. And I should have gotten there sooner. It was far too late for all that now and I knew in a way that I was just torturing myself by refusing to let her go. But I was fairly certain I deserved at least a little torture for the life I'd cost her.

"You need to work on your poker face," Anastasia's voice came from beyond my closed eyes and there was no more giggling or lightness to it. This was the girl behind the mask and I was pleased to be meeting her even if I had no desire to know her better.

"That so?" I didn't open my eyes. I didn't get the feeling she was here to kill me and I wasn't in the mood to look at her.

"Yes," she growled. "It is what it is. The way I see it, one day you and I could rule over this empire. Who cares if we don't love each other? We can be allies. And I assure you that once you get me into bed you won't be disappointed."

"Sorry, love, I don't have any intention of finding out whether or not that claim holds any truth," I told her because she needed to grasp that fact right now. Her and my cock were never going to get acquainted.

Anastasia scoffed. "Perhaps you'll feel better about the whole thing when you find out how true my claims are for yourself?"

There was the sound of rustling material and I opened my eyes to find her red dress on the floor and her fully fucking naked before me.

"Fuck me," she demanded. "However you like it, I promise you I can take it and more. Then you'll see, we can make our own alliance out of this and rise up higher than either of our fathers."

My gaze roamed over her body curiously and I could tell objectively that she was a very attractive woman. I could do it. I could forget the vows I'd made and the guilt I carried and stop punishing myself like this.

But as I thought of that, my mind moved away from the naked woman before me to my pocket-sized psycho who I had waiting back in my basement.

I disbanded that thought as quickly as it had come and took the cigarette from my lips.

"No offence," I said slowly, flicking the butt away. "But no thanks."

I turned away from Anastasia's outraged face and her equally outraged tits and headed back towards the house. I'd sleep this whiskey off in my bed then drive back home tomorrow.

I was pretty sure I'd just made myself a dangerous enemy in my new fiancé, but I didn't give a fuck. I was never going to be what she wanted me to be and I had no desire to try. Angry tits or not.

BROOKLYN

CHAPTER FOURTEEN

"**C**ome on, Brooklyn, you're not afraid of the dark, are you?" Penelope's hand was wrapped around my arm as she guided me into the trees off campus.

I hadn't wanted to come to this stupid high school dance but my uncle had insisted I get out of the house so he could have a night with his girlfriend. I'd put on the only dress I owned which was strappy, rose pink and didn't have any holes in it. I'd planned on sneaking off to spend the night in the library, but then Penelope had pounced on me and made all kinds of declarations about not wanting to graduate with regrets of being a bitch to me. She'd freaking apologised and even given me her silver butterfly hairclip when I'd told her it looked nice. It was now clipped above my ear, holding my hair away from my face. A face which Andrew Fig had told me was the prettiest one he'd seen tonight. Maybe things really were changing. It wasn't easy to forgive them for being so mean, but I'd spent so very, very long alone and maybe it was worth giving them a chance.

Penelope's nails dug a little deeper into my arm as she led me down further into the trees, the moonlight highlighting the track in silver. Somewhere in the distance an owl hooted, a boy laughed and my heart lifted *at all the hopeful possibilities that awaited me in these trees.*

I woke up screaming, reliving that night as sweat soaked my skin, my clothes sticking to my body. Rough hands took hold of me and I fought harder, picturing the one who'd touched me and thrashing like a wild beast. But he couldn't be here. There was no way he could be here. If he was, I'd kill him. I'd rip his tongue out and tear his organs from his body with nothing but my hands. I may have gone into those woods as an innocent little creature, but I'd emerged as a fully-fledged monster with sharpened teeth and claws. His death was owed to me and it was time I claimed it.

"Calm down," Mateo's gruff voice demanded of me and he pushed my hair out of my face, making me look at him.

But all I saw right then was another monster trying to hurt me. I shrank away, kicking until he let go and my back hit the bars with a loud clang. I needed a weapon. I needed to kill him. It was the only way to end this. The only way to banish the nightmare for good. I'd stab until there was nothing left to stab but red mush.

The cage door suddenly yanked open behind me and I tumbled backwards, finding myself at the feet of another villain. *Oh fucking tits, I'm in a nest of hungry beasts.*

I scrambled past Hellfire, shoving myself upright as he took hold of my arms.

"No – no, no!" I screamed, panic welling in every inch of my flesh. My skin burned where he held me because all I could feel was *him* touching me. All I could hear was laughter and taunts and the sound of my soul ripping apart down the middle.

"Spider!" Niall barked. "Snap outa it."

Mateo banged his hand on the bars as I clawed at Niall, but he only held me tighter.

His fingers dug in and I was just a bird in a cage, my wings being clipped, my freedom to fly torn away forever. *If you go down to the woods today, you're sure of a big surprise. For every beast that ever there was will gather there for certain because, today's the day the monsters will tear you to pieces.*

"Spider!" Niall shook me and my brain rattled, the memories all coming loose in my skull, dislodging from the front of my mind so I could think clearer once more.

Slowly, my body began to calm as I accepted I wasn't trapped in the past anymore. *He* wasn't here. He wasn't touching me. And even if he had been, I was powerful enough to destroy him now. It was our little secret, me and Satan's. He'd given me the strength I needed to make my first kills that day, but he'd taken my sanity in payment. I'd never been the same, but I didn't care. I was strong now. I could fight and win. And I wasn't going to let another monster come along and do the things Andrew had done to me.

"Are ya alright now, lass?" Niall asked, his voice low in my ear and I realised I was shaking.

The scent of whiskey and cigarettes clung to him and I frowned at the fancy blue pants and dress shirt he was wearing before dismissing it. He'd been gone last night but I didn't know where and right now I didn't care.

"I need to be alone!" I blurted. "A shower, I need a shower. A power shower."

"Okay," he murmured in confusion, letting me go and I didn't look back as I ran to the bathroom on the other side of the basement and slammed the door.

I tore my clothes off, stepping into the unit and turning the water on to scolding. Then I let myself come apart, dropping down to the bottom of the shower and hugging my legs to my chest. I cried, hoping the sound of the water would cover the sound, but that was a fool's hope. I was a loud crier and currently I was bawling like a wolf in a trap, its leg broken and its heart bleeding. Beasts could hurt too. There were always bigger monsters than the one I'd become and they wanted to devour me.

I hated that I wasn't over that night. Was it always going to torture me? Did I have to relive it for the rest of my life? Forever and ever and ever until I was nothing but dust and bad memories? *Ohhh, I don't want to be butt dust.*

I let myself be dramatic, wailing and allowing my grief to pour freely from me. I needed to let all the emotion out so it could wash down the drain along with the water, then I'd be okay again. The nightmare would fade for a while. Until it slowly began to build once more in the background of my mind. It was always the same. It crept up on me bit by bit until it went off with a bang like fireworks on the fourth of July.

The worst part was facing the icky truth that coated my soul in black tar; I wasn't made of stone like I wanted to be. And no matter what I did, I couldn't rid myself of what had happened. It was made worse by thinking of the men at that awful, awful club who'd touched me. The Shadow rearing over me, Señor Castillo watching, feasting on me with his dollar bill eyes. Was I destined to be a plaything for cruel men? Was I to be passed from hand to hand, owned, possessed and ruined time and again? *Maybe I've been in hell this whole time and Satan isn't my boyfriend. Maybe he watches me through the eyes of all my demons and laughs as I break. Are you gaslighting me, Big Red?*

No, that couldn't be right. He was the only one who had my back. The only one who'd answered my call in the woods that night. He'd fed me power and watched me rise from the ashes of my destruction like a vengeful phoenix.

I took in a breath which raked at the depths of my lungs. All the little pieces of me were scattering again, fragmenting further until it was hard to hold onto any of them at all. *One day my skin is going to crack apart and all the jagged shards of my soul will fall out like broken glass. I'm Humpty Dumpty's hobo cousin and the king's men won't spare me a glance if they come across my pieces. I'm not worth their time.*

The door popped open and I hugged my arms around my naked body tighter as Niall walked into the room, not looking at me.

"Listen here, Spider," he said darkly then moved to sit beside the shower unit with his back to the wall, his gaze fixed on the vanity unit opposite. He was so pretty. No, that wasn't the right word. His features were pure evil arranged into this most temptingly appetising face. "I know you're in pain. And I recognise that fucking pain. There's only one thing that ever helps me...do ya know what that is?"

I swallowed the dry lump in my throat, sure I knew. "Killing," I breathed because it was what made me feel right and I'd seen that need in him too the first moment we'd met.

Killing was like an itch that needed scratching ever since that day in the woods. It was like the vengeance in me was a creature that resided in my body now, and it was always, always ravenous. Today more than ever.

Niall breathed a sigh like that word alone brought him peace. "That's right, lass. And it just so happens, I've got a very bad man upstairs with your name on him. The type who needs killing. But you see, the thing is, ya need to do it right. I wanna show you how. You've got skill, but it needs honing. Would you like me to teach you?"

I turned my head so my cheek rested on my knees, looking out at him through the fogged up glass. The water was so hot on my back, it almost felt cold. I was sure this was how death would feel, this burning, freezing cold.

"Yes, I'd like that," I whispered, the demons in me rising to the surface, whispering my name. There was strength in this calm after my storm had blown itself out. Now I was numb and that was when I was at my most dangerous.

Mateo was banging on the bars and roaring like a beast.

"Oh-ho, the prisoner is riled up," Niall said excitedly.

I didn't understand why Dead Man was making all that noise. Why did he care if Niall was in here with me? Did he need to poop?

233

"I see you're quick to make new friends," Niall commented with a flicker of anger in his eyes and I laughed hollowly at the joke.

"I don't have any friends, not even the moon," I whispered.

"Now don't go talkin' like that," Niall said, getting to his feet. "The moon's a whore anyway, she's always sucking the sun's dick. Here. Come out. I won't look at ya."

For some reason I got to my feet and stepped out of the shower, still feeling too spaced out in that moment to really think it through. And maybe a deeply broken part of me wanted him to look, to remind me that I wasn't just a ghost and that life was still housed in this flesh. But most of all, that this flesh could be desired in a way that wasn't cruel. But Niall was true to his word, his eyes closed as he wrapped me in a large blue towel.

He opened them when I was covered, standing within a few inches of me, his head tipped down as he took in my expression. And I was lost. Lost to those green eyes which held a thousand untold horrors in them. Lost to that mouth which was always toying with a smile, and lost to the intensity pouring from him in waves. He was a bad, bad man and I wanted to know every bad, bad deed he'd ever committed. I wanted to pry open his chest and peer in at the lump of muscle pumping blood around this creature's body and see the scars which marked it. Because if there was one thing pain taught you, it was to see it in others. And I had the feeling Niall's scars were as deep and unhealed as mine.

"Your head would look nice on a wall," I told him, a blush rising in my cheeks at the admission and his eyebrows arched. He had manly eyebrows. The kind that were thick but not bushy, the kind I wanted to crawl off of his face onto my fingers and live there as little pet caterpillars.

"That's the best thing anyone's said to me in a long time, Spider." He smirked then kicked the door open and shoved me out of it. "Now get dressed, we're going killin'."

My heart lifted with excitement and I let that feeling bubble up inside me until it was all I could feel. No more sads. They needed to get gone. All the way up a tiger's butt with a coconut.

Mateo growled and I looked over at him, finding his hands wrapped around the bars, his muscles bunched and his teeth bared.

Oh my puckered nipples, he looks all kinds of scrumptious.

"I'm good," I said lightly, not wanting to go back *there* in my mind. Because there was bad. And here was, well not exactly good, but it was better than there. So that was something.

I grabbed some sweatpants and a white tank top from the cupboard, leaving the door of it open as I dropped my towel and got dressed behind it. I soon stepped out, prepared for the day, my tears dried and my spirits a little higher.

"Ready," I told Niall brightly. *I'm going killing, yippee!*

I felt Mateo's eyes drilling into us, his stance not having shifted at all though his knuckles were red from thumping the bars. He looked ready to rip Niall to pieces and I kinda wanted to join him in that pursuit. It'd be a shame to mess up Hellfire's hot body, but I'd keep his head and mount it on the wall like I'd imagined.

"Come on then." Niall grabbed my hand, towing me towards the stairs.

"You're dead if you hurt her," Dead Man spat and Niall laughed obnoxiously.

"Good luck with that while you're stuck in a cage, lad. By the way, I'll be making use of that wagging tongue of yours soon when I make ya spill yer secrets," he called, dragging me upstairs and through the basement door.

He locked it behind us and kept tugging me along and up another staircase to the second floor. Oooh, it was nice to see more places. I'd always been a traveller at heart, though I hadn't been to too many places. I'd pictured seeing the Grand Canyon while murdering a bastard or two as the sun rose above the horizon. That was some real bucket list shit. Right up there with swimming with dolphins. Although I needed to learn how to swim first before I could do that. But when I did, those dolphins wouldn't know what had hit them. Like not physically. I would never hit a dolphin. I'd kiss one though. Maybe I could cut a blowhole into my back and live among their pod. Would they take me to Atlantis and show me the secrets of the ocean? I'd probably have to marry a dolphin though and I wasn't sure I was attracted to sea creatures. But I supposed if I had to pick one it would be a dolphin. A close second would be an octopus – they'd give the best hugs. I wouldn't marry a squid though. Squids were shady, they'd probably eat my friends if I had any.

The sound of muffled cries came from a room at the end of the hall and my heart rate picked up as Niall led me to the door, picking up a large sports bag outside it. He unlocked the door and led me inside, bringing the bag with him as the sound of metal objects clinked within it.

The room was empty except for a single chair in the middle of it and a guy in check boxers tied to it with cellophane wrap. There was an orange taped into his mouth and another one was laying on the floor by his bare feet.

"Now what did I say would happen if you let that orange fall off of your head?" Niall growled, shoving the door shut and releasing me, slapping his captive across the face.

My eyes flew to the window as I wondered how quickly I could get over there, unlatch it and climb out. How far was the fall? Was it concrete at the bottom or grass? I could run with a broken arm but not a broken leg. Niall suddenly strapped something around my throat and I gasped, trying to jerk away as the clip of a padlock sounded behind me.

Hellfire released me, taking a small remote control from his pocket and waving it at me as I reached up to touch the thick, plastic collar he'd locked around my neck with a little box sitting on one side of it.

"That's a shock collar, lass. The very same one that our friend here is wearing." He pointed to the bound guy and I noticed one on him too. My heart rate spiked and I clawed at the collar to try and get it off as the man stared at me with wide eyes. When I realised it was useless, I lunged at Niall, aiming for that remote in his hand and he batted me away, his strength knocking me back easily.

"Fuck you, Hellfire," I spat.

"Calm down, it's just for if you have any crazy notions about running away," he said with a shrug. "Now do you wanna learn to kill better or what? Because I ain't got all day."

My eyes fell on the bag as he unzipped it, revealing a range of weapons inside. A steely calm fell over me as I took in their perfect curves and sharp edges. *Hell yes.*

"Teach me," I said innocently. Maybe I didn't need to seduce him after all. I'd just wait 'til he handed me one of those weapons then drive it into his heart. *Wham clam, thank you ma'am.*

He tossed the bag at my feet. "Here, your choice."

I leaned down, rummaging through the selection of knives, hammers, pliers, all kinds of tools which kissed my fingers as I ran them over each beautiful instrument of death. They were pretty plain though. They could have done with a few stickers, some glitter glue and bright paint. When I killed this motherfucker, I'd be sure to take a couple of my favourites and give them a glow up.

I chose a machete at the bottom of the bag that looked like it needed a little loving. *You'd like to spill some blood today, wouldn't you Mashy?*

I rose to my feet, weighing it in my hand and gazing at Niall as the man strapped to the chair started screaming against the orange in his mouth. I was pretty sure I heard the orange giggling.

Niall wet his lips as he stared at me and I sized him up, a deep carnal hunger for death reaching into my soul. He was scrummy, but he'd look just as scrummy dead and covered in blood.

"Alright, I'm gonna release him now and you can show me what you've got. He's gonna fight ya mind, so be ready."

Niall strode forward to start unwrapping the sheets of cellophane from the guy, walking round and round and round him to undo it. I bounced on my toes, watching as Niall moved past me once more, giving me his back and I lunged with a yell of determination, swinging Mashy toward his head.

Niall spun around, catching my wrist as I held the machete poised to kill, then threw me to the ground. His thumb slammed down on the remote button and I screamed as electricity exploded through my body. And it was the good kind, lighting up my skin from the inside like a bonfire. The pain was incapacitating, but as it stopped, a breathy moan left me and heat burned between my legs.

I panted in a heap on the floor, my veins buzzing and sparking. "Fuck me, Hellfire," I groaned, realising the double meaning to my words a little late.

I blinked innocently up at Niall as he gazed down at me, his mouth quirked in a grin and his eyes full of heat as he offered me his hand. The machete was no longer in my grasp and I growled, reaching for it, my fingers grazing the handle before Niall's boot pressed down on my wrist to stop me from picking it up. Not hard enough to crush bones, but enough to stop me. It was the nice kind of ouchy so I didn't mind so much.

"You play my game by my rules or you can go back to the basement, Spider," he warned. "Do you wanna learn to kill or not?"

I huffed my frustration. "I'm not gonna kill some random guy you tied up. I don't kill innocents unless they try to kill me first."

"He ain't innocent," he laughed and I tried to grasp for the machete again, but his boot pressed down harder, making me wince. Niall leaned forward, his face falling into shadow and all light extinguishing from his features. "If you try and kill me again, you'll regret it."

A shudder of fear ran through me that got me even hotter and I considered what he was offering here. "What did he do?" I jerked my chin in the vague direction of the guy who was struggling in his chair.

"He's a wife killer, aren't ya Henry?" he called over his shoulder and Henry whimpered as he fought wildly against his restraints. "Funny story, I went to his house by accident. He's the wrong fuckin' guy! But when I had him bloody and screaming at me feet, he just went and admitted that he'd murdered his wife and given her a shallow grave. All because his cock couldn't satisfy her and she chose to bang the gardener instead. Handy, right? I woulda had to let him go if he hadn't told me that, but as it stands, I gotta think something guided me to him last night." Niall straightened, his eyes full of hate as he offered me his hand to get up again, taking his boot off of my arm.

"Like the Devil?" I whispered in awe and Niall shrugged.

"Could be."

"So he killed his own wife, one he vowed to have and to hold and love and protect?" I asked, disgust filling me as Henry screamed against his gag.

"Yeah," Niall growled, spitting at him and making him flinch so hard that the chair toppled over backwards.

I grabbed up the machete and pushed to my feet, my eyes set on new prey. I didn't like wife killers.

Niall watched me as a potent energy ran between us, a shared hatred for this kind of scum filling his eyes. I'd been at the hands of men like Henry. Arguably worse men. All of them cowards. All of them deserving of death. *Hey Big Red, I've got a wriggler for you. I'll send him express to hell.*

Niall stepped closer, leaning down to talk in my ear as Henry thrashed like a man who knew he was going to die. Hellfire pushed a lock of hair away from my neck and a shiver of pleasure rolled through me that had everything to do with him and the scent of death in the air. I shouldn't have wanted him this close, but he'd awoken the cold killer in me and she wanted things I couldn't deny her when she took over.

"So what do ya say, lass? Are you going to let your killer come out to play?"

I nodded, stepping forward and sliding the machete into the last of the cellophane still keeping Henry tethered, slicing through it with a firm slash. He ripped the tape from his mouth and spat out the orange, leaping to his feet immediately. He was a pretty big guy, taller than me, though most people were so that wasn't surprising. No doubt he was stronger than me too. But I'd killed prey like him before. And I was gonna make a lovely mess of this wife hurter.

I dove at him, trying to run him through with the machete but he dodged aside so it sliced up his arm instead. His fist slammed into my side as he yelped and I stumbled back with a wheeze, but that wouldn't stop me. I was death in miniature form, with tiny little horns and leathery wings of doom. I ran forward with a growl of determination, but Niall was suddenly there, smashing his fist into the guy's face and throwing him against the wall.

"Get out of the way!" I shouted at him and Niall reluctantly stepped back, watching me as I held the machete above my head with both hands, slamming it down towards Henry. He jerked aside but the blade sliced into his shoulder and he roared as I spilled blood.

A vicious grin pulled at my mouth. "Aw, do you need a kiss for your boo-boo? I wonder if Satan will give you one before he plucks your eyes out?"

I attempted to twirl the machete in my hand all cool like and the guy knocked it out of my grip, his fist cracking against my jaw. *Shit biscuits.* I hit the floor and he was suddenly on top of me, his hands latching around my throat below the shock collar. I fought wildly, tearing at his arms as the blood from his wound spilled over me, but his grip was unyielding, his teeth clenched as he fought to kill me quick.

He was suddenly ripped off of me and Niall kicked him in the ribs, sending him rolling onto his back. He kept kicking and kicking and I was sure I saw actual flames in his eyes as he laid into Henry.

"Hey!" I barked. "I thought he was *my* kill." I leapt up, shoving Niall in the side to try and get him away and Henry scrambled upright, running to the window and desperately trying to open it.

Niall spun around, catching my arm as he laughed loudly. "You're no good at this. Why did I buy myself a useless little mouse?"

I gasped in anger, slapping him hard across the face, enough to make his head wheel sideways.

"Yes," he hissed excitedly.

"I'm not a fucking mouse," I spat. "I'm a unicorn."

"Sure ya are," he drawled sarcastically.

I ran toward my prey, but Niall barrelled past me, knocking me over just as Henry got the window open.

"Hey!" I snapped, fury bubbling under my flesh. "No fair."

Niall grabbed his shoulders and heaved him away from it, throwing him to the floor and kicking him to a rhythm like he was taking part in a workout routine.

My hand hit the bag of weapons and I growled furiously, kneeling up and grabbing out a bunch of knives, throwing them at both of them with screams of anger.

Niall laughed, opening his arms wide as I threw more and more and they sailed past him like he was the luckiest asshole alive. A little blade slammed into Henry's thigh and he screamed like a bitch as Niall kept kicking him, starting to sing My House by Flo Rida at the top of his lungs.

My hand locked around a hatchet and I jumped up, throwing it at Niall as I focused, trying not to let my rage cloud my vision. It sailed end over end toward his head and he ducked at the last second, the blade slamming into the wall behind him with a loud thunk.

He looked to me with his eyes sparkling. "Better!"

I snatched up a knife and ran at him with a snarl, but he shoved me down onto Henry as I made it there, dodging the swipe of my blade. I straddled Henry, turning my rage on him instead and slamming the blade into his side. He screamed, his fist cracking into my ribs harder and harder until I was sure something was gonna break. I twisted the knife as it got stuck and his screams turned to wails as he punched me so fiercely, I was thrown backwards.

Niall caught me from behind, hauling me off of Henry and tossing me away so I went rolling across the carpet.

"Hellfire!" I snapped in rage. "Is he my kill or not?"

I pushed myself up again, finding Niall carrying Henry to the window over his shoulder. Damn he was strong. It got me all tingly inside. And between my thighs. And up my butt.

"Hey!" I snatched a hammer from the bag, running to claim my kill, but Niall shoved Henry out of the window and the guy screamed as he fell toward the ground.

I ran to look out, not wanting to miss the moment the light went out of his eyes, but it was already too late. He was on the concrete with a pool of blood spreading out around him. All quiet and still and dead, dead, dead.

I pouted, punching Niall in the chest. "He was *mine*."

Niall shoved a palm into my face to push me away then slammed the window shut. "You didn't have a handle on that at all, Spider. Fuckin' useless."

My heart crushed into dust. I may have been useless at a lot of things, but killing wasn't one of them.

"I'm not useless," I said as my lower lip wobbled and he ignored me, heading across the room to gather up the weapons into his bag. "I'm not useless!"

He barked a laugh. "You just proved your worth to me, and it ain't nothing."

I trembled with rage, hate filling me from his words. How dare he? I was a killer. A good freaking killer. It was *all* I was good at. That and seduction. But killing was my best quality. And now he was just dismissing it! No. I wouldn't let him just disregard me like that.

"I survived a whole death game against fourteen other people," I snapped.

"Fourteen useless, untrained people," he taunted. "I thought I saw a glimmer of somethin' special in ya for a moment. But nah, I was wrong."

I ran at him with a shriek of fury, diving onto his back and punching the side of his head as hard as I could before sinking my teeth into his neck. He threw me off as he swung around and I hit the floor, leaping back to my feet in a heartbeat as I lunged at him again. I tore my fingernails down his jugular, wishing I had claws, because if I had he'd be bleeding out at my feet from that strike.

His hand latched around my throat and he slammed me against the wall, pinning me there as he grinned mockingly at me.

"Get out of this then. Prove yourself, Spider."

I clawed at his arm, kicked and spat, thrashed with all the strength I could muster. But it couldn't match his physical power. My ears popped as he cut off my air supply and my heart sank away into the depths of my body as I realised he was right. I couldn't beat him. But I could have beat Henry. He'd stolen that kill from me. And why? He was the one who'd brought me up here and told me to fight him. Why dangle a tasty bag of candies over my head just to take them away? It was downright evil that was what it was.

He bared his teeth at me, the temptation to finish me flaring in his eyes and I glared right back, going still. He thought I was beat. And that weakness he thought he saw made him want to end me. But I wasn't done. Nowhere near fucking done. Even if he snapped my neck, I'd come back as zombie to eat his brains. I'd enjoy them too. Make a real banquet out of them. But fighting was no good to me currently. So I fell back on the other thing I excelled at.

I lifted my thigh between his legs and ground it against his cock, my eyes locking with his as he grunted. I kept rubbing my thigh against him until

I felt him hardening against my leg and a victorious smile pulled at my lips. Lips that were probably turning blue right about now because I seriously couldn't breathe.

His grip suddenly slackened on my throat and he dropped me so my feet hit the floor. I sagged forward, gasping down air as I allowed myself a wild laugh. But my amusement was short lived as he snatched a fistful of my tank top and started dragging me out of the room by it.

"Yer on your last warning, Spider. You prove that you're worth something or I'll get rid of ya any way I see fit."

"You were the one who took that kill from me, you didn't give me a chance to prove myself!" I snapped. "Why did you keep stepping in every time I was close to ending him?"

"I fucking didn't," he growled, freaking lying to my face.

"Liar liar, France on fire," I spat.

"What?" he balked in confusion, his fist tightening in my top. "I ain't no liar."

"You just lied again," I hissed. "You threw him out the window. He was *my* kill."

His jaw pulsed with fury and he hauled me downstairs towards the basement door, a vein popping in his temple. He pushed me against the door, chest to my tits as he actually lifted me off the floor to hold me there so he could speak directly to my face. I wrapped my legs around him, trying to go all assassin thighs on his waist, but he didn't seem to notice. "I wasn't gonna stand there and watch you do a half rate job, lass. I'm too proud of a psycho for that."

He opened the door behind me and I gasped as I almost fell backwards, but he held onto me, carrying me down into the basement towards the cage. I pounded my fists into his sides as he tucked me under one arm, unlocking Mateo's cage and throwing me inside alongside the poop bucket. The barred door clanged closed as Mateo lunged at it like a wolverine on a chain, swiping for Niall through the bars. But he'd already stepped back.

Mateo snarled like a beast and I realised I was wet with blood and my body was humming with fresh bruises.

"You can go back to using the bucket today," Niall sniggered. "You didn't keep yer end of the bargain, Spider, so I won't be keeping mine."

He strode away, lighting up a cigarette and singing loudly to cover the sound of me hurling abuse at him as he headed upstairs out of sight.

Mateo turned to me, his furious eyes darting over my body as I dropped down into a corner of the cage and curled up in a ball, hiding my face in the crook of my arm.

I fucking hate that cock sucking, dick twiddling, knife humping, oafish, twat weasel!

NIALL

CHAPTER FIFTEEN

I was a royal prick. I knew it. My ghosts knew it. My entire family knew it. And now my little spider knew it too.

I'd left her in the cage for the rest of the day then I let her out into the rest of the basement again because I didn't like the way Mateo looked at her. He was a fucked up son of a bitch and I wasn't gonna stand for him getting his claws in her. Not that I was certain that was what was going on, but I'd walked in on a few too many pregnant silences down there for me to trust them. Maybe what I needed was a camera down there. But then I'd have to sit and watch it and that seemed like a whole lotta effort.

So Spider had been in my bad graces for the past week and during that time we'd entered into a glare off of epic proportions every time I went down there to feed them and change out the fuckin' bucket.

All of her fancy new clothes had been showing up all week in bags and I'd been piling them up in the corner. But now they were looking at me, asking me what I was going to do with bags of clothes meant for a tiny woman if I got rid of her. And I didn't have an answer. I mean sure, some of it might fit me, she'd mentioned hats so that was likely. But the rest...

I stood and crossed the room to the heap of bags beside the fireplace and ripped the top one open. Inside was a yellow swimsuit with the word *Gangster* written across it in black lettering.

I held it up in front of my tattooed torso and admitted pretty damn fast that it wouldn't fit and that I couldn't pull it off regardless. Mostly because it was a thong at the back and I still had four red stab wounds in my arse cheek from that fuckin' fork.

I sighed, tossing the swimsuit back down on top of the pile. I could dress Brutus up in the clothes. If he existed. Which he firmly did in my mind, but mind dogs couldn't wear real clothes.

I was sober for the first time today. Not that I'd been drowning my sorrows over the damn wedding or anything like that, but I had been forced to attend another lunch with my fiancé and her creepy arse father. He hadn't even laughed when I suggested he could start fucking all of his enemies instead of killing them then call himself Vlad the Impaler like that dude from the long agos. Nothing. Not a blink. Damn shame that. Even Anastasia didn't give me real laughs, though she'd gone right on back to trying to cock tempt me with fake giggles.

But my cock wasn't for the tempting. Not by my Russian bride anyway. And likely not by anyone ever again.

I needed something to change tonight. I needed to wake the fuck up and just have something happen or I was going to lose my damn mind.

Maybe it was time for an olive branch. At least then I could have some company up here instead of rattling around the place like a lonely butcher with nothing fun to carve up.

I grabbed the basement keys from the lockbox in the kitchen and moved to unlock the door. I did it carefully this time though, sliding the well-oiled locks opened quieter than a cheesy little mouse fart before pulling the door wide and listening.

"-see? Because that way they couldn't find me. I was all snuggled up like a kitten in cornflakes at the back of the barn and no one had a clue!"

Spider was saying enthusiastically. I waited to see if Mateo would reply but only silence followed before she moved on to talking about the importance of airing out shoes.

I crept down the stairs on silent feet, moving like a monster in the shadows and staying hidden in the dark stairwell as I made it low enough to see them. Mateo was doing press-ups inside his cage and Spider was sitting on her cushion right outside it, watching his powerful body move, enjoying a front row seat to the prison porno he was starting up right in front of her.

I watched her as she fell silent, her teeth sinking into her bottom lip and a finger twisting in a lock of ebony hair.

My gut knotted with some sharp, feral emotion and I was sorely tempted to march down there and drag Mateo into my office for some seriously fucked up questioning. And by my office, I meant my killing room. But as I took a step out of the shadows, I realised I could do one better than that, I could just take her away from here and keep her to myself upstairs.

Spider whipped around before I could get close to her and I gave her a shark's grin as a little of that talent I thought I'd seen in her on day one shone through.

She was on her feet in a blink, teeth bared like a cornered kitty cat and those electric blue eyes blazing with hatred.

"You hate me pretty good, don't ya, Spider?" I mocked and she growled. Actually growled like a lion or a bear. *Oh my.*

"That was *my* kill," she hissed, still all out of sorts even after having days to get over it.

"Salty little thing, ain't ya?" I teased and she growled again.

Mateo had stopped his workout and was on his knees glaring at me like he was picturing my death and I hoped it was a damn good one.

"Saltier than the sea," Spider agreed and my smile widened.

"I've come with a peace offering," I said, opening my arms to her in a show of innocence. I was bare chested and only wearing a pair of jeans, so it wasn't like she had any reason to think I was hiding anything.

"Is it pizza?" she demanded and I frowned.

"No. But it could be."

"Make it pizza then," she agreed, the fight going out of her as she folded her arms and gave me a glare.

"Done. Your clothes are here, you can come up and-"

She squealed excitedly and ran past me, leaping onto the stairs and thundering up them so that I was left looking at Mateo.

There was rage in those deep, dark eyes of his and I coulda sworn I tasted jealousy on the air too. I took a step closer to him, not worrying about Spider because I'd locked the door behind me so she'd only be waiting at the top of the stairs.

"You got something you wanna say, arsehole?" I offered and his lip pulled back as he got to his feet.

He intensified his glare at me but as Spider started banging on the door and yelling at me to hurry up, his gaze shifted beyond me for a moment and I got to the heart of it.

"Oh, you like my little pet, do ya?" I asked, stepping right up to the bars, giving him the chance to lunge at me through them. "Are you worried about what I might do to her when I've got her alone up there? Or about what she might wanna do to me?"

He lunged at the bars, his fist snapping out between them and catching me in the jaw.

I barked a laugh as I took it. Man had a damn good hook on him, I swear he nearly cracked a tooth. I was almost tempted to open the door to his cage and head inside for a good old-fashioned brawl with him. That would get my heart pumping, but then so did my little psycho more often than not.

"Niall!" Spider yelled impatiently but with that husky voice of hers, it was almost possible to imagine she was doing something else while calling out my name. Something I shouldn't have been letting myself think about, but which kept creeping into my thoughts with a nagging kind of intensity.

"I'm coming, love," I promised her before dipping my voice lower and speaking just for Mateo. "Or at least I will be soon, eh?"

I stepped back as he roared furiously, throwing himself against the bars and reaching for me desperately, pure venomous rage painting every line of his body. I barked a laugh and backed away from him, enjoying this new, easy form of torture I could inflict on him and wondering if I could use his little crush to my advantage even better than this somehow.

"Niall!" Spider snarled and I had to admit I liked getting her all riled up like that.

I jogged up the stairs and leaned around her to unlock the door, letting her out.

She bounded into the hall and I flipped the lights off, plunging Mateo into the dark before locking up again and following her further into the house.

By the time I found her again, she'd already made it to the front door and was rattling the locks on it as she tried to force her way out. I grinned as I stalked after her, snatching hold of the back of her neck as I caught up and whirling her around to face me.

"I thought you were gonna be a good girl for me?" I asked, crowding her back against the door and tipping her chin up to look at me.

"No chance of that," she replied breathily as my chest brushed hers. "I'm bad to the bone."

I grinned because I liked that then tugged the shock collar out of my back pocket. She pouted as I strapped it around her neck, and I twisted her around so that I could secure it with the little padlock at the back.

She pushed her arse back into my crotch as I locked it and I stilled as my pulse pounded at that little move. I placed my hands against the door either side of her head as she ground her arse against my hardening cock and a growl slipped between my lips as I tried to warn her off. She didn't know what she was doing messing with me like that, and I hadn't been tempted by a woman since the only one I'd ever loved had died because of me.

Before any wicked thoughts could invade my brain and steal the last ounces of control I held over my body, I caught her hand and tugged her after me as I headed back to the huge living room with its double height ceiling and exposed beams overhead.

I spun her beneath my arm like we were dancing and she laughed before punching me in the chest, right over the ace of spades tattoo where my heart should have been.

"I still hate you," she added in case I hadn't caught onto that.

"Well hate me and try on clothes," I suggested, pointing at the mountain of bags that were awaiting her attention. I honestly had no idea how she'd managed to order so much in the short time I'd given her access to my laptop, but she had and I was in the mood for a fashion show. "I'll order the pizza."

"Make sure mine has cheese on it," she warned. "One time, Greasy Gavin down by the bridge gave me pizza but there was no cheese on it. Or tomato sauce. And it was really just the old sole of a shoe. Very disappointing."

I snorted a laugh, not really knowing if that was a joke or not as she turned away and dove on the bags, whipping clothes out one after another and heaping them up on the end of the couch.

I had to turn away from her to concentrate on ordering the food and I did it quickly, feeling the smile on my face and wanting to get back to it. Something about her just made me smile. I mean, I smiled a whole hell of a lot because I had that unhinged psycho thing going for me, but with her it felt different on my face. More like it really was my face and not a mask. I liked that.

I hung up on the pizza fella but just as I was about to face her again, a prickle along the back of my neck warned me to move my arse.

I wasn't fast enough though and she flung the neon swimsuit over my head, hooking it around my neck as she yanked it back, creating a garrotte out of the damn thing to choke me with. She leapt up onto my back with a battle cry and let her weight do the work of choking me out as she hung from the swimsuit.

I whipped around in a circle but she clung onto me with a wild laugh, her thighs clasped tight around my waist as she locked her ankles together in front of me to stop me from dislodging her.

I ran backwards at the wall, crushing her between me and it but she only laughed louder, holding on tight. I could have done it again, harder, cracked her pretty skull against it real good, but I didn't wanna do that. So instead, I made my way to the huge grey couch and threw myself down onto it, squashing her beneath me.

An oomph escaped her as my weight drove the air from her lungs and I smiled wider as I reached for the swimsuit she'd chosen to strangle me with. Not a great choice because it was stretchy which meant that with a bit of force, I was able to rip it from my neck and back over my head again.

I sucked in a breath as I flipped over on top of her, pinning her to the couch beneath me and smirking as I grabbed her throat again, letting her see that I could end her if I wanted to.

"Now what?" I asked, my voice rough as I panted from the game, my cock hard between her thighs either from the choking, or her, or both. Wasn't gonna think about it.

"Now I put you on your ass," she growled, her eyes alight with fire.

Before I could laugh at that suggestion, she bucked her hips hard and threw her weight to the left, catching me off guard and making me fall from the couch.

I caught a handful of her arse as I fell though, tugging her over with me and somehow I ended up beneath her as she straddled me on the carpet in front of the fire.

She was wearing another swimsuit, this one orange with #Psycho printed across it and her tits pushed up until they seemed in danger of spilling out of the damn thing.

I still had my hand around her throat, but she made a gun with her fingers and pressed it to my temple.

"You wouldn't," I growled and the smile she gave me was pure evil. It made my heart race and my dick ache and a thousand bad thoughts flit through my mind before I could stop them.

"Oh, I would." She jerked her fingers against the side of my head and made the sound of a gun firing.

I let my hand fall from her throat as I jerked violently and played dead for her, closing my eyes.

Silence fell and I expected her to get up but she didn't, instead she shifted in my lap, leaning down over me until I could taste her breath on my lips and my heart was pounding with the feeling of her body on top of mine.

I hadn't felt like this for any woman in so long that I wasn't certain what to do with it, though my body was certainly getting a few ideas and as she shifted her hips again, the gasp that escaped her let me know she'd figured that out too.

"Oh," she breathed sadly, her hand landing on my chest like she wanted to make sure my heart was still beating.

"What is it?" I asked, opening my eyes and finding myself trapped in a tiny little world which only contained the two of us as a curtain of black hair fell all around us, keeping everyone else out. I quite liked it in that little world and I wondered if there was any chance we could stay.

"I just realised, I don't think I want your brains to get splattered," she said seriously and I arched a brow at her.

"Good thing you forgot to load yer gun then," I pointed out and she nodded, sitting upright again and looking down at me as her hand trailed down to my waistband and lingered there.

"I can't believe I killed you," she said, grinning and looking way too pleased with herself over it.

I rolled my eyes, plucking the swimsuit she'd used as a garrotte from her hand and shaking my head at it. "You absolutely didn't," I assured her. "This was a terrible fuckin' choice. You need something with no give in it, not something stretchy. And in the time it took ya to pull that gun, I coulda stabbed you sixteen different ways."

Her face fell into a pout and I slapped her arse to make her look at me again.

"But you did pretty good," I admitted, instantly regretting it as she beamed, looking like she thought that made her a professional hitwoman. "For a beginner," I added. "With no training and minimal talent."

"What do your tattoos mean?" she asked, ignoring my backtracking and still grinning like the cat who'd got the cream.

"Nothing," I replied. "Just nonsense and bullshit like the things that go on in my mind."

"What about that one then?" she asked, pointing at Ava's name on my arm and I stilled.

What the fuck are you doing laying here with some young girl in your lap like a fucking lech? She's more than ten years younger than you and you've got her locked up in your house as your prisoner. Are you just like those men who stole your wife now then?

I gripped Spider's hips and tossed her off of me, dumping her up on the couch before springing to my feet and striding away from her.

"The pizza's here," I muttered, ignoring her as she stared after me, those full lips parted and something painful in her gaze. "Try some more of yer clothes on and pick something to wear out tonight. I've got a job on and I think it's a good opportunity for us to figure out if you really do have any potential or not."

"I do," she growled.

"We'll see," I replied without looking back at her. "But if not, I guess I'll be dumping two corpses tonight."

A shoe hit me in the back of the head as I strode away and I cursed her but I didn't look back.

I checked the feed from the cameras then unlocked the front door to make sure no lurkers were lurking and stepped outside, taking out a smoke and lighting it up.

"Fucking temptress won't be tempting me," I muttered to myself as I drew in a lungful of nicotine and felt the sting of the cold air against my bare chest.

I plucked the cigarette from my lips as I held the smoke in my lungs and I frowned down at the cherry. Why now? Why after all these years was I getting drawn down this path? I thought I'd made my choice on this, turned my back on all that.

I tipped my head back and looked up at the stars as I released the cancerous breath, hunting out Ava up there and coming up blank. She was slipping away from me. Had been for a long damn time. I just hadn't wanted to admit it. Because if that was true then I was failing her all over again.

Looking back, I wondered why I'd ever even married her, why I'd pursued her at all. She'd been at high school with me and she'd just been so... pure. The opposite of me. And better than that, when I managed to get her to myself, she'd never even seemed afraid of me. Curious, sure, but not afraid. And at the time I'd been so taken with the idea of someone seeing something in me other than the monster beneath my skin that I'd wanted to be that man for her. At least some of the time. When I was with her.

I don't think she'd ever really known the full truth of what I was or what I did for my family. She wasn't a fool, she knew I wasn't getting my money legally and she understood the concept of me being a part of the mob. But her family thought I was a mechanic, and I was pretty sure she'd convinced herself of that lie too most of the time. I let her because...well fuck knew why really. I guessed I just got caught up in the idea of being that man even though looking back I couldn't think of anything worse than being a law-abiding citizen.

I was just a liar playing house and we both knew it, but we were happy in our deception. Weren't we?

Certainly until Tom Nelson came to our suburban paradise and stole her away to the darkness of my reality. No doubt she died knowing exactly who I was. And that was entirely on me.

I wasn't sure how long I stood there chain smoking until the pizza guy showed up and I watched him drop the stack of pizza boxes on the porch a few feet from me in silence.

He seemed to realise he was best not to mix it with me tonight and he murmured you're welcome in response to my stony silence before hightailing it back to his car and speeding away. *Smart lad.*

I wasn't worried about my little spider crawling out of the house because it was locked up tighter than an ant's arsehole tonight. The door beside me was the only one likely to be breached and that was only because I'd left it unlocked for myself. The windows were all bulletproof and the locks infallible thanks to the paranoid previous owner. Shame he'd been dumb enough to leave that window open while he was sleeping in the summer heat really, if not I'd have been hard pressed to get in here.

My phone buzzed in my pocket and I tugged it out, glancing down at the message on the screen.

Gobshite:

It's definitely the right guy this time. I followed him home and had to sneak over some massive wall with razor wire on top of it, but it's him for sure. He even has a girl in there with him – one who didn't look like she wanted to be there.

Niall:

Pictures

I wasn't gonna let my useless nephew send me to the wrong house again. It mighta worked out okay because the last one was a wife killer, but I didn't like to go off half cocked. Fully cocked was fine, as was uncocked, but if I was gonna go to the trouble of making some kind of plan then it had better be based off of good information.

My screen illuminated with several dark photographs taken through a window. There was the bastard I'd been hunting, the one who'd gotten drunk and bragged to his fancy friends that he was part of a snooty club where he could go and do anything he liked, legal or otherwise, and fuck any woman he wanted. Lucky for me, the O'Briens had ears all over this city and I'd put the word out for info on anyone mentioning Royaume D'élite.

Turns out secret clubs don't stay secret if you let loud mouthed arseholes in. Wasn't surprising really because everyone knew the only way you could share a secret and still keep it was to kill the bastard you told it to. But I guessed if you were in the business of running illegal clubs for rich fuckers you couldn't very well kill every member after initiation.

The third picture he sent showed the girl, tied up and gagged, sitting in the corner of a room with fear biting into her expression.

Something cold and dark slithered into my veins, waking me up and filling me with a toxic kind of poison that had me aching for this bastard's death even more than I usually hungered for bloodshed.

Niall:
Send me the location and fuck off outa there.
Make sure you find yourself busy tonight.

Shane would know that meant he needed to be out in public this evening which, thanks to lockdown, really just meant getting himself caught on CCTV shopping for groceries, though I had to wonder how tight an alibi would hold up when you wore a mask in all the footage. Ah well, if the little gobshite served a few years on account of me killin' this fella then he wouldn't be the first fucker in my family to take a fall for the greater good.

I stubbed my cigarette out and grabbed the pizzas as I headed back into the house, finding Spider right where I'd left her, still dressed in the #Psycho swimsuit but with the addition of a pair of chunky black combat boots that laced right up to her knees. She'd clearly bought herself some makeup too and she'd painted her lips Barbie pink.

I bit my tongue as my gaze raked over her, hooking for several long moments on the way her tits were pushed up in that thing and almost not noticing as she shifted her arm out from behind her back to reveal the big arse kitchen knife she was holding.

She shrieked as she launched herself at me and I ducked aside, dropping the stack of pizzas and barely missing the swing of that knife. I grabbed one of the huge cushions that made up the back portion of the couch and used it as a shield as she stabbed at me again, the knife sinking into the fabric before she tore it free.

She kept coming, stabbing and stabbing and cursing me between each swing of the knife until I was laughing and my blood was thrumming through my veins and I was genuinely concerned she might land a hit on me.

The next time she stabbed the cushion, she used so much force that the blade poked through on my side of it and I grabbed hold of it in my fist, swinging my leg around beneath hers and taking her down.

The blade cut into my hand as I kept hold of it, but she lost her grip on it as I refused to let go and by the time she landed flat on her back, I ripped it from the cushion and threw it across the room. The point slammed into the mantlepiece and stuck there and I dropped down to kneel over my girl with a grin.

"We're going out," I said, ignoring the punch she threw into my side.

I looked down at all of that black hair spilling out around her and wondered why I'd wanted to cut it off. Then I wondered where I'd left my scissors and considered cutting it off now to find out. Then I remembered we had something more important to be doing.

"Where are we going?" she demanded, giving up and reaching for the half open pizza boxes beside us.

I snagged a slice and held it to her lips as my smile widened.

"I just got a tip on a rapist I wanna have a few words with," I told her. "And I think I'd like to assess your work in the field."

Her eyes lit up excitedly and she leaned forward to take a bite from the pizza, but I snatched it away again faster and stuffed the whole lot into my mouth.

I tasted blood as I chewed and remembered I'd cut my hand on the damn knife.

"When are we going? And where? And how are we going to kill him? Will you let me do it this time? Can I cut his balls off? Can I stab him in the toes? Should I do something with my hair before I go? Can I pick my own killing blade? Do you think-"

"It's cold out, Spider," I interrupted her. "So mostly you just need to get dressed right for that."

She grinned at me as she raced off to start looking through the heap of clothes again.

I headed into the kitchen, poured a measure of vodka over my hand, drank a shot of the vodka for myself, remembered I fuckin' hated vodka and spat that shit back out, then taped the cut on my palm. It wasn't all that deep, but I didn't wanna be dripping DNA all over the shop. I was professional like that.

I grabbed the keys to my BMW and whistled for Spider as I strode to the door and set the alarm. Mateo would be nice and cosy down in the basement while we were gone and no one would be getting in here to hear him scream.

Spider came hurrying along with three of the pizza boxes in her arms and a black leather jacket on over her skimpy outfit. Her legs were still bare and as I held the door for her, she strutted out in her knee-high boots with her arse cheeks hanging out the bottom of the orange swimsuit.

I was so caught up watching her arse bounce that I almost forgot to grab the masks from the unit beside the door. I swiped a hand down my face to try and refocus my mind as I pulled my own leather jacket on then locked up.

I followed her to the car which was parked up beside my others and moved to open her door for her like a real gent. She looked up at me, a little closer to my height thanks to the chunky soles on her boots and hesitated with the door open.

"You have such nice eyes," she said, making me arch a brow. "Like the greenest green I've ever seen. I think looking into them while I died wouldn't be so bad. You give people a death to remember with those eyes."

"Well I could say the same for you," I replied, looking at her electric blues and wondering if they were so bright because she was so full of energy that it literally sparked within her. "If you were any good at killing that is."

I placed a hand on top of her head and exerted pressure to make her get in the car while she glared venom at me and I laughed.

I vaulted the hood and slid across it before opening my own door and getting in.

It was damn cold and the bottom half of her body was hardly dressed so I flicked the heated seats on the moment I started the engine and we took off down the drive into the dark.

Spider flipped open the lid on the first box of pizza and started demolishing it while I drove, heading to the location Shane the Gobshite had forwarded to me. He'd be holding that title forever as far as I was concerned unless he did something damn heroic to alter my opinion of him.

I reached out to snag a slice but she slapped my hand, growling like an animal. "Concentrate on driving. We don't wanna end up in the lake again," she said and I huffed, my stomach rumbling.

But before I could tell her off for telling me how to drive me own damn car, she lifted a slice of pizza to my lips and fed it to me.

I grinned as I ate. At her. At myself. At the fact that we were going killing tonight and we were hunting my favourite kind of prey. It was damn close to perfect.

"Sweet mother of the moon," Spider gasped suddenly, wriggling in her chair and looking down in alarm.

"What?" I asked.

"My chair has gone all hot and weird and is heating my ass up like it's got ideas about fucking it! It feels like I've pissed my damn self, but I'm not wet. *I'm not wet, Niall!*"

"It's just the heated seats," I explained with a laugh. "I can turn it off if you don't-"

She slapped my hand again to stop me from touching the button that controlled her seat and I wondered why I kept letting her do shit like that to me. Anyone else would be deader than dead for it, but she kept getting a free pass. It was damn strange.

"I didn't say I didn't like it," she growled, shoving another slice of pizza into my mouth to stop me from replying before switching on the radio and cranking it up.

Pink (Freak) by Elliot Lee poured out of the speakers and the two of us sang along to it between bites of pizza while we drove on into the night. She got like eighty percent of the words wrong, but I liked hers better anyway so I was okay with that.

By the time we pulled up along the road from the dead man's house, there were empty pizza boxes tossed in the back seat and Spider was complaining about me not bringing anything to drink while I rolled my eyes at her.

Damn woman expected table service in a moving vehicle or something and I wasn't rising to her nonsense.

I kept the doors locked as we sat in the dark and I pulled the two masks I'd grabbed for us from the pocket in my door, holding them out for her.

"Lady's choice, pink or blue?" I asked.

"They look black and boring to me," she said, frowning as she looked at them and I flicked the little switches to light them up. Every other kid had been wearing the damn things for Halloween last year and I'd stolen a few of them to keep for special occasions. The kids I took them from had been crying and calling me a real life monster, but they were like eight and I was pretty sure that was too old for trick or treating. They were based off of the masks in those Purge movies and had neon lights which made up crosses for eyes and a mouth that looked all stitched up.

"Oooooh." She touched the blue one, then the pink, then the blue, then the pink, then decided on the blue and put it on. "How do I look?" she asked and my gaze instantly moved between the freak show mask and her tits in that swimsuit. *For fuck's sake.*

"I'm almost temped to let you kill me," I told her and she giggled like a blushing school girl. "Switch the lights off for now though. We don't want him knowing we're here until he's already a dead man."

"If he's a dead man then why do we need the masks?" she asked.

"Two reasons. One - he probably has CCTV seeing as he has razor wire topping his walls. And the other is that there's a girl in there who we won't be killing, so we need to hide our faces from her."

"Okay," she agreed, sounding excited.

"On another note." I took the little remote which partnered her collar from my pocket and waved it at her. "Don't try and run off on me. Also, don't attack me while we're killin' this fella. I'll only warn you about that once because if I'm already in the bloodlust then I can't promise I-"

"You won't kill me, silly," she replied, opening her door and hopping out. "You like me too damn much."

I shook my head as I got out too, meeting her by the trunk and deciding not to get into a debate over the likelihood of me ending her life as I opened up the bag of tools I kept in there and grabbed some wire cutters out.

Spider reached for the bag of killing instruments next and I caught her wrist, making her look at me.

"I mean it. No trying to murder me until he's dead," I said, offering her a hand to shake.

She pursed her lips then nodded once, placing her palm in mine and I squeezed it good, wondering if she was a woman of her word or not. If she wasn't then she might end up dead tonight and I didn't want that.

She plucked a sharp little knife from the bag and slipped it into her boot. I grabbed a garrotte, a wrench and a potato peeler because why the hell not?

I locked the car and the two of us slipped into the trees as we began to circle the dead man's property.

We finally closed in on the high wall Shane had warned me about and I looked up at the curls of razor wire that topped it. The thing was about nine foot high so even I couldn't reach up and cut the damn stuff from down here. I started looking around for a tree or something I could use to get close enough to cut the wire, but Spider caught my wrist.

"I can climb on your shoulders and do it," she breathed, her eyes wild with excitement and I had to bite my tongue on another smile. The girl made me smile too damn much and I didn't need her thinking I was soft on her. I could kill her in a heartbeat and she'd better not forget it.

"Alright," I agreed, handing her the wire cutters. "Just be careful, that stuff is a right moody bastard."

"Got it." She leapt at me before I got a chance to prepare myself and I caught her by the arse as she scrambled up my body, her tits thrusting into my face before she pressed her hands down on my head then managed to get a boot onto my shoulder.

I moved close enough to the wall for her to brace herself against it as she pushed upright to stand on my shoulders, then I gripped her calves over her boots to make sure she didn't fall.

"Oh you twatting bitch," she cursed as the sound of the wire cutters filled the air. "You utter fucking tit whore."

"What's goin' on?" I hissed but she didn't reply and a moment later a chunk of razor wire sailed down to the ground beside me.

She started scrambling up onto the wall and I put my hand beneath the sole of her boot, shoving to help her tiny self make it.

Once she was up, she leaned back to look down at me curiously. "Now what, Hellfire?"

Instead of answering, I just backed up then took a running jump at the wall. My foot slipped against the bricks, but my fingers managed to curl around the top of it then I was heaving myself up to perch on the wall beside her.

"Wow," she breathed. "It's beautiful tonight."

I glanced at her and found her head tilted back to look up at the moon while she sucked on her finger, her features gilded in silver as the wind blew her ebony hair out behind her.

My gaze skimmed over her hungrily before I tore my eyes away again and looked out towards the huge house in the middle of the grounds ahead of us.

I dropped down from the wall silently then turned back to catch my little psycho when she followed. She dropped right into my arms, her fingers biting into my shoulders and her eyes widening as she looked at me.

"You caught me," she breathed like she hadn't really been expecting me to.

"You're under my watch now, Spider," I replied. "So you don't have to worry about falling. I got you."

Her eyes widened and she shook her head in refusal. "No. Don't say that. Don't lie to me and tell me I can trust you. I've heard that lie too many times in my life."

For a moment, true vulnerability flared in her eyes and I drew her closer, pressing my forehead to hers and breathing her air.

"You're mine now, little psycho," I growled. "And you can trust me to keep to my word. If I tell ya I won't let you fall then I won't. I'm not promising you the world or lying about my character - I know full well I'm a mean bastard with a violent streak so wild that no one is ever really safe around me. I'm just telling you, I won't let you fall."

She looked at me for the longest moment then reached out and trailed her fingers up the side of my jaw and into my hair before gripping the mask I still had perched on top of my head.

"You're so sad," she breathed so quietly that it was hard for me to even hear her, but we were so damn close that it was impossible not to.

"So are you," I replied and she nodded slowly.

"Evil has so many faces," she murmured, tugging on my mask so that it slid down to conceal my features. "But I think I like yours the best."

"Let's put that evil to good use then," I growled, dropping her down onto her feet and instantly missing the heat of her body against mine.

I reached out to pull her mask down to conceal her face too and she nodded then followed me as I took off towards the house.

We crossed the shadowy grounds, jogging over the grass silently before I led my little trainee around the back of the house. We paused beside the back door and I laid out the bones of the plan I had forming in my mind as simply as I could put it. She seemed excited about that, so I reached out to try the door and grinned as it swung open.

Fun fact - a shit ton of people leave their back door unlocked when they're at home because of cats or dogs or just because they went for a little wander or sat outside for a bit earlier on in the day. They just forgot all about the fact that locked doors were what kept the psychos out. They stopped nasty fuckers like me from just strolling on into their house with murderous intentions. And now look.

I mean yeah, I woulda found a way in somehow anyway, but if he'd locked his damn door maybe I'd have given myself away trying to bust in and he mighta had the chance to run, hide, call the cops, puke in fear - anything really. But no, door open, easy access and here I was, ready to kill.

A muffled sob came from somewhere upstairs and I glanced that way, wondering if he was with the girl up there or not. But orange light spilled from beneath the doorway of a room ahead of us and the sounds of a TV caught my ear just as a man laughed loudly.

I glanced back at Spider and she cocked her head, reaching up to switch on the lights on her mask so that all I could see in the dim corridor was the neon blue crosses over her eyes and stitched lines of a mouth.

I gave in to the lady's request and switched the lights of my own mask on too, my vision instantly filled with a pink glow.

I stepped forward and pulled the door open silently, creeping into the huge lounge with her on my heels. The place looked like a rich guy had puked on it. Everything was dark wood and deep green and red, heavy furniture and a roaring fire alongside one Mr Lionel Barnes who had his back to us as he laughed along to some shit on the TV.

I crept up behind him silently, getting real close as Spider waited by the door, her finger hovering over the light switch.

I took the garrotte from my pocket, holding it in one hand as I came to stand right behind him in his armchair.

I lingered there a moment, loving that feeling right before the pounce when my victim didn't even know I was there yet, and I held more power than a god. Life and death hung in the balance, all dependant on me. And sure, I chose death like ninety-nine percent of the time. And the other one percent too. But still, it was within my power to grant life instead if the notion ever took me.

I reached out slowly and snagged the TV remote from the arm of the chair by his elbow, still not raising any suspicions from him as he continued to chuckle at his show.

He was a big man, well into his sixties at a guess, his hair a dark grey which was most of what I could tell about him from my vantage point, though I knew he had an ugly pug of a mug from my investigations into him.

I looked back to Spider and tossed her the remote. She caught it neatly and I swear that even though I couldn't see her face beneath that mask, I could tell she was grinning from ear to ear.

I held the garrotte ready between my hands, the wire thin and wicked, utterly unbreakable, already sporting two deaths to her name - which was Josephine.

I watched my prey hungrily, waiting, my heart racing at the thrill of this as Spider took her sweet arse time.

Then all of a sudden, she flicked the TV off and the lights out in one move and Lionel looked around in confusion as he was plunged into darkness. I'd always wanted to kill a Lionel. There was something about that name which just screamed evil overlord to me, and I felt it was best to rid the population of them just in case they ever tried to rise up and rule the world like some kind of megalomaniac dragon king.

He spotted Spider's glowing blue mask first, sucking in air through his teeth as he murmured, "What the-" before tipping his head back and looking right at me.

"Boo," I said, throwing the garrotte around his neck and cutting off his scream before it could begin.

He kicked and thrashed in his armchair as my biceps flexed and I squeezed the life outa him. It felt so good, so fucking good. Adrenaline was singing in my veins and this sense of pure euphoria was lighting me up from the inside out as I heard the echo of Ava's screams of encouragement, begging me to make him suffer, make him pay.

I forced myself to relax my hold on the garrotte before it could end too quickly, needing to question him about that club for Kyan's sake like I'd promised. But Spider had circled the room and as she looked down at the fucker before me, she snarled viciously.

"You," she spat as Lionel gasped and spluttered, clutching at the wire which I still held around his neck, keeping my hold tight enough to stop him from escaping me while not enough to kill him just yet.

"You know him?" I asked in surprise and she nodded, pushing her mask up onto her head and narrowing her eyes.

"He was one of the men who tried to buy me from that place before I went to the death game," she hissed menacingly and hot tar ran through my veins as she admitted that. "I memorised their faces. Every one of the bidders I could see."

My grip on the garrotte tightened as I had to battle against the urge to just fucking finish this, to lose my shit and show him what a real monster could do to him. Teach him what kind of death his crimes would earn him. No one touched my spider. *No one.*

Before I'd even finished mentally calming myself down, Spider had launched herself at the motherfucker, landing in his lap and punching him over and over and over again, hitting any piece of him that she could get close to as she went full freak on his arse.

He thrashed and kicked, the chair bucking wildly and almost toppling over, and I was forced to tighten my hold on the garrotte to try and keep him under control.

"Spider," I snarled, trying to rein her in even though I could see she'd fucking lost it. She was in that place beyond reason or sense or anything at all other than the fury of bloodlust. "Hold off a minute," I growled as she went full savage on the arsehole. "I need to ask him-"

Lionel somehow managed to get a solid punch in, landing it straight against Spider's jaw and knocking her flying to the ground.

I saw red, releasing my hold on the garrotte and slamming my own fist into the side of his fucking head. Lionel threw himself out of the chair, scrambling away from me and glaring down at Spider as she bared her teeth at him.

He made it to the bookshelf beside the fire and whirled around with a pistol in his hand, clutching at his neck which now sported a bloody line from Josephine, shifting the aim of the gun between me and Spider before settling on me again.

"Stay on your knees, whore," he warned her, pointing a trembling finger at her. "Where you belong."

Spider screamed a curse as she ripped the knife from inside her boot and lunged at him anyway.

He swung the pistol towards her and panic surged through me as I grabbed the armchair, heaving it up and throwing it at him with all my strength.

The thing hit him, the gun went off and I ran straight at him, leaping over the armchair as it crashed to the ground and ripping the pistol from his grip before he could fire it again. I threw it away with a savage snarl, not wanting a weapon to make it that fucking easy as I locked my hands around his neck and squeezed tight. It was better this way. I'd be able to feel the final thump of his pulse against my hand and know the precise moment I ended him.

Something knocked against my thigh and I looked down just as Spider scrambled out from beneath the armchair and stabbed him in the groin, making his face contort in agony, but my grip on his throat wouldn't let a sound out.

"How do you like me on my knees now?" she snarled savagely and I loosened my hold just to hear him scream.

My little psycho wasn't done there though. She ripped his belt open, yanked his pants down and before I knew what the hell she was thinking, she'd cut his fucking dick off - balls and all - and was throwing them in the fire.

"Does that feel as good for you as it does for me, baby?" she purred, laughing wildly as Lionel screamed in horror and I shoved him away from me, grabbing the armchair and righting it so that it was looking right into the fire. Then I threw Lionel down into it to watch the show as blood pissed all over the carpet from his groin and Spider just laughed and fucking laughed.

It was a wicked sound, full of sin and temptation and I reached down to heave her up to her feet, grasping her chin so that I could check the bruise she'd gotten from that punch.

"You didn't follow the plan," I growled roughly, my gaze roaming down to her full lips as I drank in sight of the blood which was speckled across her skin.

"There wasn't a plan apart from me turning out the lights," she replied defiantly. "Besides, he deserved it."

Lionel was still sobbing and screaming beside us while he watched his manhood burn and I was vaguely aware that I was supposed to be asking him something, but I was too caught up in the sight of this temptress before me to remember what it was.

"Admit it," she said, her voice low and enticing. "I did good."

I dropped my hand to grasp her throat, tipping her chin up and taking in the shadow of that bruise, anger filling me as the sound of Ava's screams drowned out all other thoughts. I was left looking at her bloody corpse again, her torn clothes, the accusing look in her dead eyes.

My fault. I brought her into my dark world even when I tried to convince myself I was keeping her out. And now I was doing it all over again, putting another girl in danger and risking her around scum like the piece of shit who was currently watching his cock burn up to a crisp.

"He laid his hands on you," I snarled, the anger in me building and building until it was blinding me and I didn't know what the fuck to do with it or where to turn it.

"Yeah, and I cut his little cock off for it," she replied defiantly.

The bruise on her face was glaring at me with even more force than she was and I shoved her away from me, turning back to Lionel and realising he'd stopped sobbing.

There was a huge puddle of blood coating the floor all around him and it only took me one look to see that he was dead. Bled out or taken by the shock, I wasn't entirely certain which. And that left me with nowhere to aim my rage or seek payment for the mark on her fucking face aside from turning it back on myself.

"Look what you did!" I yelled at her. "I had questions for that fucker and now he can't answer them!"

"What questions?"

"Important questions!" I shouted. "Ones I promised I'd ask him."

"Well maybe you should have run that by me before I killed him." She smiled widely, like she was proud of that and I lunged at her, snatching her knife from her fingers and pressing it to her throat as I drove her up against the wall.

"You're a fuckin' liability," I growled. "You fucked this up. I knew you were no damn good at this."

I punched the wall beside her head and she didn't even fucking flinch as I knocked a hole into the drywall, fury pouring from her in waves.

"Are you fucking kidding me? We came here to kill that asshole. I killed him! Job done. And I did a damn good job too!"

I shook my head, striding away from her and out of the room, too goddamn angry to even look at her as my veins sung with unspent energy and I ached for another mark to finish.

I jogged up the stairs, barking a command at her to follow me as I hunted for the girl who was being held here somewhere.

The third door I tried was locked and I kicked it down, finding a terrified girl crouched in the corner with her hands over her head. She was wearing skimpy underwear and looked fuckin' freezing so I took my coat off and tossed it to her.

"Come on," I growled. "I can take you somewhere safe or you can run for the hills. Either way, it's best you get the fuck outa here."

She gave me wide, terrified eyes, and I felt a little bad about the mask, though not enough to show her my face. I didn't get the chance to hear her reply because something huge and heavy smashed over the back of my head before she could get a word out.

I cursed as I hit the floor, the shards of shattered vase falling all around me and my vision swimming with dizziness for a moment as I spotted Spider grabbing the girl's hand and tugging her out of the room. Thankfully she'd pulled her own mask back down too, but aside from that I was fuming about everything she was doing.

"Mother fucking son of a bitch arse eater." I shoved my way back to my feet and stumbled down the stairs after them.

Spider shouted at the girl to run as they made it outside and I followed them at a steady pace, stalking out onto the grass and following them as they raced down the drive towards the road.

I took the remote from my pocket and waited until Spider looked back over her shoulder at me, laughing like a maniac and flipping me off, before slamming my thumb down on the button. I watched her drop like a sack of shit, cursing me out as she fell twitching to the ground, the shock immobilising her while I closed in on the two of them.

The other girl had fallen to her knees and seemed to be praying in what I was going to guess was Polish, but I wasn't great at languages so I couldn't be certain.

I scooped my little psycho up off of the ground and tossed her over my shoulder while she mumbled threats about setting the Devil on me.

I slapped her arse to tell her off, not sure if I'd forgotten she was only wearing that little swimsuit or whether that was what had tempted me to do it, but as a breathy moan escaped her, my blood heated for a whole different reason to rage.

I beckoned for the other girl to follow us as I headed for the gate, not really caring one way or another if she did. She could run from here if that was what she preferred, but she'd be better off letting me drop her to Marlene's.

I led the way out of the gate, making sure me and Spider still had our faces covered by the masks once again in case of cameras and we were soon back to my car.

I dropped Spider on the hood, shocking her with the collar again as she tried to run and swallowing thickly as she fell back against the car and moaned lustily once more.

I opened the car door and quickly grabbed the little notebook Marlene had given me from the glovebox, flipping through it until I found the page headed with the Polish flag and pointing at it for the other girl to read.

She frowned as she accepted it but then flipped the pages, stopping on the one written in Romanian and I shrugged. I knew I was shit with languages.

Her eyes widened as she read over the note from Marlene that offered her a place to stay and explained I wasn't as terrifying as I looked - utterly incorrect but the girl could at least be sure I wouldn't hurt her like the men who'd had her before now.

I couldn't say I'd rescued a ton of girls like her, but it was enough for me to have this system for it. What could I say? I had a type when it came to the men I liked to kill, and rapists had victims. If the Castillo Cartel ever realised how many of their men and clients I'd killed for sport, they'd probably start a war with the O'Briens. But I found it hard to give a shit about that.

The girl glanced at me nervously, but I wasn't surprised when she slipped into the back of the car, deciding to take a chance on me continuing to help her. I'd drop her at Marlene's on the way home and she'd look after her from there. I certainly wasn't equipped to do it.

Spider was leaning back on her elbows, still sprawled on the hood of my car as I returned to her and it was damn difficult not to enjoy the sight of her laying there like that, thighs parted, chest heaving.

I licked my lips and tried not to think about it. I had a dead wife to consider as well as the fact that I was eleven years older than her - and a serial killer. Not exactly a catch. Not that I wanted her to think I was.

"Admit it," she demanded and I couldn't help but move closer, stepping between her thighs and leaning down to place my hands on the hood either side of her.

"Admit what?" I asked in a dangerous tone. I was pretty certain I was going to have to find another victim tonight or I'd likely kill Mateo when I got home, and I wasn't done trying to coax his secrets from his tongue yet.

"I killed that guy good. Better than you were gonna do with that dumb wire." She lifted her chin defiantly but that just put her mouth in line with mine as I leaned closer, my body dropping over hers until I was almost resting my weight on top of her.

I leaned in even more, turning my head and pressing my mouth against her ear. She sucked in a breath and the tiny bit of space between us burned with heat and fury. "Like fuck you did," I growled.

Spider shrieked furiously and I laughed as she punched and smacked me, catching her wrists and restraining her with one hand as I pressed my weight down on top of her again. My cock was very much making itself known between her thighs, but I wasn't going to bring him into the conversation, so I just wrapped my free arm around her back and hauled up with me as I stood.

Her legs locked around my waist and her teeth sank into my neck as her pussy ground against my dick and I growled again as I wrenched the trunk open.

"Naughty girl," I snapped as I tossed her into the trunk and slammed it in her angry little face.

I meant it too, she really was bad. Bad for me, anyway. Because she was the right kind of bad and I'd never said I didn't like it. I wasn't going to be telling her that though, so she could spend the night in the bad girl cage and think about what she'd done.

I refused to consider what other kinds of bad she might be because that was a dangerous thought path which could lead me to spit on the ghosts of my past, and I wouldn't do that. Not even for this wild girl who'd come crashing into my life. Not ever.

BROOKLYN

CHAPTER SIXTEEN

"I can't believe he thinks I'm no good at killing," I lamented as Mateo watched me from across the cage with a furrowed brow. "It's my best quality, Dead Man. But he's a hitman. If he thinks I'm bad at it, that means I must be bad." My eyes watered again but I held back the tears. No, I wasn't gonna cry again. I had stuff and things to prove. I was a strong, independent woman just like Beyonce.

"You must have other good qualities," Mateo said gruffly. It was the first thing he'd said since Niall had shoved me back in here and it must have been a few hours now.

I sniffed, wiping my cheeks and thinking about it. "Well…I can do this." I pretended to thread a hook through the left side of my upper lip then tugged the fake thread, moving my lip up and down in time with it.

Mateo watched then released a low snigger, but it clearly wasn't good enough to be called my best talent.

"There's other things I think I'd be good at too if I got the chance," I hurried on, tossing my fake hook away. "Like water skiing, rollerblading, wearing a fez respectfully *and* coolly, saving animals from bush fires, knitting clothes for cats, eating a pint of ice cream in under fifteen minutes, making

Moscow Mules, riding horses backwards while yodelling, guessing the sex of people's babies before they're born and if they're going to grow up to be assholes, writing books about psychos in a magical prison for Fae who are all ruled by the stars and the zodiac and the lead character would be this badass werewolf girl who wants to break out a hot, tattooed incubus with a pierced dick and-"

"I think you've gotten side-tracked," Mateo interjected.

"Blowjobs!" I blurted. "I'd be fucking great at blowjobs. I've got no gag reflex, see?" I stuck my fingers all the way down my throat as far as I possibly could and Mateo's eyebrows arched.

A low growl left his chest that sent a shiver all the way down to my clit and I slid my fingers out of my throat, not blinking. I was suddenly a deer watched by a lion, and if there was one thing I knew about the animal kingdom, it was that you needed to impersonate the beast trying to catch you if you wanted to escape. Anyway, I wasn't a deer. I was a dark pink leopard with light pink spots.

"Rah!" I shouted and he blinked, so I won. *Would it be weird to offer him a blowjob to prove I'm good at it?* I really needed the confidence boost and his cock hadn't had any attention for a long, long time. Like I was guessing a solid year. But what if I got blowjobbing wrong? Nah, I'd be a natural for sure.

I was suddenly nervous as I looked over at my dead man and I tucked a lock of hair behind my ear, remembering the other thing I was great at. I started crawling over to him on my hands and knees, rocking my hips and sticking my ass in the air seductively. Mateo's jaw ticked as he watched me approaching, his hands curling into tight fists and his knuckles turning white. I wanted to touch him again and that was weird for me. Touching was a hell no from most people, but Dead Man? Oh shit, he gave me tingles on my tingles.

I licked my lips all sexy like, giving him the full leopard experience.

That'd be my assassin name actually. The Luscious Leopard. No, the Pink Pussy. Yeah that was sexy *and* frightening. You wouldn't wanna meet the Pink Pussy down a dark alley. She'd eat up all the dicks in town.

I made a little growl noise as I crawled into his lap and his breaths came heavier as he watched me. My own breaths were quickening too as I tried to ignore the danger crawling out from every corner of this man. It made me quiver and I liked it. I drank in the fear snaking through my body because it made feel alive. This was a bad idea, but all the best ideas were. I just wasn't sure if I was going to end up ripped to pieces for this one.

"I'm gonna rock..." I slid my hand down his naked chest, over his chiselled muscles. "Your." I slid it further, all the way down onto the huge bulge in his pants. "Worm."

I lowered my head and he caught me by the throat. "World," he bit out, squeezing as he forced me to look up at him and my heart ping-ponged around my chest.

"Huh? Are you gonna kill me, Dead Man?" I rasped as his fingers tightened. "Or do you just like to play rough?"

I squeezed his huge cock through his pants, unsure what to do with it but I could totally figure it out. He grunted then pushed me out of his lap, slamming me back against the bars beside us. My pulse went haywire as he pinned me there, his eyes a sea of violence I wanted to dive into.

"Am I not your type?" I asked as I struggled to breathe. "I'm confused, Dead Man. Your dick seems to like me, or is it Niall it likes?"

He snarled, a monster taking up residence in his eyes. *Oh hello, beasty.* I reached up, stroking his hair, running my hand down the back of his neck and petting him.

He released me and I slumped down onto the floor as he hulked over me, caging me there with his giant body.

My gaze flicked down to the huge bulge in his pants again then back up to those savage eyes of his. "I'm getting mixed messages."

"I'm the monster people fear when they go to bed at night," he hissed. "Don't play games with me, or you'll end up dragged into the underworld, mi sol."

Wow, I loved the nickname he'd given me. I wondered what it meant. Probably little beansprout on account of my tininess and my beany legs. But Jack would be waiting a long time for me to grow up into the clouds so he could climb me and go hunting giants.

My heart pounded excitedly, but as Mateo placed his hands either side of me on the concrete, fear tangled with every fibre of my being. He was going to kill me or kiss me. And I wasn't sure which I'd prefer right then. Dying by this man's hands didn't seem such a terrible fate, but kissing him was the most thrilling temptation I'd ever known.

The door banged open and Niall blasted an airhorn as he pounded down the stairs. "Hey!" he barked as he saw Mateo leaning over me, jogging up to the bars and shooting his stun gun directly at Mateo's side. Mateo fell down on me with a roar and the electricity exploded through my body too, making me scream beautifully. It stopped as quickly as it had started and I panted under the weight of his muscles, writhing and moaning as static crackled through my veins.

"Give a girl some warning, baby," I panted and Niall blasted the airhorn again. *Ouchy ears.*

The sound of the cage door being wrenched open reached me then Mateo was hauled away on his chain.

"Let's see if ya have somethin' to say to me today, eh El Burro?" Niall laughed, dragging him into the killing room and I gasped, scrambling to my knees and darting out of the open door. I ran after them, slipping into the room before Niall could slam the door and his eyes snapped onto me as he shoved Mateo down on a table and strapped him in place with the metal cuffs attached to it.

"Get outa here, Spider," he growled in warning.

"No," I said firmly, planting my hands on my hips. "You can't make me."

"I can."

"You can't."

"I can."

"You can't!"

Niall lunged at me and I ran away around to the other side of the table with a squeak. He stalked around it as Mateo fought against his restraints and I kept moving to keep away from him.

"Now listen here, lass, you're trying my patience today," Hellfire growled, pointing at me. "Give me one good reason why I shouldn't just cut your head off."

"Because my neck is nice," I said instantly, lifting my chin so he could see it and Niall assessed it.

"Well alright, I'll give ya that. So then why shouldn't I cut your heart outa your chest and feed it to a guineapig?"

"Because these are perky and you'll ruin them." I pulled up my top, flashing him my bare tits and Niall froze while Mateo fought even harder to get free, glaring at Niall like he wanted to destroy him for staring at my boobs. But they were nice boobs and I never got to show them off to anyone. Janky Lou had paid ten dollars to see them once and I hadn't eaten for two days, so I'd agreed. But I couldn't remember a time when they'd just been appreciated without a value put on them.

Niall stroked his hand over his jaw as he continued to stare then blinked hard and dove over Mateo, grabbing a fistful of my sweater and yanking it down. I screamed, slapping him with both hands around the face, left cheek and right, then I twisted sharply to get my sweater free of his grip and danced away.

"Did you see that, Dead Man? He just tried to rip my boobs off!" I said in horror, clutching my hands to my chest in outrage.

Niall climbed over Mateo, landing in front of me and I ran away again, sprinting to the opposite side of the table once more. This was my super power. I was as fast as a cat with a firework up its butt.

I swung around in a fighting stance, looking back at Niall and his eyes darkened. "Fine, ya wanna watch, Spider?" He strode over to a rack of deadly instruments, grabbing a can of gasoline with a wicked smirk then returned to the table. "Alexa, play Play With Fire by Sam Tinnesz and Yacht Money."

The little woman in the speaker announced she was about to do just that and the song pounded through the room. Niall jumped up onto the table between Mateo's legs, grinning down at him like the Cheshire Cat as he started pouring the gasoline all over him.

Mateo's muscles bunched but he did nothing except glare up at Niall with those dead eyes of his and my heart started racing as I watched transfixed.

"Tell me where the money is, El Burro," Niall demanded but Mateo's lips remained sealed.

I crept closer, drinking in the peril in the air, a slave to its power. The atmosphere between the two of them was full of hate and malice. It was so potent I could taste it on my tongue like powdered chaos.

Niall took a pack of cigarettes out of his back pocket, taking his time to place one in the corner of his mouth then pulling out a silver Zippo with the words *if you can't fix it, burn it* engraved on it. He struck it up and made a meal out of lighting his cigarette and taking a deep drag on it. He tucked the lighter in his back pocket and my heart hammered as I gazed from that cigarette to Mateo, his body glistening with gasoline. His abs were all shiny and perfect and I gasped as Niall casually held his cigarette out to flick hot ash on him.

I ran forward, holding my hands up and catching it in my palms, looking up at Niall as he ran his tongue over his teeth. "Get out, Spider."

"No," I snapped. "You leave him alone. What did he even do to you anyway?"

Niall tucked the cigarette back in the corner of his mouth and arched a brow at me. "He stole some money from some bad people and hid it away like a squirrel with a fat nut."

I gasped, furious at him. "That's it? I've stolen plenty of shit from people. You can't torture him for that otherwise you'll have to torture me for that too."

"He's a job," Niall said with a shrug, drawing in a deep toke on his cigarette before holding it out to tap the ash over Mateo, the cherry looking like it might pop out at any second.

I rushed around to the other side of the table and grabbed the can of gasoline, pouring a healthy measure over myself then diving on top of Mateo, spreading my arms and legs wide as he grunted in my ear.

"If you burn him, you'll have to burn through me first!" I dared and Niall gazed down at me in surprise before roaring a laugh.

"Get outa the way." He tried to move me with his foot, but I wasn't going anywhere.

I wasn't going to let my pretty Dead Man be eaten up in a fire. He didn't deserve it. If he'd been a raper or a kiddie fiddler, I'd have struck the match and warmed my hands on the bonfire. But all he'd done was steal some stupid money. And the only way I'd survived on the streets was by stealing. What if Mateo had been homeless too? Or if he'd needed money for his sick little grandma who liked warm hugs and smelled like cinnamon buns? What then? Was I gonna let her grandson die while she was rocking in a chair somewhere in Mexico, gazing off to the horizon as she wondered where her little Matty had been taken to?

Niall snatched the cigarette from his mouth, flicking it away from us across the room and sneering at me with a world of crazy in his eyes. "Fine. You wanna burn? Then we'll all fucking burn." He grabbed up the gasoline, tore his shirt off and poured the last of it all over himself, flicking his head so it sprayed out from his hair as he laughed wildly.

I fell still as Mateo jerked beneath me, watching Niall in awe, the taste of gasoline and desire rolling over my tongue as my gaze dragged down his body. Between the sight of his colourful ink and defined muscles shining wetly and Mateo's hard body beneath mine, I was a goner. Gone, gone, gone to fantasy land where chaos reigned and they did wild and sinful things to me. I wasn't a virgin there in my mind, I knew what I was doing, and I did it with confidence and sex appeal. But then I remembered I hated this motherfucker in front of me and as he took the lighter from his back pocket while grinning like the Joker, I threw my foot up and kicked him right in the dick.

"Jesus, Joseph and Mary," he wheezed, clutching his junk, the lighter clattering from his hand.

I lunged for it, stealing it from him and diving off the table. He couldn't burn anyone without this. *Mwahahaha!*

I raced out the door and the pounding of heavy footfalls came from behind me, making my adrenaline spike.

"Get back here, you little hellcat," Niall demanded as I raced up the stairs, reaching for the door and twisting the handle. Open. *Yes, yes, yes!*

"Ha!" I laughed, sprinting down the hall and making it to the front door, twisting all the locks.

I yanked on it, swinging it open and racing outside. It was raining, pouring, the heavens falling down on me as I squinted up at the dark grey clouds. I stuck my tongue out to taste it, losing focus for a second and suddenly a huge body took me down into the mud. The lighter went tumbling away across the grass as Niall straddled my back and pushed my face down into the mud, rubbing it in as he placed a hand on the back of my head. Then he tugged me up by my ponytail and I burst out laughing at how stupid I must have looked.

Niall lifted his weight, rolling me over beneath him and I grinned through the mud coating me before throwing my fist straight into his throat.

"You little-" he growled, fighting to grab my wrists as I threw them all over the place to try and stop him. Starfish, angel, round-the-world – he wasn't gonna catch them!

He finally caught them and slammed them down into the mud either side of my head as my breaths came in heaves.

"If I had my pencil you'd be dead," I sighed.

"Pah," he laughed. "I have ya pinned down in the mud with no way out and you still think yer a decent killer?" He ground my hands into the mud and I growled, thrashing to try and prove myself, but I couldn't get away. He leaned closer, his breath hot against my face in comparison to the cold droplets of rain running down my forehead. Before I could set into a panic over being held down like this, he released my wrists and grabbed hold of my cheeks, squeezing to make my lips pucker out.

"Say it with me: *I suck at killing.*" He moved my mouth to those words and I yanked my head out his grip. He smiled mockingly, making my hackles rise.

"Well if I'm so useless, why don't you just kill me then?" I snapped and his smile fell away as he shifted his weight over me. "Go on." I dropped my arms wide into the mud and tilted my chin up to the sky, the rain pouring down on me and making my blood run cold. I was an iguana with a death wish. "I'll be with you in a minute, Satan! Warm up the bed for me, I'm all yours."

Niall reared over me so I had to look him in the eye, his upper lip peeled back like I'd angered him somehow. I stilled as I fell into the deep and captivating depths of his crocodile eyes. Was he going to snap me up bite by bite? I latched onto that green, green colour and let myself drown in it as I waited for the world to end.

"I'm not gonna kill ya," he said. "At least not today."

There was so much sin in those eyes, it would have taken a whole lifetime of confessions to rid himself of it. But I had the feeling he didn't want to. And I didn't want him to either. Because this man's heart was as black as mine and looking at him reminded me I wasn't the only creature of my kind in the world. I may have despised him, but he was my species. My kin. And that bound us in a way I couldn't ignore.

I reached up to track my thumb across his lower lip, a smile pulling at my mouth. "Oh Hellfire, I spent so long thinking I was the only one. It's been so lonely. Are there more like us?"

His brows drew together as understanding flickered in his gaze. "Not many," he said in a gravelly tone, turning his head slightly as he opened his lips and slowly closed his teeth over my thumb, biting until pain kissed me.

"Shame we hate each other," I sighed. "Mateo's my friend though. At least, I think he wants to be. Maybe. I'd make a good friend if someone would have me."

Niall's tongue ran over the pad of my thumb and I stilled, my insides going all squishy as I stared at him.

"I could bite it off," he said around it, not loosening his grip at all.

"You wouldn't!" I tried to tug it free of his mouth, but that only caused me a spike of pain as he held on. "You're as much of a dog as Mateo. Let me go, Hellfire." I smacked his forehead. "Bad boy. *No.*"

His eyes glittered with the game and he released a doggish growl in the back of his throat.

"I'm gonna do it. I'll bandage it up good after."

"Niall!" I shrieked and he reached a hand up to cover my mouth. I turned my head sharply, snatching his thumb into the grip of my teeth too.

"I'm gonna do it if you do it," I said around his big thumb and his eyebrows arched.

"Well…checkmate," he said thoughtfully. "Same time then?"

"Fine," I snarled challengingly.

"One…two…"

"Are we going on three or five?" I asked quickly, my heart beating furiously in anticipation of the coming pain.

"Three," he decided. "I've lost count now, I'll start again. One...two...hang on, do monkeys have thumbs?"

"Of course they do." I rolled my eyes. "And toe thumbs."

"What's a toe thumb?" he asked excitedly.

"Like a finger thumb but on your toes."

"Bullshit," he scoffed.

"They do!" I insisted, the taste of him running over my tongue. God he was scrummy. Like bubblegum that didn't wear out after a couple of chews.

Niall released my thumb from the cage of his teeth and I released his too as he yanked me to my feet, dragging me toward the house. "Come on then, show me. I want proof. I don't believe anythin' unless I see it with me own two eyes."

"Is that why you think I'm a bad killer? Because you haven't seen what you want to see from me?" I asked and he glanced back at me with a frown, his hand tight around my wrist.

"Yeah."

"You didn't even let me kill that guy you brought here for me. You threw him out the window," I growled.

"I knew which way the wind was blowing," he said dismissively.

"Liar," I snapped, thumping him in the back and he laughed as he tugged me along, the two of us trailing mud and water through the house. "You kept stepping in every time-"

"Every time what?" he demanded.

"Every time... he hurt me," I said in realisation and Niall wheeled toward me, bending me backwards over the couch as he got right up in my face.

"Nah, I just gave him a death you couldn't, that's what it was," he said lightly, but his jaw was working and I could see the rage in him. Though I wasn't sure it was really aimed at me.

"Give me another shot," I demanded. "I'll kill the next one so good you'll wish you could get inside my body and possess me. You'll wanna get inside me so bad, Hellfire, it'll make you ache."

His throat bobbed. "What d'ya just say?"

"Just gimme another chance or I'll scream. I'll scream and scream and scream until the whole house falls down," I vowed, throwing my head back to do it then he clapped a hand over my mouth.

"Alright," he growled. "One more chance. But that's all ya get."

He released me and I stood up with a squeal of happiness, throwing myself at him and hugging him tight before I could stop myself. I hadn't hugged someone in a very long time. I mean, I'd hugged that trash can when I was drunk on Crazy Lin's moonshine, but that probably didn't count. Especially as the trashcan hadn't hugged me back. A rat had crawled down my arm at one point, but I was pretty sure it was just using me as a bridge to the ground. There'd been no affection there. Hellfire was somehow up there on the list of people I liked to touch or be touched by. It was just him and Mateo, but two made a list, right? Or did I need three to make it a list? If I added myself, did that count? I liked touching myself after Niall and Mateo had touched me, in the shower, with the soap...

Niall was ramrod still for a moment then he crushed me to him in the fiercest bear hug of my life, my feet lifting off the ground as I squeaked. I melted against his hard body, finding myself all gooey and floaty in his arms. The Devil on his forearm rubbed against me and I wriggled in closer to him still, nuzzling my face into his neck. He smelled like smoke and a life I never knew existed and something sweet like man oil. Was that a thing? Not like the oil of a man, more like oil made to rub on the abs of ripped men. Sugary, manly man oil...mmmmm.

"Right, you can show me them monkey toes when I've finished torturing my donkey." He locked me tight to his side, half carrying me back to the basement as rage spilled into my veins.

"No," I snarled. "Don't you hurt him, Hellfire. Or I'll hurt you."

He snapped the door shut behind us, locking it this time before heading downstairs and planting me down on my feet.

"Stay here," he commanded threateningly then strode off into his killing room. I raced after him, slipping under his arm before he shut the door and for a second he didn't see me as I shot like a shadow to the table where Mateo was still tied down, fighting to break his restraints.

"Jesus, you're fast," Niall said approvingly, eyeing me as I fought with the cuffs. "You'll need a key for those." He walked over to the rack of torture implements and shouted out, "Alexa, play my killing playlist."

Killing Me Softly (Remix) by YBK blared into the room and I struggled with the restraints as Mateo stared at me like I'd lost my mind.

"Stop," he said in a low voice so only I could hear.

"I'm getting you out of here," I promised, fighting with the damn cuffs but they wouldn't come loose.

Niall sung along with the music before casually walking over, threading a bull whip through his fingers. Shit he looked hot. Like come-hither-and-murder-me-all-night-long hot. But no. Dammit, he was a cock waffle. And I wasn't going to just stand here and let this cock waffle hurt my dead man.

Niall smiled down at Mateo with no soul in his eyes. "Where's the money, El Burro?"

Mateo stayed silent, his biceps bulging as he tensed for the first strike. Niall whipped him across his chest and Dead Man hissed through his teeth before he did it again. And again and again. I started backing up, shaking my head. I didn't know what to do. I was helpless to it. My heart started beating too hard as I remembered being this helpless in the past too. Unable to get away while they did those awful things to me. A noise of panic left me as Niall struck him once more and a bundle of tiny knives lodged in my throat.

"Don't!" I cried, panic eating me up from the inside like hungry little snails, slithering and biting and leaving sticky trails against the inside of my flesh. "Stop – don't hurt him. Let him go!"

Niall ignored me, working himself up into a sweat as he whipped Mateo and the first glint of blood broke across his beautiful flesh.

My breaths came in frantic bursts and I could feel the monster in me raise her head and beg for vengeance. I knew her by the stroke of her fur beneath my skin, by the growl in my throat, by the animal stepping into my very soul.

I ran at Niall, diving onto his back and locking my arm around his throat as I wrestled with him. He threw me off and I hit the floor on my ass, starting to kick the backs of his legs. Kicking and kicking until he half buckled forward and was forced to give me his attention.

He twisted around with the whip raised and I threw out my arm, bracing for the strike.

But it didn't come. My mind was sinking down into the quicksand of those dark memories, dragging me into them. The more I fought them, the more they clung onto me. I was the horse in the Never Ending Story, growing sadder and sadder until it was impossible to escape the sludge around me.

"Calm down," Niall snarled, but I wouldn't. I wasn't going to let him hurt Mateo anymore.

I lunged at Niall, wrapping my hand around the whip and tearing it from his hold. I turned it back on him as I scrambled upright, whipping it down across his shoulder.

"Spider, snap out of it," he barked as I struck at him again but he threw out a hand so the whip twisted around it and he yanked on the end.

I didn't let go of the handle and was suddenly tugged into the cage of his arms. All I could sense was the potent deadliness of this man as I started shoving and scratching at him. I was trapped. My mind was consumed by the memories of being snared in the woods, held down, touched, ruined.

"Don't touch me, kill me if you have to, but don't touch me!" I shrieked.

He gripped my hair, forcing me to stop fighting as he crushed me to his body with his other arm.

"Breathe, Spider," he commanded, his eyes dark as he tugged on my hair to make me look up at him. I did, because I was on the verge of a full-blown panic attack. And I didn't wanna be that girl today. The girl who'd broken in the woods, under the eye of the watchful moon.

"What's it like to feel whole?" I breathed as a tear rolled down my cheek.

Niall wiped it away as his mouth pulled down at both corners. And I knew this was the real Hellfire. A sad, sad boy who felt as empty and alone as me.

"I wouldn't know, lass." He released me then walked away, grabbing his stun gun before shooting Mateo so he jerked and fell still. I stared on in surprise as Niall unlocked him from his cuffs and hauled him away through the door.

"Come on," he barked at me. "I ain't got all day."

He took a pistol from the back of his jeans, prodding Mateo in the side as he groaned, slowly coming back to life after the shock as Niall forced him to head toward the bathroom. I raced after them as Niall grabbed a chain and locked Mateo to the bolt on the wall by the shower.

"In," Hellfire barked then grabbed my arm, shoving me in after Mateo and switching the water on. It was freezing cold and I yelped as it soaked my swimsuit further and I was pressed up against Dead Man's muscles in the small space.

Niall casually aimed the gun at us and I looked up at Mateo as blood washed down his chest from the whip marks. *Oh no, so ouchy.*

I reached for the shower tap, turning it to make the water run warm.

"Hey," Niall snapped. "Turn it back to cold."

"No," I growled.

"Yes," he insisted.

"No."

"Yes."

"No!"

"I'll shoot one of El Burro's balls off if you don't," he warned, trying to aim past me to Mateo.

I weaved left and right, covering Dead Man's body with mine as best I could as I protected his balls with my life. Niall stepped into the shower with us, crushing me between the two of them, water pouring down on us as my heart rate increased. There were so many muscles and so much slippery, hard skin against me, it was a literal wet dream.

"Get outa my way, Spider." Niall tried to move me and Mateo took hold of me, trying to push me behind him but I wouldn't go easy, holding onto Niall's arm with a growl.

"Enough of this," Niall growled, reaching for the water and turning it to an icily cold flow then shaking his hair out like a dog. He stepped out of the shower, watching us shiver for a minute before gesturing for us to get out too with the gun. "Go get dressed, little psycho." He pushed me past him and I stumbled out of the bathroom on wet feet, grabbing a towel as I went and nearly falling on my ass.

I stripped out of the swimsuit and dried myself off behind the cupboard door before pulling on some pink army-style sweatpants, a pale yellow tank top and a fluffy white cardigan. I grabbed some socks too, shoving them in my pocket for Ron (first name Later).

I could hear Niall laying into Mateo in the bathroom, calling him all kinds of meanie pants names, and it got me so riled up that I made a decision. Me and my dead man weren't gonna stay here any longer. Niall had almost killed us all and for what? For something Mateo was clearly never gonna tell anyone. And I didn't wanna die here because Niall couldn't control his impulses.

I ran back into the killing room, but the second I got in there, I heard the bathroom door open. I grabbed the nearest thing I could find which happened to be a screwdriver, shoving it into my pocket and slipping out the door back into the basement, my heart beating wildly.

Niall dragged Mateo across the room as I casually floated over to stand by the cage, folding my arms as a thrill ran through me. He hadn't seen me. I was the sneakiest snake there ever was.

Niall shoved Mateo into the cage then looked over at me with his wicked, pretty eyes.

"You're in trouble too. Get over here." Niall beckoned me and I pursed my lips before complying, letting him shove me in after Mateo, locking the door tight and gazing in at me with some twisted thought in his eyes.

"You look like a girl who's seen plenty of demons in this world, Spider," he said in a low voice just for me, jerking his chin at Mateo. "So you're probably smart enough not to go giving one of ya broken pieces to that devil. But here's a reminder not to anyway. Because he'll only hand it back in shards." He turned away from me, his shoulders rolling and inked muscles flexing as he headed over to the killing room, locking it up tight before heading upstairs without another word and the door banged a second later.

I looked over at Mateo as Niall's warning rang in my head, but I pushed it away. Because Mateo was a prisoner here like me. We were on the same side. And I wasn't going to let Hellfire get in my head. I was going to tend to my dead man's wounds because I may have been a monster, but even monsters had a little good in them deep down. Besides, I'd been hurt once and no one had come to my rescue. So I wasn't going to watch as Mateo faced the same fate.

Mateo dropped onto the floor, pressing his back to the bars and a flicker of pain passed through his eyes from the lacerations across his chest. None looked too deep, but they looked ouchy all the same. I poked my bottom lip out, lowering down to the floor and crawling over to him slowly, showing him I meant no harm. *I'm just a harmless little pelican, don't mind me.*

"Poor baby," I sighed, slipping into his lap and settling my weight over him, waiting to see if he'd go all wild man on me. But he didn't.

I reached out, keeping my gaze locked with his as he watched me, his jaw ticking as darkness roiled like a storm in his eyes. They were so very, very dark. Like an eternal tunnel, cutting right to the centre of the earth. I'd like to visit there sometime. It'd be so hot and full of rocks.

"Does it hurt, Dead Man?" I whispered, taking the balled socks from my pocket, pulling them apart and sliding them onto each of my hands.

He slowly shook his head, but I was guessing that was a lie as I reached up and gently dabbed at the lasting blood on his chest with my sock mittens. The water had cleaned out the cuts pretty well but a couple of them were still bleeding a little and I didn't like to see that. Blood should be spilled from cruel, stinky little men. Not beautiful ones who held a city of sin in their eyes.

His jaw tightened as he watched me, a crease forming on his brow that said he was contemplating the whole universe. Or maybe just eenie weenie me.

"I won't let him hurt you again," I promised, pressing down on the deepest part of the whip mark to staunch the blood flow.

"It's you who needs protecting from him, chica loca," he said in that tantalising voice of his.

He leaned closer, breathing me in and a shiver tracked down the length of my spine. I could feel his soul when I was this close to him and it was a wicked, wicked thing. It reached into the depths of my own essence, calling me out and begging for the darkness in me to rise. It wasn't chaotic like Niall's, it was calm and deadly, like a praying mantis waiting for unsuspecting prey. Maybe I was that prey. And maybe I didn't mind that so much.

"I'm not the one he wants to hurt," I said, tilting my head to one side as I studied his hard and striking features. His cheeks were sharp, hollow and lovely, but it was hard to see much more than that beneath his beard.

"Not today maybe, but tomorrow the bastardo could change his mind," he said in a hiss.

"Isn't it silly?" I leaned closer to speak in his ear. "How we're stuck in this cage underground like spiders in a bathtub?"

I walked my fingers along his shoulder like a creepy crawly and his hand shot out, catching my wrist in an iron grip and making my eyes whip back to his. Oooh I really do like the touching thing when it comes to him. It makes my body hum like a harmonica. "Nothing about this is silly, chica loca. You could have died today. Why did you put yourself between me and death?"

"Because…" I dropped my gaze, heat rising in my cheeks as I prepared to be honest. Honesty was so much harder than lying sometimes. It required peeling back a corner of your heart and letting the world peer in.

He caught my chin, tilting my head up, his touch rough and demanding on my flesh. "Because?"

"Because I know what it's like for no one to come and save me," I said, not blinking, the admission making everywhere burn.

His brows lowered and a demon stared back at me from the depths of his eyes which wanted to raze the world to the ground.

"I'm not worth saving," he said gruffly, a grimace forming on his face.

"I think you are," I whispered, reaching up to brush my fingers over his lips.

He snatched my hand away and I felt his cock hardening between my thighs, my hips shifting automatically on top of it and making him growl deeply.

"Oops," I breathed. "You must have been pining for company for so long, Dead Man. I'm no Jessica Rabbit. Guess I'm more of a Bugs Bunny actually. Though he seems kinda tall. What's a small cartoon rabbit who's little? Thumper? Oh no, I'm Thumper. Actually, I bet I can do that foot thing he does."

I moved to slide off of his lap to try it out, but he grabbed my waist and pushed me down onto the ground on my back.

"You wanna try it too?" I asked, my heart doing a great rabbit impression as it bounced all over the place.

Mateo dropped over me, pressing one hand to my chest to hold me down and he must have felt my wild heartbeat beneath his palm because he smiled like a dark monster about to drag me back to its lair. But I was already in his lair. And I had no idea what he was gonna do next. I just wanted him to do it. Or not do it. I wasn't sure. Both possibilities were terrifying. But the miniature psycho in the back of my brain had already started up a loud chant of *do it, do it, do it.*

His large palm dragged down the centre of my body, over my breasts and stomach as I inhaled deeply then sliding right down to my waistband. But he didn't stop, his fingers hooking into the material and tearing my sweatpants down my legs in one furious move that made me squeak.

He found me without panties on and his gaze lingered on my bare flesh as I started wriggling away, danger and excitement twisting through my body. I wasn't sure if I wanted to escape or spread 'em wide and let him claim me. So I just writhed away like a half dead fish looking for water.

He crawled after me, grabbing my hips and yanking me back toward him, making my pulse skitter everywhere.

"Dead Man," I gasped as he shoved my thighs open and exposed me to him completely.

My clit throbbed and I could feel myself getting achingly wet for him, but I knew I should be more afraid than this. Because I didn't know what he was gonna do and the only man who'd touched me there before had shattered my soul into a million, billion pieces.

And yet…somehow, a part of me didn't want him to stop so I could find out what his intentions were. I wasn't even panicky. Not like I usually got when people tried to touch me. This was a touch I craved on some primal level. In fact, had I ever wanted to be touched as much as this? Not that I could recall, but I also couldn't remember my own name right now, so Brain wasn't much help.

Mateo hooked his arms under the backs of my knees and dropped his head between my thighs as his fingers dug into my hips. My heart was thrashing and pounding and running around in circles, but it wasn't a runaway fear, it was a I-think-I-wanna-jump-off-this-cliff fear. I didn't know what would happen when I hit the bottom, but I was hoping Mateo was about to show me.

Oh holy hell, what is he going to do down there and am I going to burst into flames if I don't find out in the next seven seconds?

The hot pad of his tongue ran up the middle of me and I screamed. Not in the help-me-I'm-being-eaten-by-a-bear way though. In the do-it-again-right-now-or-my-head-will-explode way. Shit that felt good. Like adrenaline fireworks in my pussy good. "Oh my god, oh my god."

"Quiet," Mateo snarled, his hot breath on my clit making me tingle and I clamped my hand down over my mouth. *Sure, I'll shut up. I'll stitch my lips closed too if that's what it takes. Just do it again!*

He did it again.

My eyes half rolled back as he started licking away my arousal, groaning into me as I wriggled and bucked my hips. His hand slapped down on my stomach to try and hold me still, but I wouldn't. My hips wanted to dance to the rhythm of his tongue and there was no stopping them. They were doing the bachata, I swear.

"Keep still or I'll stop," he growled and fuck if that wasn't the most difficult order I'd ever obeyed. But hell, I managed it.

He continued, his tongue moving faster like he was feasting on me, the hungry noises leaving him making my toes curl. Pleasure turned me into nothing but an animal as I moaned against my own hand. I needed more. More, more, more until the sun blew up and ate the earth. I never wanted it to stop. The human race would fall, apes would rise up to claim the planet and I'd still be here writhing beneath Mateo's mouth never letting this end.

His tongue dragged over my hot core then took a path north and flicked over my clit in the lightest of touches.

"Ah!" I screamed against my palm and he stopped. Holy mother of a duck, he *stopped*. "Do it again," I demanded, reaching out and fisting one hand in his hair as my face contorted into a snarl. "I'll kill you, Dead Man. I. Will. Kill. You. If. You. Stop." *Oh shit, did I just threaten him for this? What's happening to me?* "Okay I won't kill you but please, Mateo, *please*."

"Quiet," he reiterated in a snappy tone and I swear if a doctor had been here, I'd have made her surgically remove my voice box just to ensure Mateo continued what he was doing between my legs.

I nodded, mouthing *please* silently. Since when did I beg for anything? Never, that's when. Not anymore. But here I was, begging like a hungry goose for stale bread.

He chuckled low in his throat as my fingers tightened in his hair then his mouth lowered onto my clit again and he sucked, the sensation making me wanna scream once more. My thighs tried to clamp around him, but he forced them down as he worked to destroy me. Because I was definitely falling to ruin. My whole body was quivering and tensing as his tongue started circling over my clit and stars started popping and exploding in my brain.

I was building and building towards the best high of my life and I wasn't sure what would happen when I reached the pinnacle. I'd given myself orgasms before, but I'd never had one from a man. This was a mangasm. And it was far, far better than anything I'd ever experienced on my own.

"*Mateo*," I begged against my palm. I'd pay him however many souls he wanted to continue. I'd find a way to deliver them to his home and push them into his mailbox. Fifty souls. *Children's* souls. *Oh god, who am I?*

Was this what sex felt like? Was it better? *Oh holy fucknuts, I wanna find out. I have to or I'll DIE.*

He groaned again, apparently enjoying this too, but he couldn't be enjoying it anywhere near as much as I was. I lifted my head to watch him, his powerful shoulders tensing and his eyes moved up to meet mine as he sucked and teased my clit at his own filthy leisure. I moaned and panted as he looked at me then raked his teeth against that perfect spot and I collapsed back onto the ground again. It was so intense, so fucking everything.

"Mateo, Mateo, Mateo." His name was on a loop in my head. I wanted to tattoo it on my pussy along with a landing strip for his tongue. He could touch me like this any freaking time he liked. No warning.

His tongue started moving faster as he built me toward impossible heights and suddenly I was crashing, falling, diving over the top of a mountain and pleasure rushed through me like lava, searing the inside of my body and marking it forever, making me pant and moan and scream. I was only able to keep my hand over my mouth by sheer force of will as he laughed savagely against my pussy, continuing to stroke his tongue over me as he prolonged my climax.

My hand fell away from my mouth at last and I lay staring up at the ceiling through the bars with my chest heaving and a huge ass, smug as shit smile on my face. This was possibly the best moment of my life. I was high as a fucking balloon making its way towards the sun, ready to pop as it stared into the depths of a billion tons of burning gas.

Sorry if you saw that, Satan, but I have a second boyfriend now, kay?

MATEO

CHAPTER SEVENTEEN

I forced myself to back up even though my cock was throbbing with need and the taste of her on my lips was making me hunger for more unlike I'd ever hungered for anything. She was the sweetest poison, her flesh an addiction I wanted to ruin myself over.

Never in all my life had anyone tried to step in and protect me from anything. Least of all a woman. So despite the way my heart was racing and my dick was demanding I find out just how tight and hot her pussy really was, I forced myself to retreat until my back was against the wall and I was looking down at her as she panted where she lay, her heated gaze on me.

She hadn't done anything to try and cover herself yet and I gazed at her pussy, burning with the need to feel more of it, all of it. I wanted her tight around me while she screamed and begged and clawed at my back.

"Holy hell," she murmured, her hands roaming over her body like she was chasing down the echoes of her pleasure and I watched her with my muscles locked tight as she massaged her tits inside her top, moaning as she tugged on her nipples. "Who knew mouths had so many good uses?" she added, a hand moving between her thighs as she rubbed at her clit gently, like she was trying to keep the feeling of my mouth on her flesh alive.

I wanted that too. I wanted to mark up her pretty skin and paint my name all over it. I wanted to pin her down and make her scream in ecstasy and agony all at once while I claimed her roughly, driving my cock into her hard enough to imprint the feeling of it inside her for all of time.

"Where did you learn to get so good at that?" she asked seriously and I licked my lips, savouring the taste of her where it lingered. "Did you have to practice a lot? Or is it a natural talent?"

I still said nothing, though I could admit in my mind that I hadn't craved many pussies enough to spend time devouring them instead of just fucking them. But I'd known how sweet hers would taste with one look at her and I'd been hungering to find out for sure for as long as she'd been here.

I wanted more, though want didn't come close to the ache I felt to claim her. I needed her pinned beneath me, taking my cock hard and deep while gasping for breath around the hold I held on her throat. I needed to unleash all of the darkness in me and find a home for it inside her in every way imaginable, between those full lips then sheathed to the hilt in her tight ass. I wanted her to scream for me so loud that her husky voice got rougher and I lost my damn mind in the ecstasy of her fucking flesh.

But still I remained where I was, fighting that desire with all I had. Because I knew the beast in me would never be sated by her. Not even close. I'd want more and more and more, and I wasn't certain she could take it. Or more like, I wasn't certain I'd be able to stop. And there was no one here to force me back if I lost control with her. If my hand locked too tight, if my monsters came out to play...

"Do you think I'd be good at eating pussy?" she asked breathily as she pulled her sweatpants back up and I growled in the back of my throat. "I've thought about it a lot - other girls' pussies I mean. I wondered if my life would just be easier if I could get as wet for pussy as I do for cock. But then I get side-tracked with the idea of a huge cock driving between my thighs pushing in deeper and deeper until I can hardly-"

"Choose another subject," I snapped and she almost flinched at the harshness of my tone. It wasn't a physical movement, more a flash of something in her eyes that could have been hurt. I growled beneath my breath as my cock begged for control of my body and I refused to relinquish it.

Not on her. Not yet.

"I once spotted a chocolate bar floating along in the river when I was living under the bridge," she said, clearly taking me at my command and moving on to something else.

I said nothing and she took that as an invitation to continue as usual, sitting up and crawling closer to me until she made it to my side before pressing her back to the wall to join me sitting there, casual as anything. Like me making her come so hard she'd almost blacked out was a normal occurrence in our relationship. And maybe it would be from now on.

She crossed her legs and her thigh dropped over mine as if she wasn't even afraid of me.

"I chased it all the way along the riverbank, but it was winter and the water was deep and fast so I couldn't risk jumping in. It was so brown and chocolatey and appetising..." she sighed as she trailed off, and like with every word that spilled from her lips, I found myself captured by them and her story despite its content. "Turned out it was just a huge turd," she said sadly. "Luckily I realised it before I managed to grab it and stuff it in my mouth."

I coughed a laugh before I could stop myself and she beamed as she looked around at me. There was still a little mud smeared across her cheek and I wondered what it was about this girl that had me so captivated. She was just so unpredictable, so beautifully insane. Mi chica loca.

I pushed my fingers into the pocket of my sweatpants then tugged it inside out before ripping the fabric of the pocket clean out of them. It left a hole behind, but Niall usually gave me a fresh pair every few days so I wasn't too concerned over that.

I reached up to the tap just beside the bars and ran some water over the material before turning back to her and using it to clean the mud from her face.

My muscles were still locked tight as I fought to hold myself back from her, entering into a battle of wills with the demon that resided in my bones as I cleaned her cheek and she looked up at me with what I could have sworn was a little vulnerability in her eyes.

The moment I noticed that small sign of weakness, the fragile control I'd been holding on my baser instincts snapped and I lunged at her, dropping the cloth and pushing her down onto the cold floor beneath me as my hand locked around her throat.

Her legs wound around my waist and she clamped them tight, making my cock ride the satin smooth fabric of her sweatpants as I ground it against her and she rocked into the movement with a breathy moan.

My grip on her throat tightened and her back arched, showing me how hard her nipples were beneath her tank top too.

For a moment I was frozen again because there was one clear thing here that I hadn't been expecting from her. She liked this. I was almost certain of it. She really was a creature right out of my own favourite nightmares.

"We should run away, Dead Man," she said breathily as I rocked my hips against her again, unable to help it. My cock throbbed so violently I wondered if I could come from this alone, the friction and heat between us building to unbearable levels.

"That's a pretty fantasy."

"My whole life is a fantasy," she replied, her gaze snaring mine as she reached down and pulled something from her pocket. "And today it's looking like a good one."

I blinked at the screwdriver as she waved it before my eyes then pressed it to my throat.

"I could kill you real good, Mateo," she swore and I growled at the way my name tasted on her lips. "Do you believe me?"

"You'd paint the walls red," I agreed, seeing that darkness in her clear enough. She would. Or at least, she could.

"You think I'd do a good job of it?" she asked, her hips grinding against mine as her thighs tightened around me.

"A beautiful job, mi sol," I agreed, my eyes on her lips as they pulled into a wide smile.

"Sadly, I think I like you being alive though, Dead Man. So maybe we should just use this to escape instead?" She tentatively offered me the screwdriver and I was sure she saw the surprise flicker across my face.

This was more than her just suggesting we escape this place together. She was handing me a weapon, the means to hurt her if I chose it and yet for some reason, she had clearly decided that she didn't believe I'd do that. Or at least she didn't want to. Did she truly trust me so easily? I certainly didn't trust her. She was a woman after all, and this could easily be some new cruel deception. But I wasn't going to allow that to hold me back.

I released my hold on her throat and slowly ran my hand up her arm until my fingers were wrapped around hers where she held the screwdriver. I guided her movements as I lowered the blunt metal tip of it to her throat and watched her pupils dilate as I slowly dragged it down her body, carving a line between her tits and towards her navel.

By the time I kneeled back to sit upright and dragged it down between her legs, she was panting, her free hand moving onto my thigh and a thousand questions in her electric eyes just waiting for my answer.

"Do you trust me, chica loca?" I asked her curiously, wondering if I really had caught her in my net or if she was snaring me in hers.

"I think death by your hand would be better than a lot of others I might earn," she replied, still watching me, waiting, submitting.

I drank in the sight of her, wondering if she really was as captivating as she seemed or if I was just falling prey to some greater trap, some trick I couldn't see. Though perhaps the cost I'd have to pay to find out would be worth it.

With more than a little willpower, I pulled the screwdriver away from her body and stood, offering her my hand as I towered over her.

She took it and I pulled her up, wondering how something so small and light could be so full of life and energy that she'd captivated every piece of me so entirely. Why was she trusting me now? Did she truly have no concept of how fucking dangerous I was, how dangerous I couldn't help but be, or was there a part of her that had guessed and wanted to find out more? She definitely called to the dark in me, so maybe I should be wondering about the dark in her.

But if she took a look inside my head and saw all of the dirty and depraved things I ached to do to her, would she really still be curious? Would it excite her to give in to me, or would it send her screaming to think of me fucking her so brutally that she didn't know if she wanted to beg me to stop or beg me to keep going forever?

I looked down at the screwdriver in my hand and forced my thoughts to focus. This was my chance, the one opportunity I'd been hoping for in every moment of every month that I'd been held captive down here.

I was going to take full advantage of it, free myself, escape from here and kill that motherfucker upstairs as savagely as I could manage. And when it was done and the demon in me had bathed itself in his blood until it drowned, I'd take my little savage girl and bend her to my will. I'd paint her in his blood and let her feel the full force of the monster in me as I reclaimed my life and claimed her body at once.

The collar was fixed around my throat with a padlock and I'd need bolt cutters to remove it, but I could easily take the chain with me until then.

I moved to the wall, my heart racing with adrenaline as I pictured each and every way I'd dreamed of killing that bastardo upstairs. I wanted to make it slow, but fast would work too. All that mattered was that by the end of it I held his severed head in my hands and looked into his dead eyes knowing I'd won.

Te debo un año de dolor, hijo de puta – I owe you a year of pain, motherfucker.

The four bolts that had been screwed into the wall to contain me were surprisingly easy to remove with the right tool and a dark smile captured my lips as the anchor came away from the brickwork, hitting the floor with a heavy clang.

I stilled, listening for any sign that Niall had heard that before relaxing minutely and picking it up.

Mi sol followed me as I crossed to the door of the cage next, eyeing the padlock which kept us in here before threading the screwdriver through it. The chain was supposed to keep me away from the door so the lock wasn't massive, and I was fairly certain that with the right leverage I could break it.

I wrapped the end of my chain around the handle of the screwdriver then stepped back and pulled, forcing the lock with a growl of determination as my muscles bunched and tensed.

The padlock broke with a bang so suddenly that I almost fell, but the girl's hands landed on my back to steady me before she jumped up and down, clapping excitedly.

"You did it, Dead Man!" she cheered, leaping at me and winding her arms and legs around me before her lips landed on my cheek in a kiss that set a fire burning in my veins.

I caught her ass to hold her there, driving her back against the bars of the cage and looking deep into her bright eyes as I hunted out the truth of her.

"I'm going to kill him," I growled. "I'm going to destroy him and paint your pretty flesh in his blood."

She licked her lips slowly, hesitating for a long moment before nodding her head. "Make him pay for the bad times, Dead Man."

"Y luego te destruiré y descubriré cuánto puedes tomar. " *And then I'll destroy you and find out how much you can take.*

She smiled like she'd understood that perfectly and I lowered her to the floor before gathering the chain in my hands and heading out into the basement.

I wasted no time creeping up the stairs, moving into the best position I could for whenever Niall decided to come back. The bolts on the door were too strong for me to break without alerting him and I didn't want to lose the element of surprise.

The girl didn't follow me right away and when I glanced back down the stairs, I found her back to me as she stripped out of her clothes and pulled more on.

I watched her as she did it, eyeing the curves of her body and letting my mind run rampant as I considered all the things I wanted to do to her just as soon as I had the time to enjoy them.

She'd go from his captive to being mine and I was hoping she wouldn't even realise it. If she was enthralled by me then I could keep her without chains or cages, but if she wasn't...well, I was sure I would figure something out. Because whether she knew it or not, she was already mine. I owned her just as surely as I owned my own flesh and when I was done claiming her, she'd never be able to deny that again.

I couldn't rush it though. I needed to be certain that I could control myself. Needed to be sure I wouldn't get lost to the horrors that haunted me and destroy this little creature before her time.

A noise beyond the door made me still, the hairs along the back of my neck raising as I gripped the screwdriver in one hand and the chain in another.

I inhaled slowly, my lungs filling up with the scent of the hunt. Sometimes I was certain I really could smell my prey, that when I locked on to a victim, their very being called out to me, drawing me closer until the final act. I'd been a fixer in my previous life. The best there was. Sometimes I cleaned up other people's messes, but as often as not I had to do the actual killing too. And I was fucking good at my job.

The girl crept up the stairs behind me as I waited and I glanced at her, finding her in a pair of pale denim dungarees which had cartoons painted all over them in bright colours. She was wearing a neon orange lace bra and panties beneath it which were clearly on show under the denim panel that ran up her front. She'd tied her hair into a pair of buns either side of her head and had placed a headband with black kitty ears on top. She grinned at me with lips painted burgundy and I smiled back in a way that I was pretty sure made it clear how much I wanted to peel that thing back off of her.

"Do you like it?" she whispered, waving a foot in a white platform sneaker at me as I looked her over. "I figured escaping deserved a special kind of outfit."

The sound of the door unbolting came before I could reply, and we fell utterly still as we waited in the darkness of the stairwell for Niall to fall into our trap.

A shiver of anticipation slid down my spine as I readied myself for this fight, my grip on the screwdriver tight and demanding as each bolt was drawn back and the lock finally clicked.

Niall pulled the door wide and I leapt on him with a furious roar.

We fell crashing back into the hallway as he cursed and I slammed my arm down with all my strength, driving the screwdriver towards his blackened heart.

Niall snarled ferociously, crossing his wrists over his chest and blocking my strike as my forearm collided with them.

I swung back, stabbing at his side instead just as his fist collided with my jaw and my head snapped to the left.

The screwdriver grazed across his ribs, but before I could sink it between them, he got a knee between us and knocked me tumbling away towards the kitchen.

We were both on our feet in an instant and the girl leapt between us, not pausing for a moment, just darting by as she raced towards the door.

"My money is on the foreign one!" she yelled over her shoulder and I narrowed my eyes at Niall as he barked a laugh before launching himself at me again.

He was brutal, just as big as me and maybe even better trained, but I had the weapons in my favour and I was going to use them to my advantage.

I twisted away from him, swinging the chain that still hung from my neck and catching him in the side of the head with the heavy bolt attached to the end of it.

Blood flew and I bellowed as I charged towards him again while he was dazed by the blow, but of course he wouldn't go down that fucking easily.

"You fuckin' traitor, Colin!" he yelled and it took me a beat to realise he was speaking to the damn chain before he slammed into me, catching hold of it and yanking hard.

My stab was thrown off course and went wide, giving him the opportunity to slam his fist into my nose.

We fell to the floor once more, brawling like animals as I tried to stab him over and over and he managed to avoid every fatal blow I threw his way.

"Me voy a bañar en tu sangre," I snarled at him. *I'm going to bathe in your blood.*

We slammed into a wall and he managed to get on top of me, both of his hands locking around my wrist as he forced the hand holding the screwdriver down against the wooden floor. I punched him with my free hand, striking his ribs with all I had over and over until I was certain I heard a crack, but in the same moment he ripped the screwdriver from my grasp.

Instead of trying to stab me with it like I'd been doing to him, he just launched it away from us, a heavy thunk sounding it colliding with something at the far end of the corridor.

"Let's make it a fair fight shall we, El Burro?" he mocked before throwing a fist at my face.

I roared a challenge, rolling us over and slamming my forehead down against the bridge of his nose.

Niall cursed me loudly and suddenly his blows grew harsher, wilder, the savage in him rising from his flesh as we fought with tooth and claw, crashing through the door into the living room and beating the living shit out of each other.

I refused to back down though, I refused to allow this to end in any way other than his death.

A gunshot cut through the air and the two of us lurched apart as we found the girl standing on the far side of the room, pointing a pistol up towards the roof where a bullet hole had been carved into one of the beams. She lowered it to aim it our way and tutted loudly as she cocked her head to one side.

"Silly, silly, leaving a pistol just lying around where anyone could find it," she mocked, blowing on the end of the gun like a cowboy before pointing it at us again.

There was just something about the way she looked standing there in that insane outfit, smiling like the idea of shooting one of us was turning her on, and I couldn't help but hunger for her even more. She was all the right kinds of crazy and I was determined to find out how deep her insanity ran.

"Up you get," she commanded.

Niall laughed as we untangled ourselves and stood, but instead of raising his hands in surrender like I expected, he lunged towards me, grabbing hold of my chain and yanking so hard that I was thrown down onto my back at his feet.

"Stop!" mi sol yelled, pulling the trigger as she aimed the gun at him again, but nothing other than a dull click escaped it.

"Holy fuck, that was cold blooded," Niall laughed as he yanked on my chain and started dragging me across the floor while I struggled to regain my feet. "You really woulda killed me wouldn't ya, baby doll?"

I grabbed the edge of the coffee table and snatched a heavy ashtray from it, throwing it at him as hard as I fucking could.

Niall cursed as it struck him, dropping the chain and stumbling back against the wall as blood pissed down the side of his face.

The sound of the girl pulling the trigger again and again came from the gun, but it had clearly only held the one bullet and she screamed a frustrated curse as she realised it too.

I leapt to my feet and charged at him as he steadied himself against the mantlepiece and for a brief moment I thought I had him until he whirled around with that fucking stun gun in hand and slammed it straight into my gut.

My breath seized in my lungs as my muscles went rigid and I fell to the floor with a heavy thump, electricity pounding through my veins and blinding me with agony as I thrashed and spasmed on the ground.

I was vaguely aware of that motherfucker dragging me along by the collar as it dug into my throat and I bounced down each and every stair on my way back into the fucking basement.

The moment I began to recover, he stunned me again and the pain of the blow almost made my fucking head explode as the sound of him screwing the bolts back into the wall followed.

I rolled onto my knees as he walked out of the cage, heading into his killing room before returning with a heavier padlock and snapping it shut to lock me in again.

"Well, that was fun," Niall said, grinning at me through the blood that was dripping down the side of his face before looking towards the stairs, his expression morphing into one of excitement in anticipation of going after my chica loca next.

"It was on me," I snarled and he turned back to me in surprise, raising his eyebrows.

"Well, well, well, looks like your tongue really has started working again, hasn't it, El Burro?" he purred, stalking towards my cage with a glint in his eyes that said he was going to make me suffer for my escape attempt, but I wasn't afraid of him.

I spat at his feet and his smile only widened.

"You got a little thing for my girl?" he taunted as the sound of something heavy banging against a window echoed down to us from upstairs. She wouldn't be able to break that glass though, it was designed to stop a bullet. A tiny thing like her stood no chance.

My skin prickled as he called her his and I bared my teeth at him, wishing I could just get my hands around his fucking neck and finish the job I'd started.

"Pity for you that she has no interest in tiny cocks then, isn't it?" he taunted, trying to get a rise out of me and I snarled at him as despite my best attempts, it worked.

"Did you discover that when she rejected yours?" I hissed.

Niall barked a laugh then turned his back on me, bounding up the stairs without another word and calling out to her as he went.

"Ready or not, here I come!"

The girl shrieked and the sound of pounding footsteps came from upstairs before he disappeared out of sight, baying like a bloodhound as he hunted her down.

I wrapped my fingers around the bars of my cage, waiting, listening, wondering if she might have any chance of taking him out herself.

There was the sound of something smashing followed by another scream from her then a stream of curses punctuated by his raucous laughter.

"Do you like the new locks I put on the front door?" Niall laughed as heavy footsteps thumped back towards me a few minutes later and he appeared with her slung over his shoulder while she smacked his back and kicked her legs and called him a bad Liam Neeson impersonator.

"You're supposed to kill me!" she yelled as he tossed her down onto the bed and she bounced before scrambling to sit up again and glare at him.

One of her dungaree straps had popped open and the fabric on the front of it fell aside, revealing her left breast in that transparent orange bra. She either didn't care though or she was happy with us both staring which I definitely was, and I was pretty certain he was too.

The thought of that sent rage and jealousy warring through me and I launched myself at the bars of my cage, yelling at him to try and make him look my way instead, but his attention never wavered from her.

"What the fuck are ya talking about?" Niall asked.

"That's what Liam said he'd do, find them and kill them."

"I'm not Liam Neeson. My pa is called Liam though and he's a miserable motherfucker, so I don't want you calling me that either."

I stilled as he said that, my jaw clenching as recognition poured through me because there was one Irish motherfucker called Liam who had been causing shit for the Castillo Cartel in this part of the world for a long fucking time. A peace had been maintained between us on very uneven footing, but if anyone in the cartel knew an O'Brien had me, there would be hell to pay for it.

So what the fuck did that mean for my situation? I just couldn't believe that Santiago or anyone in his organisation would have paid an O'Brien to take on the task of locating what I'd stolen from him. Did that mean I wasn't here under the cartel's orders like I'd assumed? Did it mean that I could kill this motherfucker and stay here? Was it possible they still had no idea where the fuck I was?

"One day I'm going to be the death of you," the girl growled, pointing at Niall and he leaned down to look her in the eyes.

"You'd best start working on your skill set then, little psycho. Because as far as I see it, I got more chance of being killed by a wildly lost penguin with a taste for Irish men than I do of falling prey to your non-existent talents."

Niall turned and jogged back up the stairs and she screamed as she launched herself after him, looking like she really would try her luck unarmed as she chased him down. But his legs were longer and he slammed the door at the top with a wild laugh before she could catch him, leaving the two of us down here.

Trapped again.

BROOKLYN

CHAPTER EIGHTEEN

I was just waking up in the soft bed when a huge body dive bombed me and drove the breath from my lungs.

"Wakey wakey, little psycho," Niall's beautifully deep voice sang and I growled angrily, punching him through the material as he clamped the comforter down to trap me.

"Go away," I growled moodily and he moved to kneel over my chest, pinning my arms beneath his knees.

"Now that's not very nice, is it?" he said. "Especially not when I've decided to give you some training and make you into a real killer."

I frowned, narrowing my eyes at him. "You have?"

"Yeah." Niall grinned that crazy grin of his and it was too infectious not to smirk.

"Get off of her," Mateo snapped from across the room. He'd gone all quiet on me yesterday after our escape attempt and hadn't said a word to me even when I'd told him my best under the bridge story. It involved a stolen block of cheese, an angry cheese salesman and a pokey stick. And he hadn't even cracked a smile.

My heart lurched as Niall's weight pressed me down for a moment but then he dragged me out from under the covers and tossed me onto my feet. He sprang to my side, his inked chest bare and a clown on it grinning at me almost as wide as he was as he grabbed my hand and pulled me closer.

"What'll it be, Spider?" he pressed and I thought on that for a second.

Well I did like killing. And it might give me a chance to kill him too. So I guessed it was worth a go. "Okay."

He started spinning me around the room, taking a wireless earphone from his ear and stuffing it in mine as my brain caught up with the fact that I was awake and dancing with a killer.

Teeth by 5 Seconds of Summer filled my head and Niall's smile was so infectious that I gripped his shoulders and let him dance me around the basement, throwing my head back to gaze at the room upside down, my hair swinging out around me. "Weeeee."

He threw me back onto the bed and I laughed, shoving myself upright and striking a pose to the music, singing along as loudly as Niall was. He opened his arms wide as I whipped my hair to the beat, rolling my hips as Hellfire watched appraisingly and Mateo scowled at us.

"Jump, baby girl," Niall commanded.

Baby girl? My eyebrow arched then I took a running jump and leapt off of the bed. He caught me with his arm under my knees and one at my back and we started laughing as the song came to an end. He spun me around one final time and placed me on my feet as I caught my breath and my eyes locked with Mateo's as he glared out at us from the cage.

I took a bow, biting my lip as a blush crawled into my cheeks. A thrill danced beneath my skin as I remembered his mouth on me, his tongue rolling over my clit in a way I had never freaking experienced, but I wanted to again and again and again. The problem was, he'd gotten all withdrawn since our escape attempt last night and I didn't really know how to deal with that, so mostly I just hadn't.

"Shower, get dressed, meet me upstairs," Niall commanded and I stuck my middle finger up at him as I grinned then grabbed some of my new clothes in a bundle and raced away into the bathroom. *Oooh today is gonna be fun, I can feel it.*

I got in the shower and touched myself shamelessly over what I'd done with Mateo last night, my moans coming louder and breathier as I slicked my fingers over my clit and imagined it was his tongue. I was a sexual goddess, one step closer to my assassin seductress dreams. Mateo had looked like he enjoyed it, seeming like he was gonna go all the way with me, but then he'd run away like a pigeon down a hole. And now he was giving me the silent treatment. I hoped he wasn't having regrets. Maybe he liked blondes. Or dudes. Or carrots up his butt. No judgement, I just guessed I wasn't his type after all. And that made me all kinds of sad. *I'm still all yours then, Satan. Can you do that tongue thing Mateo did? Asking for a friend.*

I came with a loud, breathy moan and grinned as I stepped out of the shower, drying myself off with a fluffy towel. The high of my orgasm quickly tumbled away though and I pouted. It didn't feel as good as it had when Mateo had done it, but I guessed it was a close second.

I wasn't gonna get all frowny about the situation. I liked Mateo. He was terrifying and cute and yeah he made me feel all squishy inside, but I could deal with rejection just fine. I'd dealt with it my entire life. I was a seasoned pro with endless years of practice. So if he thought I'd be upset – *oh shit, I'm crying.*

I bawled for a good five minutes, wailing my anger and grief at the sink who just stared callously back at me. Stupid sink. I slapped its shiny taps before slapping myself hard enough to shut me up too. *Stop it. You're Big Red's girl anyway. You don't need sexy cage men. Put on something hot and remember that people are awful. Especially men. Especially, especially hot men.*

I put on a pale blue leotard with some pink fishnet stockings then pulled on my short furry jacket in the same colours because I didn't wanna catch a chill. Then I slipped my feet into my shiny white unicorn platform heels and moved to the mirror to do my makeup. I kept it low key, putting on a matte lilac lipstick then colouring my eyes in a range of pastels up to my brows before drawing a couple of little stars under my eyes in black eyeliner and putting on some glittery mascara.

I beamed at myself as I tied my hair up into a knot then stepped out of the room.

Niall was lying on the bed with his hands cupped behind his head and he looked up at me with an intensity that blazed against my flesh. I glanced over at Mateo as he clutched the bars, glaring at me and pressed my shoulders back, lifting my chin too, giving no shits about his attitude.

"Well are we going or what, Hellfire?"

"Jesus fuck, talk about an outfit, Spider. You know if ya keep going out killing wearing shit like that you'll be pretty recognisable," Niall said, pushing himself up as his eyes slid down to my fishnets and I felt them linger on my ass as I walked past him to the cupboard, taking out a pale blue wig and pulling it on. It had a fringe and fell down to my mid-back. I whirled on Niall, gesturing to it.

"Look, now I'm camouflaged."

Niall stood up, striding towards me and a smirk tugged at his lips. "Oh shite, where are ya?" He reached for me, pretending he couldn't find me as his hand flailed in the air and a girlish noise left me that had never come from my mouth before. Dammit, why was he so cute sometimes? No, I hated him. He was a big meanie cake with sprinkles on top.

"Found ya. Let's go." He grabbed my hand and my heart skipped as he tugged me toward the stairs. I glanced back at Mateo and he tucked his chin down, the way he was looking at me making goosebumps skitter over my body. He didn't say anything, just stared and I pursed my lips, ignoring him. *I don't need your miracle mouth. I've got my fantasies of it now anyway. And they'll be just as good. Sort of. Sigh.*

Niall tugged me out of sight upstairs and I threaded my fingers through his, wanting to do the hand holding thing because…well I didn't really have a reason right now, but that was what I wanted. He glanced back at me, but didn't let go and a devilish smile pulled at my lips.

I was gonna prove I was the best killer he ever saw today. Better than that Bundy guy or the Night Stalker or even Voldemort.

"So just to get it outa the way, why were you crying back there in the bathroom, love?" he asked.

"You heard that?" I gasped.

"It was impossible not to hear that."

"Oh," I breathed, realising Mateo would have heard it too. Dammit, what if he assumed it was because of him? I mean, it was obviously. But I didn't want *him* knowing that. "I don't want to talk about it."

"Okay… Well, I have a gift for you that might cheer ya up." He towed me through to the living room and pushed me down onto the red Chesterfield couch and I folded my legs underneath me as I looked around like an excited puppy.

"What gift? Where?" I demanded.

"Shut yer eyes," he commanded, standing before me and folding his inky arms.

The Devil gazed at me from his forearm and my eyes crept over more of his art, wishing I could give my little spider more inky friends on my body. He was so lonely on my thumb. Just like me. Though I didn't live on a thumb. Well, maybe I lived on a really, really, really big thumb if the whole universe was actually embedded under a giant's fingernail. Wouldn't that be funny? If we were just a speck of dirt in a much bigger world? And that world was fully of ogres and beasties and-

"Shut 'em," Niall pushed and I sucked my lower lip, struggling to trust him before forcing my eyes to close. He said he had a gift. And I wasn't gonna get it unless I did as he asked so I had to.

I just hoped he didn't whip his dick out and hold it up to my lips. That had happened the last time someone had said they had a gift for me. They told me to get on my knees and close my eyes. In hindsight, I should have seen that coming. I ran four miles screaming from that tiny dick. I didn't think Niall's would be so bad though. The idea of it near my mouth made me kinda thirsty actually.

His hands slid around my throat and he suddenly locked a plastic collar in place and my eyes flew open. "Ergh, I would've preferred your cock," I huffed, folding my arms and his eyes widened.

"Come again, little psycho?"

"Nothing," I mumbled and he frowned.

"This one's an upgrade. The collar's got a parameter sensor on it. So... you're free whenever I bring you upstairs from now on. You can go anywhere ya like except beyond the boundary I've set out in the yard. If you do, it'll shock you so either get yourself away from the border or you'll have to wait until I show up and turn off the power. So what d'ya think?" He beamed like he'd just given me candy.

I reached up to stroke my fingers over the collar, my lips popping open. Then I flew out of my seat, running for the front door. It was unlocked so I threw it open, tearing out into the sunshine and racing across the lawn with a crazed laugh of excitement.

Freeeedom. I'm free, free, freeee!

I sprinted towards the driveway where a blue Ford truck was parked at the end of a row of shiny cars and I glanced over my shoulder at the house, finding Niall watching me from the doorway.

He cupped his hands around his mouth as he shouted to me, "You're almost at the-"

Electricity exploded into my veins and my knees crashed into the dirt as I buckled to the ground. Pain sizzled along my limbs and my screams spiralled up into the sky. It stopped suddenly and I found the sun blotted out by Niall's large form standing above me, his eyebrow arched and his fingers wrapped around my ankle where he'd yanked me away from the sensor.

I panted as I laughed, running a hand down the centre of my body as the lasting static tingled over my flesh.

Niall crouched down, reaching out to pull a lock of dark hair out of my mouth as he regarded me. "Do you like that, little psycho?" he asked in a dark tone that made me shudder almost as much as the electricity had.

I nodded, grinning at him.

"Well don't make a habit of it or yer brain will turn into a fried egg." He pulled me to my feet and pushed me back toward the house. "Are ya ready to start training now?"

I turned to him with narrowed eyes. "Are you really going to train me, Hellfire?"

"Yeah. You wanna be a better killer, don't you?"

"I thought you said I sucked at it." I glared at him as his hand moved to rest on the small of my back. I secretly liked that. I loved how everything about him was big and made me feel even littler than I already was. It didn't make me feel weak though. It made me feel like Mother Nature resided in my chest and was waiting to be unleashed on the whole world. And he could see that in me too. At least some of the time.

"Hence the training." He led me around the back of the house and my brows arched at the sight before me.

Watermelons on tall sticks were stuck in the ground out ahead of me. And laid out on a wooden bench was a shiny collection of knives, machetes, hammers, hatchets – all the goodies. Even a gun!

I gasped, sprinting toward it, snatching it up and wheeling around to point it at Hellfire with a victorious laugh. I might have failed at shooting him yesterday, but I wouldn't today.

He stared blandly at me, waiting for me to the pull the trigger and my throat thickened with a ball of iron. My finger kissed the trigger as I stared at him, baring my teeth. "Gimme a car, let me go."

"No," he said simply. "Now what's yer next move?"

I took a step toward him, pointing the gun at his head as I tried to make myself pull the trigger. But something was holding me back today. Maybe it was because he had a lovely face and I didn't wanna ruin it. But in that case, I could shoot his heart instead. I aimed the gun lower, but it didn't get any easier.

Pull it, free Mateo, get outa here.

But I wanna learn to kill. And Hellfire's so good at it. And he's hot. Am I really gonna take this pretty devil man from the world? He's sooo pretty.

"You seem to be in a dilemma, Spider. What's the hold up? Make pastrami outa my brains." Niall walked slowly toward me and I wet my lips.

Maybe I don't have to kill him. I can just maim him. Then I can run away.

I lowered the gun to aim at his foot and pulled the trigger. Click.

Shit tits.

"Interesting choice." Niall rubbed his stubbled chin then lunged forward, snatching the gun from my grip and shoving it in the back of his jeans. Then he flicked me hard between the eyes and I winced. "That was a test. You failed, but not as hard as I expected. Now turn around and pick a weapon."

"Fine, but don't flick me," I growled and he flicked me in the ear. "Ow! *Niall.* Don't."

He flicked me in the cheek and I lunged at him with a snarl, slapping his arms and bare chest as he roared a laugh. Then he shoved me toward the bench of weapons hard enough to make me stumble, taking a handful of bullets from his pocket and casually starting to load the gun.

My heart stuttered as I moved in front of the bench, running my fingers over all the shiny pretties. Mashy was in the line-up, but the machete had had good fun with me last time. I wanted to play with someone else today. I didn't wanna leave anyone out.

I picked a serrated hunting knife with a black handle, a little shiver running through me as I took it into my grasp.

"Oooh, hello gorgeous," I whispered. *I'm gonna call you Nippy.*

I felt Niall moving up behind me, the heat of his body radiating against my flesh as I stood upright and his chest brushed my shoulder. Mmm, I didn't know if Nippy was getting me this hot or if it was him. But I was gonna say it was Nippy because I wasn't interested in kidnappers with sexy Irish accents and killer instincts. Even if I did seem to share a kindred spirit with him.

"I'm not going to take you out killing again until I know you can handle yerself," he said in my ear, his overbearing presence surrounding me, sucking me in like I was a sad little soul and he was a Dementor. "Are ya gonna play nicely today?"

"I don't do nice," I said, turning my head toward his until our lips were so close, we were only three ladybirds away from kissing.

"Good girl." He smirked then walked away from me and a shaky breath left me as I turned to follow. Damn his ass looked good in those jeans. It looked like he had two iron plates stored in there.

He yanked one of the watermelons out of the ground on the stick and held it out in front of him. "If you can get that knife in this fruit, I'll give ya a prize."

"Coco Pops?" I asked, bobbing up and down on my toes.

His brows pulled sharply together. "No, I don't have any of those."

"Then how comes you always smell like them in the mornings?" I narrowed my eyes and he shrugged.

"Must be my natural scent."

"Liar!" I accused. "You're holding out on me."

"Nah," he said, waving a hand dismissively. "Anyways, you can have something good if ya get it."

A kiss? No, no, I don't want a kiss. Well, I do. But not from him.

The only kiss I'd had involving tongue was from a cop's horse. There was a lot of teeth and it only lasted two seconds as the cop tried to mow me down. Served me right for showing up to a riot I wasn't invited to, I guess. Horses had always had an affinity for me, it was probably because I always used to carry sugar lumps around in my pockets.

Niall raised the watermelon up so it was on a level with his shoulders. "Go on then, little psycho. Kill it."

I lunged, slashing Nippy towards the fruit, but Niall swung it away then whacked me in the side with it. I shrieked, whipping around and stabbing wildly to try and skewer it, but he lifted it over my head out of reach.

"What kind of target is this?" I spat. "People don't move like this."

"No, but if ya can hit this, you can hit a human," Niall reasoned before whacking me over the head with the melon. I stumbled sideways then snarled, slashing at it again and skimming a piece of the skin off. *Yes.*

"Useless," he growled and my rage levels shot up. I wheeled left and right, following the fruit as he moved it, desperately trying to bury my blade in it. "Did all your victims fall on your blades before now? I'm struggling to see how you've got any kinda body count at all."

"Shut up!" I snapped, diving at the melon and taking another inch of skin off of it before Niall held it a foot above my head.

I lunged up, driving Nippy skyward but Niall moved the fruit in a flash, smacking me around the head with it and throwing me off balance. My unicorn heel skidded in the mud and my knee hit the ground, giving Niall the chance to hit me around the head with it again.

"Argh!" I roared, running at Niall instead of the damn watermelon as I lost my shit, but he used the stick to hit my legs and flip me off my feet.

I hit the ground on my back with an oomph, staring up at the bright blue sky as fury blazed through my flesh. *I'm better than this.*

"Why am I wasting my time on ya?" Niall mused and I leapt back to my feet, forcing myself to focus as I lunged for the watermelon again.

I took a chunk out of it this time, but Niall smacked me in the gut with it too then lowered it down by my feet. I stabbed at it, but he moved it aside and Nippy drove deep into the ground instead. I yanked the knife free as Niall moved the watermelon beside my hands and I stabbed at it once more. But he moved it every time so Nippy got stuck in the mud over and over until I was crawling along the grass as I stabbed and stabbed and stabbed. The watermelon suddenly fell off the stick and I drove the knife through it at the same time, right in the middle.

"Yes!" I cried.

"Doesn't count," Niall said instantly. "It came off the stick."

I looked up at him above me as he smirked and blind rage clung to the inside my body with bloody claws. He took the gun from his waistband, spinning it on his finger in a warning and I shoved to my feet, throwing my shoulder into him as I forced my way past then dove on the nearest watermelon perched on a stick in the ground. I sliced it in two then ran to the next one, stabbing and cutting it to pieces with a snarl of fury, then the next and the next and the next. I ripped one off its stick and threw it to the grass, slamming my heel down on it then finishing it with a furious slash of Nippy. Watermelon juice coated me and I licked a piece from my lips as I dove on my next victim. It was a massacre and the outlet it gave me was a beautiful, unfettered thing.

Niall suddenly grabbed me from behind, his hand on my stomach as he crushed me back against him. "Ya just killed a whole family." His tongue ran up my neck and I gasped as he ate a piece of watermelon from my skin, his lips burning hot against me. I felt the echo of his tongue all the way to my clit and I wondered if he knew how to pleasure girls with his mouth like Mateo did. And what it would be like to be one of those girls.

"Siblings, cousins, mammies. That's not very nice, now is it?"

"I don't kill innocents," I growled.

"Ya just did. Look at her." Niall angled my head toward the watermelon at my feet that was in pieces. "That was a grandmammy."

"No it wasn't," I gasped in horror.

He crunched a piece of watermelon between his teeth. "Tastes like one."

"No." I wheeled around to face him, gripping his shoulders. "They're all monsters. That was the game."

"I told ya to kill one specifically because he was holding all these other watermelons hostage, ya see?" Niall said, shaking his head disapprovingly and I gazed around at my massacre with my lips wide.

"Nippy and I didn't know," I whispered as tears pooled in my eyes.

"Nippy?" he questioned.

"My knife." I waved it at him, not taking my eyes off of the pieces of watermelon scattered everywhere. *What have I done? They never stood a chance.*

"Her name's Daisy," he balked.

"No, *his* name is Nippy." I turned toward him with a pout.

"Daisy."

"Nippy."

"Daisy."

"Nippy." I jabbed it at him and he caught my wrist, tugging me forward so I stumbled into his chest. My face hit the clown there and I swear I heard it laughing at me.

"Daisy," Niall growled in warning, bringing my hand up to his lips and biting my fingers to try and make me let go of the blade. Hell if I would. But his bite deepened and I found I didn't wanna let go for a whole other reason. The feel of his teeth in my skin was fucking ecstasy and as our eyes locked, I was too slow to hide how much I was enjoying it.

He lifted his hand, prising Nippy from my fingers, his teeth coming free from my skin as a swirl of shadow entered his eyes.

"Pick another weapon," he growled. "I'm going to fetch more

watermelons."

"Wait, where's my prize?" I demanded, stamping my foot as he started walking away.

"Ya don't get a prize until you make a good kill," he called back with a bark of laughter.

I gazed down at the bitemark on my forefinger and while he wasn't looking, I sucked it into my mouth and licked away the taste of him, a thrill running through my chest.

Damn bastard tastes like sugared sin.

Niall made me attack watermelons every day for weeks and weeks until I started to land strikes on them consistently. But despite the fact that I'd stuck three in a row yesterday, I apparently hadn't earned the illusive prize he kept holding over my head. Today would be different though. He said I'd gotten lucky, and luck was no good long term. It was freaking bullshit.

I'd show him what I was made of. I'd gotten stronger, quicker, more powerful. Three meals a day had done wonders for my physique too. Especially as he'd started adding in an insane workout every time I finished a morning of melon hunting. He took me to a crazy ass gym in the house and made me exercise with him 'til I almost fainted. But when I got dizzy, he fed me all kinds of amazing things. Takeaway sandwiches, pizzas, Chinese food, Thai, Mexican. But never freaking Coco Pops. Not once. I'd seen the box though. Just for a second. He'd put it away in a cupboard in the kitchen, but by the time I'd gotten a chance to go back and try to steal them, they were gone. He was Coco blocking me and it wasn't cool. But he didn't realise he wasn't just training me up to be a badass killer. He was training up a Coco

Pops thief. And I'd be getting my hands on them soon enough.

I dressed in the bathroom as I waited for Niall to show up and fetch me, opting for a leggings and crop top combo which were electric green and blue and pink, covered in lightning bolts. Then I slipped my feet into some red platform heels and pulled my hair up into pigtails with a green scrunchy and a blue one. A pop of blue eyeshadow later and the words *killer bitch* written in small black letters under my eyes and I was ready for the day.

I pushed back through the door, looking over at Mateo who was in his cage again. Niall had gotten in the habit of chaining him in the bathroom during the day which was good. Not that I cared. Because he was a pussy eating bandit who'd jumped me then didn't speak to me anymore. Barely a word in all this time. And that was fine by me because I was a cold-hearted assassin with a dark back story. Mysterious, that was me. I didn't need a dead man and his sinful tongue. Even if I did dream about him touching me like that every night. Sometimes it wasn't him in my dreams though. Sometimes it was Niall. The Devil came to party too occasionally, but somehow his face was always theirs. I didn't know what that meant or if it meant anything at all. All I knew was that people were awful and you couldn't trust any of them.

I was happy to hang around here and soak up everything I could learn about killing because it was helping me make my assassin dreams come true. But when I was all-powerful, not even Niall would be able to hold me here if I wanted to leave. Which I did. Obviously. Although sometimes I remembered how shivery and lonely it had been living on the streets and I remembered Stinky Jim's stench, then leaving didn't seem so appealing anymore. Not that my current companions were ones I wanted to keep long term. I didn't really do long term anywhere. But the regular meals and hot showers were gonna be hard to give up when it was time to go.

Maybe I should have taken Niall's plans for me more seriously. We could build a real club. Work together. Kill together. When I pictured it, it was such a temptingly wonderful fantasy that I almost forgot it would never happen. Because life didn't work out like that for me. People had painted me pretty dreams in the past and I'd been lured into them like a badger into a trap. Trust was a no-no when it came to these guys. Especially Niall. Hot as fuck, inky beast Niall. Yeah, he was a trap alright. He wanted something from me and he wasn't gonna get it. I'd take his training and his Coco Pops, then I'd steal his car and run for the hills. Maybe Mateo would come with me. In the trunk. Maybe not. I was undecided since he'd gone stone cold on me. And I wasn't bitter about that at all. *Oh shit, I'm staring at him.*

"Good morning, chica loca," he growled, the first words to leave his lips in days.

I tossed one of my pigtails over my shoulder in answer, moving to sit at the bottom of the stairs as I waited for Niall.

"You're angry with me," he stated.

"I'm angry with a lot of people," I said lightly. "Your name's a long way down a long, long list. And I can't actually remember it. What is it again? Mateo?" *Dammit.*

He slid his hand around one of the bars, his fist tightening on it. "Don't let Niall fool you into thinking he's anything other than a pedazo de mierda," he snarled.

"Yah, I'm aware he's not a pizza, Dead Man," I scoffed.

"That's not what I said," he growled.

"I think I heard you loud and clear," I said airily.

"You don't speak Spanish. The word for pizza in Spanish is pizza," he hissed.

"Good one," I sniggered emotionlessly just as the door at the top of the stairs opened.

"Spider," Niall beckoned and I jumped up, turning away from Mateo and running up to meet Hellfire.

"Hey," I said brightly.

Not that we were friends or anything now, but like, it was nice to have someone to talk to. He didn't tell me to shut up when I went off on a ramble either. So bonus points for that too. Not that I was staying. I guessed I'd miss him a little when I ran away though. Mostly I'd miss his abs. And his voice. And that crazy smile he got when he was about to do something wild. And his ink. Apart from that, I'd never think of him or this place again once I was gone. But I was a live-in-the-moment kinda girl, so for now I was gonna roll with the situation like a lost onion on a highway.

"We're not playing with watermelons today," Niall revealed as we walked into the lounge and I found all the furniture had been pushed aside to create a large space in the middle of the room.

"But I was gonna win my prize today," I complained, pushing my lips out indignantly.

"You were never gonna win the prize," he said, turning to me as he folded his muscular arms. "Yer not cut out for this, Spider. And frankly, I'm getting tired of wasting me time on you. If you can't show me what yer worth today, I'm gonna reconsider this whole thing."

I clenched my jaw, liquid hot anger spilling through the centre of my chest, but I didn't let it get the better of me right away. I'd learned that every time I did that my attacks got sloppy. And I couldn't afford to be sloppy today. I needed this butt crack to see I was an amazing killer once and for all.

He reached into his pocket, taking out a silver sharpie and tossing it to me.

I caught it with a frown, spinning it between my fingers. He didn't see the point in me learning how to twizzle weapons like that yet, but I did it anyway because the hot assassin girl I dreamed to be could do it. So I had to embody her, then one day I'd be her.

Niall pulled his black t-shirt off, revealing all of that godly ink and rippling muscle that always caught me so off guard. I never got used to seeing him like that. Maybe because the itch to explore the treasure map of art on his skin never went away. Especially the urge to explore it with my tongue.

But then I remembered he was my thirty something year old kidnapper who made it seriously clear he wasn't interested in me. That was okay, I was used to people not liking me. But I was also used to not liking people back either, so every time my eyes got hooked on him for too long or I started picturing him in bed at night, I had to force him out along with Mateo. *Pack up those muscles and take a hike, boys. I've got Big Red to keep me satisfied.*

"You're gonna try and fight me," Niall explained. "If you can draw five marks on my body that would be kill shots, I'll give you yer prize."

I bit my lip in anticipation, nodding as I gazed at him, remembering all the places he'd taught me would be guaranteed kills. The head and heart, obviously. Then there were more tricksy places like the back of the neck, the carotid artery in the throat, the axillary artery in the armpit (who knew right?), the liver, the femoral artery in the groin, and the popliteal (new fave word) artery in the back of the knee. I realised I'd shut my eyes to go through my mental notes and as I opened them, I found Niall had stripped down to a pair of dark green boxers, his tanned, muscular thighs all on show and stuff. And his ink continued down them too, a python wrapping around his left thigh and a set of burning playing cards on his right. *Mmmm...*

"Spider," Niall growled and my eyes snapped up to meet his.

"Yep?" I asked airily, totally innocent and all.

"Ya ready?"

"Yep," I repeated, shifting the pen in my grip like a knife and preparing to fight.

He chuckled darkly, shaking his head as he raised his hand to show me the gold pen in his own hand. "No yer not. Didn't ya hear what I said? I'm playing too."

Shit, I musta missed that when I zoned out to stare at your fuck-me-sideways body, Hellfire.

I grinned then pulled my top off and tossed it aside.

"Oh, you don't have ta-"

I stripped down to my shiny blue sports bra and red panties then lowered into a fighting stance once more.

"Alright," he said darkly, his deep green eyes running down my body. "Alright then."

"You already said that," I pointed out, stepping to the right as I stalked him and he arched a brow, stepping left. He'd opted for no shoes but I was still in my skull crushing heels because I was all for style. Niall had let me buy any feminine hygiene products I wanted so my legs were as smooth as a bat's butt too. Apparently I wasn't allowed razors for safety reasons (i.e. me killing him), so I had to opt for waxing. Which was now my favourite freaking thing ever. Why did people hate that crap? It was all sticky and smelled good then it went on the skin all nice and hot and gooey, then wa-toosh, the best kind of pain. I swear I got turned on every time I did it. Anyways, I'd also bought myself some scrummy oily stuff that went on my legs and made them glow like a firefly. I was sure as shit taking that stuff with me when I left here. Though how I was gonna heat up the wax in future, I wasn't sure. Maybe over Smokey Joe's fire, but he always wanted payment for the use of it with a kiss on the cheek. And I didn't like giving him those because he turned his head and tried to get my lips. Every. Freaking. Time. Hadn't got them yet though. Ha. I was a kiss ninja. And now I was gonna be a Sharpie ninja and mark up Niall's body good.

He lunged at me and I ducked his hand as he went for my throat, darting behind him and slashing my pen tip across the back of his knee. "Ha!"

He boomed a laugh, twisting around, grabbing me by the waist and flipping me off the ground. He jabbed the Sharpie tip against my liver and spanked my ass before throwing me away from him. I rolled across the floorboards, shoving to my feet with my cheeks flushing hot. Face cheeks, butt cheeks, all the cheeks and I kinda wanted him to do that again but I was in this death battle with him, so I filed that request away for later.

He opened his arms wide all cockily and I ran at him, focusing on not letting my emotions get the better of me as I homed in on his heart. I ducked his arm as he swung it out to grab me, but his hand fisted in one of my pigtails and his Sharpie scored across the back of my neck. Mine came up at the same time and I ran it from his belly button to his heart and jabbed it there for good measure, making my point. "Ka-pow!" I cried.

He caught my wrist with his other hand as it sat against his chest and both of us breathed heavily as I remained in the cage of his arms for an eternal moment, trying to tug my hand free. The scent of smoke, sweet, sweet man oil and Coco Pops reached me from him and my mouth watered at the concoction, my eyelids drooping a little as I gazed up at his lips. They looked so appetising right then, but I couldn't get distracted.

I blinked and Hellfire shoved me to the ground, dropping down with me and swiping his sharpie across my throat, his thighs clamping around my waist as he held me in place. I threw two hard punches to his stomach and he growled as he reached around to grab my leg, whipping it up to try and draw on the back of my knee. But I was one bendy motherfucker and I got it way above my head, out of his grip and slammed it down on his shoulder, forcing him back an inch. I slashed my Sharpie across his throat and he grinned like a demon, shoving his weight down again. I whipped my hand around, going for his liver, but he caught my wrist and slammed it onto the floor, grinding it into the wood. His crotch pressed to mine and I gasped as I felt how hard he was for me, my pulse pounding in my ears as his face got so close to mine, I could sense him everywhere, his darkness seeping into my skin and consuming me.

Eat me up, Hellfire, make me burn, burn, burn.

I went slack beneath him, figuring I'd use my seductive ways to draw him closer, unsure if I was just convincing myself that was what I was doing. Because right then I wanted him as close as close could be.

He ran his Sharpie down my side, scoring it along my flesh as he glared at me like I'd pissed in his cornflakes - and I would have given the chance. Not his Coco Pops though, they were sacred.

He lifted his weight and forced my thighs wider to try and bring the pen to my femoral artery in my groin. But I started bucking my hips, grinding against his hard on and crying out like a porn star, making him growl in frustration.

"Stop," he commanded.

"But that's not the game," I said huskily.

He released my hand to grip my throat instead, squeezing as he forced his hand between us and ran the Sharpie across my inner thigh towards that deadly spot. But my hand was free and I stuffed it right down his boxers, making him grunt in alarm as I swiped the Sharpie along his hard shaft for good measure before driving it hard into that fleshy spot in his groin. *End game, cock sucker.*

His fingers tightened around my throat and I yanked my hands free, abandoning the Sharpie in his underwear and raising my palms in innocence, batting my lashes. "I win."

"You…ya fucking cheated," he snarled, released me and pushing off of me to get up, turning his back on me as he carved his fingers through his dirty blonde hair.

"How did I?!" I balked in rage, shoving to my feet.

"I had ya. You were already dead," he snapped.

"So were you." I ran up to his back, jabbing the places I'd marked him with my finger and he wheeled around, pushing me back a step. "The game was five marks and I got them first." I planted my hands on my hips. "Give me my prize, Hellfire. Or I'll – I'll-"

"You'll what?" he taunted, turning to me with a twisted smile. "You're not the power in this house, baby girl. I am. And I say ya lost the game."

My mouth widened and my heart thrashed like a mad thing in my chest. "That's not fair!"

"Yer just no good at this." He shook his head, snatching his jeans and pulling them on, rearranging his dick as he did so and retrieving the pen, his brow furrowed.

I guessed the thought of killing got him hard, not me. Because this asshole hated me. And I hated him right back.

Fuck him. If he won't give me a prize, I'll give myself one.

I turned and ran away toward the kitchen, rifling through the cupboards, throwing them all open as I hunted for the Coco Pops. *I'm coming for you, you crackly little chocolate nuggets of glory.*

"Spider!" Niall snapped from the other room, but I ignored him, searching everywhere for them, but coming up empty. There was one cupboard left though, high up above the oven so I climbed onto the worktop and pushed myself to my feet, reaching for it. I may have been tiny, but I was resourceful. I yanked it open, tossing out the bags of pasta at the front of it and my eyes snagged on the Coco Pops box at the back, all yellow and alluring with that cheeky monkey whispering *come hither.*

I laughed wildly, snatching it out and jumping down from the counter with the box just as Niall made it into the kitchen. I lunged for the fridge as he lunged for me, hooking a bottle of milk out of it and ducking his outstretched hands as he tried to get hold of me.

I squealed as I ran from the kitchen, opening the box of Pops and tugging the milk cap off with my teeth. I spat it over my shoulder as heavy footfalls chased after me. But it was too late. They were mine, mine, mine!

I poured the milk directly into the box then tossed the half empty bottle behind me like a missile. A grunt told me I'd hit the angry devil man chasing me and I laughed as I made it to the stairs and started running up, reaching into the box to get a handful of milky Coco goodness. I brought it to my lips, the scent of chocolate and milk and all things good washing over my senses, but then a ten ton beast collided with me from behind and I hit the stairs beneath him as Coco Pops flew everywhere as if in slow motion.

"Noooo!" I cried as the ones in my hand were lost to the carpet and

Niall lifted me up, throwing me over his shoulder and marching me back toward the basement. I hammered my fists on his back and kicked as hard as I could, but he didn't let go, his arm locked tightly across the backs of my legs.

"Ya can have Pops when ya deserve Pops," he growled and I started sobbing dramatically as I continued to pummel him with my fists.

"You're a monster!" I cried as he unlocked the basement door and kicked it open.

He carried me downstairs, throwing me onto the bed and rearing over me with a snarl. I gasped as I saw the Devil in his eyes as clear as day and pure shadow rolled through his expression. "Yeah, I'm the worst kind of monster. And if you forget it again you might just find out why the whole world fears me, little psycho."

He shoved away from the bed, stalking out of the basement and the metallic clanging of Mateo's fists sounded against the cage as I lay in a heap of rage and sexual frustration. Because Niall may have been one bastard of a beast, but he was also the kind of evil that made me ache in all the right places. My little crush needed to remain a secret though. Because he couldn't realise his cruelty was my weakness.

That's okay. No one has to know.

NIALL

CHAPTER NINETEEN

'**D**ress smart' was one of those vague commands that really could be taken in any way. It was damn ambiguous. Confusing. My version of smart could well be different to any other fucker's out there. Though I would admit that I was fully aware of what my pa had meant. To him, smart was a three piece suit at the minimum. Tailored. In a dark colour unless we were headed out on a boat in the summer when he would accept cream or beige but never white - white suits were for wait staff and virgins. Not sure what his issue was with virgins, but there you had it.

So when I was not so casually invited to his house and not so subtly told to dress smart, I'd been well aware of what he'd been expecting of me. I was also well aware that a meeting with my fiancé and her father was not something I had any desire to dress up for, so I'd gone with a touch less than the bare minimum when dressing for this so-called lunch.

I was wearing a pair of black trousers and shiny loafers just like my pa would want, but instead of finishing up the look with a smart shirt and jacket combo, I'd opted for something a little different. My dress shirt was white with black buttons and I'd chosen to leave several of them undone at my throat so that the ink on my skin crawled up out of it instead of being choked out with a tie. And I'd decided against a jacket despite the definite ball-chilling wind out tonight. But I had put a set of braces on as a nod to the original mobsters who laid the roots for my family of miscreants a hundred odd years back. In my personal opinion I looked damn good, for my pa though, this would be almost as bad as me turning up naked.

I strolled into the dining room close to twenty minutes late and smiled widely like I didn't wish to be anywhere else in the world. The table was bursting with Russians and my siblings but there was a place at my pa's right hand set aside for little old me.

"Sorry I'm late!" I called, holding my arms out wide in apology. "I got waylaid on a job. Couldn't be helped."

Pa looked ready to shit a brick for the briefest of moments before he schooled it and I got a little rush from knowing how much my appearance would be pissing him off. Yeah, yeah, a thirty-two-year-old man probably shouldn't really give a shit about what his father thinks of him but, I challenged anyone to try livin' in my family and tell me if they could avoid the bullshit of the mob hierarchy entirely.

Anastasia was all set up in the seat beside mine, wearing a dusty rose dress with her tits spilling outa the top of it. Her eyes were icy as she watched me approach even though she had a good bullshit smile lined up for me too.

I swept down and snatched her hand from the table, placing my mouth against the back of her knuckles as if I was kissing her and breathing in the vile scent of artificial roses that clung to her skin.

"Good afternoon, fiancé," I purred, winking at her as she stared at me in shock, not having the faintest clue what to make of me.

I released her cold hand and dropped into my seat, snatching the napkin that had been folded into some kind of animal and shaking it out as I laid it on my lap.

"What job were you on?" Pa asked, clearly not buying my shit for a moment and I grinned at him as I unbuttoned my sleeves one at a time, rolling them back over my forearms so that the Devil there could smile at him.

"Just a little personal project," I replied with a shrug. "You know how I can't abide a rapist."

Connor snorted a laugh into his drink a few chairs down on the far side of the table and I turned an arctic glare on him, letting him know that I wasn't beyond diving across the table and killing him with his dessert spoon if he pushed me.

On that note, what made a dessert spoon so damn special? Why was it picked for the sweet stuff when poor old soup spoon got left with the slop? I made a mental note to cut my soup spoon a break and use it for my pudding, show it a real good time.

My brother gave me a bored look as he schooled his features while I just grinned my psycho grin at him, but he didn't dare rise to the challenge I was offering. *Fucking dildo.*

"We've been talking dates," Vlad said from his position across the table and I nodded casually.

All cards on the table, I'd taken a couple of Valium on my way over here. Trouble was, I'd forgotten that they didn't really work on me and just make me like thirty percent less inhibited. And I couldn't say I was a particularly inhibited man to begin with, so this was going to be interesting.

"Perfect," I said, reaching out to snag my pa's whiskey from the table and downing the lot. "Are you looking forward to the wedding, glove?" I asked Anastasia as I threw my arm around the back of her chair. And yeah, I said glove in place of love and no one noticed. Fucking funny that. I once had a pair of blue gloves that were like brothers to me, but better than that because they didn't talk shit or have ponytails. I shot Connor's fuckin' ponytail a glare then realised my fiancé was talking.

"-don't you think?" she purred, her hand falling on my thigh and sliding up. What was it with her tryna cock rustle me?

I glanced at my pa, wondering if he'd help me out here, but he was just giving me the deadpan death glare, so I pulled a pack of smokes from my pocket and sparked up.

"Say again, glove, I missed a bit of that on account of me staring at your tits," I said without looking at her as I held the smoke to the flame and inhaled deeply.

The Russian fella sitting next to Vlad started jabbering away in the language of... huh, French was the love one, so what was Russian? No fucking idea on that but if I had to guess based off of his tone, I'd say utter fucking rage. He was a big lad, though not as big as me and I wondered briefly if the soup spoon might like a soiree up his arse instead of serving dessert tonight.

The angry fella looked ready to throw down at the table and I eyed his shining bald spot with a mild desire to play it like a bongo.

Anastasia withdrew her talons from my thigh and leaned forward, hissing something in Russian that shut him up and the look he was giving her in return told me they were fucking. Which was handy because I didn't want my cock going anywhere near her. Good luck to them and their bald, big breasted children.

"I was saying that a summer wedding would be ideal," Anastasia said, turning her gaze back to the side of my face. I wasn't entirely sure I'd looked at her since I'd arrived, and I wasn't planning on doing it now, so it was hard to say for sure how pissed or not pissed she was at my lack of attention.

"Sure," I agreed, having no interest in any kind of wedding, therefore having no opinion on such a thing.

"Good." Pa clapped his hands together and smiled at me which was damn weird because I was clearly pissing him off right about now and he usually made no concessions for my bullshit. "That's settled then. It'll be a summer wedding."

I stilled, utterly, completely, not even a twitch of my pinky finger, still.

"Perfect," Vlad agreed. "The sooner we settle this, the sooner we can move together against the Castillos."

They descended into talks of politics and I leaned back in my chair, thinking, plotting, planning. There wasn't much to be said for any of my ideas though. I doubted I could get away with dressing a monkey in my suit and tricking Anastasia into marrying him. I probably could assassinate her and make it seem like an accident - car crash, falling piano, exploding tit implant or something equally feasible. But there were plenty more Russians in the sea. No doubt another daughter or a cousin or a great aunt Vladimir would pop up out of the woodwork and the wedding would still go ahead.

I watched Vlad's terrible face tattoo and wondered if I should just cut it off for him. Surely a hole in the face would be preferable to that blurry monstrosity? He could use the hole for plenty of fun things, like eating without opening his mouth, taking a cock in from the side (assuming he went in for a sausage suck here and there). He could allow a bird to nest in it or just decorate it with glitter. Anything would be better than that inky blob of shit.

Food was served and there were talks about dresses and colour schemes and bullshit, and I chimed in with the odd 'how about pumpkin orange?', 'I always thought rocks made nice centre pieces' and my personal favourite, 'the favours could be severed fingers. I can get them cheap from my job.'

Before long they just laughed off my input and Anastasia and an angry looking woman with a monobrow who was sitting on her other side descended into planning in Russian. There was a binder involved and colour swatches were held against my skin and all in all I was more interested in the monobrow. I mean, that shit was impressive. I couldn't grow one of those babies. I had to assume the woman was Anastasia's mother and I guessed if she took after her that would explain all the plastic surgery she'd so clearly had.

"Let's hope this one is more fun than your last wedding, eh brother?" Connor called, seeming to notice my less than enthusiastic responses to everything and apparently feeling like it was a good idea to bait me.

I grinned at him, drawing my steak knife from the table and slipping it into my pocket.

At least the food was good. Martha had outdone herself as usual and I ate like a starved man as I tried to block out the noise which was surrounding me.

At least until something Vlad was saying to my pa piqued my attention.

"-name is Mateo Ortega. Have you heard of him?"

"Does sound familiar," Pa agreed and I looked at him, letting him know I was interested in this.

"The rumour is that he didn't really die a year ago," Vlad said. "Instead there was some huge fall out and he killed a bunch of Santiago Castillo's men before stealing from him and running away like a rat down a drain."

"A man like that could be a veritable gold mine of information," Pa agreed, glancing at me. "Have you heard anything about this before? Any rumours of a cartel man on the run amongst your sources?" His lip curled back in disdain but even the great Liam O'Brien knew the value of keeping your ear to the ground. The problem was he didn't like doing it himself, and that meant that he was relying on me relaying everything I heard to him. There was a lot of trust that he was placing in me there. Some might say that was a silly thing to do.

Had I heard a rumour of a man running from the cartel after pissing them off to no end and stealing countless treasures from them? Sure had. But I'd heard the news while it was fresh, and I'd already tracked him down and locked him up in my basement. *Finders keepers*.

"Nothing," I replied with a shrug. "If it happened a year ago I'd put my money on him being far, far away from here by now. But I can ask around, see if we can sniff him out. What makes you so sure this info is good anyway?"

"Because we caught a little piece of shit Castillo lurking around our warehouses," Vlad replied calmly. "It took four days, but before he died he was singing like a canary. All kinds of things spilling from his loose lips which could help us against them, but this seemed like the biggest secret of all to me."

"I agree," Pa said. "He was high up in their organisation, so he would be able to tell us all manner of things about them which could be just the ticket we need to their destruction."

"Sounds like a golden ticket," I agreed lazily. *Nothing to see here, no need to come check out my basement.*

"I want you on this, Niall," Pa said and I woulda laughed if it wouldn't have given the game away. "You're the best at tracking down scum like that. Find Mateo Ortega and deliver him to me for questioning."

"Sounds like I'd better get to work on that then." I stood abruptly, resisting the urge to knock back another drink because I wanted to drive the fuck outa here tonight.

Anastasia stood too, seeming to think she was coming with me and I arched a brow at her.

"I'll see you later, glove," I said firmly. "I got business to attend to now."

She looked all kinds of pissed but I didn't give a fuck about that, so I just said goodnight to me pa and his new Russian bestie then circled the table on my way out.

The eyes of my siblings trailed me as I went, but none were quick enough to stop me as I paused behind Connor, snatched my steak knife from my pocket and grabbed hold of his fucking ponytail. I yanked it back hard and pressed the blade to his throat.

Everyone at the table fell silent and I grinned as I looked down into my big brother's terrified eyes. Yeah, he knew I could do it. Knew it damn well.

I leaned down so that my mouth was to his ear and spoke just for him. "You make a derisive comment about Ava again and I'll be cutting off something that won't grow back. Got it?"

"Yer a fuckin' psycho," he hissed and I let the blade catch on his skin, spilling just a little blood.

"Wanna try that again?" I suggested darkly.

"Yeah, I got it," he said with a wince and I withdrew.

I pulled the knife away from his throat with more than a little reluctance, then chopped his fucking ponytail clean off and dropped it into his drink before slamming the steak knife down into the table right beside his hand and shoving his head forward roughly.

I tipped an imaginary hat to my pa then strode for the exit, not even bothering to hurry as the sound of Connor leaping to his feet and knocking his chair back followed me.

I just kept walking and the steak knife flew past my ear harmlessly a moment later before bouncing off of the wall and clattering to the ground.

"Ya never could aim for shit," I called, picking it up and glancing over my shoulder at him coming up behind me as I tossed it back.

His eyes bugged right out of his face in fright and I showed him all of my teeth before the blade imbedded itself in the top of his foot.

I left the room with a smile on my face as he howled in pain and I wondered if he realised he should be thanking me for not aiming higher.

I strode away without looking back again, ignoring Anastasia's voice as she called after me and upping my pace until I made it to the doors and flung them open. I had my cherry red muscle car with me today and I was in the mood to drive her fast.

"Don't make an enemy of me, Niall O'Brien," Anastasia snapped just as I pulled the door to my car open and I looked back to find her standing at the top of the stone steps which led up to the house.

"Wouldn't dream of it, glove," I agreed, doing her the courtesy of waiting while she stalked down the stairs towards me, her blonde hair blowing in the wind.

She didn't stop until she was right up in my personal space and I noticed a bug landing in her hair. Did it like it in there? Was it snug and warm like her tits trussed up in that dress or cold and barren like her heart?

"We have an opportunity here," she said in an accented voice I was guessing was meant to be seductive. "We can make the most of it. Tell me why you're reluctant, is it your poor, dead wife?"

I woulda slapped her if she'd been anyone else, but I was starting to get the impression this one was a real snake and I'd do well to proceed with a little caution.

"This is how it is," I said to her, deciding to lay it out. "You and I are grown arse people. I'm a man who has lived through my fair share of shit and violence and I don't take kindly to being told what to do. That said, I'm also a member of my pa's little criminal empire and you're clearly a pawn for yours. So short of going against our families and possibly facing death over a little disobedience, it seems like this wedding is our only choice."

"I'm not a pawn," she hissed, reaching out to grasp my chin between pink taloned fingers. I let her because I was curious about what she might do.

"Pawn, whore, whatever you wanna call it, makes no difference to me." I shrugged and she dug her nails in until I was fairly certain she was marking my skin.

"I'm not a whore either," she growled.

"Good." I knocked her hand off of me and gave her a look that warned her not to do it again. "Then I'll tell you this. I was married a long damn time ago and my wife died. I made it clear I'd never be doing that again and yet my pa has decided to go against my wishes on the subject. So to keep the peace, I'll walk down the aisle and wear the dress and all that shit."

"I'm the one who wears-"

"But I won't be livin' with ya. And I won't be fuckin' ya. In fact, you can go right on fucking that fella in there with the bongo head and I'm sure we'll all be dandy."

"No," she snapped. "That won't work. The point of this wedding is to combine our families. That means we live together and we produce children."

I barked a laugh and knocked her back a step as I dropped into my car. "Good luck with that. I'm not cut out for being a daddy even if you did get me hard, so I suggest you accept the way this is going to be before you go gettin' yer feelings hurt. I've told ya where I'm at and that isn't gonna change."

The engine started with a roar and I cranked Stan by Eminem and Dido up as I started singing, driving away from her angry little face and laughing to myself as I went.

It was dark out and the time on the dash told me it was almost nine, so I put my foot down as I considered my plans for the evening.

I hadn't eaten a whole lot for my dinner – only that roast and all the trimmings, the weird tomato starter thing, three sides and two bowls of dessert - and Spider was likely hungry now too. Maybe I could invite her up to eat with me again and-

My gaze caught on the same blue Honda for the third fucking time in my rear-view mirror and I took a corner at speed before slamming on the brakes and wrenching the wheel to the left, sending my car spinning out to block the road.

I popped the glove box and grabbed my Desert Eagle out before hopping outa the car and aiming it at the Honda as it appeared right behind me.

The girl at the wheel slammed on the brakes, the car skidding towards me as I just stood and waited for her, recognition filling me as I spotted one of my brother Ronan's girls.

"Out," I barked, seeing the desire to drive the fuck away from me flaring in her eyes.

She hesitated, seeming to realise I was more likely to put a bullet in her if she didn't cooperate.

She got out of the car. "Uncle Niall, I-"

"Yeah, yeah, I got it. Your pa decided he'd like to know where I'm living in case he feels the urge to come kill me in me sleep one night."

I tucked the gun into the back of my pants and stalked towards her until I was standing right over her, boxing her in against the car. She was a pretty girl with dark skin and wild hair. Luckily for her she favoured her ma's looks over Ronan's.

"I...I - he never said that. He just wants to know where you live. That's it," she stuttered and I almost felt bad for terrifying her before remembering O'Brien blood ran thick in her veins and she was likely putting it on. I was pretty sure her name was Trixie, or Tuppence, or Tupperware, or Bernard.

"You know why he sent you and not one of yer brothers?" I asked her, wondering if she did or not and she shook her head. She could only have been fourteen or so and I hated my brother a little more for risking her like that. "It's because he thinks I'm softer on women. He thinks I believe you're all sweet and pure or some shit. And maybe he has a point about me not enjoying killing young girls. But I'll tell ya now, you follow me again and I'll make ya beg for a swift death, but it won't come. I'll drag out the sufferin' until you can't take no more and then I'll go a little further than that."

Her eyes widened as she took in the darkness in my gaze and she nodded mutely.

"Good. Now fuck off back to yer pa and tell him if he tries this shit again, I'll break into your house in the dead of night and kill every last one of ya but him. I'll just remove all of his limbs including his cock then leave him to live on knowing what he cost himself and all of you by trying to pry into my business."

"Sorry," she whispered and I scrubbed her hair affectionately - she was my niece after all.

"Just don't do it again and I won't have ta gut ya." I winked at her as her face paled then I turned away.

I took a knife from my pocket and stabbed her tire before striding back to my car and hopping in. I tossed the gun back into the glove box and noticed the unopened bottle of Valium in there. Oh. Maybe I hadn't actually taken any then. I guessed I'd just been in the mood to be a cunt. Never mind.

By the time I'd driven around a bit to double check I hadn't picked up anymore tails and I made it back to the house on the hill, it was past ten and my veins were humming with the need to shake things up.

My mind kept shifting onto my little psycho and as I jogged into the house, I didn't pause before heading straight down to the basement to find her.

She was laying on her bed, feet up on the wall and her head tipped back so she could look at me upside down as I approached her.

"Come eat with me, little psycho," I said. "I'm hungry for your company tonight."

Mateo snarled something in his cage, but I ignored him. I wasn't looking to spill blood right now, I was hungering for something else. Something I got the feeling she could give me.

"What are we eating?" Spider demanded, flipping her legs back over her head and rolling upright.

She was wearing a pair of neon green harem pants with a tight black crop top that was little more than a bra beneath a multi-coloured furry waistcoat. On anyone else it might have looked insane, but on her it just fit. Probably because she *was* insane, but I felt that that was one of her best features so I wasn't complaining.

"I can cook pasta," I said with a shrug because that was the limit of my skills. "Or order takeout."

"I'll take the home cooking thingy," she said, skipping away from me into the bathroom and leaving me to wonder where she was going.

I glanced around at Mateo and found him glaring darkly at me from his cage in the corner and couldn't resist the urge to rile him up.

"What is it?" I asked, striding over to him and standing just out of reach beyond the bars. Not that I was utterly opposed to having another scrap with him, but this shirt was clean and I wanted to keep it that way. "You jealous of our little dinner date? Sorry sweetheart, but you're just not my type."

"One of these days, you'll wake up to find me out of this cage and standing over your fucking bed," he growled in a low tone. "And then you'll realise the mistake you made in trapping me like this."

I grinned at him and Spider reappeared, moving to swing from the bars of his cage as she looked between the two of us. She'd painted her lips a bright, blood red which was inlaid with glitter that sparkled even in the low light down here. My gaze lingered on her mouth for far too long and the next thing I knew she was pouncing on me.

I laughed as I caught her, trying to keep hold of her while she scrambled around onto my back and hooked an arm around my neck, catching her wrist in her other hand and squeezing hard as she let her weight hang from me.

The move effectively cut off my oxygen and I reached around behind me, grabbing the round curve of her arse and lifting her higher to make her choke hold less effective as I carried her up the stairs and out of the basement.

I could feel Mateo's glare on us the entire way, but I didn't give a fuck. In fact, I hoped he'd fallen in love with her and his little cartel heart was breaking right about now as she ditched him to come play with me.

I paused to lock up then carried her to the kitchen, my lungs burning as I started to really struggle for breath and she laughed as I dropped to my knees. But her laughter cut off abruptly as I bucked her off of me and flipped her over my head so that she crashed down onto her back in front of me.

"Dammit," she growled and I caught her wrists as I leaned down to look at her, pinning them to the floor either side of her.

"Nice try," I said, leaning so close to her that our breaths mingled.

"You're never going to die, are you?" she huffed, making me grin.

"I told ya before, Spider, death doesn't want me. I've gotta stay here and suffer. That's the plan for me."

I released her suddenly and stood up, leaving her laying on the floor as I grabbed a pan from the cupboard and filled it with water before setting it to boil.

I was grating cheese by the time she got up and moved over to look at what I was doing.

"My dad used to make me mac 'n' cheese," she said, her voice softer than usual.

She was so damn small that I could only see the top of her head as she looked down at the counter where I was working.

I stopped what I was doing and picked her up, sitting her on the worktop beside me before going back to my grating. She didn't object and as I caught a glimpse of her expression, I coulda sworn she was sad.

"You don't talk about yer family," I pointed out. "Don't talk about much of anything before you came here. Nothin' that counts anyway."

She shrugged. "You don't talk about this." Her finger landed on my forearm where Ava's name was inked on my skin before trailing down to touch the wedding band I still wore on my left hand. I looked into her eyes and we silently agreed we weren't going to be talking about those things now either.

"Alright," I said, going back to the cheese and feeling her eyes on me. "Why don't you tell me about yer future then?"

"What do you mean?"

"I mean, what do you want outa life? You're young, you gotta have dreams, ambitions."

"I thought you were training me up to be like you?" she questioned and I stilled.

"You don't wanna be like me," I muttered. "But yeah, I'm training you up to be a killer. A decent one. But I never actually asked if that would be what you chose."

I wasn't entirely sure what I was gonna say if she confessed some secret desire to be a zookeeper instead of a gun for hire, but I was willing to hear her out.

"I wanna be like those assassins you see on the TV," she said after a pause. "The ones who turn up in their fancy dresses and killer heels and trick men into their beds and then just stab, stab, stab, stab." She enunciated all of those stabs with little strikes to my chest and for some strange reason I just let her.

I snorted a laugh. "You wanna be a honey trap? Ya don't strike me as being particularly into seduction."

"Errr, excuse you, I'm the queen of seduction."

I stopped the food prep and turned to her with an arched brow. "Since when?"

She rolled her eyes and reached around me to grab a handful of grated cheese before lifting it above her, tipping her head back and dropping it into her mouth. A fair bit of it missed and fell into her hair, down the front of her crop top and onto the counter between her thighs, making me bark another laugh. She ignored me and sucked on her fingers, moaning loudly while chewing on the cheese before swallowing.

"See?" she said, her eyes flaring triumphantly and I roared with laughter as I realised that was supposed to be seductive.

"Sorry, little psycho, but I don't think the cheese fetish is working on me. Maybe you need lessons in that too."

Her eyes flared with fury and she reached out, snatching hold of one of my braces and pulling it wide before releasing it so it snapped back against my chest, making my skin sting.

"Are you pissed at me?" I teased as she growled again before shoving away from me and stalking out of the room.

She had her shock collar on, so I wasn't fussed about her running off and I turned my attention back to finishing our food.

When it was done, I delivered some to Mateo like a perfect host then hunted her down in the dining room. I presented her with the steaming plate of cheesy pasta and we entered into our usual race to eat the fastest.

I managed to stab my tongue with my fork and burn the roof of my mouth, but I won and I tossed my fork down with a triumphant grin as she scrambled to finish the last of hers.

"I wanna go back to the basement now," Spider announced suddenly, pushing to her feet and my gut dropped at the dismissal in her tone.

Why didn't she wanna play with me tonight?

"Oh," I said slowly, trying to figure out the fury in her eyes as she folded her arms and refused to look at me. "What's wro-"

"Is it because I'm not pretty then?" she snapped. "Because one time a guy who lived in the bushes called me fuckable and I kinda took that to mean I was. But you literally just laughed in my face when I showed you my best moves and that doesn't make me feel fuckable at all. It makes me feel like that girl who everyone always laughed at when all I wanted was a friend."

She made a move to storm away from me and I caught her wrist, realising I'd fucked up and wanting to fix it for some unknown reason.

She glared down at me with a feral challenge in her eyes and I ran my thumb over the spider tattoo on hers.

"Nah, you're not pretty, little psycho," I admitted, watching her closely. Her gaze tightened and glittery lips pushed into a pout and I smirked at her as she took that as an insult.

She tried to yank her hand out of my hold and I stood suddenly too, backing her up against the wall and placing my palms either side of her head as I boxed her in and leaned down to make her look at me.

"Pretty is what you call girls who are sweet and bland and boring. You're not pretty. You're the only thing in the room no matter how full it is. You're the kind of woman men go to war for. Even beautiful doesn't cut it for you. You're breath taking in the most extraordinary way."

"Oh," she breathed, her gaze holding mine for several long seconds that seemed charged with electricity.

I drew back suddenly when I was certain I was about to be burned by it, but she gripped my braces to stop me from retreating.

"So teach me then," she murmured.

"Teach you what?"

"How to be a honey trap if that's what it's called. You told me I have to find my own style and I think that's it."

"How am I supposed to teach ya to seduce a man? I have no experience in that field, love. Were you hoping I might?"

"Well, I have had a few dirty dreams about you and Mateo doing a whole prisoner and guard porno bit," she admitted and I howled a laugh at the idea of that.

"Who was topping who?" I demanded suddenly, my humour falling away as the need to know that burned through me.

"You enjoyed him sucking your dick just as much as you enjoyed sucking his," she tossed back and I narrowed my eyes.

"Touché."

"Is that a no then? Can't the great murder teacher teach me how to seduce someone before I kill them?" she challenged.

"I can teach you to make them die with a smile on their fuckin' face," I growled in reply, refusing to back down.

"I'd like that," she agreed, tugging on my braces a little more in her excitement and drawing me in.

I slowly laid my hands back on the wall either side of her head, one after another as I leaned down to look her in the eyes again.

"How about I cut you a deal," I said to her. "You don't like me hurting Mateo, right?"

She shook her head, pouting at me. "I don't think stealing is a good enough reason to hurt someone the way you hurt him."

My smile widened, deepened, grew into something dark and cruel and big enough to eat her up like I was the big bad wolf and she was my little red.

I moved my mouth to her ear as I spoke again. "Your poor, innocent Mateo is a bad man, little psycho," I said, my voice low and rough. "He's done a whole lot worse than stealing. Enough to make even you blush."

Her breath caught and her hands ran up the length of my braces slowly as she kept her hold on them tight, not letting me go anywhere even if I'd had any inclination to.

"Tell me," she demanded breathily and I chuckled, my mouth grazing the side of her neck, stubble raking across her soft skin.

"He's a killer. A damn good one too if the stories are true - though clearly not as good as me."

"Do you think you're the best killer in all the world?" she asked me and I drew back, finding nothing but curiosity in her gaze where I expected her to be mocking.

I reached for her face, running my fingers down the side of her jaw and along her neck before dropping my hand and grasping her hip in my hand, my thumb grazing warm flesh above her waistband.

"Sometimes there's something so innocent about you," I said, breathing her in while I knew I should have been pulling away.

She was young, that was why she seemed innocent. I could tell she'd lived through her own share of pain and tortures, but they hadn't twisted her up inside the way mine had over long, hard years which made me jaded and fractured and too fucked up to return from. She'd seen a lot of pain, but she hadn't seen a lot of life. It was a strange combination, and I found it kind of intoxicating.

"I'm not innocent," she replied, shaking her head a little. "The judge said I wasn't. He said I wasn't even though I only killed them because they were...they were..." She shook her head more firmly and the ghosts which had been swirling in her eyes were banished as she fought them away. "Tell me if you're the best or not," she demanded and I decided to let her keep her secrets if she wasn't ready to trust me with them. But it might just have been time for me to go digging them up for myself.

"What kind of prize would I get if I were?" I teased and she actually looked like she was considering that as her hands slowly began a descent down the length of my braces again. I wasn't even sure she was totally aware she was doing it, but the press of her knuckles running down my body through the thin fabric of my shirt was making my heart pound faster.

"Me," she replied firmly and I frowned as I wondered what she meant by that and why I enjoyed the idea of it so damn much. "If you were the best, I'd want to die by your hand. You could take me to your killing room and make a pretty mess out of me."

My frown deepened, not liking the sound of that. "Maybe I don't want you dead."

"I don't want to be dead either," she replied, her hands making it to the bottom of my braces and resting against the waistband of my pants. "But when I'm ready I think I'd like to go that way, head to the Devil in style, all carved up by the greatest killer who ever lived."

I shook my head and she narrowed her eyes.

"Why not? Don't you like the idea of me all bloody for you?" she demanded.

"I'd see you bloody," I agreed. "But I'd sooner that blood wasn't yours."

"Why?" she asked suspiciously and I paused, surprising myself with the answer that came to mind.

"Because I like ya, Spider. I think I've met my match in you and if I have, then the world had better be afraid."

We were staring at each other again and this heat rising in my body wasn't going anywhere. I hadn't looked at a woman like this in so long, hadn't thought about a woman like this in even longer. Why her? Why now?

My gaze fell on her mouth and hooked there, drinking in the sight of that sparkling lipstick as I wondered what it would taste like on my tongue. I inched closer, drawn in by her, tempted, lured.

"So you do think I'm a good killer?" she asked hopefully, snapping me out of it and I shifted back as I barked a laugh.

"Nope." I pushed off of the wall and stepped away while she glared at me furiously. "I just see the Devil in you, lass. I see the need for violence, I see a lotta me. Doesn't mean I see any talent though."

She launched herself at me furiously and I ducked aside, pulling the remote from my pocket and shocking her with the collar that still hung around her neck.

I caught her as she fell to the floor, making sure she didn't hit her head then stood over her as I pulled my phone from my pocket and dialled a number. My phone was utterly untraceable, so I didn't have to worry about that kind of nonsense and when it connected and a sultry voice purred a hello, I just smiled.

"Hey Mel," I said, watching Spider as she writhed on the floor, a throaty moan escaping her as her hands grasped at her body and my cock throbbed in my pants. *Not gonna think about that.*

"Oh hey, baby," Mel purred, throwing on the charm in an instant, but she didn't need to run that game with me.

"I got an odd job for ya," I said, cutting to the chase. "I got a girl here who wants to learn how to seduce a fella before sinking a knife into his back without him even realising what's happening until it's too late."

"Oooh, fun," Mel replied breathily and I rolled my eyes, wondering why she still tried to pull those tricks with me after all this time when I'd made it more than clear I'd never be interested in taking her for a ride myself.

"You up for it?"

"Sure. I charge double for women though," she added, trying her luck.

"Bullshit," I growled. "But I'll pay ya double if you can tell me anything useful about my brothers."

"Well, Dermot has a big play happening this weekend. I'm pretty sure he's hoping to secure some new import deal that he thinks will make your daddy favour him if he pulls it off. He's been making me call him King Dermot while he fucks me because he's so excited about it."

I snorted derisively. Dermot always believed he was close to winning

Pa's favour, but ever since he'd gotten drunk and been arrested for trying to fuck that horse statue in the park when he was nineteen, Pa had never considered him seriously.

"And Ronan?" I asked. It amused me to no end that I had a hooker fucking two of my brothers and feeding me information on them while they both had no idea about it.

Ronan had been trying to fuck Dermot's wife for years, so it had been all too easy to arrange for him to not so accidentally see him with Mel then get him fucking her instead. He thought he was getting one up on Dermot every time he was with her, and the two of them both believed a beautiful woman like her was seriously interested in them without even realising she was paid for her time. I couldn't wait until the day they figured out she'd been paid to fake her orgasms for them for years while they'd been wasting all their money buying her shit. Dermot had even put her up in a million dollar house on the outskirts of town. Fucking classic.

"Ronan is Ronan," she sighed. "Always with the big plans and never with the execution. Kinda like the way he constantly promises to blow my mind in bed but can't actually figure out where my clit is."

I roared a laugh just as Spider pushed to her feet and launched herself at me and I was forced to catch her by the throat to stop her.

"Alright, double rate," I agreed because confirming to me that the two of them were still as useless as ever was damn good information in my books - it meant they were still no threat to me and I could go on ignoring their existence for the most part. "Here she is."

I held the phone out to Spider and she glared at me before taking it. "Who is this?" she demanded suspiciously.

"The best escort in the state," I said with a grin. "She'll teach ya your seduction shit. First lesson starts now and if you want more, I can call her for you again another time. Her name's Mel and she's nice so don't be an arsehole."

Spider gave that some thought then abruptly turned her back on me and strode from the room, saying hello to Mel in a super sweet telephone voice which she'd never used with me.

I left her to it, cleaning up after our meal and heading to the kitchen where I pulled open the boiler cupboard and snuck a handful of Coco Pops outa the box I'd stashed there. Spider thought we were all out since her stunt the other day, but little did she know I had a secret supply for emergencies. And also that huge crate out in the garage – imports weren't cheap so it made sense to bulk buy.

When I was done cleaning up, I headed back into the front room and threw a few logs on the fire, leaving the overhead lights off and turning some music on, though I was surprised to find I didn't need the distraction of the lyrics tonight like I normally did.

Talk by Salvatore Ganacci started up and I lit a cigarette, closing my eyes and leaning my head back as I inhaled deeply. Unlike most people who smoked the things, I was actually hoping they'd kill me one of these days. Nothing else seemed likely to get the job done, so why not this? I doubted it though. Maybe I'd just live forever, destined to roam the Earth doing the work of the Grim Reaper and existing on and on and on. I guessed I deserved it. But sometimes I ached for oblivion more than anything in the world.

I wasn't sure how long Spider spent on the phone as I stood by the fire, smoking and sipping on a glass of whiskey I'd poured myself, but when she returned to me, she had an excited light in her eyes that got my attention right away.

"You never finished telling me what deal you were going to cut me about Mateo," she said as she walked towards me slowly, the firelight flickering against the bare expanses of skin she'd left on show surrounding that crop top.

"Oh right," I said, trying to remember what the fuck that had been about. I'd been thinking about getting a cat and then I remembered that

Brutus wasn't a fan of cats, then I'd remembered Brutus still only existed in my head and then-

"I'll give ya two months to work your magic on Mateo," I said, snapping my fingers as I remembered it. "If you think you can be a honey trap, then I want ya to prove it on him. Draw him in however you like, seduce him whatever way ya need to, and find out where he hid that fucking money."

"You want me to have sex with him?" she asked as she reached me, her eyes glinting in a way that made rage pour through my veins.

"No," I snarled. "I didn't say fuck him. Seduce him, manipulate him, get him hard and fucking begging for your pussy but don't let him have it. That's how it works. You get him hooked on the promise of heaven between your thighs, but you make him tell you where the money is before you let him have a taste."

"And *then* I fuck him?" she clarified. "Once he tells me-"

"No," I snapped. "Then you tell *me* where it is and we have enough money to run the fuck away forever and ever. Clean money that's got nothing to do with my pa or anyone in my family."

"And what about Mateo?" she asked, narrowing her eyes and folding her arms so that her tits were pushed up.

Then I'll kill him.

I figured she wouldn't want that answer right now so I just shrugged. "Maybe I'll let you decide on that. If you get the money."

Cravin' by Stileto and Kendyle Paige started playing and Spider bit her bottom lip slowly, letting it pull free again as she considered that.

"Alright," she agreed, her voice low and catching me off guard as she stepped forward into my personal space, reaching out to catch my wrist where I held my whiskey and moving it towards her mouth. "I'll drink to that."

She was so close to me that I could smell the vanilla perfume she'd bought herself, the sweetness of it making my senses tingle as her fingers brushed over mine and she raised my glass to her lips.

I watched as her throat bobbed then she drew back, leaving me with the glass and licking her lips slowly to remove the last drops of the liquor from them.

"I always wanted to try smoking cigarettes," she said, looking at my smoke as I lifted it to my lips again. "But it makes me cough too much."

"You shouldn't try them anyway," I said. "They're bad for you."

"I tend to like things that are bad for me, Hellfire," she said huskily and my gaze fell to her lips again before I could help it. "Can I just have a taste?"

She reached for my cigarette, but instead of giving it to her, I inhaled the last drag of smoke from it and tossed it into the fire before catching her jaw in my hand and raising her mouth up so that it was in line with mine. I exhaled slowly and she breathed the smoke in like we were sharing a joint instead of a cigarette and I smirked at her as her lips parted for the taste she wanted.

"Will you tell me about this one?" she murmured, her hand reaching for the open buttons at the top of my shirt before her fingers dragged over the shamrock I had inked just above my collar bone.

"I'm Irish, love, I'm pretty sure that one is self explanatory." I hadn't released my hold on her face and I knew I should, but I didn't.

"Okay...so what about this one?" Her fingers roamed lower and my cock was pretty much bursting out of my pants and sliding inside her already while I was still struggling to catch up to what was happening.

Was that what she wanted? Was it what I wanted? I couldn't deny the hunger in my flesh or the way I was aching to close what little distance there was left between us. But I hadn't done that with anyone since Ava and I hadn't intended to. I was pretty certain I still didn't intend to, but I was still touching her and she was touching me and I didn't want it to stop either. There were a thousand reasons why it should though.

Spider was too young for me for one. It didn't matter if she was beautiful and made me burn up with want, she was too damn young and I was too fucked up. She deserved a fella her own age who could kill at least as good as she could. But even as I thought it, I mentally murdered the bastard and buried his body six feet under.

My body had some seriously strong objections to my own argument and as her hand slipped beneath the fabric of my shirt, I was struggling to maintain my stance on it.

She looked up at me and I was reminded of just how tiny she was as she pushed up onto her tiptoes, moving her lips closer to mine and drawing me in like a moth to a flame.

My hand slid around her waist until my palm was flat against the small of her back as I tugged her against me, letting her feel exactly how much I wanted her as my cock drove into her and caused her expression to flicker.

"Should I be worried about that fitting or am I overthinking?" she breathed, making me blink as half a laugh escaped me, but it was cut off again as her hand ran down to my waistband and over the hard swell which was pushing against her needily.

"Spider," I growled, meaning to warn her back but ending up leaning in.

Her lips brushed against mine and my grip on her tightened as I felt my resolve shattering for her, the need in my body winning the battle that had been waging within myself and every doubt I'd been harbouring falling aside as I leaned forward to claim a kiss which I knew I hadn't earned.

But she spoke before I could take it, her words making me freeze as her lips brushed against my mouth.

"Do you want me to call you Daddy?"

I fell utterly still, my heart racing and cock throbbing as my brain just howled a fucking laugh at how stupid I was before dousing everything inside me in gasoline and setting it alight while my dead wife's screams rang in my ears.

"Nice work, Spider," I snarled, shoving her away from me and making her stumble in surprise as I almost knocked her on her arse. "You almost had me going for a minute there. You pushed it a little too far with the Daddy kink though."

Her lips popped open as she stared at me, drinking in the change as pure, toxic rage poured from my flesh in place of whatever insanity had almost just come over me and I tried to ignore the twist of something painful that was taking place in my chest.

"Mel thought you might like-"

"Bravo." I clapped my hands loudly before grabbing the whiskey glass and launching it across the room where it smashed against the wall into a million pieces and in the next moment I was on her, my hand fisting her hair and my face right in hers. "You try and play me for a fool like that again and I'll sew your pretty lips shut to teach you not to put them near me."

She tried to punch me and I could have blocked it but I let her land it, the pain radiating through my jaw feeling so much better than the pain in my chest right now.

I grabbed her around the waist and threw her over my shoulder, unable to hear the things she was yelling at me over the echoes of the screams that I could hear rattling around inside my skull.

I unlocked the basement door and jogged down the stairs, dropping her on the bed and ignoring Mateo as he snarled something at me, lunging against the bars to his cage.

"What the fuck, Niall?!" Spider yelled but I didn't slow.

I made it back upstairs and locked up again, not hearing the way Spider was yelling my name and not caring about anything other than the way my flesh was burning and my head hurting.

I found my phone abandoned in the kitchen and grabbed it alongside a bottle of whiskey then headed back to the front room where I dropped down in front of the fire and tried not to think about what had almost just happened.

Or what I'd thought might happen while she'd been playing me.

I unscrewed the cap and drank a good quarter of the bottle straight down, aiming for comatose and hoping on death.

As the whiskey burned in my gut and began to take effect, I started up the video of Ava. The one Tom Nelson had sent me of her raped and beaten and bloody. The last time I'd seen her alive. The night I lost the last good piece of my soul.

This pain in me never really went away, but as the years passed I somehow found more and more ways to hide it, disguise it bury it. Problem was, whenever it reared its ugly head again it just hurt all the more, cutting into me, making me bleed so much worse than anything physical ever could.

I was reminded of exactly what kind of man I was. Exactly what I caused to the people around me. Exactly what would happen to anyone I ever let get close like that again. Which was why I could never let it happen. I needed to live in this pain, burn in it and let it consume me. It was the least I deserved and the surest way to make sure I never forgot.

What had happened to Ava was on me and I'd been punished for it every day since. Every day and night and all the dark places in between. She was always here and I was always alone. Which was how it was supposed to be. It was how I deserved to live.

Every time the video ended I started it up again, torturing myself more thoroughly than any weapon ever could as I drank my way through the bottle of whiskey. I didn't care what happened to me now. I didn't care. And no one else ever would either.

BROOKLYN

CHAPTER TWENTY

Niall hadn't trained me for days, only coming down to toss food into the basement before leaving again without a word. No matter how much abuse I'd thrown at him, he'd just ignored me. I didn't wanna admit it, but it hurt. I didn't think what I'd done had been such a big deal. He was the one who'd called his friend Mel. He was the one who'd told me to talk to her. So I'd discussed how to seduce men with her and she'd given me a bunch of ideas including some for him specifically, what had he expected? Did that make me a mean girl? Because like, I had definitely wanted to seduce him for more reasons than just practise. Was he offended I found him attractive because he was grossed out by me? Or was it that I'd made him think I was into him, but he thought I actually wasn't? Even though technically, I was. But only in my secret dreams.

I sat on my bed with my legs hugged to my chest as I felt Mateo staring at me while I drowned in my thoughts. My mind hooked on Penelope and how she'd lured me into those woods all those years ago. Was I like her? Was that what I'd done to Niall? Tried to lure him into my bitch net?

I'd thought seducing would be fun, but now I was having doubts. If I was doing it to nasty little men who ended up dead before they actually touched me maybe it wouldn't have felt this way, but Niall? Niall wasn't a nasty little man. Even if I wished he was. Because then I could have stabbed him in the throat and run for the hills when I'd gotten that close to him. But no, I'd just felt his huge dick grinding into my body and wondered how it would fit inside me while aching for the feel of his lips on mine.

I didn't know what I wanted or how to go about it. All of these emotions and feelings and tingles were new, and I had no idea what to do with them.

It wasn't just my captor I was pining for either. Every day I gazed over at my dead man and wished he'd touch me again too. I was lost, confused and with nothing to do down in this basement, I found myself singing or sobbing or talking incessantly until I accepted Mateo didn't wanna hear any of it. He said so few words. And I wanted all of his words almost as much as I wanted to punch him in the nose for withdrawing from me. But what had I expected? I always did this. No matter how many times I told myself not to trust people, I often got tempted in by the sparkles in their eyes then I ended up used and thrown away like yesterday's trash. This wasn't new to me. But it was the first time it had hurt this deep.

I sighed loudly, burying my face in my legs. I hadn't even worn anything particularly fun today. Just some black leggings with criss-crossing cut outs all the way down the sides and a white crop top which said 'shut yo mouth ho' in bright yellow letters across the chest. I wished Mateo hadn't listened to my t-shirt. I'd made up a whole dance routine for him yesterday in the bathroom, but I hadn't shown him in the end because he'd started working out and seemed too busy to watch it. *Siiiiiigh. What am I gonna do?*

You need to buck up and face the world, that's what. People are awful. That's not news to you, Brooklyn. So get it together.

"Mi sol," Mateo's dark, rough voice reached me from across the basement and my breath snagged in my lungs, rattling around in there like a bee in a jar. "Are you sad?"

"What's it to you?" I sniped, lifting my head and narrowing my eyes at him.

He'd moved to the edge of the cage, his forehead pressed to the bars, giving him a sinister look as he watched me.

"Significa todo para mi," he muttered.

I tsked. "I don't wanna hear about your pet parrot, Mateo," I huffed angrily, pushing out of bed and walking in his vague direction. Though I didn't know why. I just didn't wanna lie on that lonely bed anymore. And his aura seemed so tempting. I wanted to stand in it and bathe in the tantalising taste of him on the air. Just for a second.

"Come here," he said, his words an order I wasn't going to obey, even if I wanted to a little bit.

"No," I said simply.

"*Chica*," he growled in a tone that spoke of the power he'd held in a life far from here.

"No," I repeated.

He could have been the king of the world outside of this basement for all I knew – though I was pretty sure the world king's name was Phillip or something – but in here he was just a prisoner like me. And that made us equals. Besides, I'd never bowed to anyone in my life, I wasn't gonna start now. Unless you counted Queen Kittipuss of course. She was the local alley cat who lived it large back near the bridge. She had a whole army of cats at her beck and call, and I'd come *this* close to being mobbed by them. I'd had to bow to her to get a free pass. But I didn't bow to people. Not ever, not never.

"I want your name," he growled hungrily. "A real name."

I stilled at those words, glancing at him as I twisted my fingers together behind my back. "Can't give you that."

"Why?" he demanded angrily.

"Because I said so," I tossed at him and he scowled.

"Come here," he commanded again as I drifted back and forth in front of him, just out of reach like a fruitcake on a string.

"I don't want to come there. You're not my friend," I said, unable to hide the bitterness in my tone.

"Me vuelves loco," he said, bashing his hand against the bars. "You wouldn't be so cocky if I was free from these bars."

"Why? What would you do? Brush your cold shoulder against me?" I arched a brow, drifting another step closer, his eyes tempting me in, though my heart was thrashing and I knew I shouldn't lean in to the danger of him. Dammit I was such a danger whore though.

"I would punish you for your attitude," he warned and my stomach fluttered.

Tit buckets. He'd punish me? Why did that word sound so hot on his lips, and way more sexy than it should've been?

"What if I want to be punished?" I asked curiously. Not that I did. I just wanted to know what he'd think if I did. Duh.

"If you knew who I really was, you wouldn't ask naive questions like that," he said in that devilish accent of his as I slipped a little closer, the hairs on the back of my neck prickling as they tried to warn me away. But I didn't want to lean back, I wanted to lean in. Deeper, further, get tangled in his tumbleweed and never have to run anywhere again. It was so lonely being alone. For a second there, he'd been something more than just a person who slept nearby. He'd been my boyfriend. My first ever relationship. And it had already gone up in flames.

"Who are you really?" I whispered and his hand shot out, grabbing a fistful of my tee and yanking me against the bars. *Oh hell I love that. Be rough with me, Dead Man. Make me pay.*

Shit cakes, I shouldn't want that though. Why did his hands on my skin not frighten me? Why did they make me crave more? More than any flesh had ever rubbed against mine.

"I'm the villain your mamá warned you about and your papa tried to protect you from," he snarled through his teeth. "And you're my new favourite obsession, little one. When I latch on, I can't let go. So run for your life because I've got a taste for you now and the hunt is on. I won't stop until you're mine, mi sol."

"Maybe I liked being in your trap," I said huskily, reaching through the bars to stroke my fingers along the fierce angles of his face beneath his beard. "Maybe I liked it too much. But no one will ever own me, Dead Man. Not you, not Hellfire, not anyone."

"I wouldn't be so fucking sure," he said, releasing me and I stumbled back a step, my breaths coming heavier.

The sound of the basement door opening reached me and I backed up another step as my stomach knotted with adrenaline. My eyes were glued to my dead man's and his were glued to mine, the connection between us almost tangible as his chest rose and fell in time with my own. It was hard to believe I'd been in that cage with him and survived. And not only that, I'd thrived. He'd injected life into me which I hadn't known existed. He was the first man to touch me sexually who didn't mean me harm. That had to mean something, didn't it? That I hadn't shied away, hadn't squirmed from the heat of his skin against mine? That I'd craved more of it ever since...

His eyes glinted with untold horrors and I wondered if I was lucky to have escaped with my life. But why did that make me wanna go back in with him even more? Why did what he'd done to me feel so much more meaningful because I was still breathing? He hadn't killed me, he'd made me come so hard, I was pretty sure I hadn't yet recovered. But fuck him. That didn't mean he could lay a claim on me. I wasn't to be bought like some old shoe in a flea market. Not ever again.

Niall appeared in navy sweatpants and a white t-shirt, looking sombre as he glanced from me to Mateo.

"Join me for dinner, Spider," he asked in a way that was full of pain and need. His eyes were rimmed with red and I guessed he was hungover, his blonde hair scruffed up and his features drawn.

I pressed my shoulders back, not falling for his poor little broken boy act as I fixed him with a glare. "No."

He took a step toward me and I felt Mateo shift toward me too like a shadow in my periphery. I had a hell hound at my back and one sweeping glance from Niall said he knew it. He kept coming though, ignoring Mateo as his gaze fixed on me.

He reached for my hand, taking it in his large one and I frowned at it. I liked that. I liked it as much as when Mateo touched me. I still wanted to pull it back though, because I was angry at him and that was what he deserved, but the lonely little duck in my heart quacked hopefully and I had to let her have this. *Just this once then, Glenda, but we need to start remembering how to do things alone. This isn't going to last much longer.* But Glenda had been too long without human contact. And she was hungry. She had to take what she could get. Even if it was from a desperately broken looking kidnapper who hated me.

"I'm sorry, love. Come talk to me," he said, his voice low and rough, full of sharp edges.

He sounded so sad that it pulled on some strings in my chest that made me sad too. But could I really just forgive him as easily as that? He seriously did look down in the flumps though. And whenever I got all stuck in those flumps, I always wished someone would come and pull me out of them. So how could I deny him that?

"Okay," I sighed. "But I want Mateo to come too. I want all three of us to have dinner together. Like a f-" I choked on that last word, almost having said 'family'. What the flying U-fucking-O? We weren't that. I didn't really know what that was anymore. But it definitely wasn't three dark souls in a basement. "A club meeting."

"He ain't in our club." Niall's sharp green eyes shot daggers at Mateo.

"Well I say he is." I tugged my hand free of Niall's, propping it on my hip.

"I don't want to be a part of it," Mateo muttered.

"Yes you do," I insisted, shooting him a pout. "And anyway, those are my terms. Take them or leave them, Hellfire."

I walked away from them both and threw myself onto the bed, grabbing my pillows and building a small fort with them to disappear behind. I was a princess in a tower and no knight was going to come charging in to save me from the two dragons out there. I didn't want them to either. I'd save myself with nothing but a toothpick and a bedsheet. *Now where do I get myself a toothpick...*

Niall's heavy footsteps pounded back upstairs and the door slammed, making the ceiling rattle. *Guess that was a no to my request.*

Oh well, I'ma take a nap.

I shut my eyes but some loud ass drilling came from upstairs and I cracked an eye open in anger. Seriously? It was so freaking loud. It went on for a while then there was some banging and clanking and finally all fell quiet and the basement door flew open once more.

Niall came jogging downstairs, pointing at me. "You. Upstairs. Now."

"I said-"

"I'm bringing El Burro," he growled, striding over to Mateo's cage, spinning his stun gun in his hand.

"He's coming?" I asked excitedly, bounding off the bed.

"Yep." Niall shot him with the gun and I cried out, running forward to try and help, but Mateo was already on the ground, all frazzled by the strike.

"Ooh did you like that?" I asked Dead Man but he couldn't speak yet. I eyed the gun as I hungered for a little zappy playtime of my own, but Hellfire didn't seem to notice.

Niall opened the cage, striding in and unlocking the chain from Mateo's

377

collar before grabbing him beneath the arms and hauling him along toward the stairs. I skipped after them excitedly, punching Niall in the kidney for hurting Mateo before following him to the dining room where a new bracket had been fitted on the wall for the chain. Niall shoved Mateo down in a chair in front of it and he groaned, his senses reawakening just as Niall locked him in place then strode away. Mateo lunged for him, but choked as he hit the end of his chain and slumped back down into his seat with a snarl of anger.

Niall directed me to a chair opposite Mateo and I dropped into it with a smile, glancing around and sniffing the air to try and guess what we were gonna be eating. If there was one time of day I was never gonna be a moody Mandy, it was when I was stuffing my face with yummy goodness. I knew what it was like to be hungry and I was gonna enjoy having regular meals while I could. I pounded my fists on the table as I looked to Niall. "What are we eating?"

He said nothing, leaving the room with his shoulders drooping and an air of doom about him.

"What's up with Hellfire?" I murmured.

"Look at me, chica loca," Mateo demanded and my head whipped around as he fixed me with an intense look. "You need to kill him, then we can run."

"But I'm hungry," I complained as my belly growled and he banged his fist on the table which I guessed was to hurry Niall up.

"We have a chance here," Mateo hissed in his lovely accent. It was sexy, did he know how sexy it was? I rested my chin in my hand, gazing at him with a dreamy smile as he started talking about some plan involving a wife, or maybe he said a knife. It all sounded so hot whatever it was.

"Are you even liste-" he stopped dead as Niall walked back into the room and I frowned, missing his voice already.

Hellfire dropped trays of food down on the table and I snatched one, finding a roll of avocado, cream cheese and cucumber sushi inside. "Oh my sweet baby fucknuts. It's beautiful," I groaned, stuffing the first piece in my mouth. Then the next, then the next. Niall swiped some of it away from me and I growled like a dog, lunging at the dumplings he was hoarding and throwing two into my mouth. Niall and I ripped into more bags, devouring everything in sight, fighting to get our hands on the best stuff as rice and seaweed went flying across the table in Mateo's direction.

I snatched away a box of vegetable tempura before Niall could get his greasy mitts on it, then my gaze fell on Mateo just as I was about to force three pieces in my mouth at once, his brows up, his lips parted slightly in shock. *Oh no, my poor pooch is hungry.*

I pushed out of my seat, crawling across the table and sitting in front of him, propping my feet up in his lap.

"Here you go." I pushed a piece between his lips and he frowned for a second before eating it.

His hands moved to clasp my ankles and my lips hooked up at the corner despite the fact that I was still mad at him. But he was so squishalicious right now, how could I not smile at him?

Niall's large hand clamped onto my shoulder and he slammed me down onto the table, crawling past me and snatching the box of tempura, replacing it with some ramen with a plastic fork in it. "This is yours, El Burro. The tempura is mine." He smirked then started wolfing down the last of the amazing nuggets of goodness.

"Hey!" I snarled, lunging at the box in his hand as he reached for the final piece of tempura. He stuck it between his teeth, grinning at me victoriously, but I kept coming, diving on him and snaring the part sticking out of his mouth with my teeth. "Mine."

Niall tore into it and I did the same, our lips grazing as we ripped it in two and each ate half. My lips burned from the slightest touch of his mouth on mine and I realised my hands were bunched in his shirt as I was pressed close against him. I could feel the heat of him everywhere, could hear his wicked soul calling my name.

"Get back in your seat." Niall shoved me toward it and I slid back into it, wiping my lips as he cleared the table and carried the trash out of the room.

Mateo finished his meal with much more dignity than we'd managed, but sucked his fingers clean, the reverence in his eyes speaking of how much he enjoyed his food. Why didn't he join us in our savagery then? I kinda wanted to know what it would be like to see him go fully primal on me. I mean the food. And me. And Niall. *Oooh, what a party that would be.*

"If you play with street dogs, you'll get bitten," Mateo warned in a low voice, his golden brown eyes scoring holes in my flesh.

"I am a street dog, Dead Man, where do you think I got my scars?" I frowned, drawing my legs up to cross them on my chair.

Niall returned and suddenly slapped something down in front of me on the table. "Now we got the eating outa the way, do you wanna tell me more about this?"

I looked up and found myself staring at a police file. *My* police file. I was younger in the photo, just nineteen, the picture taken when I'd been classed as insane and moved to the awful hospital with the awful nurses. *No, no, no, nooo.*

I was dragged back into that hospital for a moment, hearing Madam Lucille's voice whispering in my ear.

"You're a wicked, wicked girl. You'll have to pay for your insolence, sweetie," she purred. "You'll have to stay in your room all alone for the week to give the other patients a break from you. You make it so very hard to be around you. All of us find it very hard. You'll have to wear the naughty girl cuffs on the bed while you're in there and use the bedpan instead of the communal bathroom."

My ears were ringing, my skull was cracking. Niall flipped the page and I found photocopies of newspaper articles with my name and pictures all over them. Me, me, me. He'd found me. The real me.

The 'Bully Butcher' Brooklyn Meadow escaped Eden Heights Psychiatric Hospital last night, leaving two dead in her wake. A bounty of ten thousand dollars has been offered to anyone who can provide her whereabouts. Civilians are advised to be vigilant as the convict is extremely unstable and dangerous.

My throat tightened, my eyes unfocused. Because all this did was drag me back into the past where my demons lived, and I didn't want to face them tonight. I didn't want to face them ever. But they were always lurking so close and now I couldn't escape them. They were dragging me down into a dark, dark lake inside me and I'd drown there in despair, never to be free again.

"So what are you gonna do, Hellfire?" I asked bitterly. "Are you gonna claim that bounty? Pretty sure it's gone up by now too."

I didn't look him in the eye. I didn't want to. Not him, or Mateo. I suddenly didn't want to be here at all. This was my truth. I was a runaway, good for nothing lunatic with a price on my head. People had tried to sell me out before. They'd do it again. Niall was people. Why wouldn't he be the same?

Niall took hold of my chin, forcing my head around to look at him and all I saw in his eyes was a sea of eternal pain. "I don't give a fuck about yer bounty. I spent half a million to buy ya, you idiot."

"Yeah, *potatoes*," I scoffed.

"I told ya it was dollars," he growled but it was still hard to believe that. "And I don't give a fuck about any of that. I wanna know the details of how you ended up in prison, not what's printed in those papers. I want your truth, your past. Every scrap of it. And if you give me that, I'll give ya somethin' of me in return. The one part of me that's worth having."

I tried to figure out what part he meant. There was so much of him I wanted that I couldn't guess what one thing he might put value on above the others.

I looked over at Mateo, finding him staring at me just as intensely as

Niall was.

"And what about you?" I shot at him. "If you get out of here, will you hand me over to them?" I jabbed my finger at the police file.

"He ain't ever gettin' outa here," Niall said icily and my jaw tightened, but I refused to acknowledge that, staring directly at my dead man as I awaited his answer.

"I've stolen far more money than that little bounty, mi sol," he said, tossing a hollow look at Niall.

"And you'll be handin' it to me soon if you don't wanna lose yer legs, lad," Niall warned and I huffed, getting to my feet.

"I'm not giving anything to anyone while you two are fighting," I snapped, moving to walk past Niall, but he caught my arm and tugged me back, his jaw ticking.

"I won't say another word to him, just gimme your story, love. I need it."

"Why?" I hissed, seeing a flicker of desperation in his eyes.

"You'll figure it out once you've told me," he said in a rough tone that set my blood alight.

I glanced from him to Mateo, my heart pounding uncomfortably in my chest. I hadn't told anyone this story, not since I'd stood up in court. Because it had meant nothing to anyone who heard it. And I'd sworn not to trust it to anyone else in the world. But now these two were looking at me like they might just listen, and not just listen, but really hear my side of things and it was too tempting to ignore. No one believed there was anything good in me. Not since Dad had died. Mom had stayed away after my arrest. She hadn't written to me. She hadn't even made a statement for the newspapers. She'd disowned me as viciously as if she'd never had me. And I was left alone in the world with nothing but the weight of my sins for company.

But these men had sins of their own, so if anyone could understand, it was them.

"Fine, but I want alcohol," I demanded. "And chocolate. Lots of chocolate." I was on my period, which had made the last couple of days even more emotional.

I guessed it still beat living on the streets and shoving a rag in my panties though – or that beanie hat I'd stolen from Crusty Sue that time. I currently had a fancy foof stick tucked up there for my flow and it was such a luxury that I made a mental note to rob a whole warehouse of them and give them to the poor. I'd appear in the night and leave foof products at the feet of homeless girls. They'd call me the Crimson Tide. *Saving foofs one flow at a time.*

"Deal." Niall strode away to the kitchen to fetch what I'd asked for and I chewed on my lower lip as I considered what I was about to do. *So you're just gonna tell them everything? Relive that night? Let it burn you up in the horror of it all over again?*

Well I don't want to, Brain, but what am I supposed to do?

Brain had no answer for that, but Heart was thrashing, having a mini panic attack as it knew what was coming. Because I'd made up my mind. I'd tell Hellfire and my dead man about why I'd ended up in prison. I'd kept it inside too long. It lived in me like a demon in a cage and this felt like the right time to let it out. Maybe it would set it free for good, but I didn't think so. I'd need a whole vat of holy water and a house sized crucifix to stand a chance of that.

"You don't have to do anything he tells you," Mateo growled and I looked over to find his knuckles turning white around the plastic fork from his meal.

"I know," I said. "But he knows who I am now anyway, and I don't want what he read in those files to be what he thinks of me."

"Why do you care?" he spat, rage flaring in his eyes.

"Because it's not me, Mateo. It's not my truth. And my truth is all I have," I said defiantly.

His brow furrowed and his hand slowly eased up on the fork as he nodded. "Entiendo."

I knew what that word meant, I could see it written all over his face as clear as day. He understood.

Niall returned with a large bar of chocolate and a bottle of Irish whiskey. I took both from him greedily and jumped up on the table, folding my legs beneath me as I ripped into the chocolate bar and took a huge bite out of it. I twisted off the whiskey cap and swigged a measure into my mouth, making a party of sugar and alcohol fizz around my tongue.

Niall plucked the bottle from my fingers, downing a healthy measure of it before passing it back and I held it out to Mateo.

"No," Niall snapped. "He doesn't get the good stuff."

"Shut up. It's my moment and I say he does." I held it to Mateo's lips and Niall muttered something about a greedy donkey, but didn't try to stop me as I poured a measure between them. Mateo's eyes remained on mine the whole time and his throat worked as he swallowed. I pulled the bottle back to my lips, tasting him and Niall on the bottle, making it all the sweeter as I drank another measure and it roared in my stomach.

I passed the bottle back to Niall and got to my feet, shutting my eyes as I let myself fall into that dark, cavernous place inside me. I swear I could hear some noir piano music playing in my head as I prepared to tell them everything. And as nasty as my story may have been, I never did anything without flare. So I'd tell it right. Make them feel it.

"Penelope was the most popular girl in my school," I started. "She was dating the football captain, Andrew. They were like, school royalty, the jock and the cheerleader, total cliche. And they hated me because I was poor and weird and didn't fit into their world. Back then, all I ever wanted to do was hide. If I'd had one wish, it would have been to be invisible, because then no one could ever bother me again. But I'd had as many wishes granted as I'd had kisses. Zero. No one liked the girl who showed up to class with holes in her shoes and dirty clothes. So Penelope and the football team made my life hell. They made the world hate me and I hated them all back." I swiped the bottle of whiskey from Niall, walking past him on the table and drinking a long gulp as I fixed my gaze on a clock on the wall. It had stopped working, the second hand twitching, unable to make it any further, stuck in an endless fragment of time. That was how it had felt that night in the woods. Like it would never end. Like time would freeze and the sun would never rise. Maybe in a way, it hadn't. Because I was just like that second hand now, twitching forwards but never getting anywhere, eternally trapped in the worst moment of my life.

"My uncle made me attend the school prom so he could have the house to himself and I put on my best clothes, figuring I could slip through the party unnoticed, go and hide in the library for the evening. But when I got there, Andrew and his friends came up to me and started giving me all this attention. Like, nice attention, you know? Andrew said I looked pretty and I said he looked handsome. Because he did. He always looked handsome with his dark hair and even darker eyes. I still planned on slipping away, but then Penelope showed up looking like a picture perfect prom queen and started apologising for bullying me. She even gave me her butterfly hairclip when I said it looked nice." I stroked the place in my hair where she'd clipped it and realised my fingers were shaking. I shook my head, dragged back to that very second, seeing it so clearly, feeling that blush lining my cheeks. How happy I'd felt to be seen. "People spoke to me that night. They gave me drinks and asked me questions like I wasn't plagued. I'd gone so long without any attention, I guess I just wanted to lap it up, ignore the warning alarms in my head. It was easier after a few drinks. And by the time it got late, I felt happier than I had in such a long time I was willing to believe anything in life was possible. I went to sit outside just before midnight, ready for my uncle to come pick me up. I watched everyone slip into their parents' cars as I waited. And waited..." My brows pulled down as I thought of my uncle. He had never been cruel to me, but he had disregarded me. And maybe they were the same thing when you put them side by side in a petri dish and examined them under a microscope.

"He didn't show up," I said, my eyes still fixed on the clock. "But Penelope did. She came and said nice things to me." Telling this part of the story was almost as bad as the later bit. Because it made me sick to know how stupid I'd been, to remember that silly, silly girl and her silly, silly decisions. "She invited me to come to the woods with her to meet her friends. And I said yes because…because…" I thought on that for a second, lost to those memories so deeply it was like I was standing in front of Penelope again with her flowing red hair and cherry lips. "Because I thought being liked was important. I thought things were finally changing for me, that someone had answered one of my wishes. I didn't want to be alone anymore. I didn't want that so much that I let myself trust the girl who'd tortured me for years." My brow wrinkled as I beat myself up inside over that. I'd been such a fucking idiot. "She led me into the woods on the edge of campus, further than I'd ever been into them before. And somewhere up ahead, boys were laughing. The moon was so bright, we didn't need flashlights, it carved through the dark like a silver blade, cutting into the belly of the forest to watch it bleed." I ran my thumb across my lips. "The air was warm and the taste of peaches lingered on my tongue from the schnapps we'd been drinking. I felt…fuzzy, good. But the closer we drew to those boys, the more my skin prickled and my instincts begged me to flee. I didn't though. I just kept walking, hoping I was walking towards a new life. Something sweeter than the bitterness I'd known. It's such a silly thing to hope, isn't it?"

Niall and Mateo remained quiet and I was grateful for that. Because I needed to say this my own way, without questions or interjections. It had to spill out of me like ink and stain the world blue.

"Three of the football team were waiting for us, including Andrew. They were drunk, shirtless, messing around and wrestling each other. I remember liking the way Andrew looked. He smiled when he came over to me, his fingers muddy as he pushed them into my hair." I pushed my own fingers into my hair, my heart bunching up in utter fear. His touch had been a warning I should have heeded. "I wanted to run then. But I found my legs frozen, as stiff as boards. He pushed me between his friends and they ran their hands over me like I belonged to them. I think I said no, I can't remember. My mind didn't catch up until I was shoved onto the ground and Andrew laughed. His laugh was like a bonfire crackling in my ears and it seemed to singe the inside of my skin too. I knew I'd made a stupid mistake and that I was going to pay for it. Because the moment I tried to get up, Andrew's friends held me down."

I raised my arms above my head, my fingers curling as I remembered the strong hands wrapped around my wrists and the others on my ankles. "Andrew stood over me while Penelope took her phone out and recorded me on the ground, a smile twisting up her lips. Someone hitched my skirt over my thighs, I can't quite remember who. I just knew it wasn't Andrew, because I couldn't stop looking at him. His friends were just shadows in comparison. He was haloed by the moonlight, a demon disguised as an angel. And he had a knife in his hand, a switch blade. When he flicked it out, fear spiralled through every inch of me." I was yanked into that moment so fully I couldn't breathe.

"Get away from me," I snarled, thrashing as I tried to get free.

"Scared, dirty girl?" Andrew asked. He always called me that because of the worn uniform I turned up to school in. But the way he said it now seemed to hold another meaning. "You should be."

"Hurry up, Andy," Penelope pressed impatiently.

I shrieked and Andrew's hand slammed down over my mouth. "Shh, shh," he urged.

I took a shuddering breath, clutching at my chest as my lungs seemed to contract. "Andrew sniggered as he knelt down and slid the knife up the middle of my dress to expose my bra. He smelled like pot and beer and his hand was slick with sweat. I fought as hard as I could, but I couldn't get free as Andrew slid the knife between the valley of my breasts under my bra." I ran my fingers up the path he'd taken, my eyes unfocused, my head full to the brim of that night. "He said, *'You're lucky, Brooklyn. The captain of the football team wants to see your body. Show him what you've got under here. Maybe Penelope will lend you some clothes after tonight. She'll hang out with you, you'd like a friend wouldn't you, dirty girl?'*" I swallowed the jagged lump in my throat as those words made the demons in my head scream. "Penelope said nothing, just aimed her phone at me, watching my ruin through the screen like it was easier to stomach that way." I sneered. "My body finally unfroze and I bit into Andrew's palm, not wanting to give in. I knew I had to fight, but it was so hard. I never thought I'd be the kind of girl to just lay there, but no one tells you about the shock that happens when these bad, bad things happen. The instinct to live becomes so strong it tells you to lie there until it's over, so you don't die. Not dying becomes priority. I fought that instinct, because dying seemed preferable to what they were about to do. But then Andrew wrenched his hand out of my teeth and smacked me hard enough to make my ears ring."

I felt Niall and Mateo shift at the same time, but I couldn't look at them. If I looked, I'd break. I needed to stay here, suspended in the past, letting it all out. "*'Make one noise and I'll cut you,'* he spat at me then sliced through the centre of my bra and ripped the material away. I remember shuddering, trying to shrink into the ground, praying to a god who wouldn't listen."

I wet my lips. "He looked at me like a vulture who'd come across a juicy carcass and he said, *'Fuck me, you've been holding out on us, Brooklyn,'* as he squeezed and pawed at my breasts, the icy handle of the blade licking my flesh like a threat. I started fighting again when no deity answered my call for help and managed to get an arm free from the guy to my right. I swung my fist around and it thumped against Andrew's cheek." I threw out my hand like

I had then, my fist meeting nothing but air. "*'Bitch,'* he barked at me, slashing the knife across my arm." I tracked my fingers over the faint scar there and stilled as I swear I could feel the blood washing down my skin again. "We locked eyes and something changed between us as the metallic scent of my own blood hung in the air. He'd cut me. He'd seen through on his threat. And I knew then that this was going to happen no matter what I did. No one was coming to save me, no one would answer my screams."

I took a calming breath and went on, "Luke Damsey's voice came from behind me saying he wasn't sure about this, but his grip was still tight on my arm. Then Andrew reached over my head, gripping Luke's free hand and bringing it onto my breasts. *'She likes it, see?'* he said. I'd refused to shut my eyes because I knew if I zoned out, that was it. They were going to take everything and anything they wanted from me. If I froze again, they'd destroy me. And I had to fight for the pieces of my soul that remained." I let my eyes fall closed to escape the ticking of that second hand that never moved on the clock. "Luke's hands moved over me and Penelope laughed. *'She's such a whore,'* she said. *'Look how desperate she is for it.'* Then Andrew's fingers slid under my skirt and bile rose in my throat, I could taste it sitting there like acid. My screams seemed to be locked down tight and I had the most terrifying awareness that I was all alone in the world. No one was listening, no one cared. They never had. Not since Dad died. But if no one was coming then that meant it was just me there to defend myself. But I didn't seem to have the strength to be my own saviour."

I chewed on my bottom lip as more of the memories rose up in me, all of them as fresh and detailed as they'd been right after it had happened, like they'd been branded into my brain just to make sure I'd never stop suffering over it all.

A sharp memory overwhelmed me for a moment.

"God she's pathetic. Are you gonna just lie there and let him fuck you? You must be gagging for it," Penelope laughed her high pitched laugh,

stepping closer to angle the camera down at me. "I bet she doesn't even shave her vag."

Andrew shoved my skirt up and I tugged at my ankles which were held by Matt Witby, his eyes watching everything hungrily, though he never made a move to join in.

I took a long breath and continued, "Andrew exposed my panties and ran the knife across them, making fire rise in my veins. I couldn't let it happen. I couldn't become a victim. I couldn't, I couldn't- but then my panties were being cut away and suddenly I was being touched and I didn't want to be touched. My mind was racing, tears were blurring my eyes. Something was cracking in my soul, splintering into a thousand irreparable shards and cruel laughter rang in my ears as Penelope leaned down to record what Andrew was doing to me with his hand."

I realised I'd laid down on the table, my hand between my thighs as I showed them where he'd touched me, my back arched against the wood as a tear rolled down my cheek. It was violating, humiliating. And it had hurt. It had fucking *hurt*.

The ringing in my ears built to a roar as I felt all the hate as viscerally as I'd felt it back then.

"I stopped calling on the good in the world to save me and called on the bad instead. Because I wanted vengeance. I wanted everyone around me to hurt and scream. I wanted to suck their power away and make them feel as small as they'd made me feel. I wanted them to bleed, bleed, bleed." My hands curled into fists as fury coiled beneath my flesh. It was evil, this thing in me. And I didn't care. I wouldn't have gotten rid of it for anything, because it was the only thing that had ever shown up to help me. "Finally, someone had answered my call. It was the Devil himself and he blew on the flames of my rage and gave me the strength I needed to fight. I vaguely remember that Luke's grip loosened on me just as Andrew unzipped his fly. But I no longer felt their hands on me, I felt free of all binds. Free of all laws and rules. I lunged for the knife in Andrew's grip, snatching it away from him, but he jumped back, knocking Luke into my path. I didn't hesitate, I just slammed it right up under his jaw." I acted it out with my hands, seeing Luke there above me as clear as day with his icy blonde hair and pale lips. "His blood dripped hot and fast down my arm and his eyes widened with the horror of what I'd done. I'll never forget how good it felt. How powerful. Like this act was awakening the true me, setting her free. When I drew the knife back, I stabbed again, hungry and wild as I launched myself at him, wanting to finish the kill so I could hunt the rest of them." I stabbed with my fist, my teeth bared, the scent of Luke's blood still lingering there from the past. It was as sweet as my revenge had been that day. "Penelope screamed. And I drove that blade into Luke until the light went out of his eyes and the last person on earth he saw was the one he'd helped to destroy."

I pushed to my feet on the table, numb and focused on death and nothing else, my mind a place of utter, frightening calm. It was just like that night, the huntress in me wide awake and thirsty as hell.

"Penelope ran off into the trees as Andrew shoved me to try and knock me down. I managed to cut his arm, but that was it. He ran. But before his friend Matt could follow, I stuck him in the gut. Again and again and again. He crumpled beneath me like paper and I stood over him as a monster in her true skin. The light of Penelope's phone guided me to her even without her screams. So I followed, chasing her down as she tried to escape. The fires of hell licked under my flesh and they were going to drag her into them and never let go. But it wasn't to be…" I sighed heavily, the weight of that failure still pressing down on me. "I couldn't catch her before she and Andrew made it out of the woods. So I finally dropped the blade and gazed up at the moon, the only witness to my fall from grace. But she hadn't helped me, only the Devil had come to my aid."

The room seem to come back into focus as I finished my story, finding tears staining my cheeks. But it was the good kind of tears, because I felt lighter. A little freer. I was down on my back again, gazing up at the ceiling, my hand raised to the sky where the moon had been that night.

I rolled my head to the side to look at Mateo and found a roiling sea of violence in his eyes that made my heartbeat quicken. He reached across the table to me, his fingers gripping my jaw. "If I were capable of crawling into the shadows of the past, I would string up your enemies by their necks and set a fire at their feet," he snarled and my breaths fluttered against his hand.

Niall suddenly pulled my face from Mateo's fingers, rolling my head over to look at him instead. There was a wild insanity in his eyes, his darkest demon come out to possess him.

"The past is done," he growled. "Which is why I'll offer you somethin' far better than a dead man ever can."

"What?" I asked on a breath.

"Vengeance," he said, the word echoing inside my skull and making me shiver. "Make a list, love. Of everyone who has ever wronged you deep enough to die for it. I'll track 'em down and deliver them to you with a weapon of your choice."

"You can do that?" I asked in wonder and awe, the thought making my heart pound excitedly.

"I can do any dark deed I set me mind to. Call it a gift." He pushed out of his seat, heading from the room without another word and Mateo caught hold of me, dragging me off of the table into his lap. My legs fell either side of him as his mouth moved to my ear.

"I want to be there when they die," he said in a forbidding tone that set my skin on fire. "Let the hijo de puta track them down then get us out of here and we'll kill them together, chica loca."

Before I could answer that, Niall returned and yanked me out of his arms, carrying me away from him and planting me down in an armchair across the room.

He placed a notepad and pen in my lap as he towered over me then leaned down and pressed his hands to the armrests so I was caged within his body. He had a cigarette between his lips and it lit up his eyes like two bonfires as he took a drag. "I've killed monsters like yours before," he said in a growl. "My wife was killed by them. Raped, tortured, murdered. And all because of me."

I gasped, shaking my head in refusal of those terrible, terrible words.

"She didn't get to see them die, but I promise that you will see your monsters bleed," he swore.

I reached out to brush my fingers over the name Ava tattooed on his arm and he grunted, looking like he wanted to stop me, but he didn't.

"I'm sorry," I whispered, pain blossoming in my chest for him.

"Apologies are as good as prayers," he said with a sneer. "Ain't no one listening, love."

"The Devil listens," I said firmly but he shook his head.

"No. *You're* the Devil, baby." He pressed a finger to my chest. "That evil is all you and don't go selling yourself short by saying it ain't, because you own every dark piece of that creature in ya." He lowered his head and smoke coiled between us in the air. "She's one of my favourite things about you, Spider. The sooner you start treating her with the respect she deserves, the sooner you'll become the killer you want to be."

He stepped back and my fingers moved over the notepad on my lap as I considered his words. Maybe he was right, but I wasn't sure. And if Big Red wasn't down in hell waiting for me, then what did I even have to look forward to? I didn't wanna consider that I'd been alone all these years, talking to a beastie who'd been a part of me all along.

Niall went to walk away but I tossed the notepad at his back and he glanced around in confusion. I threw the pen at him too and I bit my lip on a grin. "I don't write on paper."

"Well what the fuck d'ya write on then? A brick?" he balked.

"Close. A rock. And I'll need a shiny Sharpie so it stands out on it too."

He finished his cigarette, ashing it in a black tray shaped like a skull and nodding to me. "It's your list I suppose." He marched toward the door again and I looked over at Mateo, his gaze following Niall from the room as murderous thoughts flickered in his eyes.

I didn't like that. I wished they'd just get along. But I guessed being captured and tortured by a guy for months was tricky to form a relationship around. I hated Hellfire for it too in all honesty. But I was also a slave to the bond between us, the killer in me quietly enamoured with him. Maybe Niall was right, maybe the Devil was in me. Maybe I was bad to the bone.

He eventually returned with a flat black rock about the size of my palm and a silver sharpie, making me grin from ear to ear. I snatched them from him, tugging off the pen lid with my teeth and resting my murder rock on my knees. Andrew and Penelope headed the list then Madam Lucille from the psychiatric hospital was next, followed by the rest of her grisly team. I added Small-Willy Norman too because he was a rat. He told Lucille if he ever caught us breaking a rule. He'd liked to watch when they hurt us too and Lucille always favoured him for his ratty ways, giving him chocolate and juice and all the good stuff in life that the rest of us had been denied. Next, I added the men who'd kidnapped me, Señor Castillo – hmm how do you spell that though? I wrote out *Seen Your Case Armadillo* and frowned at it. *Yeah that looks about right.*

I wrote Rafael and Fernanda next then finally I added Cedric Rawlings. The judge who'd let Andrew and Penelope off and sent me to juvie, tarnishing my name, painting me as a wicked beast who'd hunted them through the woods for my own enjoyment, dismissing all allegations of sexual assault.

I blew on the rock when I was done, drying the ink and admiring my work before passing it to Niall, cupping it carefully in both hands. "Protect this with your life, kay?"

"Okay." He took it, eyeing the names on it as darkness seeped into his features.

"Oh wait!" I snatched it back, turning it over and writing *The Death Club* on the back of it, drawing Xs for eyes and a little stitch mouth over the A. I smiled at my work and passed it back to Niall. "I guess this was our first official club meeting." I beamed and Niall tsked.

"El Burro ain't part of our club."

"He is!" I insisted. "I'm head of the board and I say he's in."

"You're not head of anything. I'm the boss," Niall countered.

"Nah-ah," I sang.

"Ya-huh," he threw back.

"Nah-ah."

"Ya-huh."

"Nah-ah."

"Ya-huh."

"Nah-ah."

"Ya-"

"Stop it," Mateo snapped. "You're acting like fucking children."

"No we're not," I said.

"Yes you are," Mateo growled.

"No we're noooot," I sang, but Mateo didn't rise to my game, his eyes narrowing and giving me a look that said he wanted to bend me over his knee and teach me a lesson. *Ooh la la. Hello, Daddy.*

"The Death Club's a shitty name," Niall muttered, taking another cigarette out and lighting it up.

"Pfft, it's the best name," I said dismissively.

"It's shitty. It needs to be something like..." he trailed off in thought.

"The three mus*kill*teers?" I offered.

"No," he grunted. "And there's only two of us."

I ignored that last part as I went on. "The Devil's Thundercrackers?"

"No."

"The Pow-Stab-Bang Crew? Two Dicks and a Vag? Two's Company,

Three's a Massacre? The Deadly Trio? An Irishman, A Mexican, And a Shit-Hot Chica? The-"

"Stop," Mateo growled. "Please stop."

"Alright. The Death Club it is for now," I decided and Niall frowned. "We need a slogan and a mascot and merchandise and-"

"Let's just kill a few fuckers and go from there, eh?" Niall suggested, arching a brow at me sternly.

"Fine," I sighed, but I was already mentally planning out all of those things. Our mascot could be a pea-green parakeet called Greg and he could wear a tiny beret with our slogan on it which would be... *it's killing time somewhere.* No. *Killing quick, killing slow, either way there'll be a show.* Nah. *To kill, or not to kill.* Nope. *Die motherfuckers!!* Hmmm. *Killing for all ages.* Nah. *DIY killing.* That's not it - oooh I've got it!

The Death Club: Let the killing begin...

MATEO

CHAPTER TWENTY ONE

Sweat gleamed on my skin and ran between the arches of my muscles as I pushed myself harder and harder, moving into my fifth set of one hundred pull-ups for the morning.

My brain was buzzing today. Violent whispers and darkness and all the bad things in me stirring beneath the surface. Today was the kind of day when the worst of me was on show for all the world to see and the demon in me wanted to come out to haunt the world.

It was the kind of day when in my previous life, blood was most likely to be spilled at my hands.

Before coming here, before running from the man I'd been born to be and charting my own path in my escape, I'd been all the worst kinds of evil. That was what it took to rise in the Castillo Cartel. Savagery. Brutality. Cunning and forethought. I had all of that and more.

There were always a hundred men with their eyes on your position when you climbed the ranks the way I had. Each of them loyal, terrified of you and yet hungering for your downfall and aching to outplay you too. It was cutthroat and bloody and beautifully simple. Dog eat dog. And I'd been a wolf who feasted regularly.

Some men might wonder why I'd chosen to run from that, why I gave up my power and position and painted a target on my back which all but guaranteed that I'd be butchered one of these days. But they couldn't possibly understand what it was like to grow up as I had, to be surrounded by those kinds of men and be abused by those women. The whole lot of them were a rot that needed carving out. All I'd done was take the first slice.

I closed my eyes as I fought against the memories that were always trying to push their way in on me, the faces of the women who had taken such extreme measures to rid me of my darkness while only serving to make it grow.

In the silence, I could hear them chanting, reciting old prayers and new. Some directly aimed at me and my soul which they claimed to want to save so much.

The echoes of their voices bouncing off of stone walls was growing louder and louder, the Latin words they spoke to me making my head spin with the memory of them. Day after day locked in that box, forced to listen to them as they came and went, always leaving at least one person to chant on and on into the night.

I'd wait for the sound of the church bells, praying to a god who never listened to call them away to worship, to grant me the blessing of silence. *Pero mis oraciones nunca fueron respondidas.*

The scar in the shape of a cross which spread across the centre of my chest burned with the memories, the scent of my searing skin as they'd pressed the crucifix to my flesh always lingering close in my memories.

They claimed it burned me because of the demon which was latched onto my soul and I had no other explanation for it. I still didn't understand why it had burned me like it did and branded me in this way. But I had also come to accept the demon that lived inside me. If those women were incapable of banishing it then I knew I had no chance of doing so. So I'd made my peace with it as best I could and I tried not to fall prey to its wants and desires more than I could cope with.

I dropped from the bars, my chest heaving as I gripped the cold metal of the door in one hand and leaned forward to catch my breath, my free hand brushing over the old burn as I wondered for the millionth time in my life why I had been cursed with this. Why was I the one who had to bear the burden of this creature which resided inside of me? Why was I the one to blame?

The sound of the basement door unlocking made me raise my head and I looked towards the stairs hopefully.

I knew it was foolish of me to feel hope over anything, but that girl was infectious.

I'd always been a possessive man. Ever since the first job I'd run for the Castillos. I'd been gathering information and jealously possessing everything and anything of value which came my way. At first it had been food, weapons, money, property, cars, more and more and more of everything, yet I hadn't been sated by it. My hunger was a beast which was destined never to be satisfied.

Even after stealing all I had from them and burning down the house of God where the horrors of my childhood had been locked away, I still hadn't been content.

Having my new life snatched away like this had made me see that.

I was a hungry soul, ever aching, ever gorging and never full. But if that was my nature then so be it. I would devour the world if that was what it came to.

But first, I intended to devour her.

It had been weeks of sweet torture since I'd given in to temptation and taken a taste of her for myself.

Since then, I'd been fighting a battle every moment I spent with her, trying to prove to myself as much as anything that I was capable of owning her that way without destroying her. But I was starting to lose all hope of restraining myself any longer.

I heard her in the shower almost every day, moaning and sighing and sometimes calling out my name as she touched herself. At first that had ignited the flame in me to new heights and my resolve had been so close to shattering that I'd almost caved. But then she'd panted Niall's name and I had nearly lost control of myself altogether. She shouldn't be thinking about him. She was supposed to be *mine*. But if I gave in to the jealousy the thought of her with him roused in me then I knew I would lose all sense of control completely.

So I'd withdrawn. Fallen back on watching her, waiting for her to show me her true colours, reveal her true nature. I wanted to discover what trap she was setting. And yet, there had been nothing. She gave away no signs of understanding my true identity, much less having any interest in trying to uncover my secrets.

And of course, I couldn't forget the way she'd tried to save me from Niall's torture. Since that day, she hadn't been down here when he took me to his killing room. She was always upstairs doing what the two of them called training. She'd told me about the collar he placed on her which kept her within the parameter of the house and now he was using that to his advantage, leaving her up there with tasks to occupy her when he came to question me.

He'd been careful in his methods too, only using water and electricity while he questioned me, making sure there were no marks left on my flesh for her to see.

He was a trickster, a liar, cunning, deadly, manipulative. And I could see him getting his hooks into her more and more as the days went by.

I just hadn't quite decided how best to remove them yet.

Brooklyn drew my attention as she skipped down the stairs, sucking on a lollipop which had stained her tongue and lips bright red. Today she was dressed in a matching set of hot pink leggings and a sports bra with a pair of white high tops to finish it off. She might have looked like any other girl headed for a workout if it wasn't for the wild look in her eyes which promised she was anything but normal.

She carried a plate with sandwiches stacked on it and hurried over to me with a smile like we were friends.

I was fairly certain that a friend wouldn't fantasise about tying her up and fucking her in the ass until she couldn't think straight though, so I doubted I counted as that.

I reached through the bars to grab a sandwich and inspected her body as I devoured it.

"We've been wrestling today," she whispered, taking the lollipop from her mouth and using it to point towards the stairs. "Hellfire says I'm getting better." She beamed at me and I arched a brow as I moved on to the second sandwich quickly. "Okay, well what he actually said was 'I don't think anyone has ever tried to kill me by riding my face before' but it was clearly meant as a compliment."

A deep growl escaped me at that mental image and she reached through the bars to touch me, laying a hand on the slick skin of my chest so that she could feel the vibrations of that sound rolling through my body.

"Explain," I ground out because the one thing I had learned about her was that she often used poor word choices and it was worth drawing more information from her when she said something like that. She liked the sound of her own voice almost as much as I did, so she was always happy enough to embellish for me.

"I tried that thigh choke hold thing on him. You know, where you wrap your legs around someone's neck then just squeeze and squeeze like an anaconda until they're dead." She grinned as I took the last sandwich and moved away to place the plate on the stairs while I seethed over the idea of her grinding her pussy against his fucking face while she tried to execute that move. No doubt he'd had no objections to it but if I'd been there to witness it, I would have snapped his fucking neck just for getting that close to what was mine.

Heavy footsteps pounded down the stairs before she could tell me anything else and I scowled at Niall as he strode into the basement wearing nothing but the world's tiniest pair of shorts, his skin gleaming just as much as mine after my workout.

"I've gotta go off on a job for a bit," he announced, his words for her but encompassing me too.

"Oooh, where are we going?" Brooklyn asked excitedly, moving to her closet and beginning to rummage.

"Not you. Just me. My nephew Kyan just called me and he's in a bit of a jam. I gotta go get his girl outa Hemlock City before the army snatches her up."

I frowned at that. Why would the army be trying to snatch anyone? What the hell was going on in the world out there? Brooklyn had explained a little about the pandemic to me, but it wasn't something that held her attention for long, so all I really understood was that people were getting sick and everyone was looking for a cure. I guessed it didn't make much difference to me locked up down here.

"Oh, is she a really good soldier?" the girl asked excitedly, snatching a dark green camo print jumpsuit out of the closet as if she liked that idea.

"It's nothing like that," Niall said. "Don't worry about the details. It's just a little favour for the only member of my family I actually give a shit about. And after someone killed the witness I'd promised to question for him, I feel like I owe him."

"Err, I think we both agreed that that was a spectacular kill on my part and that the fucker deserved it," she said, placing her hands on her hips as she glared at him.

"We absolutely did not. We agreed that you fucked up majorly, you're not really cut out for this work and that I'm most likely wasting me time on you."

They scowled at each other for a long moment then Brooklyn turned away from him and strode over to stand beside the bars of my cage.

"If you're going to be rude, then I don't want to come on your stupid vacation," she said. "I'm going to stay here with Mateo."

"I know ya are," Niall replied. "And I absolutely wasn't inviting you to join me."

"Good. Because I'm not coming even when you beg."

"We both know I can make you come without begging, Spider," he growled, his eyes shifting to me as that taunting smirk lifted his lips again and the desire to rip his fucking head from his shoulders damn near overwhelmed me.

"Te destriparé como a un cerdo uno de estos días," I spat at him, but it only made his smile widen.

"You wanna say that in English so I can slap your bitch face for it?" Niall challenged, stalking closer to us.

I stayed exactly where I was but I raised my chin, glaring through the bars at him and thinking of each and every way I'd make him scream before I killed him, certain he could see it in my eyes.

His grin turned savage as he stalked closer, opening his arms and moving like a Viking seeking a route to Valhalla. There was something utterly animal about him. Something fluid and unpredictable and wild. It only made me crave his death more. Before coming here I'd been hard pressed to come up against a worthy opponent and I was certain a fair fight between the two of us would be brutal poetry.

Brooklyn sidestepped into his path before he could get close enough for me to reach him through the bars, her face screwed up into a scowl as she plucked the lollipop from her lips and brandished it between the two of us like a weapon.

"I think it's time the both of you just kissed and made up," she suggested, looking between me and Niall as he stood there, arms folded across his bare chest with the colourful clown tattooed on his flesh laughing at me.

"Make up?" I sneered. "That bastardo has had me locked up down here as his personal torture project for months. I'd sooner cut out my own eyes than make peace with him. Joder eso."

Niall reared back like I'd just spat at him, raising his hands in defence as I glared at him through the bars of my cage. "You're blaming me for this feud?» he demanded incredulously, his Irish accent seeming thicker as he widened his eyes innocently. «You were the one living in my house!»

Brooklyn gasped, giving me an accusatory glare as my mouth fell open and I worked my jaw for a few seconds before my rage exploded out of me. "THIS IS MY HOUSE!" I roared. "You broke in in the middle of the goddamn night like some rato cobarde and got the fucking jump on me. You're just lucky you caught me sleeping or I'd have gladly destroyed you and fed the pieces of your rotten corpse down the garbage disposal," I snarled and I meant it too - I'd done that once. Messy fucking job and I wouldn't recommend it. There were bits that just didn't want to chop down small enough and I'd had to get creative with a hammer and...I really wouldn't recommend trying that at home.

"Oh please," Niall scoffed, laughing in my fucking face while mi sol watched the show like it was her favourite sitcom. I was surprised she wasn't dipping her hand into a bag of popcorn and slowly feeding it into her mouth. "I could have beat you unconscious with my left hand while blindfolded. Don't go flattering yourself into believing any different, El Burro."

"Hijo de puta," I snarled at him, pushing my face right up to the bars as I dared him to come at me and try to prove that for himself.

"How long has he been keeping you down here?" Brooklyn asked me, her eyes wide like she was impressed with the motherfucker over that.

"I lost count," I snapped, distracted by her question. "About six months."

"Seven," Niall tossed back, counting on his fingers. "I do believe it was July. Lovely warm, summer's day. You had your window open like you were an innocent little virgin, just begging the Devil to climb in for a late night fuck. Don't get your knickers in a twist because you realised you couldn't handle me when I answered your invitation."

I ground my teeth so hard, I was surprised to find they didn't turn to dust in my mouth.

"Shit, Mateo, no wonder you look so..." Brooklyn widened her eyes and waved her lollipop at me like I was supposed to know what that meant, and I bared my teeth at her too. "But surely after all that time, you wanna just forgive him and move on with your life? You know what they say about holding grudges. It's like drinking poison and expecting your anemone to die."

"What? It's enemy not anemone," I muttered in confusion.

"I don't think so, Mateo," she laughed. "That makes no sense."

"Come on, lad," Niall said suddenly, moving around her and unfolding his arms as he held his right hand out and thrust it through the bars of my cage for me to shake. "The lady wants us to put a line under it."

"I'm scarred for life because of you," I hissed and he shrugged.

"Let bygones be bygones."

I glowered for a minute longer then reached out to take his hand. Not because I was even thinking about forgiving him. But because if he let me out of here, I was going to beat his ass to death and take my motherfucking life back from him.

I'd turn the tables on him and drag him into that fucking killing room and show him all the things I knew how to do to a man to make him scream for me. I'd rip him to pieces and make him rue the fucking day he'd ever laid eyes on me. He'd learn precisely why the people where I came from had feared me and precisely why my mother had tried to purge me of the demon that lived beneath my flesh.

Niall grinned widely as I slapped my hand into his and his fingers locked tight around mine. He yanked on my hand as hard as he could, lurching his weight back so that my face slammed into the iron bars of my cage and I

407

roared a challenge at him as I took a swing for his face with my other hand.

"Are ya ready to tell me where that money is yet?" he asked and I ripped my hand back out of his grasp and cursed him, blood running down my fucking face from my nose which thankfully didn't feel broken.

This bastardo was going to die so fucking hard by my hand whenever I got out of here. I'd take my sweet time annihilating him and making him realise exactly who I was and why he should have just killed me when he had the chance.

"I'd sooner swallow glass than tell you anything, bastardo loco," I spat.

"Come on then, Spider," he said, stepping away from me with a booming laugh, offering her his bloody hand and she took it.

I watched as he led her from the room, up the stairs towards the house and she glanced back at me with something in her electric blue eyes that looked a whole hell of a lot like disappointment. And then she was gone. And I was alone in this fucking cage once more.

The sounds of them talking echoed down to me, but I couldn't really make out many of the words as I simmered in rage, wiping the blood from my face as I waited to find out what was going on.

Before long they returned, both of them carrying boxes of food which they piled up to the side of the stairs while Brooklyn looked caught between rage and tears.

"I'll be gone a day or two tops," Niall said, not even bothering to look my way and making my anger burn hotter.

"You can't leave him in there with the bucket," Brooklyn snarled, clacking her lollipop against her teeth. "You promised no more bucket. Plus he needs a shower. He's all hot and sweaty and lickable. If you leave him like that, I'm gonna end up licking him."

Niall stilled suddenly, his muscles tensing and his movements turning all feline as he turned to glare at me. I offered him a taunting smile where she couldn't see me and he glowered darkly, no doubt thinking up new ways to torture me when he returned from his little trip.

It wasn't the first time he'd gone off and left me here for a few days, but it was the first time he was going to any effort to explain himself beyond dumping extra food down and leaving. A few times he'd forgotten the extra food and I'd just been stuck down here starving and alone for days, wondering if I would end up dying down here in the dark. *Fucking bastardo.*

"Well, we can't be havin' that," Niall growled, heading back up the stairs again in a rush.

Brooklyn turned to me, slinking closer as she pulled the lollipop from her lips and held it out to me through the bars.

I watched her for several seconds and she raised her eyebrows, waiting, watching, baiting me and drawing me in yet again. I couldn't resist her. Why couldn't I resist her? She was just so fucking tempting.

I took the candy between my lips like she wanted, surprised by the sour cherry taste that swept over my tongue mixed with the much more intoxicating flavour of her. I sucked it hard then released it from the cage of my mouth, watching as she instantly transferred it back to her own mouth again, her lips closing around it slowly and making my cock stir.

Even after all these weeks, my hunger for her wasn't diminished. If anything it was only growing stronger, more rampant, more urgent. But that was dangerous too. I knew it only put me closer to losing control and if I did that with her, I wasn't certain what would happen.

I couldn't trust myself. I wouldn't. And yet this tiny taste of her wasn't enough. I needed more. I needed it so fucking much that my skin felt like it was on fire as I looked at her.

Niall's footsteps pounded back down the stairs and I held my ground as he approached me with the stun gun.

"Wait," Brooklyn started and he turned to her with an arched brow, waiting for her to plead my case, but of course she wouldn't be predictable like that. "Can I get a hit from that?" She pointed at the stun gun and Niall smirked at her as he looked down at it.

"This is strong enough to knock out a bull...or a donkey," he said, glancing at me with a taunting grin. "But I guess I can give you a hit on the kitten setting?"

"I'm not a kitten," she protested with a pout as he caught her waist and started walking her backwards towards the bed.

"No? Then how come you purr so loud when I do this?"

He pressed the stun gun to her stomach and I snarled as her eyes widened in anticipation, her hands grasping his biceps.

"Do it, Hellfire. Make me tingle," she breathed.

He hit the button and her spine arched as the shock ran through her, a throaty moan spilling from her lips and her fingers digging into his arms until she'd marked him with bloody crescents. Niall leaned close to her, running his nose up the side of her neck before placing his lips against her ear and every muscle in my body stiffened as anger rushed through me. "More?"

"Yes," she gasped and he did it again, watching as she fell back with a louder moan, bouncing on the mattress and arching her spine as her limbs twitched and spasmed from the shock.

Niall seemed as captivated by her as I was, the two of us watching her pant and moan as she rode out the electric current spilling through her veins and for a few endless moments we were united by our hunger for her.

He turned away abruptly, crossing the basement towards me as he upped the voltage on the stun gun and I just stood there, refusing to so much as blink as he slammed it into my side and the shock hit me like a freight train.

I fell to the floor, jerking and spasming, cursing his name beneath my breath and trying to get my bearings as he made it into the cage, unbolted my chain then hauled me out and toward the bathroom.

I slurred something as I managed to roll onto my hands and knees where he dumped me beside the bed, fighting to regain control before he locked me up again, but the sound of the chain locking to the bathroom bolt echoed through my skull before I could.

I found myself looking at my chica loca on the bed, her pupils full blown as she lay there panting and smiling at me.

"Was that as good for you as it was for me?" she breathed and I was gifted a vision of her asking me that very thing after I'd spent a night with my cock buried inside her. Of course, I doubted her voice would be so clear after I'd spent hours making her scream with my hand locked around her throat so it probably wouldn't be the same.

The sound of the killing room door closing drew my attention to the hijo de puta in the room as I spotted him moving past us, carrying a sledgehammer and a bag of other tools.

"You kids be good," Niall called as he headed for the door. "If I die, you'll likely starve to death down here and I suggest you eat Mateo to buy yourself a few more weeks, little psycho. But with a bita luck I'll be back within a day or two and it'll all be dandy."

"Wait," Brooklyn said suddenly, rolling herself upright and hopping off of the bed, catching his hand before he could leave and hesitating as he looked down at her in surprise.

"What is it?" he asked and I narrowed my eyes at their joined hands.

"Be careful," she whispered like she wasn't sure she wanted the words to escape.

"You worried about me, love?" Niall asked, his eyebrows arching and she paused a long moment before replying.

"I just really don't wanna eat Mateo - he looks all gristly. So you need to make sure you come back."

Niall barked a laugh as she tugged her hand back then he turned and strode out of the room without another word.

I got to my feet as the sound of him locking the door carried down to us and headed into the shower before I lost my damn mind and punched a wall or something.

I didn't bother closing the door as I stripped off, setting the hot water running and moving beneath it as I began to scrub my skin clean. For this alone I had reason to thank that girl out there. Reason to want her. Ache for her. And reason not to destroy her. She'd given me back my humanity even if it was only at the most basic level.

My hand was on my cock before I even decided to put it there and I wasn't in any position to try and deny the desires of my flesh as I began to stroke it, a deep groan escaping my lips.

I closed my eyes and she was there, the only fantasy I ever had any more.

A sound behind me made me turn and I found her watching me, biting her bottom lip and leaning back against the sink.

"Am I squirrelling you?" she asked in a voice barely more than a whisper. "Because I know it's not cool to watch people shit, but for some reason I do wanna watch this…"

"Cómo sigues sorprendiéndome?" I rumbled in a low tone, turning to look at her as I drew my hand back and forth along my shaft once more.

The hot water crashed down over my back and the soap slid down my chest as I stroked myself, drinking in the sight of her and fighting every urge in my body to go to her.

Her eyes were glued to my cock, fingers curled tight around the sink either side of her as she watched my movements like she was studying them, memorising them, filing them away to replay later.

And I hoped she was. I hoped she hungered for me like I did for her. I hoped she'd think of this the next time she showered and touched herself in here where I could listen to her moans.

I wanted to close this distance between us, but even as I thought of doing it, my fingers tightened around my cock almost painfully as the desire

412

to grip her throat consumed me and I took an involuntary step forward.

But I'd been listening to her story the other night. I'd heard all of it from the words, to the pain, to the lingering fear of someone doing something like that to her again. I wanted to destroy the ones who had hurt her, but I also knew without a doubt that I had to be more restrained with her than ever. The dark in me wasn't something I could stain her with. She deserved better than that.

"Mateo," she breathed, licking her lips which were still red from the lollipop. "Is it weird if I touch myself too?"

Her fingertips had already made it to her waistband and I just watched her, wondering if she truly meant it or not, but the fire blazing in her eyes said she did. I groaned as she pushed her hand inside her pants, gasping softly as she began to move her fingers beneath them without waiting for me to answer.

I took another step towards her, the demon in me pressing at the confines of my skin and begging me to take her now, grip her hair, pin her beneath me and fuck that tight pussy as hard as I could. But I knew too well how the demon in me worked, how my grasp on my control was a fragile, fickle thing and how I couldn't trust myself in a situation like that.

I fought against that desire, my free hand gripping the edge of the shower door as I held myself back. It was more work than I would have ever believed possible, but I needed to hold back, I needed to bide my time, make her want it so much she was out of her mind with desire for it. I wanted her to beg. No matter how much she might be thinking about it now, I knew it wasn't enough. And I needed to test my control over and over again until I was certain I was in charge of myself. I wouldn't risk her. She was mi sol. I needed her in this place. She was all I had and I refused to give her up to anything, even my own darkness.

When she was ready, she'd want me to do my worst. She'd ache for it like I did and I'd find the way to control the monster in me for her, but that day wasn't today.

I pumped my cock harder, faster, needing the release soon if I was going to have any chance of keeping away from her. And as I watched her panting and teasing her pussy for me, I didn't find it hard to achieve that.

I came with a groan, some of the tension leaving my muscles, though my desire for her didn't lessen at all. Her eyes widened as she watched, her tongue wetting her lips and giving me more filthy ideas designed to destroy my mind with want for her.

I stepped out of the shower, water racing down my flesh as I closed in on her, meeting her gaze and loving what I found there. She wasn't afraid, she was aching, panting, working her clit for me and making it perfectly clear just how much she ached to come for me.

But I wasn't going to let her. Not like that. I could do a whole lot better than that for mi sol.

I didn't ask for permission as I snatched her hand out of her pants and pinned it against the mirror behind her.

"Dead Man," she panted as I leaned over her, dominating her, forcing her beneath me and looking her in the eyes as I pushed my hand into her pants instead, watching that desire flare, giving her a few seconds to refuse me if that was what she wanted. But I knew it wasn't. "What are you-"

"Tell me no," I growled, my fingers hovering so close to her pussy that I could feel the heat of her drawing me closer. I was a monster, but I had just enough good left in me to care about her answer. Though I doubted she understood what she was getting herself into if she gave me a yes. Because a yes meant she was giving herself to me and if she did that, I'd make sure she never forgot who owned her.

She didn't answer me but her thighs parted further, her hips bucking forward in a silent demand and I smiled darkly as I answered it.

My fingers sought out her soaking core and I growled as I pushed three fingers inside her without warning, the heel of my palm grinding down on her clit and making her cry out.

"Holy fucking man hands," she groaned, her head tipping back and eyes falling closed as I pushed my fingers deeper, curling them along her g-spot and making her moan for me.

"Look at me," I growled, my grasp on her wrist tightening until she gasped in pain and her electric eyes snapped open again, meeting mine.

"I'm looking," she promised, making the corner of my lips curl up as I moved my fingers inside her again. In and out, nice and slow, feeling how soaked she was and bathing in that look in her eyes.

She was mine. I could feel it. Right here and now there was nothing in her world but me and I was the creature controlling it.

She was panting, moaning, taking, taking, taking and I was loving being in charge of her body.

My cock was hard again already, pushing against her thigh with its own demands and her gaze dropped to it, giving me ideas I couldn't entertain.

Her hips bucked against me even as I worked to hold her still, her need to fuck my hand overwhelming the control I was taking of her as she sought out more and more.

Her free hand reached for my cock and I snarled, drawing back suddenly and flipping her around as I yanked her pants down to her ankles, baring her sweet ass to me.

"What are you-"

I cut off her question as I pushed up hard behind her, grasping both of her wrists and placing her palms against the mirror before sinking my teeth into her neck and making her cry out.

Her eyes fell shut again and I smacked her ass hard.

"Mírame," I snapped.

"Mirror me too," she gasped, biting her lip as her eyes fluttered open again.

"No, it means look at me," I growled, catching her gaze in the mirror.

"So that you know who owns you when you come."

Her lips popped open and I knocked her legs further apart, moisture beading the tip of my cock as it begged me to use it. But I could feel the demon in me rising up and as I slipped my fingers around her slender throat, I knew I couldn't allow myself to relinquish control like that. Not now.

She was a dish I needed to savour. I couldn't trust myself with her if I let myself go and I didn't want to break this creature of mine.

I reached around to her sports bra and yanked it down, making her tits push out of the top of it so that I could see them in the reflection, her hard nipples aching for the kiss of my teeth.

I grasped them roughly, tugging, squeezing, making her curse and pant and push her ass back against my cock in a silent demand.

And I wanted to give it to her. I wanted it so much that my hand wrapped around her throat again before I could stop myself and I closed my eyes as the head of my cock slid over the dripping heat of her pussy.

"Shit, Dead Man. It's so big, I don't know if-"

My grip tightened on her throat and I inhaled deeply as her breath cut off, stopping her words, my pulse racing to a violent tune as my muscles bunched and I grasped her hip, ready to do it, give in, take her, own her, destroy her.

My fingers flexed and a needy whimper escaped her, making me open my eyes again.

She was still watching me, waiting, not fighting or running or screaming. In fact, that look in her eyes made it perfectly clear that she wanted this, all of it, whatever I could give. Did she have no idea what I was? Or was she just so broken already that she was willing to let me show her in the worst ways?

I sank my teeth into her shoulder, taking my hand from her throat with a grunt of effort before dropping my fingers between her thighs and seeking out her clit.

"I'm bad for you," I told her, one last ditch attempt to warn her before it was too late. Because I was seriously close to the point of no return, of laying a claim on her and all that she was and making this dark obsession become a living, breathing fantasy which I would never allow to end.

I teased her clit as she dropped her head back against my shoulder, her eyes still fixed on mine in the mirror as I moved my gaze between her violently blue eyes, her heaving tits and the way my hand looked moving between her thighs.

"I think I like bad," she breathed. "Show me all the bad, Dead Man. I think it might help me live again."

My hips flexed against her round ass as I kept up the torment of her clit, my cock slipping between her cheeks for a brief moment as desire drove me mad with want for her.

I used that desire on her clit, teasing and circling, building her up and up as she rocked her hips against me, taking more pleasure for herself while grinding her ass against my cock and working me into a frenzy.

"Fuck," she gasped. "Oh holy, mother of- never stop. Never, ever stop."

I circled my fingers again, watching that fire flare in her eyes as I slipped my other hand behind her and pushed two fingers into her tight pussy. She tipped forward, using her hands to hold her in position as they pressed against the mirror and she moaned loudly for me, that throaty voice of hers so deliciously dirty that I wanted to consume the sound. She felt even better than I remembered from when I'd tasted her, hot and wet and so fucking sweet.

"Mírame," I snarled again, making sure she didn't forget. I wanted to see it in her eyes when I brought her to ruin.

Her words turned nonsensical as I played her body like an instrument, her gaze never wavering from mine as I pushed her harder, my fingers moving in synchronisation on her clit and inside her as she panted and moaned.

Her cries got louder, more desperate and I could feel her pussy tightening around my fingers as she drew close to her climax, her tits thrusting out in front of her as she arched back against me. I didn't even stop her as she took a hand from the mirror and hooked it around the back of my neck instead, her fingers twisting into my overly long hair as she pulled me closer.

I dropped my mouth to her neck, inhaling the scent of her, running my lips along her skin and grazing my stubble over the sensitive area followed by my teeth.

She moaned my name as she started to come and I pulled my fingers from her pussy leaving my other hand to control her clit then driving them into her ass instead, making her scream even louder, her grip on my hair almost ripping it from the roots.

She looked absolutely devastating as she fell apart for me, that fire in her eyes burning bright, her features written in ecstasy and the beauty of her searing itself into my memory for all of time.

I pumped my fingers in and out a few more times, wringing every little bit of pleasure I could from her as my gaze fell to her lips in the reflection and I pictured her taking my cock between them, sucking and licking and serving me on her knees.

"Mine," I snarled, making sure she understood that. That she knew her pleasure belonged to me just as surely as the rest of her would in time.

She just panted for several long seconds, our eyes locked in the reflection and her fingers slowly untangling from my hair as she nodded.

The demon in me purred at that and I flexed my hips, my cock moving between her thighs, sliding over the wetness there as it grazed against her swollen pussy, but I couldn't give in to what it wanted. I couldn't risk it.

I released her suddenly, heading back into the shower, closing my eyes and gripping my cock again, picturing each and every way I'd bring her to ruin once I could trust myself with her and growling with the effort it took me not to just do that now.

She'd beg for it before then. Beg and plead, open those full lips and fall at my command the way I needed her to.

I came hard, spilling myself against the shower wall and wishing it had been her full tits instead.

I stayed beneath the hot water for a long time, calming the beast in me through pleasure and determination until I was certain I'd regained full control of myself again.

When I got out I found her gone, the door closed and fresh sweatpants folded on the sink for me alongside a towel.

I dried myself off and pulled the clean clothes on, brushing my hair and teeth before pulling the door open.

I fell still as I found my way out barred by the soft bed which Brooklyn had clearly pushed up against the door frame, making it possible for me to reach it even with my chain.

"Look!" she said excitedly, hopping onto the bed and throwing herself into a roly-poly. "I can do a front flip!"

She was wrong. It wasn't a flip.

I looked down at her with a frown, trying to figure out this new mood she was in as she patted the soft mattress right beside her. She'd changed and was dressed in a pair of thigh high black socks paired with tiny black hot pants and what looked like a men's hockey shirt which she'd tied a knot into at her side. She'd also drawn a red heart on her cheekbone and for some reason, I wanted to press my mouth to it.

"I think we need to talk," she said seriously, her mood shifting again. She was like the wind but harder to keep up with.

I arched a brow at her as I slowly lowered myself onto the bed, trying not to let it show how fucking much I enjoyed the feeling of something soft beneath my body after all these months sleeping on the cold floor. This was yet another kindness she'd done me and aside from the orgasms, I still wasn't certain what she was getting out of it. Besides, I'd have given her those either way.

"About?" I asked.

"You being mad at me. You're as mad as a hatter, Dead Man, and I can't bear it."

I frowned at that because I'd just made her come so hard she'd barely been able to breathe, so I wasn't certain what part of that had made her think I was mad at her. She went on without needing me to ask though, so I assumed I was about to find out.

"Because I'm hanging out with Niall and learning to be a badass killer queen and you just have to sit down here all day with a frown on your face like a goose who didn't get to gander."

"Do you like him?" I asked her, my tone dark. "The man who took you captive and keeps you locked up like a rat in a cage?"

"Err, this cage is way nicer than my last place," she pointed out. "And I like killing, so why wouldn't I wanna get better at it?" There was more she wasn't saying about that, but if she wasn't offering it up then I guessed she wasn't about to. Maybe she wasn't even certain of her own feelings on the matter.

"If you're so good at it maybe you should be trying to kill him while you're up there," I spat.

"I've tried to kill him sixty seven times!" she said, throwing her head back dramatically and staring up at the ceiling. "He told me the Devil doesn't want him and I'm starting to think he must be right. It's hopeless."

"It's not hopeless," I insisted. "You just need to get a blade into him and then our problems will be over. I have more money than you could ever want. We could go anywhere. Be anyone."

I wasn't really sure how I was supposed to take her with me when I ran, but I would figure it out. She'd just be exchanging one captor for another, but at least I would be the kind of master willing to destroy the world for her.

"Where is all your money?" she asked curiously. "Did you draw a treasure map with X marks the spot? Bury it in a grave? Leave it with your grandma? Stuff it up your butt?"

I stiffened, wondering if this was it, the moment she revealed what she'd been sent here for. But if this was her grand plan, to blurt out random suggestions after I'd already brought the subject up, then she was the worst interrogator I'd ever met.

"Don't worry about that," I said. "Just worry about killing that hijo de puta the next time you see him and the rest will fall together."

She nodded seriously then wriggled a little closer to me, silence falling as she turned her head to look at me.

Minutes ticked by and I wondered why she didn't act differently after what we'd done in the bathroom. Did it make no difference to her? Wasn't it supposed to change things when someone made you scream their name while driving their fingers into your ass?

"Do you like me, Mateo?" she whispered finally and I was surprised yet again.

My gaze roamed over her features, but I didn't reply. What did she want me to say to that anyway?

"I think you've got a really nice cock," she added. "It's the biggest I've ever seen, which is equally terrifying and nice."

"Nice?" I grunted, wondering how many she'd seen, then deciding I didn't need to ask names or I'd just be adding them to the list of people whose deaths I desired.

"Yeah. Maybe we could agree to be camp friends if you don't wanna go all in as full friends?" I gave her nothing in reply so she just kept talking. "Camp friends are like the friend you make at summer camp and you totally think they're great, but then you get back to your real life and forget they exist. I've never been to summer camp, but I did totally forget about Old Betty the button woman once. I don't think I'd ever forget you exist though, Mateo. But if you want to forget me that's okay."

I still didn't say anything and she nodded as she bit her lip, her gaze tracing over my features before she wriggled around to get comfortable and closed her eyes, still facing me as she pulled the covers over us and it looked like she was planning to go to sleep.

I supposed it didn't matter what the time was if she felt tired. It wasn't like we had anything else to do down here.

I stayed silent as I watched her, her face scrunching up and her jaw ticking before a tear slid out from beneath her closed eyelid and my gut twisted uncomfortably.

A second tear followed the first, skimming across her nose and down her cheek before falling silently against the pillow and sinking into it.

I rolled over onto my side to face her too, the chain at my neck pulling tight as I reached the end of it before I took her hand in mine. I laced our fingers together and though she didn't open her eyes, she fell so still that I was certain she was still awake.

No more tears came and I kept watching her as her breathing slowly grew deeper until I was sure she was truly sleeping.

I could kill her so easily. She was right there, so small and fragile and vulnerable. I could do anything at all. She couldn't possibly know I wouldn't. And yet for some reason, she clearly didn't think I would. And as I lay there thinking about that, our fingers intertwined and breath mixing, an impossible thought occurred to me.

She trusted me.

At least a little. And if that was the truth then it could only be a matter of time before she gave in to me completely too.

Mi chica loca was already mine. Even if she didn't know it yet.

BROOKLYN

CHAPTER TWENTY TWO

Niall's voice woke me in the night, singing Drugs by UPSAHL loudly as he flicked the lights on and tromped down into the basement.

"Hey, Spider!" he hollered as I sat up in bed, squinting into the bright light with a scowl. "Holy fuck, what's he doing in your bed!?"

I squinted at my crazed Devil man with a pout. "Well he *was* sleeping! Do you know what time it is, you tit?" I snapped as Mateo sat up, tension rippling down his spine.

"No fucking clue," Niall laughed. "Do *you* know what time it is?"

"Time to sleep, you cocksucker!" My gaze fell to his bare chest, the blood spattering it, the duct tape bound around his left bicep with red, red blood all around it. I flew to my feet with a gasp, my heart zooming into my throat. *Oh no.*

"Hellfire, what happened?" I ran to him, clutching his forearm and reaching for the makeshift bandage on his arm.

"Pfft, it's nothing," he said dismissively. "A bullet played kiss chase with me."

"Shame it didn't plant a kiss on your brain," Dead Man muttered and I buried my face in Niall's chest, hugging him tight, hating that thought. Bullets wouldn't play nicely at all. They'd make his brain all smooshy.

"Don't say that, Mateo," I spoke into Niall's hot flesh. "Hellfire's hurt." I wasn't sure if he heard me because my voice was super muffled and my mouth was pressed up tight against the pounding thump of Niall's heartbeat. Either way, he didn't reply.

Niall stilled, slowly closing his good arm around me and rubbing his rough chin against my hair. "Wanna help out an old man, little psycho?"

"Okay. But you're not *that* old," I argued as he led me to the stairs, keeping me close and throwing a sinister glance back at Dead Man. "You're not as old as the hills, or the sky or most trees. Maybe little trees, but not big ones. You're older than most dogs though, and cats and pigeons and-"

"You," he finished for me.

"How do you know? I could be a vampire born three centuries ago." I glanced up at him, batting my lashes, taking in the scent of smoke and the trace of glitter on his flesh.

"Nah, you'd be trying to lick that blood off of me if that was the case."

I leaned forward, running my tongue up his arm where spots of blood flecked his skin and the salty, metallic, smoky perfection of him washed through my senses. *Mmm, he tastes like liquid anarchy.*

His throat bobbed and his grip on me tightened.

"Where've you been? What happened?" I demanded, glancing at that duct tape on his arm again.

"I had to help my nephew Kyan out of a tight hole," he said.

"Oh no, did his dick get stuck in someone? That happened to Nasty Nancy once. That's what she told me anyway. She said the guy had a bent wangle and it got caught around a corner in her vag. Do you think that's possible? Does your nephew have a bent wangle?"

"No and no," he mused. "Surely ya know that ain't possible?"

"Yeah, sure," I laughed loudly then hurried on. "Anyway, was he okay?"

"Yeah, my Kyan's a fucking warrior. He pissed off some army folks and needed a little distraction to get away from 'em with his friends. His girl helped me out."

"Aww, can I meet them?" I bounced on my toes. "Actually, I'd better not meet them. They'd probably think I'm odd. Most people think I'm odd. Did you tell them about me though?" I bit my lip and Niall smirked.

"Kinda," he muttered. "I told 'em to set you free if I died."

"You did?" I breathed, squeezing his arm as I blushed.

He shrugged one shoulder with a grin. "Ain't a big deal."

"It is, Hellfire." I grinned, prodding him. "It means you like me."

He snorted. "I don't hate you I suppose."

I beamed as we entered the kitchen and he grabbed a bottle of vodka and a lunchbox from a cupboard, leading me through to the lounge and picking up my shock collar on the way. He put it on me, tucking the key into his pocket and I ran my finger around the plastic, realising the thing kinda turned me on since the last time it had shocked me. *Hey Shocky. Are you gonna play zap-attack with me later?*

I dropped down beside Niall on the couch as he took a long swig of the vodka and passed me the lunchbox.

I flipped it open finding some fluffy white stuff, a funny curved needle and thread in fancy packets with some tape. "Oooh things." I took out each one, carefully laying them on my knees in the shape of a face.

"You ever stitched up a bullet wound before, love?" Niall asked.

"Ummm…well I once superglued a fig to Janky Lou's forehead while he was sleeping to cover up a huge spot he had there." I smiled proudly and Niall considered that.

"Alright, well just do as I say." He cut the duct tape free of his arm and my jaw dropped as blood spilled down his flesh from a deep gouge near the top of it.

"Ouchy," I whispered.

"Nah, I don't feel nothin'," he said, but I wasn't sure I believed that.

He took the bottle of vodka, pouring a measure over the wound, grunting as he did it. Then he drank another mouthful with a grimace and placed the bottle down by his feet before taking out a cigarette, pushing it into the corner of his mouth and lighting it up. "Fuckin' hate vodka. Tastes like a mouldy arse." He released a line of smoke between his lips. "Thread the needle with that." He pointed as he talked around his cigarette and I did so quickly before looking at his arm. "Then pinch the skin together and start knitting."

"That's it? That's your instructions?" I clarified and he nodded. *O... kay. Let's do this, team.*

I leaned forward, scrunching up my face and poking my tongue out the corner of my lips as I concentrated. "Hello Mister Ouchy, I'm going to stitch you up now," I told the wound then stuck the needle through the top flap of skin.

"Mother of a fuck," Niall barked. "Be careful, will ya?"

"Sorry." I moved my hands slower, trying to do it right, but he kept cursing while I worked. "It looks like a mouth." I pinched the skin and started moving it up and down as I sang words for it. "One, two, three, four, five, once I caught a bullet alive. Six, seven, eight, nine, ten, then I let it go again."

"*Brooklyn*," Niall snapped, spanking his hand down on my thigh and I glanced up at him in surprise as heat flushed through my body. He'd used my name. My real name. The *me* name.

"Yes?" I asked in a husky voice.

"Stop making the wound sing and finish stitchin' it, woman."

"Okay, boss." I saluted him and got back to work, frowning as I focused. I was quite good at this actually. "You put the needle in, take the needle out. In, out, in, out, you shake it all about-"

"*Argh*, stop singing them damn songs," he growled. "Or at least stop jabbing me in time with them."

"Sorry, I just love the hokey cokey. Will you do it with me after this?" I asked, biting my lip hopefully.

"Maybe. Just fucking finish up, will ya?"

"Okay, Hellfire. Hang in there, I'm gonna rescue your skin real good." I knitted the last of the wound back together and admired my work. I was no doctor, but that looked like one hell of a professional job thank you very much.

Niall twisted awkwardly to check out my work and his brows arched. "Did ya make it into a worm?"

"It's a snake, Niall." I rolled my eyes, pointing out the little fork tongue I'd done coming out of its mouth.

"I see ya stitched that bit into uninjured skin," he commented and I chuckled.

"Yeah...I did."

He barked a laugh then slumped back in his chair, his eyelids lowering halfway. "I like it."

"Are you okay? You look pale..." My heart knotted as he nodded vaguely, puffing on his smoke without bothering to use his hand, just leaving it jammed into the corner of his lips.

"Yeah, I'm alright, except..." he trailed off.

"What?" I pressed.

"I had to abandon Mary," he said, a look of pain crossing his features.

"How awful," I breathed as a little pang of jealousy ran through me. *Who the fuck is Mary? And why does Hellfire look so beat up over losing her? If he has a side piece – wait, I'm not his main piece. Or any kind of piece. I can't be jealous. Why am I jealous? Fuck, I am though. I'm all green inside. And I'm gonna slice Mary up the middle and make her scream.*

"Me best sledgehammer," he said heavily and I gasped in horror.

"Oh no," I gasped. "Poor Mary."

"She was a good girl," he said tightly. "Ten kills to her name."

"Did she go well?" I asked.

"Not half as well as she deserved, love."

I shook my head sadly, my eyes watering a little. "Poor Mary."

He looked at me for a long moment, his brows pulling together. "C'mere." He patted the spot on his other side and I headed over to sit there. He was in pain so I could do this for him. It was what I'd want if I was in pain. But it was weird how much I enjoyed touching him and Mateo considering I'd gone so long without wanting any kind of physical contact. And when I'd craved trying it before now, I'd always cringed after. But with him and my dead man, there was no cringing. It just felt...scrummy.

I curled up next to him and his arm slid around me as I rested my head on his shoulder, my gaze tracking over the ink on his chest. "How many tattoos do you have?"

"At least twenty. No, thirty. I dunno, I need to do a recount," he murmured, his eyes falling fully shut.

"I could do it for you?" I offered.

"Mmm," he agreed sleepily and I wet my lips, raising my hand to press against each one on his chest as I started counting.

"One...two...three – ooh, I like this one." I brushed my fingers around the ace of spades over his heart, noticing a thin scar that ran through it. In fact, there were lots of scars hidden under his tattoos, between them too and I found myself counting them instead, wondering how many times Hellfire had come close to death. Too many times by the looks of it.

"Thanks for fixin' me up, love," Niall murmured, his arm flexing around me and pulling me closer. His cigarette had burned right down to the cherry, a line of ash precariously hanging from the end of it.

I gently plucked it from his lips and looked around for a place to put it out. When I didn't find one, I stubbed it out between the cushions and pushed it into that mysterious dark place where a portal to all the lost keys in the world resided. Or maybe just a bunch of crumbs and lost change, who really knew? I might stick my head down there later and find out.

I continued counting Niall's scars and naming each of them after Disney characters, my head against his shoulder. He just needed a little snooze and he'd be all better. I'd done a good job of his arm, I was quite proud of myself actually. I could totally add wound stitching to my resume. Of course, I'd left my resume back under the bridge. I mean, it was really just a rock with a list of skills written on it in chalk, but that was more than even Suit Jacket Phil had. And he had a suit jacket.

"Don't go anywhere," Niall murmured and I realised I hadn't even thought to try and run. The key to my collar was stashed in his jeans' pocket, but even as I considered trying to get it, I found I didn't really want to. Not until I was sure he was okay. "It was so dark in this house before you came here," he mumbled.

"Did you get new lightbulbs when I arrived?" I whispered, but he didn't seem to hear me as he went on.

"I couldn't bear to lose you like I lost Ava, Brooklyn. We're the same, you and me…" He drifted off, his head lolling and my stomach fluttered with hungry moths.

I brushed his messy blonde hair away from his forehead with a frown, my heart beating unevenly as I stared at my captor's handsome face. He'd been so sad lately. Sadder than an owl without a raincoat. And I didn't like him being sad. I just wished there was something I could do to make his happies come back.

I lay with him for a while and softly hummed the hokey cokey, my ear against his heart so I could keep tabs on him being alive like a good doctor. *Another skill for the resume rock.*

After what must have been an hour, I got up, fetching a blanket for him from the chair across the room and laying it over his body, making sure he was good and tucked in before heading to the kitchen for a drink of water. Then I started hunting for Coco Pops. I'd earned myself a little snack after all. And once I'd located them, I could hide some downstairs for me. Mateo would probably want some, but the Pops were mine. He'd have to kill me for them and maybe he would. But they were worth that risk. Especially as he might not kill me at all, he might lick me all the way to scream town again. Or put a fourth finger in my butt if I was lucky. That would be the frosting on the Pops. I shivered excitedly as I remembered what he'd done to me. I was becoming such a sex goddess and he was my nefarious mentor, teaching me how to sin in ways I hadn't even known existed.

I moved through the rooms in the house, finding empty spare bedrooms upstairs that didn't hold a Pop in sight. Not even a whisper of a Pop.

I made it to the final room I hadn't checked, pushing the door open and flicking the light on. My heart clenched as I found myself in the only used room I'd discovered so far. The bed was a mess of blankets and the scent of Hellfire hung in the space like the darkest temptation. There were a couple of cardboard boxes at one end of the room and I crept towards them, sure I'd found the Pop jackpot – or the jackPop if you will.

"You've been holding out on me, Hellfire, stashing this many Coco Pops away and not giving me a single one. Greedy, greedy." I knelt down in front of the first box, teasing the top open and frowning when I didn't find any Pops. There were a couple of picture frames on top of a stack of clothes and I turned the first one over, my pulse quickening as I found a photo of Niall on his wedding day, his beautiful wife held against his side. He wore a grey suit, his blonde hair slicked back and glinting with sunlight. There were no signs of the tattoos he now had on his hands or neck and there was so much joy in his eyes that it made me ache. My gaze moved to his wife next, her blonde hair pulled into a silky bun and a tiara crowning her head. She was beaming at the camera, her teeth white and pearly, her eyes full of endless possibilities.

I turned the photo frame upside down again and put it back in the box, dropping onto my butt and hugging my knees to my chest as I hurt for

Niall. He'd had something beautiful, something untarnished and glowy and someone had come along and ripped it away from him. They'd shattered his soul and stolen half the shards. I knew what that was like. I knew the pain of being altered, twisted into something evil by evil itself. And there was no getting back that light. Not ever. I'd tried and tried for years. But my happies had been snuffed for good and so had Niall's. We were both just broken creatures lingering on in this world looking for vengeance or redemption or both. But it would never come. *The past is done and the future is fucked.*

I sat there for an unknowable amount of time as I stared at those boxes, feeling the weight of them in this house. I was surprised the floor didn't crack and crumble beneath them. They carried a whole life within them, a better life, a happy life. Niall would have traded everything he had now to return to it. But instead, he dwelled here seeking out happiness in a world that offered him none.

I tried to think of something I could do, any way I could make him smile again like he'd smiled in that photo with Ava. And one idea struck me like lightning, giving me sparks of energy that made me grin. I pushed to my feet, gazing at the boxes as I planted my hands on my hips. "If you can't go to Ava, Hellfire, I'll bring Ava to you."

NIALL

CHAPTER TWENTY THREE

I shifted in my seat, moving to my left and cursing as I knocked my arm against the couch, pain stabbing through the limb and reminding me I'd been shot tonight. Or last night. Fuck knew. But as I cracked my eyes open, the sky was only just beginning to lighten on the far horizon beyond the windows so it hadn't been all that long ago.

I pushed myself upright with a groan, my hand sweeping across the spot beside me where my little spider had been sitting. I swear I could feel the echoes of her fingertips tracing my tattoos and scars as she named them beneath her breath and her lips danced against my flesh.

The space where she'd been was empty now though. And one brush of my fingertips over the cushions told me that they were cold and she'd been gone a while. Her scent lingered like a taste on the back of my tongue, and I wondered when I'd started trusting her. I'd let myself sleep with her right here, given her the perfect opportunity to take me out, but here I was, alive and kicking.

So where was she?

I licked my parched lips and pushed myself to my feet with a grunt of exhaustion. It had been a long damn day and night with plenty of running about and fighting, though I hadn't come as near to dying as I'd have liked to fully banish my ghosts. Then again, I never did really.

Perhaps in the moment when I finally passed out of this world they'd leave me be, let me rest. Or maybe they'd be waiting there to drag me through to the other side, excited to have me at their mercy at last and ready to torture me for all of time.

I ran a hand down my face, wondering if my little spider had just run away. She should have. If she was smart she'd run far, far away from me and save herself from all of my bloody baggage.

Of course, if she did I was fairly certain I'd be hunting her down within the hour. I might have been aware that she was better off without me but I was too selfish to let her go. She'd brought something into this house which I hadn't even known I needed. And now that I'd gotten a taste for her beautiful destruction, I wasn't going to be relinquishing it without a fight.

I pushed my fingers into my pocket, expecting the key to her collar to be gone but finding it right there. My skin prickled as I ran my fingers over the shape of it, trying to figure out why she hadn't run. And where was she now? She was free but not free, close but not here. So where?

I grabbed a bottle of whiskey which I'd left sitting in the windowsill, unscrewing the cap and taking a healthy dose of it - alright, it was an unhealthy dose if I was being totally honest but I was aiming to blot out the pain in my arm so I was good with the liver damage.

I looked out into the dark, my gaze skimming over the pool outside then beyond it to the sweeping hills and forest in the valley beyond.

A rustle of fabric and the sense of someone at my back made me still, but I knew who it was. Call it instinct, gut reaction, the scent of her on the air, or just the fact that there was only one other fucker loose in this house, but I knew.

"You didn't run out on me then, love?" I asked her, tracing my gaze over the view once more as I took another swig of the whiskey.

"Not tonight, Hellfire. I wanted to do something nice tonight," she breathed and I swear excitement was lacing her tone.

I frowned at the blurry reflection of myself in the glass for a moment then turned to face her, a smile tugging at the corner of my lips and a joke on the tip of my tongue, but all of that fell away as my gaze moved onto her.

My heart froze in my chest and a cold, dark feeling slid through my veins as I took in the sight of her standing there, biting her bottom lip and swishing her hips from side to side as she plucked at the skirt of the flowing white dress she was wearing.

I stilled entirely, blinking against the booze and the pain in my flesh as I took in the sight of her standing there in a wedding dress that was too damn long on her and wearing a tiara that had slipped to one side.

My grip on the neck of the whiskey bottle tightened until I was almost certain it would shatter and rage rose in me unlike anything I'd ever felt before.

"Tell me I've lost me damn mind," I snarled, looking at her through a haze of red as I forced myself to remain perfectly still through pure determination. "Tell me the ghosts of my past have finally cracked me so thoroughly that I'm imagining up the sight of you standing there in my dead wife's wedding dress."

"Oh, Hellfire," Brooklyn breathed, stepping towards me and swishing the layers of white fabric around her hips again. "You've just been so sad recently and then I found the photo of you with her getting married, looking so happy and I thought-"

"You thought you'd rifle through the only things I have left of the woman who was ripped outa my life in the most bloody and brutal way imaginable? You thought you'd take an item from the biggest day of her life and dirty it by placing it on your flesh like some little girl playing make-believe?" I asked, my voice dripping acid.

Her lips popped open in surprise and she looked down at the dress, smoothing her hands over the fabric. "I'm not dirty. I had a shower today and I thought you'd like to see it again..."

I gaped at her, my eyes wide and heart pounding to a furious, dangerous rhythm which was only ever going to end in death.

What the fuck had I been thinking to bring this fucking woman into my house?

Why the hell had I thought anything good might come of it?

She was just a foul wind, blown in to shake up all the ghosts that clung to my skin and now she'd riled them beyond measure.

I lifted the bottle of whiskey and hurled it at her head a moment before I launched myself at her with a furious cry.

Brooklyn screamed, ducking aside so that the bottle hit the wall and smashed, glass and whiskey exploding everywhere as she took off outa the room.

But that wasn't gonna cut it this time. She'd gone too fucking far. I'd warned her about messing with the monster in me. I'd told her and shown her and made it perfectly fucking clear exactly what I was. And that was a creature which killed all others. Everyone around me ended up dead. So now she was going to be next on the list.

I raced after her into the hall, stumbling back a step as the dresser there was wrenched from the wall and fell across my path.

"I was trying to do something nice!" she shrieked as she ran on, ripping a picture from the wall and launching it at me.

I raised an arm and let the photo shatter against it as I vaulted the dresser and charged after her, my lips pulled back in a feral snarl as I kept my gaze focused on my target.

"I'll show you what I think of yer version of nice!" I roared, running after her as she darted into the kitchen and barely ducking as she swung a frying pan at my head.

I hooked an arm around her waist, but she brought the pan down again, clocking me in the side of the head hard enough to dislodge my hold before I could tighten it.

She kicked me in the stomach fiercely, knocking me back a step then swung the pan for my head again, forcing me to catch it.

I ripped it out of her hands but she didn't even bother to try and hold onto it, whirling away and grabbing a carving knife from the block on the counter instead, putting the kitchen island between us as she brandished it at me.

"I look beautiful!" she yelled. "And this dress was sad in that box, all sad and locked away and forgotten - it wanted to come out and play!"

I lurched towards her and she threw the knife, forcing me to block it with the frying pan. I barely managed to smack the second knife she threw aside with the pan, cursing her as she hurled another and another, making me use the fucking thing like a shield to knock each blade aside.

"I thought you wanted to die by the hand of the greatest killer who ever lived?!" I roared, launching the pan at her and caving a huge dent into the front of the fridge as she ducked it.

"Well maybe you're not the best!" she shouted back, ripping open a drawer and throwing it at me as I rounded the kitchen island to get to her. Spatulas, spoons, a whisk and a potato peeler smacked into my chest followed by the drawer itself and I snarled at her as she turned and bolted again, throwing cupboard doors open in my face as I took chase.

I smacked the doors aside, catching a fistful of her raven hair and yanking hard enough to make her fall onto her back amid the shit she'd sent flying everywhere. The tiara fell from her head, skittering away into a corner as her eyes flared with shock and outrage.

I lunged forward to grab her but she threw a fist up into my junk with a scream and I cursed as I stumbled back, wheezing in a breath as spots danced before my eyes and the pain made my lungs seize up.

"Arsehole!" I shouted after her as she scrambled back to her feet and bolted out of the room, a cloud of white material flying up all around her as she ran.

I hobbled behind her as she sprinted for the dining room and caught a chair to the chest as I stepped through the door. I bellowed a challenge at her as I grabbed it and yanked it out of her hands, smashing it against the wall as she let go and backed away again. I was left with two chair legs in my hands and I pressed forward, swinging one at her head then catching her in the stomach with the other when she ducked it.

She crumpled over it with an oomph and I was on her in the next breath, dropping the chair legs and tossing her onto the dining table on her back, sending plates and glasses flying everywhere.

I pinned her beneath me, catching one of her wrists in my hand and grabbing the top of Ava's wedding dress in my other before yanking on it hard enough to rip the sleeve, but the damn thing was laced up tight at her back and wouldn't shift any more than that.

Brooklyn shrieked at me, punching me right in my fucking bullet wound and making my vision swim as I reared back.

She tried to scramble upright but I leapt on top of her, straddling her in the centre of the dining table and snatching a butterfly knife from the back pocket of my jeans as I snarled down at her.

"This isn't how it's supposed to go!" she yelled at me as she bucked and writhed beneath me, throwing her fists into my sides and trying to fight me off. But I was bigger and badder than her and there was no fucking way I was leaving her in that dress.

"How the fuck did you expect it to go when you put on my dead wife's wedding dress then?" I demanded, the desire to punish her warring beneath my flesh, begging me to show her exactly who and what I was.

I grabbed the front of the dress in my fist, baring my teeth at her as I dug the knife into the fabric and slit the centre of it right open.

Brooklyn shrieked as I destroyed the dress, like the act of that hurt her more than any other part of our fight. She lunged at me and I had to snatch the knife away from her stomach to save it from cutting into her soft flesh, wondering why the fuck I'd done that the moment I was certain she was safe.

She bit down on my collarbone and I growled at her as I slammed the knife down into the dining table beside her thigh, skewering the skirt of the dress and missing her flesh by a hairsbreadth.

I shoved her away from me, leaving the knife where it was as my flesh burned and the bloody imprint of her teeth was left in my skin.

"You've spoiled it!" she yelled at me, her hand wrapping around the knife as she tried to rip it from the table, but I'd stabbed the fucker in there with all my strength and she couldn't pull it free.

Brooklyn gasped as I reached down for the skirt which still pooled around her legs and tore the fabric from her body. She slammed her fists into my sides just like I'd shown her, pain driving into my flesh as she hit all the right places one after another.

"You're a fucking psycho!" I yelled at her, jerking back as she swung her head forward with the aim of breaking my fucking nose and yanking the torn remains of the dress clean off of her, leaving her in her black underwear with her lips parting in shock.

I turned and whirled away from her, striding back out into the living room with the destroyed fabric bunched in my arms, the faintest smell of lavender reaching up from it and caressing my nostrils.

I didn't slow as I stalked across the huge room beneath the vaulted ceilings, throwing it into the fire with a curse.

I could hear my wife screaming in my head, the last words she'd ever said to me on that tape playing on repeat over and over, and every time I blinked I was holding her bloody corpse in my arms again.

Spider hounded me into the room but I shoved past her as I headed up the stairs to my bedroom. I marched along the walkway, throwing the door open and dragging out the boxes of Ava's things which I'd carted around with me ever since I'd lost her. They'd been pawed at, gone through, the scent of my long dead wife all mixed up with the papaya scent of that insane girl downstairs and my heart was racing as bile clawed at my throat.

You promised to love me forever.

You told me you'd keep me safe.

"'Til death do us part," I snarled in response to Ava's fucking voice in my skull.

But that never had been the case for me and her. I'd only really known her for five years. Been married to her for one of those. It had been ten since I'd lost her and yet she'd never left. If death was supposed to end this bond between us, then why was I still so tangled in this web?

I grabbed the boxes from the floor and stormed back out onto the walkway that ran above the living room where Spider stood in her black underwear, staring up at me like she didn't know what the fuck to think.

I hurled the boxes over the glass railing, clothes, photos, jewellery, a diary, all of it raining down into the room below.

I vaulted the railing and leapt over it after the boxes of shit and memories, landing hard and rolling as I hit the ground, welcoming the pain it sent crashing through my limbs and not caring if I broke something or even if I killed myself.

But of course I didn't. Death still didn't want me and the Devil wasn't in the mood for any competition.

I grunted against the pain in my body as I stood, glancing at the blood which was pissing out of my fucking arm again and welcoming the bite of pain. I deserved that much at least.

"What are you doing?" Spider asked, pointing a knife in my direction which I was guessing she'd gotten from the kitchen while I was upstairs.

I just snarled at her as I started grabbing dresses, tops, pants, any and every fucking thing I could get my hands on. All the pieces of Ava I'd been carting around with me for ten long, lonely years. They'd never done me any good anyway. Never made the slightest bit of difference to the guilt or the pain or the constant fucking emptiness in me.

When my arms were full, I threw it all in the fire with the wedding dress I'd ripped off of Brooklyn.

"No!" she gasped, racing forward and grabbing my good arm, trying to pull me away, but she was five foot nothing and no match for my strength even on a good day. And today definitely wasn't a good day.

I wrenched my arm out of her grip and grabbed the bottle of lighter fluid from the mantelpiece, squirting it all over the fabric which was half hanging out of the fire and onto the floor.

It ignited with a whoosh and a flash of flames burst to life right in my face, knocking me back a step as the heat licked my skin and promised to meet me in hell if I could only find myself a ticket.

I turned, knocking Spider aside as she tried to get in my way and I started grabbing the photographs from the floor, tossing my memories into the flames one by one and hoping it would burn them from my mind too.

"Stop, Hellfire!" Brooklyn screamed, moving to snatch some of the photographs into her grasp like she seriously believed she could keep them from me.

I grabbed more of the ones she hadn't got to yet and when I turned back to throw them in the fire, I found it spilling out of the hearth along the bridge of clothes I'd created for it, licking the edge of the curtains and climbing the wall.

I didn't care. Didn't give a single fuck if I burned up here and died screaming. I deserved it. Ava was still screaming in my head anyway, so what difference would it make to add to the noise?

When I'd thrown all I could find into the growing fire, I turned towards Brooklyn and bared my teeth at her.

"Give them to me," I demanded, pointing at the photographs she was clutching including the framed wedding photo I hadn't looked at in so fucking long I wasn't even certain I knew what I was wearing in it anymore.

All of my good memories of Ava had been scoured from my mind by the bad. The only things that had stayed clear to me were the ones of her death. Of her cold body and so much fucking blood. Her torn underwear and the way Tom Nelson had laughed about him and his men taking turns with her before I'd cut his throat.

He'd died too easy and I'd been the one left to suffer.

"Don't do this," Brooklyn begged, backing up. "Don't burn her away because of me. I didn't mean it. I didn't want this-"

"See, that's how I know how fucking young you are, Spider," I growled at her. "You're so naive - you think you know what it is to live with the things that fucked you up, but you don't. Not really. 'Cause you've barely lived at all. And you think you can just put a bandaid over all the shit that cut you and stop the bleeding. Well I'm old enough to know I'm never gonna stop bleeding. I've been bleeding so much and for so long that I'm painted red and I'm never gonna be able to scrub myself clean."

I snatched the photographs from her and pointed at a picture of me laughing at my fucking prom, Ava in my arms and an honest to shit look of happiness on my face.

"See him? He's dead. Gone. Forgotten and buried. You can't ever bring him back, not with bullshit games like the ones you play and not with anything else either."

"I don't want him," she spat, pointing at the image of me which wasn't me at all anymore. "I want *you*." Her finger slammed into my chest and I stilled as I looked down at her.

Her features were written in pain and fury and her fingers were curled so tight around the fucking wedding photograph that I knew I'd have a damn hard time trying to prise it from her grip.

I barked a laugh, stepping back and opening my arms wide as I dropped the prom photo. "Then maybe you need to take a closer look, love. Because there ain't nothing here worth having. There ain't nothing here at all. I'm the shell of a ghost of a man, all wrapped up in pain and misery and dripping in blood. I've killed more people than I can count, caused more suffering than you can imagine, and I haven't felt a damn real emotion in ten long years aside from misery and guilt and failure."

I turned away from her, ripping the gold wedding band from my finger and hurling it into the fire alongside everything else, watching the flames that were licking their way up the wall and tasting the ceiling above the curtain. There wasn't much else in that corner for them to grab hold of, but they were trying, aching to destroy the world almost as much as I was.

"You don't get to do this!" Brooklyn yelled, her hands slamming into the small of my back and knocking me forward a step, making the heat of the fire lap hungrily at my skin. "You don't get to just check out and lose your shit and destroy everything!"

"Why the fuck not?" I bellowed as I whirled back around to face her, perfectly willing to just stand here and let the whole fucking house burn down around me, not giving a single shit about it one way or another.

"Because you promised me!" she shouted right back, her hands slamming into my chest this time as she glared up at me. "You promised me I had a place here and you can't just take it away again! You can't!"

There were tears in her eyes which made them seem even brighter than usual, the blue blazing like a burst of electricity that made me want to dive into it and just let it consume me.

She shoved me again and I snapped, snarling at her as I grabbed her waist and shoved her back against the wall on the other side of the mantlepiece to the out of control fire, the flames heating my skin to my right and casting flickering light over her features.

"You keep pushing me like that and I'm gonna break," I warned her darkly, levelling her with a glare that promised her the worst of me.

"So break then," she growled. "Just fucking break and feel it. You're a genie in a bottle, Hellfire, so full up with everything that it's set to explode. You need to break free and feel all of it or you're just gonna go poof and be gone."

She slammed her palms into my chest and the force behind her strike was almost enough to knock me back a step. But I held firm, the rage in me boiling over as I forced her against the wall, my hand closing around her throat.

"You want me to kill ya?" I demanded, my fingers flexing, the ghosts urging me to just do it, punish her for what she'd done, make her see exactly who she was fucking with here. Though another part of me held back, a voice I didn't often hear from, one which hungered for something more.

"I'm not afraid to die," she hissed defiantly, raising her chin and glaring at me. "I'm afraid of not living."

The rage in me burst over, but instead of squeezing her throat, I shifted my hand, capturing her jaw and holding it tight as my mouth collided with hers.

She gasped as I kissed her, full lips parting for my tongue as I pressed forward hungrily, desperately, devouring her and drawing her in even as the fury in me begged for an outlet of its own.

Her arms wrapped around my neck, fingers twisting tight in my hair as she pulled me closer, pushing up onto her tiptoes as she tried to make up for the difference in our heights.

I grabbed her arse with my free hand, hoisting her up and she jumped to accommodate me, her legs wrapping around my waist as the kiss deepened and I pinned her back against the wall.

My heart was racing as the fire raged beside us and the echoes of those screams in my head roared louder and louder, threatening to split me in two.

Her teeth sank into my bottom lip and I snarled as she spilled blood, the iron tang of it moving between our mouths as my cock ground into her though the barrier of our clothes and she bucked her hips against me.

Something slammed into the side of my head and I jerked back as she dropped the metal vase she'd snatched from the mantlepiece to attack me with.

I snarled at her, releasing my hold on her jaw and gripping her hair in my fist, forcing her to tip her head back as I looked down at her, my blood staining her lips and running over my chin.

She dropped an arm to my bicep, squeezing the freshly stitched bullet wound and almost making me drop her before she kissed me again, harder, hungrier, this dirty fucking dream of a kiss that made my heart race and my cock ache as my entire body came alive for her.

The fire blazed hotter beside us and I dragged her away from it, carrying her to the Chesterfield on the far side of the room and dropping her onto it, pressing my weight down on top of her as I followed.

Her fingernails carved lines down my chest and drew blood as I crushed her beneath me and kissed her harder until I was breathing her air and she was breathing mine and I knew I never wanted to come up for more.

I hadn't done this in so long that it felt brand fucking new. My skin was on fire everywhere she touched me, my heart racing like I was some lovestruck boy and my cock aching like a virgin desperate for its first taste of pussy. Ten long, empty years I'd avoided this at all costs, I'd denied myself in every way and for what?

Because you're the reason your wife is dead.

The screaming in my head grew unbearable and suddenly I was right back there, coated in the blood of the woman I loved, too fucking late to save her, no fucking use at protecting her.

I couldn't do it again. I couldn't let someone get that close to me ever again.

I wrenched myself back so suddenly that I almost knocked Brooklyn from the couch as I stood, my heart racing and panic flooding through me as I looked down her, panting and confused beneath me.

I shook my head as I backed up, swiping the back of my hand across my mouth to banish the taste of sin from my lips. Because I knew the more I gave in to that, the worse this was going to get. For me. For her. I couldn't do it again. I wouldn't. Not to her.

"Niall?" Brooklyn breathed, confusion and hurt flashing in her eyes as she pushed herself up and I just kept backing away, shaking my head.

I whirled away from her, grabbing the grey couch closest to the fire and hurling it over with a furious roar that shook the foundations of my soul loose from its cage.

"Did I do something wrong?" she asked and the pain in those words cut me deeper as I kept my back to her, swiping my hand across my face again.

"You need to keep away from me," I snarled, still not looking at her because my body had some very different ideas about how this was going down and I knew I was too weak to resist her if I looked.

"Why?" she asked as if she seriously had no fucking idea.

I snatched my cell phone from my pocket and linked it up to the TV, playing that video. The one of Ava right before the Nelsons raped her again and murdered her. I cranked the volume right up so that the screams at the end echoed around the house, then I flicked it onto the photographs of her body. All the blood and pain and everything I'd caused right there on the screen.

Brooklyn watched it all, tears rolling down her cheeks as she absorbed it and I knew then that she finally saw what I was. The truest monster she'd ever known.

"Niall," she whispered, but I turned and stormed away from her, passing the fire which was starting to die out with nothing but bricks to feed it and feeling a faint flicker of disappointment in knowing that I wouldn't burn tonight after all.

I kept going until I made it to the basement where I unbolted the door and ripped it open.

She finally seemed to understand then. Silence falling at last as she passed me, tears sliding down her cheeks and enough pain between the two of us to make the whole universe hurt.

She looked back at me as I swung the door closed in her face and I knew exactly what she saw.

A man whose worth had been tested and found wanting. A man who had taken something pure and beautiful and destroyed it beyond all possible return. A man who was broken and ruined and worth nothing at all.

A ghost who should have just accepted he'd died a long, long time ago.

BROOKLYN

CHAPTER TWENTY FOUR

I ran downstairs and launched myself onto the bed with a wail, mourning the loss of everything that had burned because of me. I was so stupid. I couldn't do anything right.

"What's happened?" Mateo demanded in a gravelly tone full of fury, his weight dropping onto the bed. "What did he do to you? Where are your clothes? If he hurt you I'll-"

"He didn't!" I cried, rolling onto my back as a shuddering sob wracked through my body. "He hurt himself, he hurt his Ava."

I thought of what I'd seen in that video and I knew it would haunt me forever. That poor, beautiful, innocent creature ruined and cast into death. Those men were monsters of the most sickening kind, the kind I'd known first hand. I pitied Ava, and a piece of my heart chipped off for her, swirling down into the abyss inside me like a precious coin down a drain, never to be retrieved.

The smell of smoke and burned up dreams clung to my skin like they were accusing me of destroying them, but I hadn't meant for that to happen. I hadn't wanted that.

"Where. Are. Your. Clothes?" he gripped my jaw, turning me to face him where he knelt on the bed, his chest bare and his muscles as tight as a coiled spring.

"He was mad. He cut off her dress and burned it," I choked out.

"Whose dress?" he hissed, endless fury swirling in his golden brown eyes.

"Ava's. His poor, dead wife. I put her wedding dress on. I thought it would be a nice thing to do. Hellfire looked so sad, I just wanted to make him smile, Dead Man. But I messed up. He got the angries instead of the happies."

He released a slow breath as he took in those words. "Tal vez al menos ahora se mantenga alejado de ti," he muttered, dropping his hold on my jaw.

I gazed up at him as my lower lip trembled, aching for him to come closer to me, to wrap me in his arms like my Daddy used to do when I cried. "Will you cuddle me, Mateo? Just…for a minute," I whispered and his brows descended like I'd asked him to do something far worse. "Never mind," I said quickly, but he lay down beside me and scooped my body into his large arms, holding me to his chest.

My ear rested against his heart and I shut my eyes, listening to the powerful drumming of it. It was slow and confident unlike my wild heart which beat all over the place like it was a one man band putting on the show of his life. I liked Mateo's heartbeat, that steady, reassuring tha-thump seeming to beat through the centre of my body. His skin was as hot as an oven and it baked me through like a cherry pie. But I didn't want to be put on the windowsill to cool just yet. I wanted to keep baking, get over crispy, my fruity insides turned to sweet, gooey mush.

"I've never been held like this before," I whispered against his flesh, my lips grazing the crucifix burned into his body. "Did it hurt very bad when someone did this to you?"

"Yes," he said in a dark tone full of hate.

"Poor chest." I kissed it and he stiffened in two senses of the word, his cock driving into my thigh and his body as rigid as a ruler.

"I'll fucking kill him for making you cry," Mateo snarled and I realised no more tears were falling now.

"It's okay, Dead Man," I whispered. "He's just a big bad wolf with a big sad heart."

"That's no excuse," he growled. "This time he's gone too far." His fingers brushed down the length of my spine and the best kind of shivers tickled me from the inside.

"I hurt him too," I said. "That's how we play, me and Hellfire. It's honest and brutal sometimes, but that's what I want, it's what I like. I'm not a china doll, I'm a serial killer in the making."

He growled, shaking his head, but said nothing more.

We fell quiet and my tears dried up as I snuggled against him. I was so tired. The world was so heavy sometimes. It must have weighed a thousand, million, billion, zillion tons…

I woke to a loud clanking sound and cracked my eyes open, the light so glarey and blindy.

"Mateo?" I reached into the sheets but they were cold and as the clanking sounded again, I lifted my head and saw him holding onto his chain and tugging hard. His biceps strained as he fought to break it off the bathroom wall. He was like a wild animal, yanking on it so fiercely I swear the bolted thingy in the bathroom groaned.

"Stop it, you'll hurt yourself, Dead Man," I gasped, reaching out to him.

"I'm going to kill him," he growled. "Today's the fucking day."

My fingers grazed his back and he turned sharply, yanking the chain furiously once more as sweat gleamed on his skin. His eyes were full of the desire to kill and the sight of it lit me up from the inside like a distress flare wheeling through the sky. But I didn't want Niall to die, even if he deserved it a little for what he'd done to my dead man, I still hated the thought of it. He was my, well not friend. But like, my...bosom buddy? No that wasn't right.

The door to the basement flew open and Niall stormed down the stairs, marching toward me with a fierce intent, his stun gun in hand. I gasped as he grabbed me, pulling me away from Mateo as he took a swing at Niall and pushing me to sit on the far side of the bed.

"Get off of me," I snapped, shoving his hands away and clawing at him as he tossed the stun gun away to get a better grip on me.

"Stay still," he commanded, but I wouldn't. I didn't like being held still, not one bit. I wanted to flap my arms like a bird and take off into the sky.

"Ca-caw!" I landed a solid punch to his gut, making him grunt from the impact and I punched harder, kicking, thrashing and going fully wild as he tried to restrain me. It brought up memories of straitjackets and straps holding me down on hospital beds. I heard my own screams echoing in my ears from the past and suddenly they were ripping from my throat right now too.

"Get away from her!" Mateo roared, but Niall ignored him, grabbing my legs and yanking me off the bed so I fell onto the floor on my back.

"Niall!" I yelled as he dropped over me, straddling my hips before I could manage to get a knee up to crush his dick. He fought to get hold of my wrists, but finally managed it, pinning them above my head with one hand.

"Get away!" I begged, bucking my hips, unsure what the fuck he was going to do and his face kept changing from his to Madam Lucille's, her laughter ringing in my head. He reached into his pocket, taking out a syringe and utter dread coiled in my gut as he tugged the cap off with his teeth to expose a jabby needle.

"No, I don't like it. Get it away from me!" I could see the white coats, the hands holding me down. So many hands. A needle sliding into my neck, the poison stealing me far, far away into the dark. Madam Lucille's smirking face came into my mind as her vile team of nurses held onto me. *"It'll hurt more if you struggle, sweetie. And then we'll have to punish you by putting you in the cold room all on your own. You don't like the cold room, do you?"* her voice twisted through my head like she was right here, right now.

"No – don't send me away!" I screamed, thinking of that horrible cold place with all the frozen food that hurt my teeth when I tried to eat it.

"You're dead, you're fucking dead!" Mateo roared.

"Calm the fuck down," Niall barked at me and his face came back into focus. He was just Hellfire. My devil man in the flesh. "It's a vaccination for the goddamn Hades Virus. My nephew Kyan gave 'em to me for helping out with that job and I forgot I was supposed to give 'em to you sharpish."

I stilled, my breaths coming raggedly as I looked from him to the needle in surprise.

"I'm not gonna hurt ya, little psycho," he said in a low tone, leaning down with a look of regret in his eyes. "Just stay still."

I stared at him, unsure if I trusted him anymore or if I ever really had. People were awful. People did terrible things. Was this one of those terrible things? Was he lying to make me accept that jabby into my flesh? What if he was going to sedate me then sell me to someone else? I could wake up in the basement of a far worse monster than Niall, someone who really wanted to hurt me. Someone with teeth and claws. Like a bear!

"Please don't sell me to a bear," I breathed desperately. "I know I was bad. I didn't mean to make you so angry. I didn't mean for you to burn all of her things. I'll be better. I'll be a good psycho. You can go back to teaching me all the stuff and things. I'll listen. I'll make you proud. I promise."

His brows stitched together, his eyes full of flickering green flames as he sighed. "I'm not gonna sell ya, Spider. You're my killer. *Mine.* Ain't no one gonna take you from me. This really is a vaccine." He held the syringe in front of me then released my wrists, shifting back on my legs so I could sit up.

Mateo was still fighting to break free, snarling furiously as he yanked on the chain again and again. I appreciated his efforts. It really was sweet that my boyfriend wanted to murder for me. I just didn't want him to snap Niall's neck. It was such a nice neck, there was a shamrock inked on it among a bunch of other interesting things.

I took one long breath, fighting against my instincts not to trust anyone at all in this world. But if it really was a vaccine then it was as rare as stardust and would keep me safe from the mean virus storming through the world. So many people were dying out there beyond this house and I didn't wanna be one of them if Hades came knocking at our door. I'd seen people die on the streets from it. The coughing, the rash, the weakness. I'd probably only managed to avoid getting it because I couldn't stand being too close to people regardless of social distancing and all that jazz. But that wasn't the case if I was really going to work with Niall to become a killer. I'd have to get up close and personal with my marks while I was gutting them. And what if splashy blood carried the virus? I couldn't put myself at risk from the splashies.

"Okay," I gave in, offering him my wrist but he shook his head.

"It can go in the top of yer arm or yer arse, what'll it be, love?" he asked and though I doubted he liked me very much anymore, I still felt that bond between us, buzzing and humming, telling me I should be here. With him, with Mateo. My instincts had failed me before though, so I couldn't always rely on their flutterings. This time, I guessed I'd try to.

I rolled over and stuck my ass in the air. "I'll take one order of jabby in the butt with a side of ouchy."

"Right, sure," Niall muttered, gripping my hip, his thumb skimming over the lacey fabric of the panties I was wearing where they curved around my ass. His palm ran over my skin as Mateo roared something in Spanish which I was pretty sure meant he didn't wanna have his vaccination in the butt.

"It's okay, Dead Man," I called. "It's just a little jab -ah!" I squeaked as Niall stuck me in the ass with the needle and pressed the plunger. "Ohhh it's quite nice actually."

Mateo roared again and there was suddenly a bang and the clank of metal then Niall was ripped away from me. I twisted around with a gasp, finding Mateo having broken free from his restraint. He had his chain wrapped around Niall's throat and was hauling him backwards through the basement by it.

"Stop!" I screamed, springing to my feet and chasing after them.

Niall grabbed hold of the chain with a snarl, yanking it even tighter so Mateo was tugged closer. I gasped as he threw a furious punch at his head and Mateo snarled as Niall yanked on the chain so hard that Mateo fell down on top of him. They launched into a furious fight, punching each other and rolling across the floor as they battled to get the upper hand. It was kinda hot actually. Like, lemme-pull-up-a-pew-and-touch-myself-hot. But I couldn't do that. I needed to stop them before one of them ended up deadified.

When Mateo got on top of Niall and cracked his head down on the floor, I leapt onto his back, throwing my hands over his face. "Stop it! Stop hurting each other!"

Niall slammed bone-crunching punches into Mateo's sides with a wild laugh, managing to throw him off and sending me rolling away from them. I scrambled back upright as Niall started kicking Mateo on the floor, but my dead man grabbed his leg, uprooting him once more and diving on him with a dark, cloying hate in his eyes. Mateo locked his hands around Niall's throat, squeezing so hard, his biceps bulged. *Oh holy tits, this is premium porn I'm getting for free.*

Niall managed to get his knee between them and force Mateo away, throwing a hard punch into his gut too.

"Hellfire! Stop it," I demanded, running at him and grabbing his arm as he swung it back to hit Mateo.

The moment cost him his advantage and Mateo threw himself at Niall once more, knocking us both down to the ground. The air was crushed from my lungs with the weight of them both and I wished I could call cut on this porno now. No one's clothes were coming off and it didn't look like anyone was up for some dick sucking. Except me maybe, but I wasn't sure how to pose the question right now.

They quickly rolled off of me, wrestling on the floor as they fought like wild animals. Testosterone burned through the room and I drank it in like a little girl with a sippy cup.

I got up again, spotting the stun gun beside me and picking it up, running toward them with a snarl as I fired it up. "Come on then Zappy, let's finish this."

Before I could strike either of them, Mateo flung out an arm, knocking it from my hands so that it skittered across the floor and I swore, pushing him to try and get him off of Niall.

"That's enough!" I shrieked as Niall suddenly lunged up from the ground, shoving Mateo hard in the chest. He lurched back into me and I was thrown away, smashing into the cage with a yelp of pain as something cut into my shoulder. "Ow ow ow ow!"

I crumpled to the floor as the heat of blood wet my back and I cursed between my teeth. "Tit blanket on a fucking tuna baguette with a side of shit tarts! *Ow!*"

"Mi sol." Mateo dove toward me, his eyes focused on me and nothing else. But before he made it to my side, Niall shot him with the stun gun and he fell like a stack of dominoes before me, jerking and twitching on the ground.

Niall stood above him bloody and victorious, looking as hot as a flaming crouton as his chest heaved and his muscles flexed. *Um, yum. But also, that was so not cool.*

He hauled Mateo to the cage, shoving him inside and sticking him in the thigh with the vaccine then bolting his chain to the wall in there before locking it tight. Then he strode toward me, scooping me into his arms without a word and marching up the stairs to the exit.

"Where are you taking me?" I demanded, trying to get free, but he clung on tight, his features fixed into a steely mask that I couldn't read. *"Hellfire."* I tried to get down, but he growled low in his throat, crushing me to his chest and I pouted up at him.

He walked me through to the kitchen, sitting me on one of the worktops before grabbing the lunchbox which served as a first aid kit from a cupboard.

"I'm as fine as a dandelion," I said lightly, waving him off as he approached, but he just flipped me around to face the window. I crossed my legs as I gave in, rolling my eyes. He gently brushed my hair over my shoulder, his fingers skimming across my skin and sending a shiver right down to my toes. His fingers felt as zappy as his stun gun right then and I bit my lip as I pictured those fingers caressing other parts of my body. The dirty parts.

"This'll sting like a jellyfish," he muttered then pressed something cold and wet to the cut and I moaned. It stung real good in the best kinda way.

"I've never seen a jellyfish before, have you?" I asked, but he didn't reply. I twisted my fingers together, gazing out the window as rain pattered against the glass. "I think I'd like the sea. It's all big and washy and blue. Blue's my favourite colour. It's the colour of all things free. The sky, the sea, some special types of starfish, bluebirds. What's your favourite colour?"

"Red," he grunted, gently cleaning the wound then tossing the bloody swabs in the sink.

"Is it deep? Will it leave a scar? I like scars. They're like little clues to the past. You've got a lot of scars... I like finding them in your ink."

The hot press of Niall's lips against my shoulder made me gasp. The heat that ran through my flesh was like an inferno and I knew for sure that this man was forged in the fires of hell.

"I'm sorry," he said darkly. "Sorry I lost my temper over Ava's clothes."

"Oh...that's okay, Hellfire. I guess it seemed like a good idea at the time. But I don't tend to be the best judge of good ideas. I just wanted to see you smile again. I don't like seeing you sad."

His breath skated against the back of my neck and more warmth curled through my veins like a thousand tiny flames under my skin.

He didn't answer me and a question knotted up in my throat, a bundle of words just sitting there like a razor blade. They came bursting out before I could stop them, even though I was pretty sure this was one of those ideas which were bad. "Do you still love her?"

Silence. The kind that echoed on into eternity and made you feel like you were sitting on a termite hill getting bitten all over. I was about to retract that question and run for my life when he answered me.

"I don't know if I even really remember her," he said in a deep voice full of guilt. "That's the worst thing about time. It steals everything. Even memories."

I dropped my head, bunching my fingers together as I felt his pain clinging to my body like a second skin. "I know. It eats it all away like a hungry maggot," I agreed. "My dad used to be so clear to me in my mind, but every day it gets a little harder to see his face. I don't even have a photo of him." My heart hung like a lead weight in my chest as I ached for him. The one person in this world who had loved me unconditionally. "Misty Jean used to drink Dad's favourite beer back on the streets and I'd steal a can or two from him when he passed out, sniffing them just so I could get a piece of him back. It always sparked memories. Like little rockets going off in my head, reminding me of all the good times."

"I used to get that from her perfume," Niall said hollowly. "Doesn't work anymore. Sometimes I think the girl in my mind ain't nothin' like the one I really married. I've been filling in the gaps for too many years, trying to recreate pieces of a puzzle I lost years ago."

"Do you think she's out there somewhere, waiting for you?" I asked.

"No," he muttered. "She's gone. There's no after, there's just hell or heaven on Earth. It's a toss of a coin which one ya get."

I glanced over my shoulder at him, meeting his gaze. "Well if this is me burning in hell, it's not so bad. Not right now at least."

"Yeah," he agreed, grazing his knuckles down the length of my spine until goosebumps spread everywhere across my body. "It ain't so bad right now. And I have some good news." He eyed me with a look I could have sworn was hunger then pulled his black t-shirt over his head, making my heart race as I drank in every inky inch of his chest. I was getting ideas, the best kinds of ones about how his mouth had felt against mine and how his tongue had driven between my lips when he'd given me my first ever kiss and the heat of it had almost been enough to set me on fire. I licked my lip as I tried to remember the taste of him and how good his weight had felt on top of me, how hard his cock had been driving against me and how much I'd wanted to know what it felt like inside me.

But then he passed me his shirt, shattering my filthy fantasies as I realised he was giving it to me to cover up with. I pulled it on before spinning around to look at him, hanging my legs over the counter. "What news?" I asked excitedly, hitting my disappointment over the head with a shovel and burying it deep underground.

He popped open a cupboard beside my head and took out a box of candy, rattling it under my nose. I picked out a Coca Cola lollipop, unwrapping it and sticking it in my mouth with a grin. "What's the news?" I pressed and his eyes darkened to pitch as he rested his hands either side me on the counter.

"I found those people who hurt you. Andrew and Penelope," he spat their names like they were dirty and tasted bad in his mouth, making a flare of excitement shoot through me.

"Well where are they? Let's go!" I tried to get off the counter, but he blocked my way to keep me there and I bumped against his hard chest instead, making my heart flutter as I looked up at him in confusion.

"It ain't that simple, love. The lad's a cop and the girl's his Stepford wife."

I sucked my lollipop, considering that news. "Motherfuckers. That is a problem."

He nodded and as I pulled my lollipop from my lips, he leaned forward and sucked on it too, looking at me as he did so. It was weirdly fucking hot. And that made two lollipops I'd shared now. *I wonder if I can get Niall and Mateo to share one...*

I tugged it from his lips and pushed it back between mine, savouring his taste as much as the lolly.

"We gotta be smart about this," he said as a smirk twisted his features and I caught a glimmer of my Hellfire back in his sad eyes. "But I'll hand ya them, Spider, don't you fucking worry about that."

I laid my hands on his shoulders, placing my faith in him. It wasn't much. I was a squirrel with a lot of trust nuts which I was hoarding, but I could give him one for this. Because he was the best killer I knew, and I'd give anything to get my hands on those fuckers who'd haunted me all these years. "I'm going to kill them real good. My best kills yet."

"Well, we'll see about that." His smirk grew, but I suddenly slapped him hard across the face.

"That's for hurting Mateo," I growled and he bared his teeth at me.

He pinched my arm. "That's for getting involved in that fight downstairs."

I jabbed him in the cheek. "That's for being a meanie bambini."

He flicked me in the forehead. "That's for being a crazy daisy."

I scrunched my fingers in his hair and he wrapped his fingers in my hair too. As I started pulling, he did as well, and we growled like dogs as we each pulled harder.

"Truce?" he asked.

"Truce," I agreed. "Let go on the count of three. One, two…three."

I let go half a millisecond after he did, but he didn't seem to notice as he walked away and I mouthed at his back, *"I win."*

MATEO

CHAPTER TWENTY FIVE

I watched her in the light and the dark, day and night, not even certain I slept at times with my attention so riveted on her.

Was this how I met my downfall? At the hands of a chica loca with violently blue eyes and a free pass to hell?

My neck was bruised almost as much as my ego after my attempt to get us out of here. I'd failed again. Every time I'd gone against the bastardo, I'd ended up on my ass at his fucking feet and I was done with it.

I needed to break free of my chains permanently. I needed to reclaim something in me which I was afraid I might be losing. I was a demon where I came from, feared and avoided, spoken about in hushed whispers behind hands and closed doors. People knew to fear me. Yet now I was reduced to this shadow of a man locked away beneath ground and neither of the two people I had contact with feared me like they should.

Without the shield of that fear, I wasn't certain of who I was. Just a broken man with a fucked up past and a taste for blood which had been left wanting for far too long.

I was in the cage again. No doubt being punished for fighting against the injection he'd forced upon us. And I had to admit that after five days it seemed as though nothing had come of it. Maybe he hadn't been lying. Maybe he really had just given us immunity to the virus which was plaguing the world. I guessed it made sense - he wouldn't want me catching it via him then dying before he got done torturing information out of me.

Not that he'd ever prise so much as a word from my lips. One day he'd grow tired of trying to tear my secrets from my flesh and follow through on his threats to finish me. I needed to get out of here before then, but every plan I'd tried to execute had failed, leaving me in this limbo eternally.

Brooklyn was doing a headstand on the far side of the basement, her little pink panties showing beneath the fabric of the loose, lime green shorts she was wearing as the material slipped down over the curve of her ass.

"Are you counting?" she demanded.

"Si." I wasn't. I was just watching her, my cock growing hard as I looked over her body, taking note of the ways it had filled out since she'd been here. Regular meals and workouts with the hijo de puta upstairs certainly hadn't hurt with that much. Her tits and ass were fuller, muscles stronger and body more fuckable than ever.

"Have I made it to five minutes yet then?"

"What do you get if you make it five minutes?" I asked, gripping the bars above my head and licking my lips as I drank her in. I was going to destroy her when I gave in to this desire. I just wished I could trust myself with her to do it.

"Ummm, maybe a fish? Orrrr a new tattoo? A cute one of a bloody knife, or of a skull…or a kitten. Or maybe a bunch of flowers? Or Niall might give me Coco Pops at last? Orrrr what if you do that mouth thing to my pussy again?"

I bit down on my tongue, pressing my forehead to the bars and looking between them at the pink sequinned top she wore. It was slipping down, catching on her tits and almost exposing them. A few more moments and I was certain her nipple would slip free of it. Would I refuse her request?

Doubtful. I dreamed of her pussy near constantly and the idea of owning it again was more than a little appealing.

Before I could reply to her suggestion, she fell to the ground in a heap, shrieking angrily and ripping her shoe off before launching it across the room. It hit the bathroom door and disappeared inside, a splash suggesting it had fallen in the toilet.

"Dammit - that was only three minutes!" she snarled, tipping her head back to the ceiling and closing her eyes as she shrieked again, thumping her fists down on the ground as she threw her little fit.

It had been more like thirty seconds, but it didn't seem like the time to point that out. She looked like she needed an outlet for all of that frustration though and my mouth had been watering from the moment she'd suggested I take another bite of her.

"Come here," I commanded, jerking my chin and tightening the grip on the bars above my head.

Brooklyn dropped her hands over her face, but then split her fingers apart to peek out at me with one eye.

"I don't deserve to come," she breathed.

"I'll decide that," I replied darkly and her eyes widened as she caught the double meaning to that statement. "Now come here. Don't make me ask a third time."

If she knew what was good for her, she'd do as she was told. I didn't like people backchatting against my orders and I'd punish her for it if she made me wait.

She licked her lips slowly, drawing my attention to the bright plum coloured lipstick she was wearing before she started to crawl across the floor to me.

"What will you do to me if I don't do as I'm told?" she asked roughly, her eyes wandering over my torso, drinking in my scars and the memories of my pain like she was hoping for a taste of it.

"The man I was before I came here would have killed anyone who disrespected him," I replied thickly, wondering if I was that same man anymore or not. Sometimes I wanted to be, other times I hated him with all the passion of a thunderstorm set to break over the sea.

"How would you do it?" she asked me curiously, a hungry look in her eyes as she crawled closer still. I watched the way her hips moved before eyeing her tits thirstily as they threatened to spill out of the sparkly thing she wore. She went without underwear more often than not and I was consistently getting hard for her because of it.

"I always favoured a blade," I replied slowly. "I like it to be personal. Like to look into someone's eyes as they die for me. I like the heat of their blood on my hands."

"Shit, that's so hot," she said, biting her bottom lip. "I think you'd look really good all red and bloody, Mateo."

"I'd look a lot fucking better with a haircut and a razor," I put in bitterly.

"I think I'd like that," she said. "I think I'd like to see who's hiding under all that hair. Are you a heartbreaker, Mateo?"

"I've never gotten close enough to a woman to break her heart," I replied coldly.

"Why not?" she breathed, stopping just out of reach and crossing her legs beneath her as she looked up at me.

Flashes of my past whipped through my mind. Of nuns and chanting and the burning kiss of hot metal searing away my skin. Of dark rooms and hunger and bible verses repeated over and over and over until I couldn't even make sense of the words.

"I hate women," I admitted, watching her closely, wondering if she would understand that. If she even could. I hated her entire gender and no matter how much I enjoyed watching her or listening to her or wanted to fuck her, I was always going to hate her for what she was too.

"Oh." She chewed on her bottom lip, taking an elastic from her wrist and slowly tying one side of her hair up in a pigtail. "Is that why you don't like me? Why we can't be friends?"

"We can't be friends for a number of reasons. Not least because when I see you, I want nothing more than to sink my cock into you and hear you scream," I growled. "That's not how friends normally treat each other."

"So...you're my boyfriend then?" she asked, cocking her head.

"No," I snapped, my grip on the bars tightening as she flinched. "Boyfriends are the nice guys you bring home to your mamá. They're the kind to keep you safe and whisper sweet nothings in your ear. I'm not that kind."

"So what kind are you?"

"I'm the kind who only brings trouble," I said. "The kind you know you should fear even when I draw you closer. I won't whisper sweet nothings to you, I'll deliver death threats while fucking you so hard you can't think straight and reminding you that you had time to heed the warnings before getting close enough for me to burn you."

"Being burned by you doesn't sound so bad," she said breathily. "But if you're not my friend and not my boyfriend then what are you? What am I to you?"

"You're mine," I said firmly. That much was true, no matter what the rest of the fucked up truth amounted to.

"So you're mine too?" she asked, chewing that lip again and making me ache. I'd never hungered for a mouth the way I did for hers. Those full lips, that sinful tongue, the husky voice that poured from it, the words which spun insanity into the air and allowed me to breathe it in and get high on it. I was addicted to her mouth and I fantasised about it incessantly.

"If you lay claim to me, you won't easily give me up," I warned her. "And if I lay claim to you, I never will. Beware chica loca, you're dancing with the demon in me every time you get close and if he gets his hooks in you, you'll be ruined beyond repair."

Excitement lit her features like she didn't think that sounded so bad and I watched her as she moved even closer.

"Why do you hate women?" she asked, shifting towards the bars, moving into my trap even if she didn't know it yet.

"That's a long story," I said slowly, biding my time, picking my moment.

"Did they hurt you like Andrew hurt me?" she breathed, scooting closer again.

"Not like that," I said with a shake of my head. I didn't know why I was telling her this, but I felt my tongue loosen around a few more details so I pressed on. "My mamá realised I had a demon in me when I was young, so she took me to her church to have it exorcised. Between her and the nuns who worked to rid me of it, I found more than enough reasons to hate your gender."

"Men are cruel too," Brooklyn said, frowning at me like my story didn't make sense to her.

"Yes," I agreed. "But men are simpler with their cruelty. Their intentions are clear and their actions swift, perhaps more brutal, but there are no lies there. Women are the fouler beast. They're cunning and savage with their evil, it's the kind that creeps beneath your skin and scars you on the inside."

"Do you think I'm cunning?" she asked, getting to her feet slowly and running her hands up the bars until her fingers slid over mine where I grasped the cold iron.

"I think you have an agenda, mi sol," I murmured.

"What agenda?" she breathed, watching me closely like she was aiming to find out too.

"Well, you're hoping I'll lick that sweet pussy of yours for a start," I replied darkly, not that I was wholly against that idea. "After that, I can't say for certain, but I do know that dark in you is real."

"People are awful," she murmured in agreement. "And I'm people too."

I tilted my head as I looked at her, wondering if she meant that, if she was truly capable of admitting that she herself was just as flawed as the rest of us.

I reached through the bars suddenly, gripping the single pigtail she'd tied in her hair and tugging her close enough for our lips to touch if I were to lean forward an inch. "Take your panties off, chica loca. I want to have a taste."

Her gaze met mine and I saw the defiance there, but if she wanted to use me for her pleasure she'd do it under my terms or she could get herself off without my assistance. Not that I wanted that. I ached to be the master of her pleasure more than she could possibly imagine, but I ached to be the one in control of her even more than that.

She sucked in a breath as she released her hold on the bars, pushing her shorts and panties off before kicking her remaining shoe away too.

I didn't make a move, my gaze running down her body, hand still fisted on her pigtail.

"Touch yourself for me, bonita," I purred, wondering how far I could push her.

She fell to my command so easily, her eyes on mine as she slid a hand between her thighs and began to slick her fingers over her needy clit.

"Tell me what you're thinking about," I said, watching her movements as my dick thickened and chafed against the inside of my sweatpants.

This was dangerous, but I was caged, locked on this side of the bars and unable to hurt her really. All she'd need to do to escape me would be to jerk back, move away. I could push a little harder with this barrier between us. Just a bit. The darkness in me craved it and I'd been forcing it back for too long.

"You," she breathed, her other hand reaching between the bars like she planned on touching my chest.

I snatched her wrist before her fingers could reach the old scar of a crucifix which marred my flesh.

"Be specific," I warned.

"Your mouth," she gasped, moving her hand between her thighs until she was pushing two fingers inside herself. "I want your tongue on my clit, playing it like a harmonica. I want the bite of your teeth on my flesh like you're so hungry you can't help but try to eat me up."

I smirked at her as I pulled her hand closer, letting her slide her fingers down the centre of my burn scar from the point just beneath my clavicle almost down to my navel. The feeling of her skin on my body was an exquisite kind of relief laced with the pain of the memories which haunted me. I'd never let a woman touch me there. Not since the mark had been branded on my flesh, but the feeling of her fingers running down it awakened something primal in me which I didn't want to cage.

"I want your cock," she added suddenly, trying to move the hand I held lower while continuing to finger herself for me. "I want to know what it feels like, looks like, tastes like and how something so big will fit into-"

"Hold onto the bars and don't let go," I commanded her, gritting my teeth against the power of her words as I placed her hand against the cold metal.

She didn't stop pleasuring herself with her other hand until I tugged that away too and as I wrapped her fingers around the bars between us, she scowled at me.

"I want to come, Dead Man," she hissed like an angry cat. "And I want your cock. Give them to me or I'll find my own relief."

"Not yet," I replied in a low growl, knocking her hand away as she reached for my waistband and firmly making her take hold of the bars again.

I dropped to my knees before she could protest further, reaching out to grasp her knee and encouraging her to put her weight on one foot as I tugged her leg between the bars.

"Lean back," I said, looking up at her as she watched me and I pulled the leg I held to rest it over my shoulder.

She caught on to what I needed and she did what I said, leaning right back and pushing her hips forward so that I could find the wet heat of her pussy between the bars.

Cold iron pressed to my cheeks as I moved forward, gripping a handful of her ass tightly in one hand and tilting her pelvis to give me the perfect access to her.

The first sweep of my tongue around her entrance had her groaning my name and I smiled as the taste of her overwhelmed my senses. My addiction to her was only growing more potent as time went on, but it was pointless for me to consider quitting her now. She was all I had down here in the dark, so I was going to gorge myself on her and damn the consequences.

I lapped at her again, tasting, teasing, licking softly several times all around the edges of her pussy before sucking her clit into my mouth and making her cry out.

"Quiet," I warned her, my lips dragging over her clit with my words and making her pant louder.

"Fuck, Dead Man, do it again," she begged, her heel driving into my spine as she tried to force me closer with her leg.

"Who owns you, chica loca?" I asked, licking and kissing all around the place where she wanted me most, waiting for her to say it, needing her to admit it.

"You don't own me," she groaned, bucking her hips to try and force me where she needed. "But you might just own my pussy."

On balance, I was okay with that, so I decided to remind her pussy of exactly why that was.

I began to feast on her, licking and sucking and making her moan far too loudly, but I was moving beyond the point of caring.

When I pushed two fingers inside her to further her pleasure she actually screamed, her hips bouncing and thrusting as she fucked my face and I lapped at her clit, driving my fingers in deeper and faster until she was coming hard, moaning my name. Her back bent over so far that her hair brushed the concrete floor behind her and her heel drove into my spine hard enough to bruise while I pumped her pussy a few more times, wanting to be certain I'd wrung every drop of pleasure from her.

"Oh tits," she panted as she straightened, sliding her leg back off of my shoulders and staring at me with wide eyes. Her knuckles were white where she gripped the bars and I got the impression that she was holding herself up while her legs went weak.

"What?" I asked, my cock throbbing as I licked the taste of her from my lips.

"I didn't make five minutes. I didn't earn that orgasm." She pouted at me and I couldn't help the breath of laughter that escaped me.

"Well, it's a little late for that," I pointed out.

Brooklyn continued to pout as she pulled her shorts and panties back on and I stood, looking at those plum painted lips and thinking up all the ways I'd like to satisfy the throbbing of my dick with them.

I caught the front of her shorts and tugged her flush against the bars again as I rolled her sequinned shirt up and dropped my mouth to her hard nipple, palming the other in my hand and squeezing until she gasped.

"I have to cancel it out," she forced out through her laboured breaths. "I need to make you come too, then it's even Simons."

"You think that would cancel it out?" I asked in amusement before biting down on her nipple just enough to make her drag in a sharp breath before sucking and kissing the pain away again.

Fuck, she has nice tits.

"Please, Mateo," she groaned, grasping my chin and forcing me to look up at her. I growled a warning, squeezing on the nipple in my hand and making her whimper but she ploughed on with her line of thought all the same. "Just let me suck your cock. I want to prove how good I can be at blowjobs anyway and I want to make you come like you do for me."

The darkness in me rose up to the surface of my skin at her words, the thought of those plum painted lips wrapping around my cock making me impossibly hard as I considered it.

I was still in here after all, still caged and unable to fully unleash the worst of me upon her even if I did lose control. Could I risk it? Would I? I'd been hungering for the feel of those lips on my dick for a long fucking time now and it was beyond overdue.

Before I could fully decide on my own limitations, Brooklyn dropped to her knees before me, reaching through the bars to tug on the waistband of my pants.

"What are you doing?" I growled, catching her wrist to stop her, frowning at myself more than her for this hesitation.

"I want to own you too, Dead Man. So I'm making your cock mine."

She snatched her hand away from me and yanked my sweatpants down before I could stop her, my hard length springing free before her face and making her gasp.

"Hello, Dead Dick, can I make you feel alive today?" she asked curiously and I cursed her insanity half a breath before she placed a kiss on the head of my cock.

"Fuck," I growled as the whole thing jerked, sliding over her lips and smearing the bead of moisture from the tip across her mouth.

She licked her lips hungrily and raised her eyes to me, the mischief in her gaze battering down any and all protests I'd been considering.

I gripped the bars either side of me as I gave into this, wanting it too fucking much to deny myself and stepping forward so that my cock slid along her cheek and she nuzzled against it like a cat.

"Tell me when I do it good," she said, looking up at me seriously. "I need to get a feel for it."

"Well, I can tell you that just staring at it isn't doing a whole lot to get me off, chica loca," I growled as I watched her, my fingers biting into the bars as I fought off the desire to just grab her hair and thrust my cock between those fuckable lips of hers to stop this conversation. Normally, I would happily listen to her talk all day but right now there was something else I wanted that mouth to be busy with.

"Okay, okay, I'm just getting my cock bearings. It is pretty fucking big and there isn't a map."

I was about to curse her when she leaned forward and ran her tongue along my shaft from base to tip, moaning softly as she went.

I fell still as she did it again before dropping down and sucking my balls into her mouth, making me grunt before she pulled back.

"Are the balls kinda like a clit or-"

"Why are you acting like you haven't done this before, mi sol?" I demanded, watching as her eyes widened and wondering what the fuck she was playing at now.

"I have!" she spluttered. "I've sucked dream cocks twice as big as this and licked dream balls for at least eighteen hours too. But if you don't wanna tell me what you like then-"

"I want you to take that loud mouth of yours and wrap those full lips tight around my cock and suck it like you did that lollipop," I said, holding her gaze. "Is that clear enough for you, chica loca?"

"Yeah - I know I've gotta suck it, duh." She leaned back and stared at my dick with a serious expression on her face. "It's you and me, so be a good boy and come in my mouth, kay?"

I muttered something that started off in Spanish but turned unintelligible as she leaned forward again, her mouth sliding over the head of my cock and making me groan as those plump lips tightened around my shaft. She slid me in further and further and I cursed as her lips made it to the base of me, her claims about her lack of gag reflex clearly true. It felt so fucking good that I growled her name, wanting more and more of this and fighting to allow her this moment of control.

She drew back again just as slowly, the head of my cock rubbing across the roof of her mouth and sending prickles of desire racing all over my body.

As she began the same slow descent again, I bucked my hips forward to urge her on, earning myself a gasp as I growled, "Faster."

Brooklyn moved a little faster, her tongue swirling around me as soft, muffled moans slid from her.

She drew back suddenly, looking up at me as my cock fell from her mouth and I noticed the plum lipstick smeared around my shaft. I swore as she stopped, wondering what the fuck she was playing at and if her intention was only to tease me. If I had to use my hand after that beginning, I was going to be seriously pissed.

"Should I do the tongue thing faster or-"

"If you want to suck my dick, mi sol," I growled, unable to hide the hint of frustration in my tone. "Then why don't you wrap those pretty lips around it and stop making conversation?"

"I just want to get it right. It's hard to ask questions when my mouth is so full and I don't know how fast or slow or-"

"Do you want me to fist my hand in your hair and show you exactly how fast I want it?" I asked in a growl, expecting some smartass remark in return but her eyes widened with excitement instead and she nodded.

"I think I'd like that Dead Man," she breathed huskily, that fucking voice of hers making me so hard it felt like I might come from the sound of it alone. "I think I'd like that a lot. Will it be rough and dirty and all the bad things that feel so good?"

"That's pretty much the best way to describe me, chica loca," I replied darkly, wondering if she could possibly enjoy what I did or if I was just indulging in a hopeless fantasy.

"Then do it, Dead Man. I want it to be the way you like it. Show me how you want me."

She leaned forward and licked the end of my cock like it was an ice cream cone and I growled with the need for more.

The last of my control snapped, the demon in me rising up and taking control. Any doubts or hesitations I'd been clinging to evaporated as I reached down with my right hand, tangled her pigtail in my fist and pushed her mouth down onto my dick.

Brooklyn moaned as I drove my cock all the way to the back of her throat in a punishing thrust, the vibrations of that noise rattling through me and making me groan.

I drew back, my fingers biting into her scalp before I thrust forward again and she moaned even louder, her hands sliding up my stomach and over my abs.

As I thrust in again, her fingers curled against me, her nails ripping into my flesh and making the beast in me snarl as she dragged them down, marking me with bloody lines.

The pain only urged me on, made me want it more, crave her more. I upped my pace, taking her moans of pleasure as encouragement as I fucked her pretty mouth hard and fast, loving having her on her knees for me.

I kept my left hand locked around the bar above my head as I drove my cock in and out of her mouth, her full lips smearing lipstick all over my shaft and making me so fucking hard that I could barely breathe.

She kept moaning and sucking, her nails scraping over my flesh and making me bloody for her as I took and took and fucking took from that beautiful mouth of hers, snarling like a beast and drinking in the sight of her down there.

I wasn't going to last long, it had been months of celibacy in this hell and weeks of lusting after her. I needed this release more than I needed air in my lungs, I needed to use her and let her own me like she claimed to want to and feel like anything other than a prisoner.

The sound of the door opening drew my attention for a brief moment, but I was so fucking close to the edge that I couldn't force myself to stop.

Brooklyn's teeth scraped along my shaft as I pulled back once more, the bite of pain exactly what I needed to send me spiralling as I thrust into her mouth once more, groaning loudly as I came hard, my head tipping back as ecstasy burst through me.

I spilled my cum down her throat and she did as I asked, sucking on me like that lollipop and swallowing it down with a moan of pleasure that made the hairs along the back of my neck stand on end.

"What in the ever loving fuck is going on down here?!" Niall roared as he leapt off of the stairs and barrelled towards us with fury flaring in his eyes.

I released my grip on Brooklyn's hair with my upper lip peeling back, yanking my sweatpants up as I tried to drag her to her feet on the other side of the bars.

But before I could pull her away from him, Niall had snatched her into his arms, hurling her away just as fast so that she landed on the bed and bounced to the other side of it. Her legs went up over her head as she tumbled across it and she squeaked in alarm and fury as she went.

He bellowed like a charging bull as he launched himself at me, swinging a fist through the bars of my cage with a wild and furious jealousy burning in his eyes. "I'll fucking kill you!" he yelled. "And then I'm gonna kill your mamá and your papa and your great aunt Dahlia's pet chipmunk. I'll get every fucker you ever so much as looked at fondly and kill 'em worse than I've ever killed anyone. I'll make you watch it all before ripping yer fucking eyes from yer head and wearing them on a necklace so that you're forced to watch every other horror I ever commit from the afterlife!"

"What's the matter bastardo? Did you think the beautiful girl might want *you*? The hijo de puta who kidnapped her and locked her in a basement like a dog?" I spat at his feet, laughing at him as he continued to try and reach me through the bars, the tables finally turned between us as he found himself unable to get to me.

"Stop it, Hellfire!" Brooklyn shouted as she leapt off of the bed, running at him and jumping onto his back. She locked her arms around his muscular neck and hung there like she seriously thought she might be able to pull him away.

"Get offa me, you little monster," he snarled, grabbing her ankle and whirling around as he tried to yank her loose. But she just scrambled around his body like a monkey until she was clinging to his front instead, locking her arms around his neck and her legs around his waist, frowning in his face and baring her teeth like a beast.

"You don't get to ignore me for days then come down here hollering like a baboon," she snapped. "If you wanna shout at me then just do it - don't take it out on Dead Man."

"You just expect me to let him get away with that shit?" he yelled at her in outrage.

"If you've got something to say to me then just say it," she snapped.

Niall glared at her, then at me over her shoulder. "I'll talk with you in private," he gritted out, looking to her again then he turned away abruptly, carrying her up the stairs and out of sight.

The door banged solidly, quickly followed by the sounds of the locks bolting shut and I was left down here in the dark, alone and seething, wondering if I'd ever see the light of day again.

BROOKLYN

CHAPTER TWENTY SIX

Niall carried me upstairs and the second we reached the hall, I leapt free of his arms and backed away with a furious frown.

"That piece of shit is using you." He rounded on me, stepping forwards with intention and I stepped back. "I told ya to seduce him, not to fuck him!" He kept stalking toward me and I kept retreating, anger flooding every inch of my core.

"Mateo is my *mine*," I said.

"Yours?" he spat, lunging at me, but I leapt back, lifting my chin as I dared him to come for me again.

"Yeah, we're a thing. Not a boyfriend and girlfriend thing apparently, but something. I have feels in my heart for him and I think he maybe, possibly has them back."

"You sucked his fucking cock, men don't get *feels* over a girl on their knees for them," he threw at me and a knife dug into my heart under my skin. "He doesn't care for you, love. He's a fucking snake." His eyes blazed greener than ever before and I shook my head in denial.

I opened my mouth to argue that he did care, but the words wouldn't come out. They got all choked up in my throat like a lump of used coal.

Because I couldn't see any reason why Mateo would care. But he was the only man who'd ever touched me and made me feel good, didn't that count for something?

"I know I'm just some unlovable street rat, but he might be my Princess Jasmine," I pressed, trying to make myself believe that as much as Niall.

He laughed mockingly, lunging at me again to try and catch me, but I darted around a corner, snatching a picture frame off the wall and smashing it over his head. He roared angrily, shaking glass out of his hair as he kept coming.

"You're not unlovable, woman," he snapped. "But ya are naive and El Burro is taking advantage of you." His hands clenched into fists as he moved quicker to try and match my pace, but I kept retreating, hunting for another weapon to beat him around the head with. I was all in my angries. He'd come down there and embarrassed me, thrown me away from Mateo like a frisbee. Like, what the tits, Hellfire?

"Fuck you," I spat. "I want his hands on me and he wants mine on him. So why would he try and take advantage of me?"

His face turned redder as I said those worse, rage etched into every corner of it. He was so huge already, but he seemed to take up the whole hall in that moment, an enormous shadow surrounding him like death itself.

"To use ya to get himself outa there," he hissed. "Tell me he hasn't brought it up with you and maybe I'll consider believing ya." He laughed coldly and the sound was so cruel it made my cheeks burn.

My lips parted then closed again because I couldn't say that. Mateo *had* asked me to help him, to kill Niall, find a way to set him free. Was that really all he wanted? Was I being led into a fisherman's net without knowing? Was I just a hungry little shrimp hunting for some krill to eat up with my little shrimp whiskers, unawares that a fisherman was luring me in for his dinner?

I blinked hard, shaking my head violently as I pushed out those thoughts. I knew my Dead Man, I felt the connection between us. Didn't I?

"He's using you," Niall said just as my back hit a wall and I tried to flee, only finding I'd walked myself right into a dead end. Niall took his time stalking closer, savouring the kill as he cocked his head to one side, his entire being seeming to swallow me up. "He doesn't deserve a single fucking touch from you, Spider."

"I like him and I'm lonely. Is it such a bad thing to crave affection when I've never had any, Hellfire? It's like a drug." I lunged forward and clutched his shirt in my fists, feeling that ache in me now. "I've gone so long without it, but now it's in my system and I *need* it. And I need it right now because one day I'll be back on the streets with no one around me and no chance to be touched again. Not by someone I actually want to touch me. I've never wanted that from anyone until him."

Niall's face fell entirely into shadow as he stepped so close to me that I couldn't inhale a single slip of oxygen, my hands crushed between us and his heart pounding against my fingers as frantically as my own. He walked me backwards until my spine pressed to the wall once more and there was nothing but us in this hallway, everything else a blur of emptiness.

"Just him?" he asked in a rough tone that made every piece of my soul ignite like a match.

I gazed up at him, feeling everywhere the cold wall kissed my back and finding a deep, primal ache for more of the warmth of his flesh against mine.

He reached out, gripping my face with both hands, leaning down so his mouth was just a whisper away from mine.

"Answer the fuckin' question, love," he demanded and I tasted his desire like it was candy on my tongue.

The answer sat inside me, wanting to pop out and shout surprise. And I couldn't stop it as it sprung free.

"No," I breathed. "Not just him."

He released a low noise in his throat, his fingers pushing into my hair and fisting tightly as he forced me to tilt my head back. I loved it. I fucking adored being touched like that. I'd gone so long without feeling any kind of touch, these rough ones were making up for lost time. I needed the pressure of his fingers on my skin, the bite of teeth, the torture of his grip on me. I was a stress ball to be squeezed and squeezed, nails leaving crescents in my soft flesh. And I wanted to feel the total power of his hold. I could take it. I wouldn't break. In fact, I had a feeling I'd be forged.

His mouth collided with mine and I moaned, melting against him as his tongue pushed between my lips in fierce and hungry movements. My heart raced and happiness exploded through me in waves. Sparks popped beneath my skin like fireworks and I could hear them banging in my head with flashes of colourful light.

I dragged my hands down his body, gripping his belt and pulling him against me by it, making him growl as his hard cock drove into my stomach. I thought of Mateo, how I'd wanted him as keenly as this and I wondered if I could claim them both, tattoo their dicks with my name and lock them in a cock cage or a dick dungeon whenever I wasn't playing with them.

I gasped as his mouth broke free of my lips and dragged down to my throat, painting a line of pure ecstasy across my flesh. When he met the muscle of my shoulder, he sank his teeth in, making me cry out and my back arch. I felt him get even harder as he ground into me, his mouth returning to mine as we started kissing more frantically.

I unbuckled his belt and my pulse skittered everywhere under my flesh as his hand moved into my shorts and kneaded my burning pussy through my panties. He pushed them aside and I clung to him, trying to rock myself into his rough fingers, but his lips broke away from mine once more, his eyes turning to the darkest shade of green in the world. I walked into the forest of those eyes and found myself lost. Lost in a vast wood where there was no way out.

Then he tugged his hand out of my shorts and stepped back again and again until he was so far away it felt like an abyss stood between us.

Heat crawled into my cheeks as I panted, rearranging my panties in my shorts as he turned his eyes away from me. I felt the rejection like a slap to the face, leaving a stinging mark on my skin that blazed.

"Ava," he muttered his wife's name and my throat tightened. "I can't, Spider."

"Because of your wife?" I asked, needing the confirmation because I was about to tailspin into my insecurities and I needed a solid reason to hold onto that wasn't simply...me.

"Not just her," he grunted. "You're too young for me."

I released a hollow laugh, holding back the tsunami of emotion in my chest. "Sure, okay."

His head snapped around to look at me and his jaw flexed. "It ain't just that neither, I'm engaged. I'm wrapped up in shit with my family that-"

"You're engaged?" I blurted, my gut knotting, my heart throwing itself against my ribs in a suicide attempt.

"Yeah," he said gruffly. "She's just some Russian girl with big tits who I have to marry because-"

I didn't hear the end of that sentence as I marched past him down the hall, my brain bashing against the inside of my skull. *I've been as stupid as a snail in a top hat.*

"Here I was thinking it was just the three of us against the world, The Death Club, but you have a whole other life outside of here, don't you?" I tossed over my shoulder, his booming footsteps following me. "You have a fucking *fiancé*."

"What do you care if I do?" he snapped from behind me.

"I don't," I said airily, my lower lip shaking. "I don't care at all."

"Well you sure seem pissy for a girl who doesn't care."

"I just realised it's me and Mateo against the world, that's all," I spat. "You're off with your la-de-da life and we're stuck here together alone. I thought you were only off killing when you left the house, but it was all bullshit. You were off fucking your big boobed fiancé with her big boobs and her fucking…tits."

"What do you care if I was?" he barked.

"I don't," I snapped. "Just like you don't care about me and Mateo."

"I don't care if you've been fucking him every colour of the rainbow, I was just tryin' to give you a heads up that he's trying to manipulate you. I won't bother in future, love."

I made it to the kitchen, yanking the utensils draw open and taking out a bread knife, pointing it at him. "That's the only reason he'd fuck me, I suppose?" I snapped, hurt flashing through me. Holy fucking ow, Batman. I could see in his eyes that was what he thought of me. The little useless, sad pathetic hobo girl with her meagre tits that didn't measure up to his fiancé's. When you had that, why would anyone want me?

"Yeah, it is. And you couldn't even suck his cock good enough to get me my information, could ya? So I hope you're pleased with yer efforts." He glared at me, his eyes full of some fiery emotion that built a wall in his gaze and forced me out.

"I am!" I roared, pointing the knife at him threateningly, daring him to get near me right now. I swear to god, I would cut him from dick to nipples. "I am very pleased. As pleased as a crab in a nice dress actually."

"Why don't you just fuck off outa my house then, because you're clearly no good to me. Yer a useless honey pot, useless at killin', useless at getting information and just plain *useless*."

Pain spilled through my chest as I felt that word down to the pit of my soul, where it echoed on and on and on. My hand shook around the knife, my eyes blurred with unshed tears that I refused to let fall. I tossed the blade into the sink with a loud clatter and he turned, striding away, the sounds of locks clicking making me follow him through the house. He threw the front door wide open then gestured for me to leave, sneering before marching away and pounding back in the direction of the basement.

Rage burned through me and I picked up a lamp, launching it across the room with a shriek that made the walls quiver. "Fucking lamp! Stop looking at me!" I bellowed at it.

I knew what I had to do. I'd go. I'd fucking leave forever and he'd never see me again. And I was going to prove I was worth something, even if it was only as much as an ant on a cantaloupe.

I ran to the cabinet in the living room where he'd put the file on Andrew and Penelope. I took it out then snatched a car key from a bowl on top of it and strode back through the kitchen to the laundry room. My clothes were hanging around the place and I stripped out my outfit, grabbing a holographic mermaid green dress and some snuggly socks. I pulled them on and put on a little pair of rabbit panties underneath with a tiny white fluffy tail on the back of them and a bunny face on the front. Then I pulled the other half of my hair up into another pigtail with the tie on my wrist and marched out of the room, dragging on my knee high boots by the door. Then I left, walking straight out into the night without a backwards glance, saying goodbye to the house, to Niall, to Mateo. I didn't like leaving my dead man, but I had no choice now. This was goodbye.

I ran over to the line up of cars on the drive, pressing the button on the car key I'd stolen and the lights flashed on Niall's blue Ford truck. I climbed in and found a bag in the footwell full of weapons. Everything I'd need to prove I could kill better than he ever could.

I'd driven my uncle's car a few times when I was younger, but I was well out of practise as I started it up and accelerated down the drive with the engine roaring as loudly as my soul.

I knew only one thing as I weaved off of the property and sailed into the dark like a ghost leaving her body behind. This night would end in the screams of my enemies and their blood decorating my skin. And when the world heard my name in future, they'd fear the girl who'd killed so cruelly, ruthlessly, beautifully. They called me the Bully Butcher, but I hadn't done a thorough job the first time. So it was time to finish what I'd started and live up to the only name I'd ever be remembered by.

NIALL

CHAPTER TWENTY SEVEN

My feet thumped down the stairs into the basement as my pulse pounded so violently that I could hear it hammering against the inside of my skull.

I'd been a godawful prick and I couldn't even make myself regret it. Because now she'd run. She'd run and run and fucking run and hopefully she'd be far away from me before I ever gave into the desire to chase her. That was the best thing I could do. I was rot and poison and I didn't want to blur her sharp edges. She needed to be gone and now she was. Fuck the consequences for myself and my damned soul.

I didn't see red, I saw black, this hopeless, endless void of nothing and no one but death, death and more death.

"Where is she?" Mateo demanded, glaring through the bars of his cage at me like he was hungering for bloodshed almost as much as I was.

"What's it to you? You think she's yours now, do ya?" I asked with a sneer. "You think because she got on her knees for ya that you have some claim on her? She's my property - *mine!*"

"No lo creo," he snarled at me.

"Use English, El Burro, you know I can't speak yer fancy language,"

I snapped.

"I said I don't think so," he hissed, striding towards me until we were practically nose to nose through the bars of the cage. "You might have bought her and told her she was your property, but I'm the one she came to in the dark. You're just jealous she hasn't been sucking *your* dick, hijo de puta."

"And who's to say she hasn't?" I asked him cockily, my smile wide and fake, my soul dead and cold as something inside me twisted up into a knot so tight I knew it wasn't ever coming undone.

"Mentiroso," he spat, giving me the translation before I could demand it. "That means liar in case your ignorant little mind couldn't catch it."

I wanted to break his fucking face. I wanted to unlock the door of his cage and move in there with nothing but flesh and blood between us. I wanted to fight him hand to hand and see which of us came out on top and which was beaten into the ground. I'd kill him with my bare hands and fuck the money, fuck my chance to escape this life, fuck all of it. It was the stupid dream of a broken fool anyway.

There was no getting out of my family. There was no light at the end of my tunnel. I was an O'Brien. An attack dog. Nothing more. I'd marry Anastasia and be the puppet my pa wanted, baring my teeth on demand and seeking out happiness at the bottom of a bottle. But I'd never find it. There was no nirvana for people like me. My soul was cast into damnation the day I dragged Ava into this world, and I'd come damn close to doing it again with Brooklyn.

Maybe I should head into that cage and let Mateo finish me. Let it be over and done and stop lingering in this eternal torment.

But even as I considered that, I knew the stubborn little bastard inside me wouldn't allow it. He wanted to live, even if only to suffer. And though I couldn't easily call what I'd been doing for the last ten years living, I was still breathing, moving from place to place, killing and smoking and drinking and just fucking existing.

I was good for nothing and no one but death and cruelty and with that in mind, I leaned forward, pressing my face to the bars and speaking low as I looked into Mateo's dark eyes.

"Did you like her, El Burro?" I purred. "She told me you call her mi sol and I looked that up. *My sun.* So romantic for a piece of shit cartel fixer. Did she light up your dark little world?"

"A real man would let me out of this cage and test his mettle against me," he said in a low tone, the challenge in his gaze clear, tension in his posture oozing violence, but I wasn't done toying with my meal yet. I could spit venom like the best of vipers – I'd proven it just now upstairs. I had a special kind of knack for figuring out all the best ways to hurt a person physically or otherwise and I could always strike true when I wanted to. It might have meant I was an utter cunt, but I'd never been one for gathering friends anyway.

"I picked her out specially for ya, did you know that?" I asked and he frowned at me.

"Stop speaking in riddles and spit it out."

"I bought her for you," I said. "A sweet little gift with nice tits and a mouth good for sucking cock. She was playing you, El Burro, playing you and using you and working to steal your secrets while you fell for it like the desperate arsehole I knew you'd be."

He lunged at me, punching my jaw so hard that the inside of my cheek split open against my teeth and blood coated my tongue. I stumbled back, laughing at the pain and spitting blood onto the floor. It didn't come close to what I deserved.

"Every word she offered you, every look and touch, every kiss and caress was all just bullshit," I said, grinning at him as he raged and threatened and tried to taunt me into coming closer again, but this was so much better. I was finally giving him the kind of pain that cut him, and I hoped the blade was deep enough to pierce his heart.

"Where is she?!" he roared and I just laughed louder as I backed away.

"Gone," I said with a shrug. "She ran away from here and left you all alone without a backwards glance. She used you, but apparently her skills weren't up to scratch because I still don't have what I need from you."

"Mentiroso!" he yelled again and this time I remembered that he was calling me a liar. And maybe I *was* full of shit, but there wasn't a whole lot else to me, so I wasn't inclined to give a fuck.

"I hope you enjoyed the feeling of her lips on your dick, El Burro, because I've got the sudden inclination to cut it off. I'm sick of this dragging on and on, I'm sick of giving her time to break you and ending up with nothing to show for it aside from her giving you a good time. So I think you and me need one last appointment in my office." I pointed to the killing room on the far side of the basement and his eyes went stony as I got nothing but silence in response to that. "But I won't be holding back this time," I warned him. "This needs to end. So I'm gonna go upstairs and get a few more interesting tools. Then when I come back, I'll be strapping you to that table and cutting pieces off of you until you tell me where you hid everything you stole from Santiago Castillo. Either I'll be earning myself a ticket outa here with your hoard or you'll be dying today. Then I guess I'll be sticking with the Russian bride and my prick of a father. Either way, I doubt my position in life will improve all that much."

I turned and strode back up the stairs without another word and he let out a bellow of pure fucking rage which told me all too plainly how much he hungered for my death. But unfortunately for him, I was the best at what I did. He may have been a close second, but that wouldn't save him now. I was done. I was feeling bloodthirsty. And I didn't much want to keep house guests any longer.

I threw the basement door closed behind me, but I couldn't be fucked with locking it up. I stormed away, the fury in me not lessening a single bit as my brain accosted me with memories of Brooklyn's mouth against mine, her hands on my skin, my cock hard and aching as I ground it against her. I hadn't wanted a woman that way in so long that the feeling itself seemed alien to me.

But there were more reasons than I could count for us to keep away from each other. She was too young for me for one. Too naive and innocent and pure despite the blood on her hands. I was decay and blight and the reason for all the worst things. I'd already proven that I couldn't look after anyone besides myself. I'd been Ava's death and I'd have been hers if she'd stayed.

But I still wished she would have stayed. This selfish, hopeless part of me wanted her here despite all the reasons I had for her to go. Which was exactly why I'd had to do it now. If it had gone on much longer, I'd have talked myself into it. I'd have let the devil in me take everything from her and I would have convinced myself that it was okay for one reason or another.

So it was good that she was gone. I could rage about it and go on a killing spree, drink myself into oblivion, chain smoke the regrets away then hopefully she'd be long disappeared before I got around to convincing myself to hunt her down.

Because I couldn't do that. Even if she made this place brighter and gave my life...more. It didn't matter. Because I was nothing but bad. All the bad. And I needed to keep the fuck away.

But looking down the barrel of my life was a pretty fucking depressing thought. I had a wedding coming up and from the few events I'd been forced to attend, I could tell my pa was done with letting me hide in the shadows. He had plans for me, and I was about to lose what little control I had left of my life. I'd be marrying that fucking woman and I got the impression I hadn't even figured out the half of what I was getting myself into with her.

I had planned to go straight on out to the shed to gather up some more tools to use on Mateo to loosen up that reluctant tongue of his, but I took a detour to the whiskey first, heading into the front room and trying not to think about Brooklyn or how fucking barren this house felt already.

I strode towards the cabinet where I kept my liquor and fell still as I found the one beside it open, the shelf inside empty.

I dropped to my knees as I inspected it with my pulse racing. Gone. She'd fucking taken it. The one thing in this house I should have made certain she couldn't get her hands on.

She was going after the motherfuckers who had hurt her all those years ago. She was going to walk straight in there and do her fucking jazz hands bullshit killer thing and get her damn self killed.

Those people weren't simple targets. I'd been working on the perfect plan to take them out and it hadn't been fucking easy. I didn't like killing cops. Not because there weren't any bad ones or any bullshit like that. But the police tended to do a whole lot more investigating when one of their own was killed than they did with anyone else. Even if they were a perverted monster who deserved the worst kind of death.

I'd been planning this out and it was going to be fucking perfect, but now she was going to go blazing in there and end up shot.

This was bad. Fucking tortuously bad. And I was responsible for it. I'd found those fuckers, I'd written it all down and I'd left it out for her sticky little fingers. I couldn't let her go in there half cocked. That daft bitch was going to get herself killed. And then history would repeat itself and all the worst things I'd always known about myself would only be confirmed.

"Fuck!" I roared as I stood, kicking the cabinet door hard enough to rip it from its hinges.

I had to go after her.

And once I saved her life, I'd give her some money to go with the car she'd already stolen from me, point her in the direction of the horizon and make certain I never laid eyes on her again.

BROOKLYN

CHAPTER TWENTY EIGHT

The drive was pretty smooth to the outskirts of Hemlock city. I mean yeah, I hit that stop sign, and yeah that old man with the cain almost lost a butt cheek, but maybe he shouldn't have been loitering in my way on the sidewalk. He had a freaking death wish I tell you. You just can't teach common sense to some people.

I parked half a block away from the address, saluting the GPS in the dashboard for getting me here and unzipping the bag of weapons in the footwell. I strapped a hatchet to my hip and a motherfucking sword to my back. There weren't any guns in the bag, but whatever. I didn't need Mr and Mrs Bullet fighting my battles tonight. I could do it covert style with a side of bloody. Simple, stylish and savage. That would be the moto for my new club which I'd set up on my own. I'd call it The Lone Pickle. No, The Lonely Foreskin. Nah, The Pubetastic Bombastic Society. Hmm no, The Clit Clan. Yup, we had a winner. Except I didn't have a clan. But I did have a clit, so I was halfway to a full membership.

I shoved the door open, stepping out on the sidewalk and replaying the argument I'd had with Niall in my mind. "Ergh, fucking twat of a fucking Minpin!" I yelled.

A cat sitting on a low wall opposite me shrieked, leaping into the air before falling out of sight beyond the wall.

I didn't even apologise to her because I was still in a rage over *him*. *Niall the crocodile. Nah, more like Niall the crocodick. Yeah, Croconiall the crocodick. That's him.*

I didn't even wanna think about my life beyond tonight. I was just gonna rain vengeance down on my enemies and when their blood slid over my tongue, I'd deal with where to go next. Okay so maybe I was thinking about it a little bit. I didn't wanna go back to the bridge. It was so windy there and someone would have taken my sleeping spot by now. Sure, I could dress up like Chucky and creep up on them in the night to scare them away, but my heart just wasn't in it. I didn't want the stupid bridge. The bridge was cold and never spoke to me. It was a place where souls went to die and mine had barely survived its last stint there.

I sighed, my heart tugging over Mateo, wishing I could have saved my dead man. But I was no hero. I'd known that a long time ago. I just really, really, really hoped Niall didn't kill him. But maybe if he did, his soul would find a way to fly all the way to me and hang out sometimes.

Sickness made me lean over and retch loudly. *No, don't kill him. Don't fucking kill him. He gives me the flutters. And I don't want them to go away.*

New plan: I'll kill these motherfuckers then go back and break out Mateo. Yeah, that's what I'll do. Then we'll run away together like Bono and Claud. I'll learn the harp and play it on the roadside, busking for money. People will be so entranced by my music they won't even realise when Dead Man slips his hands in their pockets and steals their wallets. I'll smile at him with stars in my eyes and he'll smile back. A real smile - his beard will be gone so I can see it properly. And his hair will be all pushed back like those movie people, and when we steal a car and drive off into the sunset, he'll kiss the back of my hand and say, "I'd steal the moon for you, baby pie."

I stalled on the road, my breaths coming quicker as the urge to go back hit me like an earthquake. But there was no going back. Not yet. My path was written out before me like the Yellow Brick Road.

Get moving, you big turnip. This is your moment. You're gonna shine. You're gonna make the world see that you're the best killer they ever knew. You're better than Hellfire. Better than that Ripper man and Eminem in those songs he sings about his ex wife. You. Got. This. Sugar. Tit.

I am so right. My 'in the brain me' is always right dammit.

I started skipping past the fancy rows of houses before turning onto a quiet street and jogging almost half a mile to the end of it where there was just one lonely house surrounded by trees. And I was gonna break into it like a sneaky snake.

There was an iron fence circling the property and the twinkling lights from the red brick house beyond it brought a wicked smile to my lips. My heart beat hungrily as I slipped off of the sidewalk into the trees that ran alongside the fence.

I stroked my hand over the bars, the cold licking my fingers as I hunted for a way inside.

"Hello little bars, are you going to let me through? You're very strong, but I'm stronger. I bet I could break right through!" I lunged at the bars with my head bent down like a battering ram and a clang rang out as I smashed into them.

"Owww you *bar*stards." I stepped back, aghast as I rubbed my head then I pointed at them with a pout. "I don't like you very much."

I kept going and had to go pretty far through all the brambly bushes and the twigs kept poking me in the head. One even got me in the eye. Like ow, what the fuck foliage? Why didn't anyone like me tonight? First Niall, now the whole world. It was so unfair.

I finally found a hole tunnelled under the fence where some sort of animal must have made its way beneath it. It wasn't too big, but the soil was soft and I was as bendy as a bendy thing so I could definitely make it with a

503

little digging. I crouched down, taking my hatchet from my hip and using it to help me dig the hole deeper, tossing dirt out either side of me.

I pictured Niall's face as I did it, getting a little too aggressive once or twice as I slammed the hatchet into the ground with a growl. "Fucking big man with his big attitude, big head, big dick – *ergh*. I'll chop his dick off, make a dildo out of it and only use it when I'm angry. That'll teach him."

I finally got the hole big enough and tossed my hatchet and sword through to the other side before dropping down, ducking my head beneath the bars. I could totally fit. I was as small as a baby squirrel. A runt baby squirrel.

I wriggled my way through, my hips jamming against the bars and I cursed. "Come on squirrel hips, you can do it."

Those hips were tricksy, but they made it through with enough wriggling and I scrambled across the ground with a laugh of victory. I pushed my fingers into the grass as I searched for my weapons and made kissy noises.

"Where are you Hacky and Swordline?" I hissed, hunting for them, my hands running all over the dark ground. *They were right here, where'd they go?*

Great they've fucking eloped together, haven't they? I should have brought less attractive weapons, I've only got myself to blame. I even talked about eloping with Mateo right in front of them. Wait, did I say that out loud though because I'm pretty sure I only said that in my head. Oh my god, my weapons are psychic.

My heart snapped like a twig as I thought of Mateo again. Who was I really kidding? He wouldn't run off with me or drive me into the sunset. Once he was free, he'd leave. People always left.

"Stay right where you are," a dark voice barked and my head snapped up as shock jarred through to the centre of my being.

My eyes locked on my own personal demon, spat straight outa the bad place. Andrew was older, bigger, fiercer. He was shirtless in just dark sweatpants and had a gun in his hand. Hacky and Swordline were under one of his booted feet. Trapped.

"Put your hands above your head," he snarled, stepping forward with a phone in his grip, his dark hair blowing back from his forehead in the breeze. He tapped on it while keeping his eyes on me and a flashlight flared from it, shining right in my eyes.

Dread pooled in my gut and panic swept through me like wildfire consuming a whole forest and all the baby animals in it. Suddenly I was just a girl on her back in the woods beneath a monster, being held down, touched where I didn't want to be touched.

"Wait…" Andrew stepped closer, leaning down to look at me as the gun barrel stayed aimed straight between my eyes. "Holy fucking shit. Brooklyn Meadow, is that you?"

My throat knotted up, but I couldn't freeze up. Not again. I wasn't that girl. I was a dangerous predator here for my kill.

"Yeah, it's me," I growled, lifting my chin and his mouth twisted thoughtfully. He was just as handsome as he'd once been and something in his dark eyes told me he was more dangerous than before.

"Well fuck me, Penny will be surprised…" He jerked his chin. "Get up. We were just about to plan another little party and now one's walked right into our back yard." He smirked in a way that set my nerves prickling.

I lunged for the weapons under his boot, but he grabbed my arm and yanked me to my feet, pressing the gun to my temple. "Let's not get feisty. Not yet anyway." He took in my outfit with an arched brow, an appraising look on his face as he glanced down at the weapons. "Is that revenge I see in your eyes, dirty girl? Or have you just been hungering for my cock all these years?"

"Get your hands off of me or I'll cut them off," I snarled.

His fingers on my body made my skin prickle like it was being stabbed with tiny knives. I wanted to pull away, to attack with everything I had, but I knew the move would cost me my life.

"Make any move against me and I'll pull the trigger," he warned. "You're trespassing on a cop's property, I'm well within my fucking rights to shoot. No one would question it."

He was right and I hated that. Hated myself for this failure. But maybe there was still a chance yet. I just had to go along with him for now, wait for another opportunity to strike.

He started walking me toward his house, my enemies' lair. I'd bide my time for the kill. Because as terrifying as it was to be back in the clutches of this vile creature who'd broken me beyond repair, he had no idea that he was walking his death into his house with the Devil at her back.

Roses are red, violets are blue, watch out beastie, I'm going to kill you.

NIALL

CHAPTER TWENTY NINE

I threw everything I might need and more in the trunk of my cherry red muscle car and tossed a devil mask and my new axe onto the passenger seat last. I hadn't had a chance to test her out yet, but I'd named her Evangeline on account of her lovely red blade.

I'd lost time having to look up the address again thanks to my little spider stealing the only easily accessible copy I owned, but the moment I got the damn thing hooked up on my phone, I was off.

I cranked the radio up, blasting Bohemian Rhapsody by Queen into my ears until I felt like they might bleed and drumming my fingers against the steering wheel as nervous energy rocked through me.

I kept my foot flat to the gas as I tore down quiet streets and raced towards my destination and my little psycho.

Every time I blinked I pictured my girl's body lying there waiting for me when I arrived, cold and bloody just like Ava's had been.

It was happening again. All over again. History had decided to repeat itself and I was stuck in an eternal loop of loss and grief and guilt. I never shoulda brought her into my world. I was stupid and selfish and just so damn alone. But none of that shoulda made a blind bit of difference. The moment I'd bought her I shoulda given her some cash and a fake ID and sent her on her way.

I'd rescued her from that fucked up club. I'd done good by her. The rest had been my selfishness and greed. I'd seen a pretty, broken little thing and I'd wanted to keep her because she looked like I felt inside. All cracked and fissured and so fucking lonely it hurt.

But why hadn't I been strong enough to let her go? It was all happening again now, just like I'd always known it would if I ever let anyone get close. Especially someone like her. Too good for this fucked up world and too tempting for sin to resist tainting her.

There was a reason why demons didn't have loved ones. It wasn't because they couldn't love. It was because their love was toxic and ruined everything it touched. I'd tainted her with my nearness, infected her with my own desperate need and desire for blood. She might have had it in her to kill, but without my interference she never woulda found the pair of motherfuckers she was heading towards now. She never woulda been in danger like this.

She was too small, too fragile, too fucking everything to end up prey to that kind of scum, and yet I'd wrapped her up in a bow and practically sent her their way gift wrapped. What the hell had I been thinking telling her I'd found 'em? I shoulda kept the information to myself until I was ready to act. But oh no, Mr Big Balls had wanted to make her smile. I'd wanted to see her look at me like I was something worth seeing. Like I was good for something. And my own greed for that kind of attention from her could well have cost her her life.

I wanted to believe that she could do what she was setting out to, but there was a lot more to that couple than their squeaky clean exterior. They were hunters just like us. And she might have been a spider with a lethal bite, but they were buzzards used to pecking bones clean.

The roads flew by in a blur and the screams in my head grew louder and louder. Ava's. Brooklyn's. Mine. None of it real and yet all of it entirely overwhelming.

If she died because of me then I'd take the choice outa the Devil's hands and deliver myself to him personally. I couldn't survive it a second time. I wouldn't.

But right now I couldn't dwell on that. I had to hope I wasn't too late, that she wasn't too far ahead, that I could get there in time to fix this, help her, save her. And then I'd send her far, far away from me and make sure she was never burned by the poison of my presence in her life ever again.

BROOKLYN

CHAPTER THIRTY

Fear was a foe in a bowtie, and I was wearing it ready to attend the ball.

My heart beat rampantly as I fought against the ziptie on my wrists, shaking my head violently to try and dislodge the scarf that had been wrapped around my head too. My breaths were hot and stifling, and all I could think about was how stupid I'd been to believe I could pull this off.

No, Brain, don't think like that. We can find a way out of this. We're good killers you and me. And Heart, don't leave her out. She loves a little thrill, can't always handle the big ones though, but don't tell her that.

My throat tightened as I fought harder to free myself from the ziptie, thrashing like a wildebeest in a net. What if Andrew was calling his cop friends and they were all heading here to take me away? Back to that terrible, terrible place with the nurses and the needles and the padded walls. The thought made my stomach get all twisty-turny. If Madam Lucille got me in her claws again, she'd make my life in that place insufferable.

I have to kill tonight. I'm not a wounded animal anymore, I've mutated, grown bigger with razor sharp teeth and claws. And I'm starved for blood.

Andrew had brought me into his fancy house, but I hadn't seen much else before he'd grabbed this scarf from a coatrack and blinded me. I'd kicked and fought but the kiss of his gun to my temple had been enough to make me fall still. I had to go along with what he wanted for a little longer. Because I wasn't gonna die without taking him with me. So that was what this had boiled down to, this was the egg left in the pan. And now I needed to crack it open and hatch a plan.

So focus, Brooklyn. Use all those brain cells, rub them together good and come up with the plan of dreams.

Wherever I was, it was creaky. The floorboards beneath me were hard and scratchy and from the amount of stairs Andrew had dragged me up, I was guessing I was either in an attic or a barn on top of the roof. There wasn't any hay about or the scent of horses, so I was gonna go with my first guess.

Female laughter carried from beyond the room and I held my breath as I recognised that laugh, the sound of it sending a shard of dread into my heart. I used to have nightmares about that laugh, back when my fear of her bullying and humiliation tactics were the only things I had to fret over. Back before I realised that all of the taunting and mocking and making a fool of me in front of everyone was nothing, nothing at all compared to what she was capable of. Penelope was here.

Andrew's answering laugh told me the two of them were stalking closer, coming to finish the job of destroying me.

A door opened and footsteps creaked across the floorboards towards me.

"Are you sure it's her?" Penelope asked excitedly and a growl built in my throat, the hunger to kill so fierce it took over everything in my soul. I was nothing but the Devil's messenger here to send them express to hell. And I'd find a way to do it no matter if I had to go with them. Maybe a part of me wanted to go too. Big Red would welcome me into his arms, congratulate me for the kills.

But what about Mateo? I can't leave my dead man.

"Yeah," Andrew said. "It's her alright."

A hand took hold of my blindfold, wrenching it off and I found myself looking up at Penelope with her long red hair and smirking face which was just as beautiful as it had been the last time I'd seen her. She wore a revealing green silk nightdress that showed off a lot of tit. I bared my teeth like a wild beast and lunged forward with the intention to bite and maim her any way I could. This bitch had stood and watched me suffer, recorded it on her phone, laughed while I'd cowered. I would show her what it was like to scream and know no one was coming to save you.

Andrew was suddenly there, pushing me back, his gun in his hand. "Come and play nicely, dirty girl," he said, dragging me to my feet and holding me against his body. Penelope's fingers pushed into my hair and she cooed as she examined me.

"You almost grew into something pretty," Penelope commented in that bright, bitchy tone of hers.

I jerked against Andrew's hold and flinched away from his wife's touch, my upper lip curling back.

"You just brought your death into your home," I promised, snapping my teeth at them.

"Did we now?" Andrew purred, dragging me away from his pawing bitch and shoving me down onto a large bed with red silk sheets.

I could finally see the attic I was in, with the exposed beams overhead and the scent of dust in the air, my breaths growing shallow. There was a video camera set up to take in the whole attic, aimed at the bed where I sat. All kinds of sex toys hung on racks on the walls and a large mirror sat above the bed. My gaze flitted between all of that as I tried to piece it together. *What am I seeing? What's all this stuff? Why is it here?*

"What the fuck is this?" I spat, moving to get up, but Andrew levelled the gun at me and I stilled.

Don't die, not yet.

Penelope moved beside Andrew, stroking his crotch as they both stared at me like hungry hyenas who'd just stumbled across a fresh kill.

"You were our first, dirty girl," Andrew spoke to me, his eyes never wavering from my face. "But not our last."

A chill rushed into my bones and froze them solid as everything clicked together. This room, this lair. It was evil. And not the good kind. The kind that made my skin crawl with vomiting ants.

"This is our playroom for our guests," Penelope said with a girlish giggle that made my blood rise. *I'm going to rip out your throat and stuff your giggle box up your ass.*

"I'm not your guest," I hissed.

"That's what they all say," Penelope mocked. "She's just like the rest of them, isn't she Andy?"

"Nah," he said darkly, his gaze moving over my body thirstily. "She's special."

Penelope stopped rubbing Andrew's dick and moved over to the camera, taking it off its stand and turning it around so I could see the little screen before pressing play on it. My heart clamped up into a fist as I watched a girl being held face down on the bed by Penelope while Andrew fucked her from behind. She released a desperate kind of noise that made so much rage spill into my blood that I could barely contain it. They had to die. Maybe this was my calling in life. To be here now, take them from the world once and for all, even if I ended up with a bullet in me and my life spilling out on the floor.

"Are you a screamer or a crier?" Penelope asked cruelly before placing the camera back on the stand and pressing record, a little red light blinking at me.

Andrew moved toward the bed, tucking the gun into the back of his sweatpants before taking a small flick knife from his pocket and cutting the zipties on my wrists.

"I like when they fight," he said as he put the knife away again, speaking to Penelope like I was just a pet in the room who couldn't understand his words. But then he spoke directly to me and I wondered if that was worse. "I still have a scar from you." He held his forearm up, showing me the place where I'd slashed a blade across his skin all those years ago. "You made me like this," he accused and disgust ran through me.

"I don't make monsters, monsters make themselves," I growled.

"And how would you know how monsters are born, dirty girl?" He crawled onto the bed, reaching out and pushing a lock of hair behind my ear.

I snarled like a beast, smacking his hand away. Hatred seeped through my blood like venom and I was going to inject it into this assfuck and watch him die.

"Because I was born the night you broke me," I said in a deadly whisper. "But it wasn't by your hands that I was made. I needed a saviour, so I became my own. She didn't ride in on a white horse, she came with hellfire at her back, her body coated in a suit of sin. I'm not the girl you dragged into the woods that night. I'm your darkest nightmare brought to life."

"Yeah, yeah, well let's see how long you keep up the big talk once I'm inside you." He grabbed my throat, but I used a move Niall had taught me to break his grip then threw my head forward, my forehead smashing into the bridge of his nose.

He roared in pain, leaping backwards and clutching his face as blood pissed out of his nose. I jumped off of the bed like a prancing deer, diving at Penelope and grabbing a fistful of her hair before she could get out of my way. I swung her around and she screamed as I launched her onto the bed and scrambled off the other side of it.

"Bitch!" she shrieked. "Get her, Andy!"

Andrew wiped the blood from his nose, smiling viciously, his teeth stained red as he jumped onto the bed to hunt me down. I swung around, grabbing a wooden paddle thingy from the display of sex toys and running to meet him. His fist cracked into my side as my paddle whacked across his head, making him stumble a step while I devoured the pain he offered me. He had nothing on Hellfire. I ducked his next fist, jabbing him the gut with the paddle hard enough to make him wheeze then kneeing him furiously in the balls aiming to make them go pop.

"Fucking whore!" he yelled as he cupped his junk then yanked the gun from the back of his sweatpants. But I was ready for that, smashing my paddle into his arm and sending the weapon skittering across the room with a clatter.

Penelope screamed, chaos reigned and the beautiful madness within me came out in full force. *Hello pretties, I've come for tea. Is there cake? I do like cake. But only when it's served with a side of murder.*

Andrew snatched the paddle from my hand and threw it over his shoulder with a sneer. I reached for another weapon behind me, my hand closing around a huge pink dildo which I immediately whacked Andrew around the head with. He came at me with a bellow, trying to get his hands on me, but I ducked and weaved, beating him with the rubber dildo with furious whacks that made him grunt and growl.

A weight collided with me from behind and my vision was lost to a sea of red hair as Penelope took me to the ground, punching me furiously in the kidneys. But she was weak, her arms like string beans and I laughed through the mild irritation her blows delivered in place of pain before rolling us over, straddling her waist then taking hold of her throat as I abandoned the dildo on the floor.

I squeezed, grinning down at her as I clamped my thighs tight around her waist, relishing having her beneath me like the weak little Barbie doll she was. Her hands flew at me, clawing and tearing and I just smiled wider as my fingers locked on her slim neck, never to let go.

"Mark me, sugarpuff. Decorate my skin," I encouraged. "I want something to remember your death by."

Penelope's eyes slid over my head and I glanced back just before

Andrew's strong hands grabbed me, ripping me off of her and shoving me back onto the bed. I scrambled backwards as he came for me, crawling up the mattress with a wild look in his eyes. He was enjoying this and I could see that violent creature possessing him. He needed to hurt me like I needed to kill him. It was in his blood like it was in mine. But we were entirely different breeds of monster. And I'd show him which one was more powerful. But right now I needed to move faster, get back up, gain the advantage.

He leapt forward before I could escape, pinning me beneath him and dragging one of my arms above my head, the clinking of a metal chain making panic wash through me. I was small enough to lose this game if I didn't think fast. I couldn't let him lock me down or that was it. It was K freaking O for me.

I grabbed hold of the chain before he could lock my wrist in place against the headboard and whipped it backwards. It smacked against the glass mirror on the wall and it shattered, the pieces tumbling down in a shower of sharp shards as I covered my face to try and avoid them. Andrew flinched back and by some miracle the glass didn't cut me, just cascaded down around me on the pillows. Oh holy hell yes, the Devil was watching me tonight.

I grabbed a shard, lunging at my enemy with a laugh of victory and he cursed as he tried to make it off the bed.

"Andy!" Penelope wheezed, still on the floor where I'd left her as she clutched her throat like an overturned turtle.

I slashed the glass across Andrew's bare chest and the glimmer of excitement in his gaze extinguished as blood spilled down his body. His eyes widened and he turned tail, trying to get away. I got up and bounced off the bed, landing on his back and latching on like a monkey as I stab, stab, stabbed him. Blood flew and Andrew screamed a beautiful scream. He stumbled to his knees as I stabbed everywhere that wouldn't kill right away, making this last, making him hurt.

Penelope crawled frantically away as Andrew reached for her and I laughed louder as he collapsed beneath me. That wasn't good enough though. Not for this piece of shit, the one responsible for breaking me. The boy who'd tried to claim a piece of me. And maybe he had. But now I was cutting it out of him, taking it back alongside the pound of flesh I was owed.

"Hurt motherfucker," I snarled as he screamed once more, flailing uselessly. "Hurt and bleed and suffer for me."

I lifted my weight, rolling him over with a growl of effort and straddling his waist as he stared up at me, his mouth spewing blood, his eyes full of panic.

I whipped up Dilly – the pink dildo I'd lost earlier - as he jerked and tried to fight, but the strength was leaving him fast. And Dilly still had work to do.

I pinched his nose and he gasped as he tried to breathe through the blood in his mouth, giving me room to shove Dilly in. I pushed her deeper, leaning down with all my weight to look Andrew directly in the eyes as my hair created a curtain around us. It was just me and my monster in here and the terror in his eyes said he knew who the real beastie was now.

"I told you," I said with a smirk. "But you didn't listen."

He choked violently beneath me, the light fading from his eyes. *Yes, yes, yes. Go into the dark where all your sins await you. They're demons now and they're coming to eat you.*

The barrel of a gun suddenly pressed to the back of my head.

"Stop!" Penelope commanded. "Get off of him!"

I ignored her, lost to the kill, needing to do this even if it cost me everything. I shoved Dilly in even further and Andrew spasmed one final time beneath me before his eyes went glassy and I could almost hear Big Red's laughter as he was dragged away into the depths of eternal suffering.

A click sounded, echoing through my skull and I knew Penelope had pulled the trigger. But unless death was very, very, very similar to life, I didn't think my brains had just been blasted out.

I swung around, facing the barrel as Penelope pulled the trigger again, her eyes wide with fear. I grabbed it from her, twirling it on my finger and examining it as she backed up, falling onto the bed with a yelp of terror. It was like a moment in a horror movie, the stupid prom queen stumbling away from her killer, making all the dumb choices. And just like in those movies, she wasn't going to get away.

"It's got a safety catch, see?" I showed her. "It's tricky on this model. You just do it like…this." I flipped the catch then raised the gun. "Hellfire taught me that." A lump built in my throat at his name on my lips, but I pushed it away. This was my moment. My single shining, gleaming one which would likely be the peak of my life.

I pulled the trigger and Penelope screamed as a bullet ripped through her chest, clutching at the wound with a look of shock like she couldn't believe I'd really done it. Then I jumped onto the bed, bouncing up and down before firing again and again and again, emptying every round into the witch beneath me as I laughed and fucking laughed.

She fell still, her face twisted, making her look ugly and more like who she really was.

I grinned like the Cheshire Cat, doing a few more jumpies on the bed before I noticed the phone on the floor beyond her, the call connected to 911. *Oh tampons up a monkey's butt.*

I leapt off the bed and grabbed the phone, putting on the voice of an old woman as I held it my ear, "Hello dear, nothing going on here, just dialled a wrong number. Silly me. I've lost my glasses too, have you seen them?"

"Who is this?" a woman asked frantically on the other end of the line and I threw the phone at the wall so it smashed into three pieces.

I took one glance down at the blood splattering my body before running from the room, tossing the gun back on the bed with what was left of Penelope as I went.

I couldn't even find it in me to feel panicked. I was swept up in the high of the kill. I was free. Free from the beasts who'd ruined me, the monsters who'd tried to destroy me for good. And even if I was doomed for what I'd done, it didn't matter. Because they'd never break another soul again.

NIALL

CHAPTER THIRTY ONE

I skidded to a halt right outside the house of the motherfuckers who had hurt Brooklyn when she was a kid, my front wheel bumping up the curb while I gave absolutely zero shits about being seen. If she was here I didn't have the time to waste on subtlety, though as I glanced around at the dark street, I didn't spot my truck so I couldn't be certain she was.

I pulled the Devil mask down over my face and got out of the car with my axe in hand. I had a gun stowed in a holster beneath my leather jacket and four knives in various pockets too, and it would have to be enough.

I skirted the high fence surrounding the house, using the shadows to hide me. There was a gate half way up the drive and I slipped towards it, trying it out and finding it unlocked. Rule one of breaking and entering: always try the path of least resistance. Any other fucker would probably take off into the trees, skirt the fence, look for a weak point, but nine times out of ten people couldn't be fucked locking a gate. Mostly because they never imagined a serial killer would slip through it, but look where that had gotten them now.

The large house stood in the centre of a wide yard ahead of me and I glanced between the windows, noticing lights on within a couple of them, but it was late and in all likelihood they were asleep. Or they would have been, assuming my little psycho hadn't woken them up.

I still couldn't see any sign of her here, but I wasn't a fool. This was definitely where she'd been headed so I was almost certain she'd be here somewhere. Though I hoped she mighta fucked up, gotten lost on the way, stayed far from these monsters and left them here for me. Because there was no way I'd be leaving them alive now that I knew she was on the hunt. If I didn't find her here I'd finish them for her, make them beg and scream and die hard just the way she'd want and protect her from their wrath in the process. Fuck, I really hoped she wasn't here.

I closed in on the building, forcing myself to stay quiet so I could listen for any sign of anyone inside even though I wanted to yell her name and call her out of hiding. But there was nothing. Not a peep.

A shiver ran down my spine and I quickly made it around to the back of the house.

I had my axe ready to force entry if I needed to, but Evangeline was going to have to wait because I found it open a crack, inviting me in.

I silently tugged the door open and paused as I spotted the outline of a bloody shoeprint on the tiles just inside the door. It was small, like a pocket sized girl kind of small and it made a knot tighten in my chest.

I held Evangeline ready, easing my way into the house and glancing about at the illusion of normalcy on display. There was a coat hanging beside the door, a cop's baton beside it alongside his badge on a little shelf. I took the badge and pushed it into my pocket then carried on into the house.

Beyond the porch, dark carpet lined the floors so it was hard for me to make out any more footprints but I followed my gut, heading for the stairs in the centre of the building.

I looked around in the dim light, spotting a smear of blood on the bannister and creeping up the stairs as my instincts paid off. Up and up I went, passing through the halls and following the blood trail as it got thicker, my pace hastening as my heart pounded in anticipation of what I was about to find. Ava was begging and pleading in the back of my skull, reminding me of what I was, what I'd cost her and I was getting the godawful feeling that fate had come full circle.

I reached another set of stairs hidden away in a corner behind a door with a smear of blood on the edge of it and headed up into the attic on silent feet, my gun ready as I ascended, finding a closed door at the top of the stairs.

The scent of blood and death reached me and I gritted my teeth against the visions of what I was about to find in there. My girl had been here recently, I was certain of it. And when I stepped though this door, I was going to find out exactly what had become of her because of me.

I swallowed a thick lump in my throat, hefted Evangeline higher in my grasp and knocked the door open.

It was dark inside, but enough moonlight spilled in through a window on the far side of the attic to show me the bloody lump of flesh which had once been a living, breathing human being where it lay face up on the floor in front of me.

My fingers shook a little as I reached out and prepared to flick the lights on, needing to see, to know, to find out even if it could be the end of me. Because I was too late yet again. Whatever had happened here was already done and dealt with. Fate had run its course and when I flicked that switch there would be no changing what I discovered.

I steeled myself and flicked it, the lights turning on and revealing the utter devastation of the room before me and making my chest seize up as I drank it all in.

Andrew Fig lay dead and bloody before me, stuck full of holes and choked on a giant pink dildo with his eyes bugging outa his face in horror. Beyond him, laying on the bed shot full of bullet holes was his dear wife, her blood splattering the walls and shattered glass pooling around her from a broken mirror. It was a work of art. Beautiful in its poetry and simplicity.

My lips curved up as I took it all in. Every detail. I could see where things could have gone to shit and could almost taste the moment where my little psycho had gotten the upper hand. A bloody sliver of mirrored glass lay abandoned beside Andrew's corpse and a gun had been dropped on the bed beside Penelope's.

Pride swelled my chest, a wide smile filling my lips as I looked all around at the carnage, a laugh falling from me. She'd only gone and done it. She'd only fucking faced her demons and shown them what she was truly made of.

I noticed a camera set up in the corner of the room and my brows dropped as I stalked towards it, stepping over the rubber cock-choked corpse of Andrew and taking it from the stand.

I rewound the footage, playing it from the start and gritting my teeth as I watched them manhandle her, saw him pin her to that fucking bed and read exactly what he'd been planning to do to her in the evil curves of his too-pretty face. If he wasn't already dead I'd have killed him good for that, I'd have made it last longer and hurt more, but the way she'd done it was perfection in itself. It was exactly what she'd needed. Justice. Carnage. Mayhem. A bloody victory in payment for what they'd tried to do all those years ago and the life they'd stolen from her.

I took the SD card from the camera and pocketed it. Best case scenario, I would return it to Brooklyn and let her keep it to watch and enjoy at her leisure. Worst case scenario, it was evidence of her innocence and I could use it to get the truth out into the world. But ideally the cops would never catch her anyway and it wouldn't be necessary to do that.

I looked all around, swinging my axe through the air and apologising to her for her spotless appearance, but there wasn't anything for me to do here. No heads to chop or blood to spill. Nothing. Though I guessed it wouldn't hurt for me to make sure there wasn't a scrap of evidence left behind.

I could do that.

Then I had a choice to make. I could either keep chasing after my little spider, find her, try to make it right between us and bring her back home with me... Or I could let her go. Leave her to make her own choice and stick to it. She was better off away from me anyway. I knew that even if I hated it.

I headed back out to my car and popped the trunk, glancing around for any signs of some nosey fucker looking my way, but it was quiet here, secluded, perfect for the kind of shit those animals in there had enjoyed.

I grabbed a can of gasoline outa the trunk alongside a handful of fireworks then lit a cigarette and placed it between my lips. I tossed Evangeline into the car and slammed the trunk, toking on my cigarette and strolling back towards the house with a casual gait.

I splashed gasoline everywhere inside the building, all over the corpses and the walls and everything in sight. Probably kinda dumb to do it while toking on a smoke but as per usual, death gave me a solid fuck you and let me keep on breathing my nicotine laced air without setting me alight and ending my fucking misery.

I tried to smile as I backed away from the house, looking at the outline of the building as I tossed all but one of the fireworks into the doorway.

I raised the other to my mouth, using the cherry of my smoke to light the fuse and holding the rocket tight in my fist while I waited for it to burn down.

A second before it could explode and blast my hand off, I tossed it straight into the building.

Red and green sparks erupted from it half a second before the entire place went up with a whoosh and a wave of heat damn near knocked me on my arse.

The rest of the fireworks went up with it, multicoloured sparks exploding in every direction as they were shot from the burning building and I stood there watching it for a while, waiting for the joy to come from my destruction.

But it didn't.

The flames were hot but there was a coldness in me which wasn't going to budge. It was an emptiness. A lack of her. But I knew that was for the best. She was better off well away from me and free of the shackles my presence would place upon her. I was a burden she didn't need to bear, and if I was half the man I wished to be then I knew I had to let her run. Run, run, run far away from me and never look back.

I turned away from the blazing fire and the stench of death on the air, not even bothering to watch the rest of the fireworks as they shot from the flames and exploded all around me.

I made it back to my car, tossed the empty gas can into the trunk then got in the driver's seat, sitting in silence behind the wheel as I looked at the street.

Thunder cut through the air overhead and I sighed as I tipped my head back to look up at the dark sky, taking another cigarette and placing it between my lips. The sound of sirens called in the distance and I wondered if a nosy neighbour had spotted the fire that quickly or if someone had heard all those gunshots Brooklyn had fired and called the cops. Either way, I needed to get my arse away from here.

I started the car and slowly drove to the end of the street, looking left and right and wondering which way she'd gone.

Left would lead me back home, the way I'd come and though it was possible she could have taken a different route, I doubted it. I would have passed her on my way here and I would have recognised my truck. Which meant she'd gone right. Away from me.

"Clever girl," I muttered, spotting the flash of red and blue lights in the distance, my fingers tightening on the steering wheel as I considered my options and just let the car idle.

The need to hunt her was filling me like a warring army full of desire and violence and death. I wanted to do that. I wanted to chase her into the dark, track her down and force her to come back with me.

And if I was being wholly honest with myself, I wanted more than that. I wanted her. Just her. I wanted her hot mouth against mine again, her body pinned beneath me, my name on her lips and her soul wrapped around mine. I wanted to drown in the darkness we could create together and paint something beautiful out of it.

I lowered my window as it began to rain, that scent of rising dust mixing with the taint of smoke on the air and making my hackles rise. The sirens were louder now, that flash of red and blue brighter. I was running out of time and I needed to decide.

If I hunted her down now that was it. I wouldn't let her go again. I'd lay claim to her more fully than I ever had until this point and once I had, that would be it for me. For her.

I closed my eyes, inhaling deeply as the sound of Ava's screams rang in my ears alongside the sirens and I reached out to crank the music up as All The Good Girls Go To Hell by Billie Eilish started playing.

I exhaled a harsh breath, flicked the cigarette butt out the window, threw the car into drive and turned left.

That girl had made her choice and if I dragged her back into my life, I knew she wouldn't ever escape me again. This was her shot. Her one chance at a life that wasn't ruined by me. She deserved that.

So I'd do what I could to give it to her.

I hit the gas as red and blue lights flashed in my rear view mirror and let the song pour gasoline into my wounds and set them all alight. I'd been burning for a long damn time though and I could take the pain. I'd drown it in blood and booze and try to forget.

I had my own kill list waiting for me and enough merchandise in the trunk to paint the town red. I'd throw myself into a different kind of hunt, block out the part of me which was tearing apart with blood and brutality, and when I couldn't find the energy in my limbs to heft my axe anymore, I'd return home and drown my sorrows until oblivion found me.

Maybe I'd get lucky and death would find me tonight. If not, it could keep me company on a killing spree. I hadn't had one of those in a long damn time and I had the names of a good few fuckers who deserved a hard death, some jobs from my pa which I'd been neglecting and others I could take on.

The radio roared and I forced myself not to think of her as I drove further and further away, giving her this one opportunity to claim something better. Because I knew I wouldn't be able to stick to this. Sooner or later, I'd find myself hunting her.

I just hoped for her sake that she'd be long lost before I gave in to temptation.

BROOKLYN

CHAPTER THIRTY TWO

I ran down the road, my heels clipping along the pavement as blood trickled down my body, already starting to dry against my skin in the night air. But as rain began to lick my skin, it became wet all over again, reigniting the scent of death on my flesh.

Holy fucking potatoes. That was awesome. I was free. Freer than a bird with a passport to anywhere. I'd totally gotten away with it. No cops had found me, nothing, nada. I was as subtle as a gooseberry on a merry-go-round.

I was buzzing with the thrill of the kill and I wanted more. More enemies at my feet, more monsters in the dirt because of me. I'd hunt out the bad in this world like a plague for as long as I could. I'd kill and kill, leave my mark in the most glorious of ways. But first, I was hungry.

I jogged onto a street where bright lights highlighted a superstore up ahead and a grin bit into my cheeks. I ran up to it, practically salivating as I headed through the parking lot, gaining a bunch of stares from the few people hanging about.

A woman actually screamed and ran away from me, diving into her car. It felt good. I was all powerful. A bloody demon crawling out of hell for snack time.

I walked into the store, grabbing a basket and heading down the first aisle, picking up an apple and sinking my teeth into it, the juices spilling over my chin. *Mmmmm.*

"Oh my god!" someone wailed behind me, but I didn't look. I was too hangry to see what they were yapping about.

I tossed my apple away and threw a pineapple into my basket followed by a couple of clementines before rounding the corner and heading straight along to the snack aisle.

I walked up it, sucking my lower lip as I took in all the rows of chips and chocolate. I ran over to a huge bag of Doritos, tearing into them and throwing a few into my mouth.

"Ah!" a woman screamed as she rounded the aisle and I offered her the bag of chips as I crunched my way through a few more. She turned and fled and I shrugged. "Suit yourself, screamy lady. More for me."

I tossed the Doritos away in favour of some Cheetos, ripping the bag open and scoffing down a few cheesy puffs. *Ohmagooood I love a cheesy puff.*

Then I made it to the chocolate and had a quick binge on Hershey's Peanut Butter Cups before falling completely still as I considered what I wanted next. Belly was doing a happy dance, shaking its ass and singing a little song about all the food it wanted to eat. *But what next, Belly?*

"Bread!" I blurted and ran out of the aisle, my basket bouncing against my hip as Perry the Pineapple and his cousins Clive and Clemmy the clementines bounced around in there with him. I made it to the bakery and started squishing all the loaves to find the best one. "Which of you is crumbly, squeezy perfection?" I wondered.

Then just as my fingers squeezed the bread roll of dreams with its white, crunchy, doughy goodness, a weight collided with me, throwing me to the ground. Perry went flying and I screamed, reaching out for him as he bounced across the floor with Clive and Clemmy rolling after him. "Wait! Come back!"

My arms were yanked behind my back and cold cuffs were snapped into place on my wrists, making shock jar through me. *What the duck in a tutu?*

"You're under arrest," the man growled in my ear and shock rattled through me as he kept prattling on and I stopped listening, needing to figure out a way to escape.

I lifted my head, finding another cop standing there pointing her gun at me, then I looked to the perfect bread roll which had been crushed during the attack.

"Oh no, you'll never fulfil your destiny, Barney."

The man weighing me down dragged me to my feet and I tugged against my restraints as panic set in. Realisation often hit me a little slow, but it was setting in now. I'd been lost to my post-murder high and had forgotten the stuff and things. That always happened after I got killy. I hadn't murdered in so long, that now I'd forgotten to check myself before I wrecked myself.

I was in trouble. They were going to find out who I was, then they'd throw me back into Eden Heights with Madam Lucille and all the horrible beasties who'd haunted me before. My heart started a bar brawl in my chest, throwing chairs and smashing glasses.

"No! Let me go! I'm innocent!" I yelled, thrashing wildly and the cop took his baton from his hip in warning.

"Ma'am, stop fighting. I will use necessary force to apprehend you," he warned. "Why are you covered in blood?"

"It's tomato sauce," I insisted, but he just dragged me along to the end of the aisle where a group of customers had gathered to watch. Some of them recorded me and my cheeks flushed. *Ohhh are they looking at little ol' me?*

"Can't a girl walk into a store covered in ketchup without getting arrested?" I demanded, thrashing and fighting until the other cop levelled her gun at my head.

I didn't wanna die. I was having such a fun night. Why did it have to end like this? Why had my brain gone all fuzzy and made me do a stupid thing?

I was hauled outside toward a cop car and shoved in the back of it, my ass hitting the seat and my arms crushed behind me. *Ouchy*.

The door slammed shut and I pouted out the window, pressing my face to the glass as the small fan club I'd gathered spilled outside. My nose smooshed to the window and I licked it to taste the cold, but it didn't bring me any happies.

I flopped back onto the seat with a wail, knowing exactly where I was gonna end up if I didn't find a way to get myself free. I started kicking the seat in front of me as I fought against my cuffs, but they were hard and hurty and they wouldn't let me go.

"I don't wanna go back there, don't take me there Mr Cop man, please. I'll be good. I only killed bad people."

"You killed someone?" he gasped, sharing a look with Mrs Cop woman beside him.

"Um, no," I backtracked. "I mean metaphorically. Like, I murdered them in my mind, that's all." They didn't reply to that as the woman started talking in a low voice on a radio.

"If you let me out, I'll owe you a favour," I tried. "A big favour. Whenever you wanna call it in, I'll be right there, kay? Just lemme sneak out the door and I'll leave my phone number on a rock-"

"Quiet," the guy barked and I fell back in my seat with my lower lip trembling.

I was all alone and heading back to a place far worse than hell. It was my nightmare, and Madame Lucille would make me suffer for getting one up on her when I escaped. She'd probably been plotting ways to rip my spirit out of my body ever since I'd gotten free.

A choked noise of anguish left me as I thumped my head back against the seat again and again. I was a bird in a cage once more, my wings clipped, my beak and talons about to be cut off. And there was nothing and no one in the world who cared.

NIALL

CHAPTER THIRTY THREE

Three days. I only knew it had been that long because I was staring the date dead in the eye as I looked at the TV. I musta left it on before I passed out, but it was muted so I couldn't hear a damn thing, the newscaster warbling on about fuck knew what while I groaned and pushed myself upright in bed.

I was butt naked and the new tattoo I'd gotten on my cock was staring me in the face alongside the piercing. I'd been drunk off my arse when I'd stumbled to my tattooist's house a few mornings ago and demanded some dick decorations, and I was wondering what the fuck I'd been thinking to have wanted a bolt put through my fucking cock. I wasn't surprised that Ronnie had done it though - he'd figured out a long time ago that whether I was shit faced or not it was best to just do what I asked. Hence the reason for some of my more interesting tattoos. But why had I decided to go for a piercing in my goddamn cock?

Oh yeah, I'd been wondering what could hurt more than getting stabbed or shot because I wanted to know what my pain threshold was like and I'd asked that nice fella I'd been talking to. He'd reckoned anything that happened to your cock would be worse and I'd begged to disagree. In order to win the bet, I'd gone to Ronnie and gotten my new ink and piercing then gone back to where I'd left him tied up in the woods and I'd shot him in the head so we could compare.

If I hadn't been so fucking pissed I mighta remembered not to aim for something so vital because we couldn't compare the pain with his brains all splattered like that. But in hindsight, I'd been there to kill him anyway, so the conversation had just been dragging out the inevitable. Safe to say, I'd won and now my dick was all kinds of fancy.

No doubt my right hand was getting all sorts of sordid ideas about it already, but seeing as my cock was still fucking tender, I wasn't gonna give it a whirl just yet.

The Prince Albert piercing winked at me as I looked between it and the Celtic design that had been inked around my shaft.

I musta been fucking insane. Too late to do anything about it now though. I'd just be a celibate drunk with a pierced dick for fancy masturbating from here on out. Sounded pretty good to me.

My gaze skimmed to the dark sky out of the window and I sighed, wondering how late it was. Too damn late. Or too damn early I guessed, depending on how I looked at it. It was definitely night-o'clock anyway.

I pushed outa bed and into my en suite for a shower, my tongue thick and fuzzy in my mouth and my stomach rumbling. I guessed I'd neglected food while I'd been drowning my sorrows in blood and whiskey.

I set the water to cold in some attempt to push the haze of alcohol away and as I reached for the shower gel, I noticed a tally score marked on my palm in Sharpie. Six. Six what?

Six potatoes?

I started scrubbing at my flesh, washing flecks of dried blood away with the general dirt and grime on my body which I guessed had something to do with whatever the fuck I'd been up to while I fell into the dark place.

It was often like this for me when my ghosts became too much to bear.

I liked to blame the booze, but in all fairness, I could get shit faced with the best of them and wake up with my memories intact when it suited me. Nah, this kind of oblivion was my brain's way of trying to forget the pain I'd been in. When I was drowning in my loss and failures like that, it was kinder to forget it. And when I began to rise from the fog of that pain, I was just left with the lingering ache of knowing I was never gonna be right in the head. Never gonna move on from this place of grief and rage at the world.

It had been a while since I'd fallen this hard, but I shoulda known it was coming. Now that my girl had seen what I was and I'd chased her away, what else did I have left anyway?

Six kills? I started counting on my fingers. I'd gone after two fellas my pa had been harping on about, then I'd stalked that rapist fucker who had been on the news the past few weeks. It always amazed me how the cops failed to put the pieces together and figure out who these fuckers were or at least where their hunting grounds were. I mean, I'd caught a slice of luck because my hunch had paid off and I'd caught him trying to break into the rear entrance of that hospice. I guess he was trying to break in to find his next helpless victim, but it hadn't been hard to figure out his patterns.

Anywho, he was currently laid out on the hood of a squad car with his throat cut and a pomegranate wedged half way up his arse in the parking lot where the cops stored their vehicles. I'd even included a little note telling them that he was the man they were hunting for so that they could test DNA and at least give his victims a touch of relief when they found out he'd died a nasty fucking death. And he really had - I'd taken my foul mood out on him for a long damn time before losing my temper and bleeding him out.

So no, it wasn't six kills because those were the few parts of the last three days that were still pretty clear in my mind. Maybe I shouldn't have gotten so fucked up on the whiskey and I coulda killed a few more.

Why had I gotten so fucked up on the whiskey?

Electric blue eyes and long ebony hair swam through my mind and

I grunted as a little stab of discomfort drove itself into my gut and lodged there.

I blew out a harsh breath and scrubbed my hair clean, trying not to think about her and failing spectacularly.

I'd done the right thing by letting her go. I had. She wasn't safe here with me. No one was ever safe with me.

But if I was being totally honest with myself, I hadn't sent her away because I was some benevolent soul just wishing to save her. I'd sent her away because her lips had tasted too fucking good against mine and her body had been tempting me every damn time I looked at her. I'd kissed her and kissed her again and I'd wanted to do so much fucking more than that, but I'd made a promise to myself a long damn time ago that I wouldn't ever walk that path again.

And despite how it might have seemed, that wasn't because I was a kind and nurturing creature with a warm heart and buckets of compassion. It was because I was a selfish motherfucker and I didn't want to feel that pain ever again. I didn't want to live with that guilt.

I wasn't saving her. I was saving myself.

A few more days or weeks in my company and I would have stopped fighting. I would have kept corrupting and corrupting her until I got between those sweet thighs of hers and-

Holy mother of a fucking goose, what the fuck has happened to my cock?

I cursed as I stumbled out of the shower, slipping on the tiles and falling against the sink so hard that I ended up half sat in the damn thing with the tap making an attempt to get real friendly with my arsehole.

I looked down at my hard dick and gritted my teeth against the pain from the piercing where the skin was being stretched. I'd been shot about seven times, stabbed and cut up countless times, been strangled, broken five bones, dislocated my shoulder and had a hacksaw taken to my ankle - only for a few strokes before I managed to snap the motherfucker's neck but still - I had *never* in my life experienced this kind of pain from getting turned on. What the fuck had I been thinking?

Jesus.

Maybe I should just take the fucker out.

I frowned at the bar thing hooked through my damn dick as I considered it, but the pain was doing a good job of banishing my arousal and it was pretty shiny. Everyone liked shiny.

Maybe I'd been wrong though. Maybe this *was* worse than a gunshot. Ah well, that fucker was dead and I wasn't paying up. But I decided to leave my new dick jewellery in place. At least if I couldn't jerk off over my runaway girl, I had an extra reason to avoid thinking about her tits.

Oh fuck, not again.

I cursed as I scrubbed a towel through my hair, making it stick up all over the damn place and fall forward into my eyes. The Sharpie was almost all gone from my palm, so I decided it didn't matter what the six was about.

I tried to think about the things I had to do this week. Some fancy dinner I'd agreed to have with Anastasia. More work meetings with my pa and I wanted to go visit my nephew Kyan while he was still staying at the house too.

But none of it was all that appealing. Nothing was all that appealing.

I was a big barrel of nothing inside and even as I tried to distract myself with thoughts of bloodshed and carnage, I found it all a little...empty.

I headed back into my room, my eyesight clearing even if I wasn't walking entirely straight and my stomach growled. A decent meal would likely banish the worst of the drink from my system and then I'd be...well, a less drunk miserable bastard with not a lot worth living for. But I didn't quite desire death enough to just fucking do the job myself either.

Dandy.

My gaze scoured over the dark sky beyond my window and I groaned as I realised I'd gone and fucked my sleeping pattern up. Though that said, if I filled my stomach, I would likely be able to pass out again and get rid of another boring as fuck night of nothing in the life of me.

I pulled open the top drawer on my nightstand and took a cigarette from the packet I found there, sparking it up before grabbing a pair of jeans and pulling them on.

Fire blazed through my cock as the rough material rubbed along the piercing.

Nope.

I dropped the jeans and switched them out for a pair of black sweatpants which were nice and airy in the crotch then turned back to head from the room.

But before I could take so much as a step, I froze, my gaze falling on the muted news broadcast which was still playing on the TV.

My lips parted and the cigarette nearly fell from them as I dove onto the bed, hunting for the damn remote and finding it in a tangle of sheets.

I quickly flicked the volume up and looked back at the screen where an old mugshot of my little psycho was plastered alongside the newscaster as she spoke.

"-dubbed the Bully Butcher has been arrested and sent back to the Eden Heights secure psychiatric facility after being on the run for over a year. Brooklyn Meadow is a mentally unstable and volatile woman who had been a danger to the public during her time on the run. We will all sleep a little better in our beds knowing that she has been brought to justice once more. In other news, Billy the Bunny has been doing the rounds visiting care homes after-"

I shut the TV off and released a roar of anguish as I grabbed the side of the bed and flipped the whole thing over with an enormous crash.

This wasn't how it was supposed to go. She was supposed to be far away now, somewhere sunny getting a tan on those perky tits and making me ache while I fought the urge to hunt her down.

She shouldn't have been caught. Hadn't she listened to anything I'd told her about how to escape the cops?

Ah fuck, had I even given her those lessons?

Maybe not. I'd thought I'd be right there beside here to look after her when we went out killing so I hadn't given much thought to it. So this was even more my own fucking fault than I'd first realised.

I ripped my closet door open and grabbed shoes and a shirt then threw a holster on over the top of them and cursed as some foreign pain drew my attention to my ribs on my left side. I hoisted my shirt up to get a look and found a spider tattooed there. Of fucking course there was a spider tattooed there. That way if I failed her, I could have her inked on my skin for all of time just to make sure I never forgot about it just the same as Ava's name mocked me daily from my arm.

But this wasn't the same as Ava. Brooklyn wasn't dead. And I wasn't leaving her to rot in some psych ward for the rest of her damn life. If she was crazy, then so was I and I didn't for one second believe being a psychopath was a sign of insanity. We were just a persecuted profession and we needed to stick the fuck together in this world of judgemental bastards.

I dropped my shirt and entered the code on the hidden wall safe before pulling out two Desert Eagles, a couple of boxes of ammo and a hunting knife which I jammed through my belt.

I snatched my cell from the nightstand and quickly did a search on Eden Heights to get an address and a lay of the land. The place was pretty tough on security, big walls and razor wire with guards and dogs and all that shit. Good. I was up for a challenge.

I made it to the foot of the stairs and stumbled over my damn feet, catching myself on the wall and snarling as the room spun. *Fucking whiskey. Why do you gotta be such a lingering bastard?*

I shook my head to try and clear it a little more then headed to the kitchen, downing a pint of water and taking a couple of pain pills for the impending hangover. This was gonna be fucking rough.

But I wasn't waiting. My girl had been in that damn place for too fucking long already and I wasn't leaving her there.

I strode through the house, ignoring the furious yells which came from the basement. No doubt El Burro was hungry, but I didn't have time for his shit. Besides, I distinctly remembered giving him some pasta before stumbling up to my bed this morning, so he wasn't exactly starved.

Although, come to think of it, I mighta just hurled a packet of uncooked penne down the stairs and warned him not to crack a tooth on it. Ah well, no time to deal with that now.

I opened the front door and paused as I spotted the stack of thin boxes on the step. *Well shit. At some point I musta ordered pizzas. Go me.*

Wait a fucking second - that was six pizzas! I musta wrote that tally on my hand so that I wouldn't forget about them and like a gobshite I'd gone and forgotten anyway. Or passed out. Yeah, I was pretty sure I'd passed out. Ah well, a hungry yesterday meant a full belly today. And I needed the food to help get rid of this fucking whiskey.

I unlocked my black Jeep and tossed the pizzas on the front seat, flipping a box open and stuffing two slices into my mouth in an attempt to soak up some of the alcohol. Then I opened up the trunk and headed over to my shed, grabbing a bunch of smoke grenades, some blow up in yer face grenades, a flame thrower, a box of fireworks, a few more guns, a baseball bat named Dave and Evangeline the axe before tossing them all in. I paused for a second, offering a moment of silence to dear Mary me best sledgehammer. I hadn't had the heart to replace her yet.

I threw the door shut and rounded the hood to get in but I managed to slip on something, my hip crashing into the car and before I knew it I went arse over tit, smacked my fancy cock piercing on something and ended up spread eagled on the fucking ground.

I groaned as my dick throbbed painfully and the world spun in slow circles as I stared up at the moon. She was laughing at me, glowy bitch.

Shit.

I really was wasted. Really fucking wasted and really fucking angry. I couldn't drive like this. I needed a wheels man. An angry little donkey of a wheels man. And I just so happened to have one in my basement.

A throaty laugh spilled from my lips as I realised I was about to set a fucking psychopath free after spending months and months torturing him. I hoped to fuck that my drunk arse could control him well enough to save my girl.

It was a dumb arse plan destined to end in spectacular, bloody failure. But it was also the best I had, so I pushed myself to my feet and headed back towards the house. I had a deal to strike with a demon and I was going to make sure he took my bargain.

MATEO

CHAPTER THIRTY FOUR

I slammed my palms against the bars of my cage again, cursing that piece of shit upstairs in English and Spanish and every other language I could think of or make up. Fuck him. Fuck him for everything he'd done, but fuck him for this most of all. I was a king of monsters where I came from. I deserved blood and pain and suffering and any kind of brutal death imaginable, but I refused to sit in this cage and starve.

Three fucking days since he'd given me food. He'd left me in the dark down here with nothing and no one and I was left to drink water from the tap and wait to die.

He'd done this before. Forgotten me or been away for a day or two at a time. The worst thing of all was that it wasn't intentional. Like my life and existence generally meant nothing to him and he just forgot I was here half the time or couldn't be bothered to look after me even if he remembered. He was the only person in the world who knew where I was and he didn't even give all that much of a fuck. At least he *had* been the only person until she came along. But now she was gone too.

I didn't know what to think of the things he'd said about her. I didn't want to believe them. But it didn't really matter anyway. Because now I was going to die down here due to nothing beyond neglect from that fucking O'Brien pedazo de mierda upstairs.

The door at the top of the stairs banged open and the lights flicked on so suddenly that I couldn't help but cringe away from them, raising a hand in front of my face to screen the bulb on the far side of the room.

Niall stomped down the stairs, his feet crunching on the dried pasta shells from the bag he'd hurled down here as supposed food for me and I sneered at him as he stumbled a little on the last step.

"I'm drunk," he announced. "Fucked up to be entirely accurate - though I'm working on sobering up. I could still kill ya about nineteen different ways, but if I wasn't this shit faced I could do it in a good fifty without even breakin' a sweat."

"I need food," I snarled, my stomach aching as weakness clung to my limbs. I was a big man and I needed a lot of food to sustain me. Going days without any was akin to the worst torture he'd subjected me to.

"Yeah, yeah. I got ya this to start you off." He raised a hand and shook a family sized bar of chocolate at me tauntingly before tossing it through the bars.

I caught it and ripped the wrapper off before taking a huge bite and devouring it as fast as I could. Pride was irrelevant to me in that moment, I just needed the fucking food.

"Can you drive, El Burro?" Niall asked as I worked on taking more and more bites, my mouth watering and stomach growling in pain and relief.

I didn't reply, focusing on my food and not giving a shit that he could see my desperation.

"I'll take that as a yes then. We have a problem you and me," he went on, pulling his cell phone from his pocket and tapping something on it. "A five foot little firecracker of a problem."

I managed to give him a little more of my attention as he spoke of the girl, and I wondered briefly if she was alright before trying to remind myself

I wasn't supposed to give a fuck either way.

"Ah, see, you're interested now, aren't ya?" he asked, taking a step closer and holding out a second chocolate bar.

I snatched it, dropping the wrapper of the first and ripping into it. "What about her?"

"Tell me, do you actually care?" he asked seriously. "Do you actually feel anything for her? Or is it just because her mouth felt so damn good wrapped around your cock?"

The thought of her lips hot and wet around my shaft made my dick shift in my pants and I smirked at him as I continued to eat. No matter what else she might have been or what her motivations were, I couldn't deny how fucking good it had felt to fuck that pretty mouth of hers.

"What difference does it make?" I asked him.

He held his cell phone out to me and I stilled as I spotted the image on the screen. It was an old mugshot of the girl who had come bursting into my life like a beam of sunlight, her eyes cold and dead - drugged I'd say if I had to place a bet on it. She looked fucking miserable and as my gaze moved to scan the article attached to the photograph, my blood began to boil and my grip on the phone tightened until my knuckles were bleached.

"So she does mean something to ya then," he said with a nod like he'd been expecting that.

"How did this happen?" I demanded.

"She ran off, killed those fuckers who hurt her and then she kept running," he replied, his voice rough from the alcohol though I doubted I would have spotted how drunk he was if I hadn't seen him stumble.

"And you just let her go?" I asked angrily.

"Seemed like she'd be best off away from me," he replied, some old pain flickering in his eyes. But I didn't care about his fucking pain or self-pity or any of that bullshit.

"Maldito idiota," I growled, dropping the second wrapper and feeling a little stronger as the sugar hit my system.

I never would have let her go. She was mine and that was all that mattered. I wouldn't have cared if she wanted to leave or if she hated me, I'd have kept her precisely where she belonged by my side and she would have been safe.

"Yeah, yeah. No doubt you woulda done a much better job of it," he replied with a scoff. "But you don't know a fucking thing about me or what I am. I'm a curse and I wanted her to be free of it. But now she's in there and I'm gonna get her out. And it just so happens, I need someone to drive me."

"You want my help?" I sneered at him in disgust, wondering if he really had lost his damn mind.

"No, I don't *want* yer fucking help," he snapped. "But I'm not leaving her in that place any longer than I have to which means I'm going right now. She's the one who needs your help so are ya gonna give it or what?"

My mind whirled with the possibility of this being a trap, but I couldn't see how the fuck it could be. Besides, if he got me out of this cage and brought me with him to save her then I could kill him once it was done. Then I could take her and run, retrieve everything I'd stolen from Castillo and take my life back.

"Yes," I said firmly. "Let me out then."

"Don't go getting excited, honeypie," he warned as he took that fucking stun gun from the back of his pants and brandished it at me. "You'll still be my caged dog while we're out there. I'll just be walking you on a leash instead."

I took the hit from the gun, countless volts of electricity pouring through my body and knocking me on my ass where I jerked and spasmed involuntarily.

The cage door opened and the most intense relief flooded through me as he unlocked the collar around my neck and freed me from it for the first time in months. Even just the brush of his rough fingers against the flesh that had been locked away for so long felt like bliss, the skin needing to feel something other than the bite of hard leather.

I struggled to get my limbs under control as thoughts of violence and mayhem reigned inside my head and the desire to beat him to death with my bare hands flooded my body. But before I could regain enough control to do that, a new, thick plastic collar was locked into place around my throat and he was backing away from me.

As the electricity finally faded from my limbs, I managed to roll onto my hands and knees then grasped the bars of my cage to heave myself upright.

"Fifteen minutes," Niall said firmly as he watched me, holding something in his fist. "Clean yourself up and put some proper clothes on. I'm gonna try and drown this whiskey in coffee and sober the fuck up."

He looked like he had more to say but with the chain around my neck gone and the door to my cage open, I lost all sense of control over my body. A feral roar escaped me and I launched myself at him with the desire for his death burning hot in my veins.

Niall grinned his clown's grin at me and a moment before I could collide with him, he hit a button on the thing in his fist and electricity poured from the new collar he'd given me, sending me crashing to the floor in a twitching heap once again.

"That was Spider's collar," he told me through the agony in my limbs. "But I upped the voltage for you, big boy. I may be drunk and in need of your driving skills, El Burro, but I'm still the best hitman in the state. Probably the world. Don't go thinking you can get one up on me just because you're outa yer cage for a bit."

He turned and jogged up the stairs, leaving me to scramble back to my feet as the shock faded and I regained control of my body.

I cursed him beneath my breath and followed on after him, fingering the new collar and finding it locked just as tightly as the other. But at least there was no chain.

When I made it to the top of the stairs, he directed me up towards the bedroom which used to be mine.

"I couldn't be fucked clearing your shit outa here," he said. "So yer clothes are still at the back of the closet. Hurry the fuck up."

I bared my teeth at him, eyed the remote in his fist then turned and headed up the stairs.

My mind was whirling with ideas of all the ways I was going to kill him and how I'd bathe myself in his blood, drink it, colour the walls red with it. But another set of more insistent thoughts kept pushing in on me. My chica loca was all alone in that hospital. She was locked away from the light after giving so much of it to me. I couldn't leave her to rot in there. Which meant the best thing I could do would be to use Niall to get her out.

Once she was free, we could kill him together. Then I was going to claim her body in all the ways I'd been dreaming of and teach her how good it could feel to be caught by a sinner.

I glanced at the overturned bed with a frown as I made it upstairs then strode into the bathroom with my stomach still rumbling and tried not to get caught up in staring around at the rooms which had once been mine. This place was so familiar and yet so alien with Niall's things cluttering it. He'd taken it from me and I wanted it back.

There was an electric razor beside the sink and as I glanced in the mirror at my thick beard and long hair, I grabbed it. Mi sol didn't need some wreck of a tortured prisoner coming to her aid tonight. She needed the man who had been feared throughout the whole of my home town. El diablo de la montaña.

I picked up the razor and switched it on, making quick work of stripping away the beard until my strong jawline was coated in nothing but a layer of black stubble. I took the sides from my hair too, reaching around to do the back and not caring if the lines were uneven. The man I used to be was emerging from beneath it and my dark eyes glinted as I set the razor down and stepped into the shower.

I made fast work of scrubbing the dirt of the last few days from my flesh then stalked through my old bedroom to the closet to find my clothes. Everything I chose was black just as it always had been when I embodied the worst of what I was and worked for Santiago. Jeans, a wifebeater and a leather jacket coupled with heavy boots which I could use to stamp Niall's smiling face into the dirt just as soon as the opportunity presented itself.

I clawed my fingers through the longer hair on the top of my head and pushed it out of my eyes as I looked into the mirror. This was the man mi sol needed to come for her in the dark. This was the man who had never been told no.

When I emerged in the bedroom, I found Niall waiting for me, finishing off a huge mug of coffee and arching a brow.

"Wanted to look pretty for her, did ya?" he asked, murder flashing in his green eyes.

The weight of our hatred hung between us in the room alongside the promise that we would end this feud in death. But not now.

"At least I'm not too drunk to drive a fucking car," I sneered.

"Touché. Though I think the worst of it is lifting," he replied and I had to admit, he didn't look drunk. "I think I'll still bring ya with me though - you'll be a nice distraction for the guards and while they're killin' ya, I'll grab the girl and spirit her away."

"Voy a bailar en tu tumba," I said darkly.

"Yeah. That too," he agreed before pointing me towards the door.

I gave him my back as I moved away ahead of him, down the stairs and through the house to the front door which was standing open.

I hesitated a beat before stepping out and inhaling deeply as I tasted the first fresh air I'd known of for months.

It was a cold night though there wasn't a frost and the moon hung fat and low in the sky amid a blanket of stars.

"Don't worry, mi sol, the demon in me is coming for you," I murmured before striding towards the car that Niall pointed out.

He tossed me the keys as we both got in and he passed me a box of cold pizza before piling five more on his lap.

I flipped the lid open and shoved a slice into my mouth without hesitation. The chocolate had helped, but I was in desperate need of more food and I was clearly going to require my strength tonight.

"Eat and drive, lad," Niall growled, setting a destination on the GPS.

Eden Heights was about an hour from us which meant I'd be stuck in here with him until then. I gritted my teeth but started the car. I'd use him to get Brooklyn free then I'd gut him like the pig he was.

"I'm not your lad," I replied darkly. "I'm older than you for a start."

"Really?" Niall cocked his head at me, turning the remote over in his hand. He looked casual, relaxed, though I could tell he was anything but. He was buzzed, on edge, ready to cause death and carnage at the drop of a hat and in no way letting his guard down around me. We were beasts of the same design after all.

"By a year," I added as I started the car and pulled away from the house.

It had been so long since I'd driven that it almost felt foreign to me, but my muscles remembered all the movements even if my brain was scrambling to catch up to the reality of being out of that fucking cellar.

"Well, I stole the best part of a year from ya in the basement," Niall said. "So I think we can agree I'm older, lad."

I didn't see the point in arguing with a madman so I dropped it, keeping my eyes on the dark drive as we headed out. It was easy enough for me to focus my thoughts anyway. I only had to keep them pinned on my chica loca locked up in some hospital for insane people and I knew I wouldn't falter. I'd get her back then I'd punish her for leaving me behind. She should have killed Niall and freed me then I could have protected her from this fate. Once I got her back, I wouldn't make the mistake of letting her out of my sight again. She needed to learn what it meant to be owned by me and stay in her place where I told her to be. Where I could keep her safe.

We made it half way down the drive and pain erupted through my neck, driving into the rest of my body as the collar exploded with electricity. I lost control of the car and almost blacked out from the sudden assault, biting my tongue as Niall's laughter echoed in my skull and the car hit something hard enough to throw me forward into my seatbelt.

"Whoops," Niall said as the pain faded away and he slapped me around the face to bring me back to full consciousness. "Forgot to disable the parameter sensors on yer collar. My bad."

I snarled and lunged toward him, but the barrel of a gun pressed to my forehead before I could tighten my hands around his neck.

"Easy now," he warned, his laughter falling away and a dark, soulless creature peering out at me from within his green eyes. "Don't go thinking I won't kill ya just because I need a ride and could do with some help. I've got an army of O'Briens I could call on if I have to. You're not my only option here."

"So why don't you?" I hissed, easing my hands off of his throat reluctantly.

"Because I hate them," he growled and for once there wasn't any bullshit in his words. This was his truth. The real honest to fuck bones of it. "I hate them and I don't wanna rely on them or associate with them more than I have ta. They're the reason my Ava died. They're the reason for a lot of shitty things in my life and beyond. I might be loyal to them, but I know what they are and I don't want them getting their claws into Brooklyn. You got that?"

I glared at him for several long seconds then nodded. Yeah, I got that.

"Good. Let's get our arses moving then, yeah?" He holstered the gun again and I backed the car away from the tree we'd hit.

It still seemed to drive fine so I just bumped us back up onto the drive and headed out into the night.

I'm coming, chica loca, and may God help anyone who stands between us.

BROOKLYN

CHAPTER THIRTY FIVE

I sat in the middle of my padded cell as the cushy walls bulged toward me like fluffy candy floss. Couldn't eat it though. That was a no-no. Teethies didn't like that. And it made the walls cry.

Oh whoooosh.

I fell onto my back, my brain sizzling like a red pepper on a barbeque. My mouth still tasted of pills. They were yucky. I'd spat them right out. But then someone had stuck a jabby in my arm and everything went all quiet. I didn't much like the quiet. It was pressing, so loud, louder than a bee in my ear. I'd rather the real loud. The one where people talked and music blared.

"Hellllooo?" I called to the lonely walls. "I'll be your friend," I whispered conspiratorially. "You and me, me and you, we'll form a club."
Oh, aren't I part of another club? Can I be part of more than one?

No…wait, I got kicked out of that last one. The Devil man didn't want me anymore. But I was in The Clit Clan now.

"Enrolment day!" I cried to the walls, but it came out all slurrish. "First rule, you have to be an upstanding citizen." I snorted then fell apart laughing, silent waves of utter amusement ripping through me. "Not really. I don't like upstanding citizens. They're judgey. I won't judge you, walls. This club is a judgement free zone. Unlike the last club I was in. Hellfire judged me every day." I stuck my finger up in the air, waggling it as I impersonated him perfectly, except I actually didn't because I was in a straitjacket. "Yer bad at killin', love. Yer useless, good for nothin'."

A lick of pain caressed my heart and I welcomed it into my club as a new friend. It could bring the others too if it wanted. The hurts and the sorrows and the lonelies. Might as well bring them all in now before they started breaking the doors down. "He was probably right about Dead Man too. He just wanted me to help him get free." I sighed, sad that I'd left him behind. Maybe he would have stuck around if I'd gotten him out of his metal net. Probably not though.

I flapped my arms, making a snow angel and a fwoomphing noise sounded as it rubbed against the padding. "Hey, Big Red?" I whispered. "Are you still there? I think I'd like to go to hell now…"

Silence, unending, unnerving silence.

A tear wet my cheek, slipping down into my hair to make a nest for all the other tears about to follow. "Don't leave me too. I'll do better. Are you mad at me?"

The ceiling seemed to shudder and ripple like water and my mind swirled too. I tried to reach toward it, but my arms remained locked to my body. "Stupid jacket, I'll Houdini my way out of you if you don't let me go."

Jackie didn't listen to my threat. Jackie was a bitch.

There was a distinct clunk then light spilled over me in a rectangular shaft. I wriggled my way upright, sitting with my legs crossed as my enemy stepped into the room. She was tall with broad shoulders, slim-framed glasses perched on her upturned nose and her black hair greased back into a tight bun. She wore the white uniform that all the staff wore here, her purple lanyard marking her out as head nurse on this ward. Madam Lucille. Queen Cunt of Eden Heights.

"Hello Brooklyn," she said in that sultry, don't-fuck-with-me tone of hers. "How are you?"

I blew at a strand of hair that was crossing my vision, but it remained stubbornly there, probably trying to shield me from her ugly face. *Thanks buddy.*

She walked forward then crouched down in front of me, the black Crocs on her feet offending me. "Ugly shoe bitch, I'll cut your feet off and beat you to death with 'em," I slurred, the drugs still clinging firmly to my brain like leeches sapping my strength away.

She pulled something from her pocket, reaching out to my face and I refused to flinch, gritting my jaw as I remembered all the shit this bitch had done to me. She liked punishing me in all kinds of ways, like making me sit in dark rooms alone for hours, sometimes naked, sometimes with my hands bound. Other times, she'd like to call me names, make me look in a mirror and point out all the nasty things about myself. Whenever she was working, the patients were always sad. No one wanted to be the centre of her attention, but since I'd come back that was all I was.

She took hold of the piece of hair covering my eyes and suddenly sliced through it with a small pair of scissors.

"That's better." She smiled that sadistic smile of hers and I lunged at her, snapping my teeth as I aimed to bite her piggy nose off.

She moved back and I face planted the floor, growling as I bit into the padding.

"Mind your manners, Brooklyn," she warned. "Perhaps you'd feel more comfortable without that mane of hair. I can arrange to have it shaved off, would that suit you better?" Her tone was mocking, belittling as she waved her winning poker hand in my face. She was the queen here and I was just a little peasant she liked to amuse herself with from time to time.

"Take what you want," I spat out, my throat working a little better than before. I managed to sit back up and found Lucille standing upright again, regarding me like a hunter with an injured animal at its feet.

I realised she had a bottle of water in her hand and the desperation to drink it filled me to the brim. She saw me looking and brought it out in front of her, grinning darkly. "Oh are you thirsty, sweetie?"

I glared at her, giving no answer because she knew I was. I hadn't had a drink for hours.

She twisted the cap off of the bottle, bringing it to her lips and taking a long gulp of my water before releasing a dramatic sigh of satisfaction. "Here you are then." She tipped the bottle up, pouring it all over my face and I was so thirsty I dropped my head back, opening my mouth and took what I could get, but most of it just soaked me through.

Lucille chuckled as she emptied out the last drop and I swallowed down the tiny mouthful I'd salvaged.

She gazed down at me with a sneer on her lips. "Your behaviour has been most unsatisfactory, Brooklyn. You're going to have to work very hard to earn my favour again, do you understand?"

I spat at her and she leaned down to grab my jaw in a pincer grip, her nails digging hard into my skin. "You will remember who owns you, sweetie," she growled as I felt her thumbnail pierce the skin. Her face seemed to pulse, falling in and out of focus. "For your insolence, you will spend the next two days in the dark."

She turned sharply away, stepping out of the door and the lights switched off just before she swung the door shut. My heart crumpled like a ball of paper, my breaths coming quicker as the darkness coiled around me like a python hungry for its next meal.

All of my friends vanished until there was only me, floating adrift in an eternal, lonely black sea.

NIALL

CHAPTER THIRTY SIX

"Pull over here," I directed, pointing towards the thick woodland at the side of the road and yanking on the wheel to make Mateo drive into the trees out of sight.

"How are we going about this?" he asked in a rough tone as he killed the ignition, eyes on the trees surrounding us and muscles coiled with tension. This was the fucker I'd hunted down all those months ago. A machine of a man with deadly intent and all the instincts of a cold blooded killer. Not really my M.O. I was more of a suck it and see kind of killer, all unpredictable and shit. I guessed both methods had their plus points. "Do you have a blueprint? Where exactly is she being held?"

I barked a laugh and got out of the car. Blueprint? Who the fuck did he think I was? The Queen of Sheba? I bet that one had blueprints for days, all tucked up safe in her crown of cat food. Not me though.

"I'll tell ya what I've got, lad," I said, ignoring the scowl he shot me over the roof of the car as he climbed out too. "I've got a few grenades, a couple of guns and the determination of a madman."

"But what's the plan of attack?" he pushed, moving around to look as I opened up the back of the car and started loading myself up with weapons.

"Well, on this occasion I'm going to wing it," I told him. "Big places like this tend to work best like that."

"That's madness," he snarled, reaching towards a grenade and earning himself a gun to the temple for his efforts.

"Back up, gobshite, I'm not giving you any heavy artillery or long range weapons just so that you can turn them on me. You'll have Evangeline and a few smoke grenades. Maybe Greg will allow you to take him too."

Mateo glowered at me as I exerted pressure on the gun and he was forced to back up several steps.

"Who are you talking about?" he asked as I returned my attention to loading myself up with weapons.

I grabbed the axe and gave her a goodbye kiss before tossing her to him. "That's Evangeline. She's a virgin so make sure you go gentle with her first kill. Once you've got her good and wet you can have at it though - I get the impression she's gonna be a real goer once she's been broken in."

"You name your weapons?" Mateo asked, swinging the axe to and fro as he got a feel for her.

"Of course I do. There ain't a hitman worth his salt who doesn't take good care of his weapons and I make sure to treat mine like old friends."

"I have no idea how you aren't dead already," he muttered, beheading a sapling and giving Evangeline a good swing. I could tell she liked it too, dirty bitch.

"Because death doesn't want me," I replied, sounding like a broken record, but it was true. It didn't. And I hadn't sent myself to hell yet because... Well, shit the first thing that popped into my mind when I thought about that was my little spider. What the fuck was that about?

"Well I'll make sure death reconsiders once this is over and I have mi sol back at my side," Mateo promised.

I glanced at him, half surprised that he hadn't tried to kill me yet and taking in the determination in his gaze. It was her. Had to be. And I didn't know if I should be grateful for that or if I should be gutting him for it.

He couldn't have her though. I wouldn't allow it. She deserved better than me and she most certainly deserved better than this piece of shit. Hell, maybe I should just challenge him to a fight to the death and make sure we both fucking lost to protect her from us.

But not yet. Not while she was still stuck in there.

I strapped the flamethrower to my back then locked the car, jerking my chin to encourage Mateo to walk with me, the two of us taking off into the trees as we stalked towards the Eden Heights compound ahead.

We kept a good few meters between us and I made sure to have the remote for his collar to hand, but I got the feeling I wouldn't need it. Not yet. He was fixed on the idea of getting my girl back just as plainly as I was, and it seemed we were going to stick to this truce between us until then.

My steps were sure footed as I walked, the effects of the whiskey lessening now that I had a full belly and a taste of the fresh air. I wasn't exactly sober, but I was damn deadly half cut so I wasn't worried. In fact, I was fairly certain I could take it from here, but I guessed having backup in the form of a former cartel fixer wasn't the worst idea I'd ever had. Unless he turned on me of course. Or stole my girl away. Or fucked everything up.

I took Greg from my belt, running my thumb over the sharp point of the blade as I eyed all the best places on Mateo's body for sticking it. His death would be fucking glorious. But I wasn't so certain he'd earned it yet.

"Here," I barked, tossing him the knife as he glanced at me.

He caught it neatly, eyeing it like a pro, weighing it in his hand and giving me a look that said he was considering gutting me with it.

"Are you going to tell me the plan now?" he asked.

"Simple," I replied. "Just follow my lead and don't get dead until after we rescue my little psycho. After that, if you've gotta bleed out on me I can take it, but I would prefer you tell me where you hid all that shit you stole first."

"Ni siquiera después de mi muerte," he sneered and rolled my eyes. I'd take that as a no. Stubborn bastard. I'd crack him one of these days though. Somehow.

I placed a finger to my lips as a wire fence came into sight up ahead and we stalked forward on silent feet. Just a wolf and lion on the hunt for a kill. Clearly not friends, but hungry enough to tolerate one another until our needs were satisfied.

The fence met up with a cosy little guard hut thingy-majig beside the barrier which crossed the road and I set my gaze on it as I counted the men inside.

"I'll take the two by the window, you get the one on watch over the gate," Mateo breathed, moving almost close enough for the two of us to reach each other but not quite.

This trust between us was a fragile, brittle thing and neither of us would be willing to lean on it too heavily.

"What about the fucker on the roof?" I asked casually.

"Where?" he asked.

I rolled my eyes. "There's always a fucker on the roof."

Mateo drove his tongue into his cheek as his dark eyes scoured the top of the building ahead of us. "I don't see one. But just in case, we can take the uniforms from the men we kill while we walk up to the building."

"I suppose," I sighed dramatically. "But that sounds awfully like a plan, El Burro, and I don't want you tryna stifle my dramatic flare once we get going. Got it?"

Mateo sucked his teeth with a sneer then took off ahead of me, not answering but clearly deciding that now was the moment.

Irritation flickered through me because I was the damn boss, but I thrust it aside as I jogged on too, staying low as we crept up on the hut.

Mateo headed to the left of it where the two targets he'd picked for himself were playing cards at a small table inside the cracked open window and I headed around to the hatch where the remaining fucker was keeping an eye out for any approaching vehicles.

I squatted down low and crept beneath the hatch before reaching up and rapping the tip of my knife against the glass.

As expected, the fucker in question opened up and leaned out, looking to see where the noise had come from and I swept my blade above me, cutting him a new smile across his throat as he bared his neck for me.

Blood rained down on me as he jerked and spluttered and I caught him before he could fall out of the hut, shoving him back inside before hopping up after him.

Mateo stood over the corpses of the other guards in the low lit space and I grinned at him as I swiped a hand down my face and smeared the blood across my skin. He was fucking spotless somehow and he didn't look too impressed by the bloody mess I'd made of myself.

"Two to one," I commented, gesturing at him with my knife. "I bet my body count will top yours before the end of the night though, sweetheart."

"I'm not interested in some foolish competition with you," he growled. "I'm here to get mi sol out of this place."

"Yeah, yeah, yada, yada. We'll see if you don't care when you're not in the lead anymore."

I looked around at the little guard hut and grinned as I spotted a map on the wall which marked the different wards making up the building we were heading into. I started playing eenie, meanie, minie, mo with them before noticing the one marked *high security* and tapping it with the tip of my blade.

"What's the betting they stuck the little cop killer in there?" I asked as the shadow which was Mateo drew closer to take a look.

"I agree," he grunted, sounding less than pleased about being on team Niall. "So what's the plan?"

He took a coat from one of the dead guards and tossed it to me while I rolled my eyes and tipped my head back to the ceiling. "Please Lord, save me from the hell of planners. I cannot take the constant questions. Just deliver me into the freedom which true carnage requires, and I promise to make many sacrifices in your honour."

"The Christian God doesn't claim to want sacrifices," Mateo muttered as he pulled his own jacket on then placed a baseball cap with the word *security* emblazoned on it in yellow on top of his head. "Perhaps you'd be better to turn to the pagan deities if you want to praise one with blood."

"Perhaps I will," I shot back at him, tugging on the damn jacket and a cap of me own. It was bulky over the flamethrower on my back, but it covered it up okay.

I snatched a security lanyard from a little tray by the door and the two of us headed outside again.

I gave Mateo the side eye, wondering where he'd stashed Evangeline and noticing the very end of her handle poking out from beneath his coat. *Sorry about him pawing at ya, girl.*

She winked at me in the moonlight and I scowled. She was clearly enjoying herself and if I didn't get her back soon enough, she was gonna start bonding with El Burro and acting like a right little whore.

We walked up to the main building, its grey walls bare and barren and oh so fucking mind-numbingly boring. This was a place where chaos came to die under the utilitarian regime of complete and utter boredom.

I felt the prickle of eyes on me as we walked, certain there was someone on the roof despite Mateo's doubts and resisting the urge to glance up and hunt for them in case they spotted my blood-stained face.

We reached the heavy metal doors of the building where a little reader for the key card sat waiting and I swiped my stolen helper through the slot.

A panel beside it flashed to life requesting a fingerprint ID too and I cursed just as Mateo elbowed me aside.

"There was a scanner like this on the door back there," he muttered irritably like I shoulda noticed that, as he lifted a severed thumb and pressed it to the panel.

When the fuck had he even had time to sever that thumb? Had he seen the scanner before or after deciding to do it? What would he do with the thumb now? Was it a keeper? Would he hang it around his neck on a little chain and let it rot there? Where was he planning on getting the chain?

A low buzz sounded and the door clicked open, making me forget the thumb as I shouldered my way inside with Mateo right behind me. He coulda killed me then. Probably shoulda. But he didn't, staying close and silent at my back, hounding the same little bunny as me.

A woman looked up from behind a desk in front of me, a frown marring her features a moment before the full shock could set in and I quickly pointed one of my Desert Eagles right at her face.

"Be a lamb and tell me, love, where are you keeping Brooklyn Meadow?" I purred, my heart ticking faster at the fear in her eyes and the hilt of a knife kissing my palm as I took it from my belt.

"P-patient records are confidential," she stuttered but her little pinky fingers were creeping to her left, no doubt hunting for a panic button somewhere there.

I flung my knife just as a little bout of dizziness swept over me from the lingering booze and the woman screamed as instead of slamming into the wood just by her fingers, I somewhat impaled her hand on her desk. *Damn whiskey.* Not that I'd be admitting that was a fuck up though.

I leapt forward just as another scream burst from her lips and managed to slap my hand down over her mouth before she could get it all the way out, crouching on the desk in front of her.

"Maldito idiota," Mateo snarled, striding up behind me as I slid over the desk and looked around for the sign of anyone else coming to help this little screamer out.

I gave it a beat but there weren't any sounds of approach and I grinned down at my prey as I leaned in close to speak in her face. "I guess working in a place where people scream all the damn time makes it hard to tell when someone really needs help, huh?"

She whimpered and my smile widened as I yanked the knife back out of her hand - thank you Gilbert - and shoved her backwards on the wheels of her chair, keeping my hand over her mouth as I followed her, pushing until it bumped against the row of filing cabinets behind her. She cradled her bleeding hand to her chest and looked up at me like she was looking upon the face of pure evil, and maybe she was, though I liked to think I had some redeeming qualities too. Like my fancy newly decorated cock - at least once the swelling went down.

Mateo started tippy tapping on the computer at her desk and I slowly removed my hand from her mouth, giving her a stern look which warned her in no uncertain terms not to scream again. I wasn't really all about killing random bitches, but I wasn't wholly against it either if she turned out to be an arsehole.

I flicked the name badge on her shirt and read her name Gemma Whelan before taking Brooklyn's death list rock from my pocket and hunting it carefully.

"Looks like it's your lucky day, Gemma Whelan," I said with a grin like a Cheshire Cat. "You're not on the list."

I stepped back and reached down to unbuckle her belt, rolling my eyes as she squirmed and whimpered some more.

"I'm not gonna rape ya," I growled, hating when women thought that of me. I had some fucking lines. Not many, granted, but some.

I whipped her chair around and grabbed her arms, forcing them behind her and tying them to the back of the chair with the belt before spinning her to face me again.

"Got it," Mateo said and I glanced at him as he pointed at the screen. "Ward G. High security."

"What did I tell ya?" I asked excitedly as I read my spider's name there and grinned.

"Let's go." Mateo made to walk away but I held a finger up to stop him before shrugging out of the guard's coat and tossing the cap away. Then I carefully lifted a grenade from my belt and turned back to Gemma Whelan.

"Open wide, poppet or I'll shove it up your arse," I urged and she quickly opened her mouth, tears spilling down her cheeks.

I pulled the pin outa the grenade and tossed it aside, keeping the trigger depressed beneath my thumb before pushing the whole thing into her mouth.

"Shh," I said, placing a finger over my lips and wiping her tears away. "Just stay nice and quiet, lass, and you won't go boom. No doubt some helpful fucker will find ya before long." I patted her on the head then pushed the button to open the door which led through into the rest of the hospital.

"Let's hurry," Mateo urged, tossing his coat and hat aside too as we headed inside and started jogging down the dimly lit corridor.

After a couple of turns, the sound of laughter called to us and we slowed our pace, slipping towards the source of the noise with weapons ready and blood on our hands. Mateo held Evangeline poised for her first kill and I hoped for her sake she had a good time. She deserved to have a memorable moment when she popped her death cherry.

I paused at the next corner, glancing around it and watching as a nurse in a white uniform laughed once more then walked away from an open door, pushing a cart stacked high with meds and disappearing around another corner.

I slipped out of the shadows and moved towards the open door with Mateo at my side, looking towards the pale blue light that spilled out into the corridor.

I made it to the door and peeked inside, finding a room full of security monitors which showed all kinds of views from around the hospital.

There was a guard sitting there, observing the screens while eating a pot of noodles and looking bored.

Before I could decide what to do with him, Evangeline went whistling past my ear and embedded her sweet self in his skull.

The guard fell to the floor, noodles spilling everywhere and I raised my eyebrows at Mateo as he stalked into the room.

"Well, you made a whore out of her fast enough," I muttered, pouting at Evangeline as he tugged her back out of the dead fucker's skull. "Not even a whisper of foreplay."

"She was hungry for it," he growled at me and I considered killing him as I got the impression he was referring to my goddamn girl and not the axe at all. "And I wasn't afraid to satisfy her."

I huffed irritably, considering his death once more but he didn't seem concerned.

I watched him as he reached for the name badge which was hanging on the jacket the guard had left on the back of his chair and turned it to show me. I read the name and arched a brow at him.

"Observant little fucker, aren't ya?" I teased, taking Brooklyn's rock from my pocket and striking the name off with a sharpie I'd brought for the job.

"Three to one, bastardo. For a competition I don't care about, I seem to be winning rather easily," Mateo taunted.

I scoffed like I didn't care, but I did. He wasn't gonna win. Oh no. I'd be the killer of the day and I'd lay the most heads at my little psycho's feet by the time we found her, mark my words.

The two of us looked up at the security feeds, taking note of the locked doors between wards, patrolling guards and nurses moving between cells. It was gonna be a bitch to get all the way to the far side of this facility without alerting all of them to our presence and two against fuck knew how many weren't good odds, even if we were two of the best killers around.

"Alright, time for plan B," I announced, taking the flamethrower gun from my back and grinning widely as I got ready to light her up.

"I didn't think there was a plan A," Mateo muttered scathingly.

"There wasn't. But when in doubt, burn them out."

"You think setting this place alight will help?" he asked, giving me that look which said he thought I was mad, and he'd be right about that.

"You know what happens in a place like this when it gets set on fire?" I asked casually, my fingers moving over the gun of the flamethrower in a loving caress. Her name was Rhonda and I loved her deeply.

Mateo tipped his head to one side as he considered it. "They open the doors so that the inmates can get to safety?"

"Damn straight, El Burro. They open the doors."

The motherfucker actually smiled then and I looked into his eyes as I pulled the trigger, blasting the wall of CCTV monitors with a line of pure fire and watching the reflection blaze in his dark pupils.

A fire alarm blared almost instantly and the sprinklers sprung to life overhead, soaking us and washing some of the blood from my face.

I tipped my head back and laughed as I continued to burn the CCTV monitors before turning my attention beyond this room.

No doubt my little psycho was praying for the Devil to save her, so here I was delivering her own personal slice of hell. I wouldn't ride in like a white knight to rescue her though, more like one of the horsemen of the apocalypse – and my steed would be a grumpy cartel donkey with a taste for blood of his own.

"Giddy-up, Mateo!" I cried as I led the way back out into the corridor. "We have a fucked up little damsel to find."

BROOKLYN

CHAPTER THIRTY SEVEN

Time was nothing and everything, swirling together in my head as I sat in the dark and tried to remember who I was.

I'm a beanstalk with a taste for golden eggs.

I'm a dog called Tallulah who likes her dinner served at four o'clock sharpish.

I'm a pretty little Fae with lilac hair being screwed by a sexy snake man in the land of Solaria.

I'm Mr Tumnus the fawn and you're going to fall asleep when I play my magic flute, Lucy.

I'm an inanimate object lost at sea, floating away like Wilson the ball. Do I even have a face like him?

I tried to reach up to feel my nose, but the straitjacket held my arms down tight. *I think my nose is still there...I hope so anyway. I wouldn't want to look like Lord Voldemort. Though, I guess I could pull it off. I'd make a great Death Eater. I'd eat death for breakfast if I could. Nom, nom, nom. Wouldn't beat Coco Pops though.*

I scrunched my nose up and it started to itch, making me thrash as I tried desperately to scratch it. I managed to roll over and rubbed it against the padding.

Somewhere far, far away there was an alarm going off. It sounded like the Purge alarm, but it couldn't be that. They weren't going to let all crime be allowed for a day or else they'd let me free, wouldn't they? They wouldn't make me miss out on that. That would be a crime in itself.

A clunk sounded and I twisted around as a crack of light spilled into the room, so bright it burned, like a beam straight from heaven. *Oh no, I'm going to burn up in that holy light. I'm too full of sin.*

I tried to roll away from it, but the door kept opening until it was flooding over me and I screamed, writhing like mad as the light exorcised every demon in my body – and there were a damn lot of them. I jerked and flexed, expecting to catch fire at any second, but I didn't.

My eyes adjusted to the light and I sat up, squinting out into the hallway beyond where water was spraying down from sprinklers on the ceiling. Wait, I wasn't dying. I was freaking free!

Patients were running back and forth out in the halls and my eyes snagged on Angry Jack as he stepped out of a cell opposite mine. He was huge with a mess of long, white-blonde hair – not in an old guy way, more in like the Witcher way. He was built like a tank and his face was fixed in a constant snarl. Those huge hands had done a lot of murdering in their time from what I'd heard, not that he ever talked about it. In fact, he only ever talked in one syllable words. But that was what I liked about Jack. That was why we were friends. *Best* friends.

I struggled to my feet, leaping outside, but my head spun and I crashed into the wall beside Angry Jack's door. The drugs in my system were still keen to play havoc with my head, but nothing was going to stop me getting out of here.

Jack grunted as he looked at me and I beamed brighter than the sun.

"Hey, big man, my legs are all wobbles. Will ya give me a ride?" I asked and he sneered a moment before shrugging.

I ran around him and he lifted me onto his back. I wrapped my legs around his waist as I gazed over his shoulder, my arms crushed to his spine within the strait jacket. I dropped my chin over his shoulder to get the best grip I could, my thighs locking around him tight so I didn't fall.

"Yah!" I cried and he took off down the corridor like a charging rhino, shoving anyone out of our way with his huge fists.

Cannibal Carol was knocked flying and I flipped her the finger inside my jacket. Eating people was so unhygienic. I only ate the veggies, the fruities and the candies. All the good stuff. Ain't no one ever gonna get me eating people. Ick.

We made it to the security door at the end of the hall where a bunch of nurses were holding back the patients, injecting anyone they could get near with sedatives.

I clutched Angry Jack's waist tighter with my thighs as he started running and a bellow left his lips. I joined him, screaming like we were charging into battle together as he blasted through the wall of nurses, sending everyone flying as we made it to the other side.

I laughed wildly as he turned down the next corridor and my eyes snagged on a needle sticking out of his arm, but the syringe was still full of the sedative and hadn't made it into him thankfully.

"Jack, you've got a little friend in your arm," I told him and he ripped it out, slamming it into a nurse's neck as we rounded a corner, knocking him over in the process.

I gasped as my gaze locked on Madam Lucille at the far end of the corridor, trying to lock the security door that led into the rec room. She was typing in codes frantically on a keypad but it kept flashing red, not listening to her fat fingers. *Oh what fat fingers you have, I shall cut them all off and shove them up your nose holes.*

"Knock her down, Jack," I growled in his ear, the desire for blood curling under my flesh as I remembered who I was. My mind spun like a washing machine for a moment and I fought back the drug fog trying to claim me. They made my head so floofsome. My decisions could always be a little thrown by them, but they weren't going to stop me from escaping this place. No siree Bill.

I'm Brooklyn Meadow, the Bully Butcher, Spider, the little psycho. And today I am death.

"This kill's mine," I whispered to him and he nodded, starting to run faster, barrelling towards Lucille as she fought to get that door locked from the other side.

Jack charged through it with a roar, throwing Lucille to the ground and she screamed wildly, trying to scramble away. I jumped down from Jack's back as she grabbed a taser from her hip to try and immobilise me. But I wasn't scared of a little zippy zapper. I threw myself at her, headbutting her in the tit just as the taser slammed into my side. I fell with a scream that turned into a moan, my mind awakening like I was coming up from beneath a dark sea. The drugs tugged me back down a little, but I was gonna get my ass out of here before they consumed me completely.

Not before I'd made this cunt of cranberry suffer though.

I blinked out of the dark, a bellow filling my head as I found Angry Jack pinning Lucille to the wall by her throat, the taser abandoned by my side. I rolled over, picking it up between my teeth as the zappy end continued to crackle with electricity, then I pushed myself to my feet and poked Angry Jack in the ass with my toe.

"She's mine," I said around the taser, jabbing his ass again as Lucille started turning blue, her feet kicking as Jack lifted her up above the ground.

Man, he was muscly. He had a big scar running into his hairline too where he'd had some sort of brain operation. Rumour had it, he'd had a tumour removed, but the process had switched on his angries forever. He'd murdered people in their dozens like a fox in a chicken pen. He'd never hurt me though, and I guessed that meant we really were best friends. *I should make us some friendship bracelets with our birthstones on. I wonder when Jack was born. I bet he's an Aries, he has such Aries energy.*

I stopped jabbing Jack and full on kicked him in the ass. He grunted, wheeling around, his face twisted in a snarl, but as he lunged for me, I ducked under his arm and jammed my taser into Lucille's thick neck before she could get away. She fell with a shriek at my feet and I glanced back at Jack, finding him taking his angries out on the rec room, throwing chairs everywhere before starting to punch a wall repeatedly. *Aww, he's so happy when he's destroying things.*

I dropped down to kneel on Lucille's gut, balancing there as I grinned at her around the sparking taser. The water from the sprinklers cascaded over me and slicked my hair to my back.

"Get back!" she commanded as she came around from the first shock. "You loathsome freak! Get away from me! Guards!" She screamed and I bent down jerking my head forward like I had a beak and forcing the taser between her open lips.

She spasmed beneath me so hard I nearly fell off of her, but I rode that bitch like a mechanical bull. I was made for riding things. It was a freaking gift. Bulls, horses, cocks. I knew I'd be a pro at all the riding things given a chance.

I jerked my head back, not wanting her to die too fast, but ducked as a chair flew over my head and smashed against the wall. Jack was in a full on rage, his face red, his hands balled into fists, bloody from the beating he'd just given the wall. He started tearing up the carpet and I looked back down at Lucille as she panted beneath me, blood trickling out of her mouth.

She'd locked me in rooms alone for days, made me shower naked in front of her and her team, poured hot tea on my skin, made me pee in bottles and cups and outdoors in the open yard, made me beg for food and water. She was a power hungry pelican with a big beak full of turds. And she was soon to be a dead pelican. But first, she'd suffer for me and for everyone else she'd tortured in this place.

I started jabbing at her randomly, bucking my head back and forth like a chicken pecking seed as I blasted her with stabs of electricity over and over again. She screamed and fought, but I was going nowhere. This was my kill and I was in a blood fog. It wasn't gonna clear until she lay dead beneath me.

"Guards," Angry Jack growled. "Move."

I jabbed faster, focusing on her chest as her heart rate went up, my eyes flicking to the fitness watch on her wrist as the numbers cycled up and up and up. I kept the taser directly over her heart this time, watching as I wondered if the whole organ would go bang and a shower of blood would coat the room.

She started convulsing and kicking, a gargling groan leaving her lips as she stared up at me in horror.

Die, die, die, Pelican tits!

A final shudder ran through her as the heart attack ended her for good and I tossed the taser away from me with a swing of my head. Angry Jack suddenly plucked me up, tucking me under his arm so I was looking out behind him like a happy little Gucci purse. He shoved a hand in Lucille's pocket, snatching out a security card then ran across the room while I stared back at her corpse with a manic laugh.

"Goodbye, whoremonger!"

Angry Jack smashed through another door across the room and I winced as a bang made my head ring and my drugged up brain swirl. Armed guards were chasing us, guns raised and eyes wide. As we rounded the corner into the next hall, I heard them crying out in alarm at the sight of Lucille.

I grinned from ear to ear as the afterglow of death held me in its manic pincers and I shouted to Jack, "Yah!"

MATEO

CHAPTER THIRTY EIGHT

My flesh was alive with adrenaline, the demon in me purring with pleasure as screams rang out and water poured over us from the sprinklers while Niall continued to set everything he could alight.

I used my axe - which I wasn't calling fucking Evangeline - to take the heads off of the sprinklers, making them less effective at stifling the fires while Niall whooped and laughed every time he blasted something with flames.

Guards and nurses crossed our paths, either running or falling beneath the power of our weapons if they tried to fight us. Though I knew that wouldn't last much longer. The men stationed inside the building didn't carry guns, but those outside most definitely did and it could only be a matter of time before they made it inside.

We moved quickly, doubling back more than once as we got lost in the warren of corridors until a roar of frustration escaped me.

An alarmed shriek caught my ear and I turned, finding a nurse cowering behind a padded chair in some kind of recreational area as she attempted to hide from us.

"Get up," I commanded, stalking towards her and brandishing my bloodstained axe.

She shrieked again and tried to run but I caught a fistful of her brunette hair and yanked her around to face me.

"Take us to Brooklyn Meadow," I demanded, holding the bloody axe to her throat. "High security ward."

"I...I...I don't have clearance for that-"

"Just get us to the door, lass, we'll figure out our own way through it," Niall said, grinning at her through the blood which still speckled his skin despite the flood of water washing down on us.

I shoved her towards the door and she fell to her knees before scrambling upright and making a run for it, a squeak of, "This way," escaping her as we followed.

We turned left and right, ignoring fleeing inmates and panicked staff members as we stalked after her.

Niall suddenly whipped his flamethrower towards a nurse who was trying to run past us and lit him up like a bonfire, his screams colouring the air and making everyone close by panic and turn tail.

"That's Karl Regan – I saw it on his name badge," he announced proudly. "He was on the list."

I cursed beneath my breath and turned back to find that the nurse we'd been following was gone.

"For fuck's sake," I growled. "Nunca la encontraremos así."

"Don't get yer knickers in a twist," Niall growled, heading on down the corridor and turning right.

I glanced around, kicking up water from the puddle that had formed on the ground before carrying on after him.

"Here it is!" Niall announced loudly and I broke into a run as I turned the corner, finding him there before a set of reinforced doors with the words *High Security Unit* emblazoned across them.

There was an access keypad to the right of them and Niall swiped his stolen key card down it before cursing as the thing flashed red.

I tried the severed thumb in my pocket but that did fuck all and I snarled as I tossed it away.

"Stand back," I commanded as I hefted the axe in my arms and moved before the doors. If we couldn't open them the usual way, then I'd gladly tear them down for her.

I swung the axe with a bellow of exertion, cutting into the thick wood with a bang that reverberated around the now empty corridor.

The whole thing rattled and a small piece broke off, but it wasn't enough.

I swung the axe again and again, my muscles bunching and flexing, each strike reverberating back up through my arms and into my chest. But I wouldn't give up, no matter how slow the progress was. Mi sol was beyond this door. She was waiting for me. I wouldn't give up.

"Stop right there!" a man yelled behind us and only my quick reflexes made me drop in time to avoid the bullet that had been destined for my skull.

I whirled around as Niall howled in excitement, whipping his own gun out and firing back at the guards who had appeared to apprehend us.

They dove into cover again and my heart thrashed as I looked towards Niall while he kept firing, holding them back but unable to hit them while they remained beyond those walls.

"Give me a gun," I commanded and he laughed wildly.

"I'd sooner give a kitten to a hungry pitbull, sugar. You just keep workin' on that door and leave the killin' to the professional," he replied, not even bothering to look at me as he kept firing at the group of guards every time one of them poked their heads out.

"Just give me a-"

"Bullseye!" Niall roared as a guard was thrown back against the wall, his blood splattering the paintwork and causing more bullets to fly our way.

We were exposed here, like fish in a fucking barrel and we needed to get through this door.

"Te odio," I growled fiercely, turning my back on the gunfight despite every instinct in my body, swinging the axe at the door again.

I'd break it down and find mi sol and get her out of this place no matter what it cost me.

Niall ran back and forth, drawing the attention of the guards and covering me while he continued to fire at them over and over again.

"Grenade!" he bellowed and I flinched as I heard something hitting the wall behind me, but instead of an explosion rocking the walls, pink glittery smoke encased us in a cloud.

Niall laughed wildly as he dove into it and I looked back at him for a moment, watching as his silhouette disappeared into the smoke before swinging the axe again.

Screams and gunshots sounded behind me, panic in the voices of the guards as they yelled between each other.

"Where is he?"

"I can't see!"

"Oh holy mother of fuck!"

"Help!"

"Shit, shit, shit, shit shiiiiiit-" That last one cut off with a gurgling scream just as the doors gave way and burst apart before me.

Niall reappeared, splattered in blood and grinning from ear to ear as he slapped me on the shoulder like we were friends. Fucking bastardo loco.

"That brings my count to eight - where are you at again, El Burro? Six was it?" He cackled wildly and took off through the doors as I snarled, hounding after him.

"I'll finish my count by striking your head from your shoulders, hijo de puta, and then who will be the winner?"

An unearthly shriek sounded from an open cell to my left half a moment before a heavy body collided with me and I was knocked from my feet beneath them.

Nails gouged at my face as a woman screamed and cursed, bible verses pouring from her lips and suddenly thrusting me back into my past as panic washed over me. I was just that boy again, caught at the mercy of those women who claimed to serve a god who had never had any love for me. I was a child so in need of love and gifted hatred instead. I was lost and screaming out for my papa to come home, hoping he would realise what my mamá was orchestrating whenever he was gone, but he never did and I was left here to suffer on and on and on until-

The woman was heaved off of me and tossed aside and I found myself staring up at a bloody Irishman with his head cocked to one side and a hand extended to me.

"Come on, lad. I can only be a decent human being for ten minutes a day and you're cutting into my allocation."

For some unknown reason, I let him take my hand and pull me to my feet then found myself staring into his bright green eyes.

I couldn't thank him. I hated him far too much to ever even consider that. But I couldn't quite bring myself to take advantage of his closeness and stab him either.

"Men like us are all haunted by something," he growled. "I think it's best we don't give the ghosts any extra ammunition when we can do something to stop it though, don't you?"

He slapped my bicep then turned and jogged away, calling Brooklyn's name and looking all around for her, leaving me to stare after him in confusion.

I followed him, my heart pounding and brow furrowed. Where the fuck was she?

In fact, where the fuck was everyone who should have been in this wing? The woman who had attacked me had scurried out the door I'd broken down after Niall tossed her away from me, but the others couldn't have gone that way.

A lead weight dropped into my gut as a feeling of dread pooled through my limbs. We were missing something here. Something vital. And if we didn't figure out what was going on soon, I got the terrible feeling we were going to be too late to save my chica loca.

"Brooklyn!" I bellowed alongside Niall, upping my pace as I ran after him and we hunted for her together. "Brooklyn!"

BROOKLYN

CHAPTER THIRTY NINE

Angry Jack slammed the key card he'd stolen from Lucille onto the door panel that would lead us outside and I craned my neck around to try and see better as he stepped out into the night air.

He suddenly threw me behind a bush and I yelped as the prickles got me. Jack leaned over me like the Leaning Tower of Pisa, his eyebrows lowering. "Hide," he commanded in his gruff voice.

"What about you?" I gasped.

"No." He glanced over his shoulder as shouts carried from close by and his jaw flexed with rage. He looked back at me and shoved my head lower beneath the bushes. "Stay." He marched away and the sound of shouting carried from nearby. *Oh fucking chipmunks.*

I poked my head up above the rose bushes, gazing out at the large concrete courtyard where the guards and nurses were frantically filing patients onto transport buses shouting things about fire procedures and emergency evacuation.

Jack strode straight up to a truck parked at the end of them as the driver aimed his gun out the window at him. I opened my mouth to warn him as the shot went off and Jack didn't even flinch as the bullet sailed past him, grazing his arm and spilling his blood. I gasped as he lunged forward, yanking the man out of the window and taking hold of his head between his hands, digging his thumbs into his eyes. My lips parted and I watched the beautiful display as he killed him mercilessly and tossed him onto the ground. He got in the truck, starting it up, his eyes set on the rose bush I was behind. *He's coming for me. My big angry giant is on his way!*

But suddenly the guards were tearing toward him, their weapons raised as they barked orders at him to get out. My heart beat like a rabbit bouncing around inside a cage as they hauled him out of the truck and forced him to the ground, locking his hands in cuffs.

"No...Jack," I breathed in horror.

The world was falling apart, mayhem descending. But not the good kind. The patients were losing the upper hand. It wasn't a fair fight. So why the hell had they let us all out? Just for a shower time in the sprinklers? Honestly, who were the crazy ones around here really? Not I.

I tried to grasp some ideas to get myself out of here and run, run, run all the way to the sky where it was safe, but my thoughts were all swooshy, whirly from the drugs they'd forced on me, and every time a plan formed in my mind it shot away again before I could grasp it.

I snagged a rose bud between my teeth and chomped it down, wondering if it might give me some ideas. But it didn't. *Silly rosebud, where are your thoughts gone?*

As Angry Jack was hauled away to the most heavily armoured bus, my heart yanked me toward him. He could have been a part of my club. He didn't have a clit, but I'd have made an exception this one time. And anyway, I could paint a little clit down there. We could decorate it too, make a real day of it.

Ergh my head is still so smooshy, why is that again? Oh yeah, the drugs. Freaking head fuck those things. Can't do anything stupid. Must stay sane. Well, semi-sane. As sane as a plane down a drain. Oh dear...

"Rook!" Jack barked like a beast and I guessed that was me.

Okay, maybe we hadn't been *that* close of friends before tonight seeing as he'd forgotten my name, but that was okay. I wasn't even a hundred percent sure his name was Angry Jack. Like, who would call their kid Angry? It was a mighty coincidence that he turned out to be so angry. Freaking destiny that was.

I ate another rosebud, considering my options. I could go gung-ho, ninja style. Kill as many assmunchers as I could and see how far I could get. *Or* I could run to the outer fence and hope I wasn't spotted then brave the razor wire. *Or* I could pretend to be a snake and casually slither out the front gate after picking up Jack on the way. *Oh my god, I'm actually a genius. It's kinda frightening sometimes.*

I shuffled out from behind the rose bush and flattened myself to the ground as I started wriggling across it. "I'm coming Jack, ssssss. I'll get you off that busssss."

I slithered my way towards the armoured bus, struggling not to scrape my chin on the rough ground and wincing against my crushed fingers in the straitjacket. I really needed someone to cut me out of this bitch. Maybe Jack could do it with his big hands when we got free. Were we going to run away together? I'd never had a best friend before. What other kinds of things did best friends do together? Sit side by side on swings? Play chess? Braid each other's hair? *Oh my goddd, his hair would look so good braided. I need to tell him.*

I slithered faster, but as I made it into the edge of the light from first floodlight illuminating the courtyard, a shout went up and heavy boots pounded my way.

Shit, act for your life, Brooklyn!

"Ssssss," I hissed. *I'm just a harmless little viper coming through, don't mind me.*

Strong hands hauled me to my feet and I flicked my tongue out.

Dammit, what else do snakes do?

"Fuck me, this is the Bully Butcher," the guard gasped. "Get her on the high security bus." He shoved me into the arms of another man and I tried my best not to panic.

"I don't know who - sssss - you mean - ssssss," I tried, but they still weren't buying it. Man, I really shouldn't have paid for those acting lessons from Earwax Willy back at the bridge. Fucking rip off. I'd had to give him my entire bottle cap collection for that.

I started fighting as best I could, but I was walked straight up onto the bus, skipping the line of inmates who were being corralled outside it.

I was shoved down onto a bench at the back of the bus by a small square window. Two men cuffed my ankles to a bolt on the floor and I snarled at them, snapping my teeth savagely. Small-Willy Norman was sitting in front of me and he glanced over his shoulder with his beady eyes. This snitchy snitch was on my death list for all the snitching he'd done to Madam Lucille. I tried to kick the back of his seat, but my feet were yanked back by the chains.

"Look away!" I shrieked at him and he licked his greyish lips before he did what I said, hunching his head down and hiding behind his long curtain of lank brown hair.

Cannibal Carol was hauled onto the bus, her short black hair sticking up in every direction as she fought to bite a chunk out of the closest guard's flesh. A weird muzzle cage was snapped over her face a second before she was pushed down into the seat beside mine.

"Ohh nooo!" I wailed, cringing away from her. "I don't wanna sit beside Carol!"

"Tough fucking shit," the guard barked, locking Carol in place who started breathing like a maniac beside me. *Gahhhhh, I hate mouth breathers. And she's such a mouth breather.*

"Can you breathe through your nose at least?" I snipped at her and she shot me a glare, her teeth gnashing together inside her muzzle.

"I bet you taste like sugar dipped in honey, my dear," she purred and I shuddered, leaning right against the wall and pressing my face to the window. *Eeeew. Whhhhhy me?*

"Rook," Angry Jack's voice came from behind me and I turned, my brows raising as I found him in the cage at the back of the bus behind me, his hands still locked at the base of his spine. The look he gave me with those steely grey eyes of his was intense enough to burn a hole in my forehead.

"Hey bestie," I whispered. "Total shit-show, right? Maybe we'll get another chance to run later, eh big man?" I wanted to believe those words, but my heart was falling into a dark well inside me.

And as Angry Jack started thrashing angrily inside his cage, I turned back to face the window with a pout, sadness descending on me. We weren't getting out again. They'd never take the risk of that happening now. And as much as I wanted Jack to be my bestie, I knew we'd probably just go back to how things used to be between us. He'd stare at the wall, out of his head on sedatives strong enough to kill a horse, and I'd float around in cuckoo la la land pretending I was a pigeon on an updraft thanks to the pills they forced on me.

At least Madam Lucille was dead. That was something. But not enough. Because I was still a captive and I'd sworn never to be owned again. The law had me in its grip and wanted to squeeze until my crazy head popped and I was no longer a drain on their perfect little illusion of a normal world with normal people in it.

A tear wet my cheek and suddenly I was sobbing, kicking and thrashing against my chains and the straitjacket while Carol started sucking in air beside me, trying to eat my lifeforce or some shit.

I stared out the window as it started to rain and my soul rained with it.

We rounded a corner and I gazed at the building where fire blazed and two men caught my eye among the carnage as they climbed out of a window one after the other. My heart turned into a marble which ping-ponged around my body so furiously I couldn't breathe.

My throat was stuffed with a lump of coal, my legs weighing me down like tree trunks, my tears as hot and sticky as tar on my cheeks as I stopped crying and just gaped.

My devil, my sinner.

My captor, my boyfriend.

Hellfire, Dead Man.

Niall, Mateo.

Holy fucking tits!!!!

———————————————

AUTHOR'S NOTE

Jesus! That was…something. If you've read our books before now you will know that if we promise some kind of something we don't do half measures and I can tell you that getting inside the minds of this crazy bunch has been pretty intense. But we don't need to talk about the killing spree me and Caroline inevitably ended up on, or how we are now wanted women hiding from the cold hard rod of the law. Haha rod…

Anyway, as we are finishing this book it has officially been a year(ish) since the world went to shit because some fucker ate a bat (wasn't us – we don't eat meat and this is why!!!) but what a weird/crazy/intense/mind numbing/sad/hard/insert-every-other-emotion-here year it has been! For us personally, though we have desperately missed seeing a lot of our loved ones and venturing out into the world, we have been incredibly blessed by gaining more and more of you wonderful readers and by living our dreams of doing this whole author thing full time for another year. Each and every one of you has changed our lives just by diving into these worlds with us and we really just want to thank you for taking the plunge with us and falling headfirst into our literary insanity no matter which direction it takes us.

We hope you've enjoyed getting to know our gang of psychos and that you aren't feeling too harrowed by that cliff – don't worry, we'll be back to see The Death Club soon and you can find out how the fuck they're going to move on from that shit fest of an ending. In fact, they're probably going to need a name liiiike, Gang of Gangsters orrr The Hot Dogs orrrr Society of Psychos – yeah, I think that one works, feel free to pre-order it now ;)

Love you guys, Susanne & Caroline

ALSO BY
CAROLINE PECKHAM
&
SUSANNE VALENTI

Brutal Boys of Everlake Prep
(Complete Reverse Harem Bully Romance Contemporary Series)
Kings of Quarantine
Kings of Lockdown
Kings of Anarchy
Queen of Quarantine

**

Dead Men Walking
(Reverse Harem Dark Romance Contemporary Series)
The Death Club
Society of Psychos

**

The Harlequin Crew
(Reverse Harem Mafia Romance Contemporary Series)
Sinners Playground
Dead Man's Isle
Carnival Hill
Paradise Lagoon

Harlequinn Crew Novellas
Devil's Pass

**

Dark Empire

(Dark Mafia Contemporary Standalones)

Beautiful Carnage

Beautiful Savage

**

The Ruthless Boys of the Zodiac

(Reverse Harem Paranormal Romance Series - Set in the world of Solaria)

Dark Fae

Savage Fae

Vicious Fae

Broken Fae

Warrior Fae

Zodiac Academy

(M/F Bully Romance Series- Set in the world of Solaria, five years after Dark Fae)

The Awakening

Ruthless Fae

The Reckoning

Shadow Princess

Cursed Fates

Fated Thrones

Heartless Sky

The Awakening - As told by the Boys

Zodiac Academy Novellas

Origins of an Academy Bully

The Big A.S.S. Party

Darkmore Penitentiary

(Reverse Harem Paranormal Romance Series - Set in the world of Solaria, ten years after Dark Fae)

Caged Wolf

Alpha Wolf

Feral Wolf

**

The Age of Vampires

(Complete M/F Paranormal Romance/Dystopian Series)

Eternal Reign

Eternal Shade

Eternal Curse

Eternal Vow

Eternal Night

Eternal Love

**

Cage of Lies

(M/F Dystopian Series)

Rebel Rising

**

Tainted Earth

(M/F Dystopian Series)

Afflicted

Altered

Adapted

Advanced

**

The Vampire Games

(Complete M/F Paranormal Romance Trilogy)

V Games

V Games: Fresh From The Grave

V Games: Dead Before Dawn

*

The Vampire Games: Season Two

(Complete M/F Paranormal Romance Trilogy)

Wolf Games

Wolf Games: Island of Shade

Wolf Games: Severed Fates

*

The Vampire Games: Season Three

Hunter Trials

*

The Vampire Games Novellas

A Game of Vampires

**

The Rise of Issac

(Complete YA Fantasy Series)

Creeping Shadow

Bleeding Snow

Turning Tide

Weeping Sky

Failing Light